UNEARTHING IDYLL

DHARA PAREKH

To you Mummy, for passing down your curiosity, and Pappa, for teaching me humanity. Thank you for cloning me. This is for all the times I should have called but didn't.

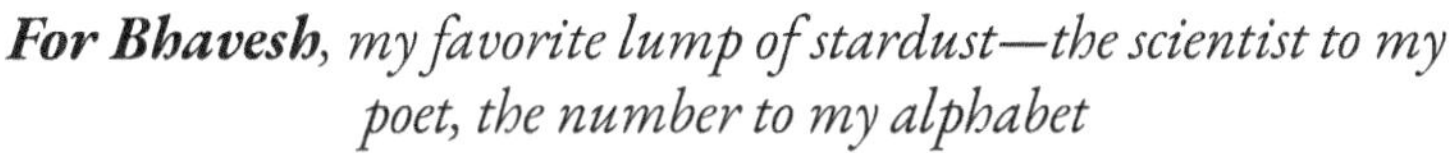

For Bhavesh, *my favorite lump of stardust—the scientist to my poet, the number to my alphabet*

To quote Carl Sagan,
*"In the vastness of space and immensity of time, it is my joy to spend a planet and an epoch with **him**."*

A good science fiction work is framed around challenges we currently face, dramatizing the ways we draw on science and technology to meet these challenges and aspire to new and better methods of organizing ourselves. Even dystopian sci-fi is optimistic in a way, hoping that those terrible futures will warn us away from bad choices and toward collective survival. In the best science fiction stories, however, science and technology operate like fellow characters along with humans, and together they interact about essential humanness in strange and unsettling environments. Think of 'beaming' in the Star Trek universe or haptic body suits from Ready Player One. Even in those galactic and virtual universes, the technology unearths the ethos of human nature—exploring, fighting, falling in love, finding joy, nostalgia, and purpose, and never being quite content.

In Dhara Parekh's Unearthing Idyll, the first book in her new Asymptote Universe, a curious-minded individualist is thwarted in her attempt to escape an asteroid-based utopia that has limited her understanding of herself and her society. How much will the technological prowess of the future help her or us understand our essential nature? We will have to find out. But learning is possible, and our ability to grow remains powerful, as you will learn from this cerebral yet moving piece of fiction by Dhara.

This book, like the best sci-fi works, uses science and technology to focus on human desires and quandaries — wanting to escape a society you don't fit in, thinking happiness lies in the next best thing, the dread of living in an oppressive state, the drive to find answers far away, the constant struggle of comprehending our self as a separate entity, forming bonds, and returning to principles and ethics that are foundational to human thriving.

In the end, Unearthing Idyll makes us question our own humanness. What would we do if we were living on an asteroid or our own earth a hundred years from now, with new tools and new abilities? Do we assume improvement? Do our desires change? Do we still seek human connections? How would we define our utopia? Would we be seeking that idyllic world? What lengths would we go to in fulfilling that?

When you flip this page, you will walk a step further in discovering those answers.

Hollis Robbins
American Academic and essayist
Dean of Humanities, University of Utah

UNEARTHING IDYLL

DHARA PAREKH

CHAPTER 1

PacaSpace Transit Station

July 13, 2125

"I am not lying!"

Lyra had raised her voice for the second time in her unremarkable life of twenty-seven years. It sounded like she spoke through a throat spiked with shards of glass.

"I had my documents with me just a while ago. There, at the café."

She rummaged again through her luggage, her sweaty tresses blinding her vision. In the last fifteen minutes, she had stubbed her toe, injured her shin, and bitten her inner cheek. This was not how she had imagined her first trip to Earth would be.

Lyra sucked in quick short breaths and pulled the neck of her sweater for some air. Despite the warmth, her body trembled. She would have blamed the centrifugal force of the rotating transit station, but the two delightful hours she once spent reading about the station's mechanics didn't allow her.

"Miss," an officer in a sharp, black uniform warned, "you are breaking Earthler laws by attempting to enter Earth's immigration without papers. You could be arrested for it."

A rotten taste swam up Lyra's throat as the soft buzzing of the station tingled her eardrums. She glanced at the travelers scattered around. Then she looked at herself—an ink blotch on a fresh sheet of paper. This was not how it was meant to go. She had dreamt of this day all her life. Her mind wasn't supposed to toss her the visuals of her comforting bedroom, the bedroom of the house inside an asteroid she had finally escaped.

The terrifying stare of the officer brought her back to the security line.

How is it even possible?—Lyra thought. How could her documents disappear? She had placed the folder back in her bag at the Spacebucks café...or had she?

Asteroid Zenith
24 hours ago

"I've seen you wearing the same pair of pants all the time. Have you packed enough clothes?"

"Yes"

"Did you pack preventive meds? Your body will go through a lot, Lai."

"Yes, Dad."

"Did you convert enough ferrics into PacaDollars? You might need some as soon as you land. Don't forget; one Earth PacaDollar is one-twenty Zenith ferrics. Spend wisely."

"I did and, yes, I will."

"Did you submit your university application? The deadline is before you return."

"I did," Lyra lied.

Beethoven's *Ode to Joy* provided the background score to Keid's interrogation. He had been quizzing his daughter ever since he had woken up.

Lyra glanced at her father and thought of the pain she was about to cause him soon. He looked older than his age, his body frailer than it had been on his fifty-eighth birthday last year. His untamed, gray hair was greasy, as was the mustache that he once flaunted.

She shook her head and concentrated on packing.

The manual that came along with her Earth visa was aggressive and detailed. It had a long list of things she was not allowed to carry, some specific and silly. Lyra was okay with everything until she read 'pens/pencils' and 'books' on the list of restricted items. She had never left home without a notepad and two pens just in case she lost one, which she often did. It bothered her that she would be traveling 60,964 miles, all the way to Earth, without carrying her essentials. She had hoped that by books, the Earth government meant only printed books, because she had packed her great-grandmother's diary.

"What if you get lost?" Keid asked. He was sitting at the foot of Lyra's bed, massaging his neck. "There are four billion people on Earth!" His eyes fell on her messenger bag and he saw the diary in its mouth.

"Why are you carrying this? Did you also pack a pen? Lai, you don't know these Earthlers. They are…"

"No, Dad. I am not taking a pen."

Lyra zipped her bag and shoved a lock of her wavy hair behind her ear. Its ends rested torpidly on her shoulder.

"If you can't control your kids, pack and send them away to Earth!" The screeching voice of Ms. Tara, Lyra's front-door neighbor, tore through her bedroom window. "If I see their filthy footprints on my farm again…"

Lyra took a deep breath and ignored the noise. Nothing was going to ruin her mood. This was the most important day of her life.

"Lai, did you pack extra jackets?" her father spoke again. "Earth's climate is different from ours. They not only have different seasons, but their weather changes throughout the day."

Of course, Lyra knew that. Earth had fluctuating weather, unlike Zenith, where the temperature was set between 68 and 72 Fahrenheit throughout the year. She imagined Earth's foggy mornings, scorching afternoons, cloudy evenings, and frosty nights. Just the thought of it spiked her energy.

"Clothes can be bought, money can be wired, and pens can be discarded at our spaceport. Documents—those are fundamental," Sagan interrupted the conversation.

Lyra's twelve-year-old brother had been standing by her bedroom door for the last twenty minutes, petting a fist-sized spider.

"Did you take your visa? Did you pack your passport?" he went on. "Did you check their validity? Did you make enough copies of your travel documents? Are you leaving a set of copies for us? That has proven to be a fruitful precautionary measure. Your baggage will be subjected to extreme pressure and reverberation. Did you wrap items in shock-resistant bags?"

Lyra spaced out for a second, more thrilled by her brother's interrogation than her father's. When she finished running Sagan's sentences in her head, she smirked. From her bedside drawer, she grabbed a big, blue envelope-shaped folder and waved it at him. The folder had a map of Earth printed on it.

"Your documents?" her father asked.

"Yes...my passport, my badge, my tablet, my Earth visa, and other travel papers I might need. Oh..." Lyra remembered something. She removed a vintage compass sticker from the folder and glued it on the cover of her great-grandmother's diary. Keid and Sagan shook their heads when they saw her smiling at it.

After verifying the contents, Lyra placed the folder and diary in her messenger bag.

"Good work, sister," Sagan said.

"Thank you!" It was not every day that her brother was impressed by her organizational skills.

"We should also digitize all our IDs and documents like the Earthlers do. I hate carrying them around all the time," said Keid as he dusted toast crumbs off his crumpled T-shirt.

"Contrary to popular Zenither belief, digital documents are less secure, and more prone to misuse than hard documents," Sagan said, still looking at his pet spider.

Keid wrinkled his forehead and changed the subject.

"What about your ocean and planeair trip from Earth spaceport, Lai? Will you be able to handle them?"

"Airplane." Sagan corrected his father again.

"Dad, I will be traveling in a space shuttle and a space elevator after that. I think an airplane and an ocean train will be fine. Besides, planes are not as scary as we think. They only fly at about 35,000 feet."

"And a metal bus flying that high is not scary?"

"That is only twice as high as our asteroid's roof," informed Sagan.

"I don't know about others but our roof looks fairly high to me."

"Our perception of height will always be subjective," Sagan concluded. Then he circled his sister's room like he was taking his spider on an evening stroll and left.

Keid shook his head and got back to quizzing Lyra.

"What's the name of that place again... the one you are traveling to from Earth's spaceport?"

"VacaRealm." Lyra hoped it would be the last question. "That's what they now call the place great-grandpa was from. VacaRealm is an enormous Head. It's located in Earth's 2nd Stratum, a few thousand miles away from spaceport, which is in the 1st Stratum." She stopped, remembering that not everyone was as obsessed with Earth's geography as she was.

"Enormous head?"

"Earthlers call their big cities Heads. The towns are called Trunks and the countryside is called Tails."

"Can't say they lack creativity," Keid mumbled under his breath.

"Okay, I'm all packed." Lyra rubbed her back. "I will make a quick lunch for you both before I leave. There are enough prepared meals in the freezer. Heat them directly without thawing. If you are out of food or don't want to cook, call Gryffy. She will send you packed meals from the hotel's kitchen. And Dad, please..."

"What?"

"Please be patient with Sagan."

Apparently, Keid took the request as an attack, for he left the room without a word

Lyra sighed and took one last look around the room to make sure she had not missed anything. She glanced at her favorite spot—a small bench squeezed between the window and the head of her bed. A part of her was sad that she might never see this room again. It was her comforting cocoon.

She made two rounds and carried the two big bags downstairs. Then she went to the kitchen and grabbed a bottle of oil.

"Your shuttle leaves in five hours," Sagan spoke from the upholstered bamboo couch in the living room without looking at her. "As time draws near, your heart rate will increase and your adrenal glands will produce neurotransmitters, which will journey into your bloodstream. This will expand the air passages of your lungs, elevate your blood pressure, and jumble your nervous system. In your case, you will soon start feeling dizzy, your stomach will churn, and your palms will perspire. Given your past mental response to these physical symptoms, you will begin to believe that you've forgotten something important. Stress will take over you, and your self-professed journey-of-a-lifetime will look vexatious."

Lyra tried her best to keep up with her little brother's babbling.

"What?"

"Vexatious. Meaning unpleasant."

"Not that. Why are you stalking my nervous system?"

"Because you are doing chores two hours before you leave for an outer space journey. Also, you hate chores."

"The departure time is four pm."

"You are supposed to reach the spaceport at least three hours before departure."

Lyra turned to look at him.

"I know, Lord Sagacious!"

The back of the couch concealed his tiny body. The only part visible was the top of his head, which was buried in a book.

The thought of leaving her brother to fend for himself hijacked Lyra's brain again. It was this moment that she had dreaded ever since her visa had been approved. She had flung the thought somewhere in the cluttered corner of her head where all her suppressed feelings went to hibernate, but it was time to leave and she could not stall it anymore.

Lyra had told everyone that she was leaving on a one-month vacation. Her father believed that she would return and enroll in the university for her advanced degree. The hotel she worked at as a chef had already sent her the work schedule and menu-planning chart for the next month. But she felt worst about lying to her brother. It was easier, she had decided, to tell him the truth right before leaving.

Lyra looked at her father's bedroom door. It was shut. With a heavy heart, she walked up to Sagan and confessed her true intentions. She told him that she wouldn't be returning in a month, that she had plans to stay on Earth permanently. As soon as she landed, she would apply for a visa extension. In the extended period, she would get in touch with the right people and apply for Earth's citizenship.

"No one in the history of Zenith has ever done that. I have no data to tell me how it's going to turn out," she mentioned.

Sagan took it all in, stayed quiet for a moment, and then spoke,

"I am aware of your plan. You are terrible at veiling secrets when you are over-enthused."

"You knew? How?"

"That's not important."

Lyra saw a hint of disappointment on Sagan's face which he was trying hard to mask.

"I am so sorry for keeping it from you. Please don't think I was going to abandon you here. I would never do that." She knelt on the floor and placed her hands on his knees. "Would you like to move there too, to Earth, once I am all settled in?"

When Sagan mentioned countless reasons for not wanting to move to a strange world, one being "I don't like change", Lyra bribed her bug-obsessed brother with the idea of having access to innumerable insects on Earth. She explained how he would never have to take multiple permissions to borrow them from the Goodall Sanctuary.

"Even spiders?"

"Yes. Any insects you can think of."

"Spiders are not insects; they are arachnids," Sagan specified in a judgmental tone. It still amused Lyra how a preteen could throw shade like a finger-wagging 90-year-old Terraformer.

"You are right. I forgot. I remember Mom telling me that." Her head turned upward and then back at Sagan. "How is this for damage control—there are over fourteen million known species of insects on Earth?"

"I assumed that was a myth."

"It's not. They estimate close to thirty million, actually. So...you in?"

"Thirty million species of insects is a good incentive."

"Yes!" Lyra stood and sat next to her brother. "Thank you."

"You might now feel the need to exhibit physical affection, but as we are both aware of our uneasiness with it, I'll let you get back to your infused oil."

Lyra laughed. It sounded as if she was reading the sound of a laugh.

She grabbed Sagan's head and gave him a warm squeeze. Sagan freed himself from his sister's scrawny arms and flattened his soft, brown hair.

"Call me if you need anything, okay?" Lyra straightened the collar of Sagan's formal button down shirt. By now, she was used to his grownup clothes. "I haven't told Dad anything yet. Give me some time. I'll figure everything out."

Sagan nodded.

Her father was not included in Lyra's plans, because she knew it was impossible to convince him to leave his wife's memories behind.

Lyra went back to the kitchen and made a big batch of vegetable daal. She left notes about meals on the fridge and explained them to Keid.

"I am flogging a dead horse, but Lai..." Keid rubbed his shoulder "...this place you are going to look for, where your great-grandparents got engaged, you don't even know what it's called now. Your mother didn't know it either, and she was their granddaughter! I made a huge mistake by giving you that diary."

"Dad, I'll be okay. Besides, I am not going there just for that place. I have a long itinerary. Maybe I'll go wherever India was, see the land of my ancestors. Afterall, that's where great-grandma grew up." Lyra checked her watch.

"No, you can't..."

"I have time. I'll check the laundry. I hung them to dry early today."

In two hours, Lyra had put away the laundry, swept and mopped their entire house, and made herself a snack for the trip. She was perfectly aware that guilt was driving her system. After contemplating a lot, she also finally cleaned up the space under the edge of the living room rug where she would often shove the dirt.

When Sagan announced the time, which he had been doing every fifteen minutes, Lyra realized she was late. She ran back to her room and changed. Sagan was right; her nervous system was jumbled.

She quickly combed her hair with her fingers and hung her messenger bag across her chest. She pushed her feet into a pair of black canvas shoes and tied the laces so tightly that she flinched with pain.

Just when she got down, she heard a honk.

"Your auto is here, Lai. It's Trac." Keid got up and carried the bags outside.

Lyra walked up to her brother who was sitting on the couch.

"I know you don't like hugs," she said.

"You loathe them too."

"I like yours."

Sagan gave her a tight-lipped smile and hugged her.

"I'll miss you," he muttered under his breath.

Lyra bent down and clutched him. Sagan patted her head thrice, a habit from his childhood.

"Me too," said Lyra, as a sliver of guilt rose in her chest. Her eyes glistened. "Be nice. Don't worry about school too much. Just go and be your best self, okay? In no time, you'll be there with me, on Earth." She gently rubbed his forehead. "Go, now. Your army must be starving. It's lunchtime."

Sagan imitated a smile, and with hands in his pant pockets, went up to his room to feed his pet insects.

Lyra rushed outside and looked at the auto. Like always, the staple transport of Zenith reminded her of a computer mouse. She flickered her index finger as if to click its roof.

Keid dropped his conversation with the middle-aged driver and spoke to her, "I'll see you in a month. Don't forget what I said. Keep in touch with your university."

"I will."

Lyra blocked the mental slideshow of all the mishaps her dad might experience in her absence and gave him a half-hug. She got in the solar-powered automobile and shut the door. Three spherical wheels set into motion. The iron pavement beneath was still warm from the heat of the simulated lights attached to the asteroid's roof. She looked at her father through the back window. He was staring at the ground, lost in his thoughts.

"So...visiting Earth, eh?" Trac's shrill voice pulled Lyra back to her seat. "Why didn't you tell me, Lyra?"

"Sorry, Trac."

"That's a first if I must say. Even my mum doesn't wanna go back to that place, and she emigrated from Earth only forty-two years ago. Zenith is the best! They will be expanding the Earth Park in three months. Lyra, I hear a lot of things. They say it's going to be so similar that you'll almost feel like you are visiting Earth. And it will cost a thousand times less than what you're spending on the ticket."

He failed to get a response, and so he continued, "And you know...these Earthlers, not very nice people to mingle with, if I must say." Trac's potato-shaped head shook with disapproval.

Lyra decided not to acknowledge that statement. She gazed at the bright Zenith afternoon from her window and toyed with the Earth-shaped pendant that Sagan had gifted on her twenty-fifth birthday.

As the auto drove down the Archimedes Street, she observed the houses of her sloped district. They all looked the same to her. The afternoon commotion was no different, either. Vendors selling fruits and vegetables in solar wagons and children busy with their shenanigans as they returned from school.

In five hours, the simulated lights would be turned off and these streets would be blanketed in the cold darkness.

Lyra, however, felt warmer than usual. Whether it was the Power Sat division that had cranked up the asteroid's temperature a few degrees higher or the adrenaline humming in her blood, she was not sure.

"Two weeks ago, an Earthler left me a huge tip," Trac looked back and whispered. "A thousand ferrics!" He faced the street again and switched to his normal volume. "He even gave me a fancy watch, but not for one minute did he stop treating me like a slave. Not one minute!" His short, stubby body bounced as the auto passed over a bumper.

There, in the back seat, Lyra gave a last look at everything in her scope of vision—from the faraway cratered terrain of factories, trees, and fields to the blinding roof of the asteroid. It reminded her of Earth's sky. The mere thought of experiencing sunlight directly from the sun exhilarated her. It didn't matter how many times she read about the size of the sun; she could never imagine it the way she saw it in the pictures of Earth. For her, the sun meant a light bulb in outer space which she had seen numerous times from the observatory.

"The bastard disinfected his hands after he accidentally touched me!"

Lyra remembered reading not just about nature but about tall skyscrapers and the bustling life of Earthler cities, or as they called them, Heads. She imagined herself as a part of that grandiosity. Her heart raced.

"I'd kick him in the nuts if I could..."

When they reached Bhabha Street, Lyra saw the bookshop where she had worked for a year when she was fifteen. She shrank in her seat when she saw its owner, Kish, looking towards the street. She didn't want to indulge in another goodbye conversation.

"I told him, it's T-R-A-C, Trac. Just four letters. How hard is it to learn, eh, Lyra?"

They reached the spaceport. It was on an extended platform constructed outside the perimeters of Zenith, next to Ramanujan District. Lyra always imagined the port to look like a soap bubble stuck to the huge piece of rock that was Zenith.

Welcome to Zenith Spaceport, a big sign read.

Trac stopped at the security gate where an officer checked Lyra's documents and badge—a Zenither identity card that looked like a flat, metal wallet with their photograph and a unique code on it. When he gave the green signal, they entered a dark tunnel lit with bright halogen lights. A chill swept through the auto as they entered an incubated space.

"So, later when I asked him how his day was, he said, 'Shut up!'" Trac continued his conversation in an awful Earthler accent.

Lyra checked her bag again as she saw the final gates approaching. Everything she would need was in its place. She touched her great-grandmother's diary and imagined all the strange stories she would get to write in hers.

"You're here. Seriously, you take care, Lyra, eh? Come soon. It's not very nice there if I must say...and while ya there, don't forget to disinfect your hands after touching an Earthler driver, eh?" Trac twisted his mouth.

"I won't. Thank you, Trac." She paid him. "Give my love to T. rex. Tell him I will miss him a lot." T. rex was a mountain gorilla at the Goodall Sanctuary where Trac and Lyra both volunteered.

"Ya know I will." Trac turned his auto and left.

Lyra checked in all her baggage and went through a thorough physical examination. Next was a nine-and-a-half-hour shuttle to the PacaSpace Transit Station which was located between Zenith and Earth in the Geostationary Equatorial Orbit. After a three-hour halt at the station, she would board the PacaSpace elevator. The carbon nanotubes composite ribbon which was anchored to a platform on Earth's equator would descend her to Earth in fewer than six hours.

She was as nervous as she was excited.

At the shuttle door, a pair of mechanic hands handed her ear pods. They dictated the rules and regulations of the shuttle.

Hours later, when she woke up, the shuttle was already attached to the transit station. All she remembered was entering the shuttle, which was a tad bigger than Zenith buses, and being coldly greeted by an Earthler attendant. He handed her a bottle of water with three pills, which he asked her to take in his presence.

There were many passengers on the shuttle, mainly elite

Earthlers, who were returning to their planet after a Zenith vacation. Lyra even remembered the passenger who sat next to her—a tall, silver-haired young man in a business suit.

Her head buzzed as she exited the shuttle, but the uneasiness faded when she entered the transit station. It was a whole different world—a gargantuan, confined metal cabin packed with Earthlers in lavish garments. They talked in whispers and glided through the crowd with poise and elegance. Each face like its own different island, unlike Zenither faces that seemed like different pieces of one big puzzle.

Lyra checked her attire. Canvas shoes, black tapered pants with their cuffs folded above her ankles, and an oversized blue sweater under a cheap jacket. They did not exactly scream sophistication. Her sweater had a picture of T. rex in a spacesuit. She had thought it was funny, but after noticing everyone around, she chained her jacket up to her chin and unrolled the hems of her pants.

There were a lot more people at the station than she had imagined. In addition to being a transit station, it was also a tourist destination. Earthlers paid hefty amounts to enjoy the view from an altitude of 22,236 miles above Earth's sea level. The station also hosted the space to fine-dining restaurants, bars, and fancy stores.

Lyra checked her watch. T. rex's arms on its dial informed her that she had an hour and a half to kill before she entered the security line to board the elevator. The only place she could afford was a modest café. As she searched for the right place, she remembered something. A suggestion: "Get Estlechino at Spacebucks while you are at the transit station. Don't forget or you'll regret it."

She collected her baggage from the carousel, placed it on a surprisingly light trolley, and headed straight to Spacebucks.

No one who knew her would have identified the smile on her face and the spring in her step. It could not be said for a large part of her life, but she was incredibly and wholeheartedly happy.

Lyra thought of her mother. She had missed her on several joyous occasions, such as when Sagan had spoken his first words or when she had been promoted at the hotel, but she missed her the most today.

When she was eight, she had crafted her piggybank out of a round metal ball that she had found at the recycling center. "The concept of a piggybank is alien to Zenithers," her mother had told her. It was natural for them to spend whatever they earned as the asteroid took care of most of their future needs. To grow up a saver in a world where saving money was considered greedy was a challenge for Lyra.

On the metal ball, she had painted random shapes in green and blue. She had cut a slot on the top for depositing money. She called it the 'North Pole Slot'. It had made her mother giggle. The metal ball that looked exactly like the planet Earth had been on her bedside table ever since. Her mother had made the first deposit in the piggybank. Even though Lyra was just a child, Poona never belittled her daughter's unrealistic dream of visiting Earth. Every Zenither knew it was a luxury, unaffordable to most of them.

"Here are the first fifty ferrics for your trip, Lai. Don't spend it," her mother had said.

Every single saved ferric, including her mother's fifty ferrics, had gone towards buying the ticket to Earth. She had never desired anything as passionately as this trip.

As soon as she got her first job, she started depositing a huge percentage of her salary in the bank every month, the receipts of which went into her piggybank. It had taken her almost two decades to save enough to move to Earth.

For Zenithers, Earth was only a planet around which their habitat orbited, but for Lyra, her entire existence revolved around the blue planet.

She took a deep, tired breath when she finally found Spacebucks. As a kid, she had imagined the station to smell like space or the stars, but it smelled like how she imagined the inside of her watch would smell. It reminded her of an interesting fact she had read—because the station is a confined space, just like Zenith, it traps all the odors. To prevent that, the station has what they call a micropurification unit. The mechanism eradicates all trace contaminants and smells that build up in the environment.

When Lyra's eyes registered the coffee shop's board again, she shook her head to break her chain of thought. This was not the time to think about how PacaSpace dealt with human odors.

She entered the café and ordered the recommended coffee at the counter. The young man gave her a stiff smile and requested her to take a seat. Lyra sat at a corner table and pulled her luggage trolley beside it.

An attractive, towering woman approached her and asked if she wanted some water.

"Sure," Lyra said with a nervous smile. She noticed that the server had a sharp scar on her forehead. Strangely, it made the woman less intimidating.

"Perfect! I'll be right back with a whole glass of refreshing, cold water," the server said with an enigmatic smile. The importance she placed on a glass of water pushed Lyra towards another train of thought, but she resisted.

"Your water, miss." The server placed a sparkling glass on the table. "My colleague just told me you ordered an alcoholic coffee. Do you mind showing me your ID?" She bent to make comfortable eye contact with Lyra.

"Not at all." Lyra removed the documents folder from her messenger bag. She retrieved her passport and showed it to the server.

"Perfect! Your drink will be here in a moment," said the server and left to clear the table behind Lyra's.

When the coffee arrived, Lyra took a careful sip and involuntarily began to identify the ingredients—cognac, cherries, sugar, and coffee. She touched the tip of her tongue to her lips to identify a foreign flavor. She couldn't. If she had tasted eggs before, she would have detected the egg whites. But the failure did not upset her like it always did. This time, she was heading to Earth where she would get to learn and experiment with all Earthler ingredients.

She looked in the distance and smiled. A line of passengers was waiting to pass customs and security. A line she would soon join.

"I am not lying!" Lyra lashed out loud. "It was with me when I had my coffee at Spacebucks just...I showed my passport there barely an hour ago. Give me a minute. I am sure I'll find it."

"Miss, we've been through all your bags. Twice!" The security officer, who stood a foot taller than her, raised two fat fingers at Lyra's face.

"Hang on," Lyra said and lunged towards the coffee shop.

"Miss!" the officer yelled at her. "You cannot leave your bags unattended!" His voice sent a tremor through the customs area. Lyra had never heard a tone as scary as his. She looked around to find everyone staring at her. She paced back to the officer, lifted her bags, and walked back to the café, embarrassed and out of breath.

At Spacebucks, both the server and the young man helped her look for the folder. When they found nothing, they got back to work.

Lyra returned to the queue, seesawing with two heavy bags on both side, and another across her tiny frame. The loose laces of her shoes followed her. When she neared the officer, she realized that her bags had wheels and she could have rolled them.

She swallowed the frustration.

"I just checked at the café. They couldn't find it..." She panted. "Just think about it. Why would I visit Earth without my passport and visa? They wouldn't even allow me to check-in at Zenith without it!" She had never felt so helpless and desperate. Tears stung her eyes. "Please, trust me. I am not lying. Check your system. I..." Her voice cracked. She shoved her hands back into her messenger bag and searched again.

"I am afraid, I have to take you to the side, miss. A line is waiting behind you."

"Please."

"You cannot enter the Earth perimeters without valid documents. You have to return to your port of boarding," the officer dictated.

"This is a mistake. I am sure something can be done. Please don't send me back!" Agony swept her insides as she saw her life's biggest dream fade away.

Her stubbornness disgusted her, but she had to try. She continued pleading until the officer escorted her to the departures, the gate that would deport her to Zenith on the next shuttle.

"You are lucky you are only getting deported. Fewer than three words out of my mouth and you'd be sitting in cuffs across the Earth immigration officer. Now go back to your tin-can and make sure to bring the one thing that's needed when you visit Earth again, miss," said the officer and left.

As if the planet below had magnetized her feet, Lyra couldn't lift them off the floor. She dragged herself to the nearest sitting area, not believing how close she had gotten to the space elevator before being mercilessly plucked by misfortune.

She collapsed on an uncomfortable chair. Her problem-solving mind suggested that she run back to the immigration office and talk to a higher official, but instead she rubbed her scalp and massaged her head. She knew she would be thrown out or, worse, put on a No-Fly list.

Her face fell into her hands and she let out a sob.

Then a thought crossed her mind. She took out her phone and typed a message-

URGENT: I am being sent back to Zenith. I lost my documents. What do you think I should do?

The walls of the transit station stood tall in front of her. She visualized herself tearing through them, diving into space, and

disintegrating into dust within seconds.
    Her phone beeped with a reply-
    Find a new hobby.

CHAPTER 2

THE EARTHLER NEWS

July 15, 2125

ANTI-PACA CORPORATIONS SHUT DOWN IN SOUTHERN 1ST STRATUM

The Pacamounts raided multiple Trunks of southern 1st Stratum last night and seized seven corporations that have been known to assassinate NonCreamers for their missions. A BuyingBan of fifty days will be imposed by PacaDiscipliners on their entire customer base...

He read the headlines and shut off the news portal. It's not news, he knew. It is fabricated information written not by journalists but by psychologists who are omniscient about the best methods to indoctrinate the population.

His lenses switched to a black-market book-

On January 27, 2027, we learned about a near-Earth asteroid that was to pass by close to Earth. For years, Earth had salivated over the idea of outer-space colonization. Now, they had the perfect venue.

The M-type asteroid was discovered in 1884 and is roughly 30 miles x 11 miles x 3.5 miles in size. While passing by Earth, the asteroid was thrust by propellers and pulled into Earth's orbit. A human-made Yarkovsky effect. To everyone's surprise, Earth gained its second moon that day. The asteroid revolved smoothly in the High Earth Orbit, roughly at a quarter of the distance to the moon.

Three years later, when the Pacamounts clawed their way into Earth's politics, they decided to mine the asteroid.

The metallic asteroid, which was shaped like a barrel, was mined from the inside out, keeping its protective outer layer intact. They created a network of tunnels and then larger caverns within the structure. It was then encapsulated in a thin polymer shell and inflated with carbon monoxide at low pressure to the desired radius. The entire collection was heated until the nickel and iron in the asteroid began to react with the CO gas. By keeping the shell at a constant temperature, the metals were deposited evenly on the interior surface of the shell. The entry point into the asteroid was sealed with an airlock relatively early in the process, and the hollow space was filled with an atmospheric mix essential for humans to breathe. The dense and non-porous composition of the asteroid helped in sealing the atmosphere which was introduced over time. By the time the digging was done, a large cavernous space was ready to be colonized.

He had dozed off last night while reading the illegal book written by an anti-Paca. An arduous find. He bookmarked the page and turned off his lenses. The blue in his irises turned back to its natural color. His apartment's chipped ceiling reappeared in his vision.

The dead silence that rode in the air soothed him even as a musty stink tried to break open the room's closed windows. It was hard to get a moment of peace in Sonmanto.

He went to the bathroom, popped a TeethBot, and shut his lips tightly. The stubble on his cheek wiggled as the tab scrubbed his teeth. He pulled wet napkins out of the dispenser and wiped his face, arms, and upper body. The TeethBot burst in his mouth and thick minty liquid flooded his teeth. He spat before the last cycle ended, cringing at its taste.

The mirror in front of him reflected the tired face of a twenty-seven-year-old Earthler. He turned his head and pulled the ends of his thick black hair across his nape. They were half an inch longer than he preferred but he ignored that. He couldn't, however, ignore his facial hair. The PacaDiscipliners had already caught him and imposed BuyingBan on him twice. Not that he cared about the inability to shop, but today was not a day when he could afford to play on the edge. He shaved, which would make his face easily recognizable to the PacaEyes, just like the Pacamounts wanted.

From the bathroom shelf, he grabbed a slate gray T-shirt and one of the two denims he owned. After putting them on, he walked to the kitchen, which was twice the size of his small, single bed, and opened the door to an even tinier room inside.

The sight of the secret room comforted his deep gray eyes. Even though he was alone in the house, he looked around to make sure he was not being watched. Reflex. All the walls of the storeroom were lined with plastic shelves. Each shelf was stacked with worn-out, dusty books. What pleased him the most was the knowledge that each of those books belonged to a time different from today; that they came from an era when shelving them was not a punishable crime.

He reached for the thickest book on the top shelf. The title read *War and Peace*. His caffeine-infused dark lips sneered at the irony. A pocket was carved into its pages. That was how he had found the book when he bought it. He grabbed the heavy package that was cozied inside it and scanned the room again. Despite spending time in his only favorite place on the planet, he still felt groggy.

A red bottle on his desk enticed him.

He hid the door of his secret room and popped an AwakeTab from the red bottle into his mouth. Within seconds, the caffeine molecules shot through his membranes and alerted his brain cells.

A widget beeped on his bed. It was a reminder he had set for the arrival of his new roommate tomorrow. He ground his teeth and buckled the widget on his wrist. From his desk, he picked up an empty chocolate box and slid the heavy package from the book into it. He threw on his backpack and got out of his stale apartment.

The pavement outside his building brimmed with pedestrians; the addition of a couple more might have spilled everyone onto the street. He looked at the faces walking in different directions.

I hated them. Every single face. The mere sight of them nauseated me. I saw faces that were deep-fried in stress and loneliness with no dreams or ambitions of their own. They moved about, wearing ignorance and indifference like a winter coat. I didn't see people walking or driving to their jobs; I saw customized robots trudging to their programmed destinations to fulfill their programmed tasks. I didn't see homes; I saw warehouses that stored these robots when they were not in use. I pictured them returning to their storage rooms and plugging themselves into outlets to recharge for the next day. I saw a man getting on the bus and knew that the only goal of his life was to provide surplus blind loyalty. To exactly what? He wouldn't know. I saw children who didn't know they were children. They moved and talked like adults, carrying the lack of innocence within them.

From where I saw, it was a big pile of muck and it suffocated me. I knew that one day this planet is going to suffocate too and burst into a hot volcano of wrath and agony.

And I sure as hell didn't want to be here to witness it.

He clicked on his widget, switched on his lenses, and inserted pods in his ears. He preferred using the keypad, but he was late and so he had to speak to command his lenses.

"Prapsico Circle, Main Street, on foot," he spoke to the air in his gruff voice that was weakened by the AwakeTab addiction.

Public transportation disgusted him, and owning a car was a luxury he could not afford. He looked to his left. Heavy traffic was on the ground level. Cars and buses mostly stood at a specific spot, moving a foot at a time. Ten times fewer cars hovered over the ground-level traffic. They darted at the speed of bullets.

"Good morning, Aryabh. Welcome to PacaMaps," a voice spoke in his ear pods.

Two transparent routes formed in his peripheral vision.

"Your destination, one of Sonmanto's biggest hubs, is twenty minutes away by foot, with medium-level pedestrians on Route A and high-level pedestrians on Route B. Please select a route."

"Route A," Aryabh said.

"As you walk on the strong pavement built by Robust Constructions, select a product that interests you. Specially designed to enhance your walking experience. We have mind-boggling products ranging from shoes, sunglasses, blinkers..."

He memorized the route and turned off the lenses.

The sun was out. Even though the canopy of skyscrapers shielded the pavement from sunlight, the asphalt of Chase Street smoldered from the ever-growing heat.

Around fifty feet ahead, Aryabh saw Neslo, a homeless man he often encountered. He was sitting at the same spot, drinking the same spunky liquid in the same old, dirty glass. Like always, he was sitting on a stool and singing at the top of his voice.

Aryabh frowned. He had an urge to change the route, but he knew this was the quickest path to where he was going.

"We must not look at the goblin men, we must not buy their fruits," Neslo sang. "Who knows upon what soil they fed? Their hungry thirsty roots? Come..." He stopped as his eyes fell on Aryabh.

"Lookit, who is here! It's Mr. Grumpet," he yelled and raised his glass at Aryabh. His voice sounded drunk but he didn't look intoxicated. His balding head was covered in leftover grays and his face was a land of craters.

Aryabh hated Neslo with a deep passion. He was repulsed by his voice, his face, and his daily taunts. By ridiculing him for years, Neslo had entered himself into the endless list of people Aryabh would kill if he could. As always, he ignored his remarks and kept on walking. Neslo had an insatiable need for Aryabh's attention, which was why he enjoyed the pleasure of not giving him any.

"Lookit, who is too clever to lookit me. This ugly bugger, that's who!" Neslo announced again. His hoarse voice complemented the stuffy air of Sonmanto. People going in and out of the supermarket next to him ignored him, just like everyone else around.

Through the corner of his curious eye, Aryabh glanced at the signs and symbols painted on the legs of Neslo's stool and the board that leaned against them. Like always, he couldn't identify the art.

It also baffled him how Neslo was the only one who sat on a stool. All the other homeless people, who often endured his bullying, lined the floor of the pavement.

Aryabh stopped himself from thinking about the other homeless people. Their mere sight struck a nerve within him that he didn't know existed. He didn't hate all the faces. Not theirs. Those were the faces he had had to watch on every street ever since he was a child, the only faces he related to.

On hundreds of random nights, when their thoughts had kept him awake, he had walked past them, dropping pieces of gold on their bodies as they slept.

But not on Neslo's. An official complaint at the supermarket would be enough to have his stinking body get kicked out off the street, Aryabh always thought.

"Yah, yah, walk away, Grumpet, gallop away on your mighty horse," Neslo yelled at Aryabh's back.

"Asshole," Aryabh mumbled to himself and walked on.

It would have been easier to handle this business at his apartment but he didn't. He knew that in Sonmanto, when it came to secretive meetings, crowded places were safer than secluded ones.

Twenty minutes later, Aryabh reached the circle and stood by a bus station. He skimmed the PacaEyes around and above. They weren't capturing him. He stood at a perfect blind spot.

Once he felt secure in his surroundings, he looked for Shiaya.

In a crowd, Aryabh had always felt like an alien, an outsider who didn't belong. His existence, as he knew, was like oil to the murky water that was Earth. As different as he felt he was, he and the crowd around him seemed like one coalesced complexity of Sonmanto—the capital of planet Earth and the biggest Head in all the three Stratums.

The bustling horde and the loud traffic stifled him, as if a million nails were scratching drywall inside his head. But he resisted. Nothing was to ruin this. Today was one of the most important days of his life, the day he had waited for a long time.

He was glaring at a huge interactive hoarding in front of him when a voice from behind startled him.

"Gold first!"

She stood like a rock with her arms folded on her chest. If it weren't for the roughness of her mannerisms, she could have passed for a star at PacaEntertainments. The crispness of the early twenties boosted her flawless face. The waves of her dark magenta hair swayed with the wind of whooshing upper-level cars, even as its pointy golden tips teased her waist. Her nails were of gold, and sharp like daggers. She wore a deep magenta dress under a black, ankle-length vest that fluttered in the air like a cape. Her lips were the same color as her hair, as were her eyes. The ink of her tattoos blended like paint with her sharp features. Her tall frame spoke of her confidence, and her posture of self-importance.

Despite her undeniable beauty, Aryabh smelled vodka on her breath and looked at her forehead scar. Not because they corrupted her beauty, but strangely, those were the only things that made him feel comfortable.

"What?"

"Gold first," Shiaya said firmly.

Aryabh handed her the chocolate box and before he could explain, Shiaya spoke again, "Neat idea." She juggled the box in her hand to feel its weight.

"The rest of the gold after I verify the contents."

"You should know the damage I can do if you start babbling my name around," Shiaya threatened. "I can make your life difficult, not just with the Rodents, but with the Farm too. Don't forget; I've risked my life *and* my job trying to get this lousy folder for you. Cool T-shirt, by the way," she added. "Didn't you just wear this...let me recall...every day?"

"Folder," Aryabh demanded.

She opened her purse and took out a big, blue envelope-shaped folder. Aryabh snatched it in a heartbeat. He turned around to leave when Shiaya discreetly removed another item from her purse.

"What's the hurry, freakbox? Look what else I scored. Contraband." Shiaya sang the last word. The tiny diamond that hung from her septum piercing flailed. "That chick is either a fool or a badass, trying to bring something like this here. Now, how much extra for this? I know you are a sucker for such shit."

Aryabh looked at an old, worn-out notebook, a diary he had heard a lot about. The faded mustard color of its cover seduced him. A few extra ounces of gold were nothing compared to what was in her hand.

"Goodbye." He seized the diary, shoved it in his backpack, and walked away.

The twenty minutes back to his apartment were the longest twenty minutes of his life. As soon as he entered the house, he went through the contents of the folder like a sniffer dog. They smelled like rusted metal. From the contents, he only needed two things; the rest was useless. But his curiosity got the better of him.

He sat on the desk chair and pulled his right foot up to his butt. After he looked around, he inspected every single item. Apart from the documents, there was a thin sheet of screen, of the kind the Earthlers used some eighty years ago.

> Only Zenithers would know their way around the newest technology, but would still prefer to operate outdated gadgets to keep their lives simple and their environment clean.

The sheet had a button at the bottom, which he pressed. The screen lit up. It had a picture of a small boy holding a large spider. On its congested home screen, there were dozens of random files and folders. The one folder that grabbed Aryabh's attention the most was named 'Earth'. He tapped on it.

Hundreds of documents, images, videos, and audio files of Earth appeared on the screen.

Every byte in the folder infuriated Aryabh. He was stunned. The intense passion for Earth offended his core and insulted every second of his life. He wanted to smash the screen and break it into a million pieces.

How can someone be so naïve?

He lifted his wrist to his face and materialized the keypad from his widget to type a message. Hot anger flushed inside him when he re-read the last incoming message-

URGENT: I am being sent back to Zenith. I lost my documents. What do you think I should do?

Chapter 3

Zenith

July 15, 2125

She sat on the lawn outside her house, rocking herself back and forth on her late grandmother's chair. To her right, she saw a line of passengers waiting. A chatter of noise exploded from the left.

The loudest voice was of Ms. Tara telling everyone how little Lyra had failed to visit Earth.

"Twenty years of saving, all down the drain..." Her father's voice killed Ms. Tara's.

"Get. Your. Degree. Get. Your. Degree..." the rest of the crowd chanted in a chorus.

"We are glad to announce that the Earth perimeters are permanently closed for all Zenithers." An automated voice announced from the asteroid's roof.

"It's the repercussion of your self-serving dream and your audacity to leave me alone," spoke Sagan robotically as tears rolled down his cheeks.

Lyra struggled to run away, but the chair had turned into a jaw with sharp teeth around its rim. It was swallowing her up.

"Help. Help. I am sorry. Help," she screamed.

The officer from the transit station approached her and bent down to face her. His scary eyes flashed at Lyra. He shoved two fat fingers in her face. "Two more minutes and you'll turn into dust!" A maniac howl came out of his guts.

The thundering sound of his laughter perforated her eardrums and she woke up with piercing ear pain.

Lyra took quick breaths and relaxed when she heard *Moonlight Sonata* mixed with a sound clip of Earth's ocean waves. It had been playing on loop since last night.

She wondered if it was a dream or a conjuring of her half-awake mind. And yet, she was not new to nightmares. Over the years, she had seen the craziest of dreams. One of her unreasonable fears was the invention of a technology that could record people's dreams. She was sure she'd be certified a psychopath that day.

It was two days since she had returned home from the transit station. She was surprised that she had slept for eight hours. It was better than her usual four to five hours of sleep per night.

Her throat was scratchy and her scalp burned. Years of teeth-grinding had already stiffened her jaw, but the ache in the ears was new. She grabbed a glass of water from her nightstand and took two big gulps from it. It tasted like failure.

Fresh tears rolled over recently dried tears. Her bloodshot eyes resembled a fiery ocean of grief.

Ever since she could remember, she had felt a weight of aspirations within her. She wanted to do and be many things but could never figure out what they were. Every morning she had woken up questioning her future. Earth was the only concrete element of her identity. She was not certain about anything else as much as she was about moving there.

In this constant mental battle, she had lost her physical quintessence. The unceasing stress had disabled every muscle of her body from bringing strength to her posture. Her eyebrows were always knitted from constant thinking and her muscles always flexed from persistent anxiety. What she still possessed were the curious mud-brown eyes and a meek stoic face. She had retained the ever-present knots in her coffee colored hair and the nail scar below her left eye that looked like a dried-up tear. She still conserved her extraordinary, overworked mind.

Lyra hurried to the bathroom and splashed cold water on her face. She applied a liberal amount of moisturizer on the white trails that her nails had left on her skin and various bruises and stitch-scars from childhood trips and falls. Then she ruffled her hair to bring some life to them. At last, she looked at the mirror and tested a smile.

Her bedroom which was always littered with books, empty mugs, and organized clutter, was overflowing with her travel bags and scattered documents. Lyra climbed on her bed and walked across it, squashing and soiling her sheets. She stepped on the pillow and grabbed three dried-up mugs from a small bamboo bench between her bed and a window.

Like every morning, Lyra left her disordered room to clean the rest of the house.

As if her dexterity had been hijacked, her hands worked through the house like automated claws. She soaked the laundry, watered the garden, and swept the floors. Like always, she lifted the edge of the living room's rug and swept the leftover dust underneath it. She even gathered her old clothes, some from her now unpacked bag, and dropped them in the recycling bin outside the house. The clothes would travel to Zenith's Textile Recycling Center and be back in the market as brand-new in no time.

"Morning, Lai!" Keid walked up to Lyra in the kitchen and stroked her hair. He picked the pot from the counter to make tea.

"Why are you up so early? Let me get this," Lyra faked an uplifting tone and grabbed the pot.

"You seem upbeat. I thought you'd be..."

"I am fine, Dad," she said and opened the kitchen windows. A draft of fresh oxygen bathed her face. The rooflight hit her eyes and journeyed to the dining table where Keid sat.

"Good. I know I was okay with you leaving for this trip, but I wasn't exactly happy about it," Keid confessed.

Lyra maintained her gaze outside the window.

"It's not easy visiting a foreign planet." Keid rubbed and stretched his neck. "It doesn't matter how much you read about Earth, you will never understand how their world works. I've heard scary stories, Lai. Those people are strange."

Not many things enraged Lyra, but if there was one thing that boiled her blood, it was Zenithers making blanket statements about four billion Earthlers when they barely knew a couple. She despised how many say it because some say it.

Lyra lugged her sight over to the pot. The water was burbling with violent uproar.

"Don't take this the wrong way, Lai, but in a way, I am thankful they sent you back. It's for your good." Keid hesitated with his words but didn't choose to censor them.

Lyra found a lump building in her throat. She switched off the stove and grabbed a can of black tea.

"Now that there are no distractions, you can concentrate on your academics. It's time to leave these silly fantasies behind and get your master's and doctorate. You know you tried it all. The sanctuary, the bookstore, the hotel. They were all just phases and they passed. You'll be glad it's over. A bright future is in front of you, Lai. You have so much more to give. Zenith needs your contribution."

Lyra wanted to tell her father to stop talking, but instead, she placed the tea on the table and went upstairs to her room before her theatrics were exposed.

After finishing high school, Lyra had pursued a bachelor's degree in Food Science, an exciting field when you are living inside a hollowed-out asteroid. Science, in general, had attracted Lyra the most because she understood and accepted the universe through it. Plus, she was part of a civilization that was less than a century old. Zenith was always in a need of new inventions and discoveries.

She realized that the life of the Zenithers was fairly comfortable, with most basic needs met. But the one thing they craved more than anything else was food. Zenith needed to grow, cultivate, and modify food items that were available on Earth, items that had homed on the palette of the Terraformers who first moved to the asteroid from Earth seventy-five years ago. That was why she had picked Food Science.

The instinct to think about the asteroid's needs came from her parents. Keid and Poona had contributed their fair share to this world in the field of Botany and Zoology. Her father was a botanist who, along with other scientists, had successfully cultivated more than forty plants on Zenith, a once-impossible task. Her mother had played a vital role in convincing Zenithers and Earthlers to inhabit the asteroid with animals. She worked on methods to integrate wildlife on Zenith, which eventually populated the once human-dominated asteroid with gorillas, baboons, bats, and lemurs. With the help of her research, Zenith's forest was also incorporated with bees, insects, and butterflies, and the Alvariño pond with fish, frogs, and plankton.

Both her parents played vital roles in strengthening the flora and fauna of Zenith which turned the asteroid into a full-fledged ecosystem. Not just them, but her maternal grandparents had also played an important role in setting up the foundation of Zenith when they colonized the planet. Her parents' important education and grand achievements pressured Lyra to make the most of her potential too.

For four years, she studied Food Science and worked part-time as a research assistant at Zenith's only university. She ate up everything the university had to offer. Until she hit a brick wall. The field's rigid structure and lack of autonomy pushed her away.

But money had to be earned and saved for her future on Earth.

So, after graduating, she left the field and worked at the Goodall Sanctuary for two years. Keid was disappointed but he assumed that it was Lyra's way of commemorating her mother's memory.

During one of the events at the sanctuary, Lyra volunteered to help the catering staff. That was when she discovered that her passion lay not in the science of food but in the art of it. Cooking was the one thing that relieved her from being her logical, scientific self, a way to feel less robotic.

After she studied culinary arts, she took a job at the only luxury hotel on Zenith—Faraway Paradise. Because she was strongly attached to the animals at the sanctuary, she continued to volunteer as the animal caretaker.

Her father wasn't the only one who was bothered by her impulsive decisions. She was baffled too and had relied on her trip to Earth to put her life into perspective. She was sure she would know what she wanted once her feet were standing on Earth. All she needed was room to make errors and Zenith didn't provide that.

Instead of stewing in the web of her erratic thoughts, Lyra decided to head to work.

She walked to her usual kitchen corner and tied a white apron on her waist as tightly as she could. In the space between the walk-in freezer and the kitchen, she saw Wan, her coworker, napping on a stool. Pretending she didn't see him, she wiped the kitchen counters and prepped the ingredients. It was not her job but she liked doing it.

As a ritual, she was supposed to sprinkle salt over a whole lime and crush it under a pestle. That was what their executive chef had instructed the kitchen staff to do every morning for good luck. Lyra had lied for years, saying that she did it. She didn't believe in superstition or luck, or in wasting a perfectly good lime.

She had joined Faraway Paradise as a kitchen apprentice. All she did was clean the kitchen, open food cans, boil rice and pasta, and make sure the chefs had clean aprons. But while her limbs did the menial job, she observed the chefs constantly. The way the food danced in woks and pans amused her. She would learn a recipe each day, go home, and recreate it with her twist, using ancestral spices of her grandparents' land. She got hold of as many culinary books as she could and mastered major facets of their theory.

Her knowledge in the scientific aspects of food made her an expert in storing and preserving imported Earthler ingredients. Her thirst for learning the art of cooking and her dedication towards it was well-known among the staff. Hence, the executive chef, a person Lyra had come to know as the hardest person to impress, was impressed. She promoted her twice in two years.

Lyra now worked as the station chef or chef de partie, as her executive chef had always insisted on calling. She had no plans to return from Earth, but in case she had to, she wanted her job back. Therefore, she had taken a month's leave.

She stood in the hotel's kitchen, tying her neckerchief, when she remembered how her request for a lengthy leave had irked the executive chef, Balin. She stared at a floor tile and tried to board a different train of thought. Wonderful memories started to reel inside her head.

She was wearing blue overalls over a soft black T-shirt. On her feet were her favorite shoes with animals painted on them by the sanctuary's volunteers. For a seven-year-old, Lyra was mature, well-read, and analytical, thanks to her mother. When she was taken to the Earth Park for the first time, she headed straight to the interactive live exhibit.

As she walked through a tunnel-like entrance, she smelled Earthy scents that galloped inside the dark cave. An overwhelming sense of excitement overtook her. She started with the Seven Wonders of Earth. There were seven, twelve-foot replicas of architectural and natural wonders. She goggled at them with her jaw on the imitation mud floor.

After enjoying numerous exhibits, she had walked up to a stall that offered various choices of Earthler music. She pressed a button next to a song titled Symphony No. 5, and for the first time in her life, Lyra heard Beethoven. She was touched in a way no seven-year-old is emotionally wired to.

She gaped at the replicas of famous paintings from Earth. Her mother, who enjoyed painting as a hobby, explained their origins.

The two hours she had spent in the exhibit were glorious, but they were nothing compared to what she had experienced outside. When she got out, she was met with a huge green structure, which to her, looked like a gigantic dome. As she circled it, she saw water droplets sprinkling from above. When she looked upwards, a few drops pricked at her face. She giggled and ran back to her mother, who looked surreal in an emerald green tunic. A small pair of earrings carved from the iron of Zenith swung at her ears.

"Mom, what is this huge dome?" she had asked.

"That's a mountain," Poona explained. "Earth is covered with giant hills like these, kind of like the rocks here on Zenith, but bigger and taller, and those water droplets...Do you remember I told you how Earth doesn't have the same temperature throughout the year as we do; they have seasons?"

"Yah..."

"There is one hot season called summer when the sun heats the oceans and rivers of Earth. Oceans and rivers are like our pond, but larger. When the water heats up, it evaporates. Like when we boil water for tea."

"Yes, the steam!" Lyra exclaimed.

"You remember what happened when Dad overheated water one morning? A lot of steam reached the roof of the stove and water droplets dripped down. That's called condensation. It's the same concept on Earth, but on a huge scale. The water evaporates, the vapor rises up towards the sky and forms clouds, and they shower water back on Earth. Earthlers call it rain. It falls exactly like this, but from clouds, not sprayers."

Her mother's intelligent voice had sounded like a poem to Lyra.

"So the water falls from the roof?"

Poona chuckled. "Yes, Lai, Earth sky is kind of like our asteroid's roof."

"Wow!"

"This process is very important for the survival of Earthlers. They don't have a Regenerative Life Support System like us. Without rain, people and animals die."

"Oh!" Lyra's face fell.

"But it always falls," her mother reassured. "Your grandma used to play and dance in the rain."

"Really?" Lyra said, mesmerized.

She stared at the fake rain on the fake mountain. The imagery of the real version had thrilled her.

Keid had then dragged the mother-daughter to various Earthler food carts and they ate food that Lyra had never seen before.

It was the happiest day of her life, a day she would never forget. Because that was the day the thought of visiting Earth was seeded in her brain.

'The Earth Park is a sad by-product of the Terraformers' nostalgia.' — Lyra recalled an old comment. Her executive chef's cynical opinion about the park overran her memory. Before she realized it, her mind wavered in the wrong direction.

She thought of all the times she had visited the Earth Park, which was not many since the park was open only for a month every year. It consumed a lot of Zenith's energy and resources, which could be put to better use.

Lyra asked her mind to shut up, and tried to think of ways to go back to Earth, something she did all around the clock, but the memory of the last time she had visited the park pounced on her.

She was fifteen when she had gone to the Earth Park on a school trip. Coming home tired from physical and social exhaustion, she had gone to bed without changing. When she opened her eyes, it was to the unbearable sob of her father informing her of her mother's demise.

Keid had come home to find the lifeless body of his wife and a weeping six-month-old Sagan beside it. Poona had died on their living room floor after calling Lyra repeatedly for help.

She needed her inhaler. Lyra knew this because she had several missed calls and a message on her phone from her mother. In her slumber, Lyra had felt the phone vibrate, but had ignored it like she always did.

Since her mother's death, Lyra had played that night in her head countless times. Every time, she imagined herself waking up to the yelp of her mother or answering her call. She would rush down the stairs, get the inhaler from her parents' bedroom, lift her mother from the floor, and help her pump the medicine into her airway. Her mother would breathe normally in less than thirty seconds.

But that was not what had happened. She had not woken up. Medically, her mother had died of an asthma attack, but to Lyra, she was the murderer. Her indolence had killed her.

"Why the fuck are the asses of these ladles next to the faces of these spatulas?"

Balin's commanding voice filled the kitchen. It brought Lyra back from her living nightmare. She watched as the executive chef rearranged her drawer and moved around like turbulence. Even though Balin's head tossed, her short burgundy hair stood stiffly, as if she had threatened them not to move.

Lyra also noticed that the entire morning staff was in the kitchen. Everyone was either looking at her or following Balin's trajectory.

"Pre-shift, Gryffy." Balin clapped twice. She removed her sparkling white apron from a bag and tied it around her plump waist.

Lyra observed her own faded apron and tiptoed behind the counter. When she found her shoes just as dirty, she polished her left shoe with the socked right foot and vice-versa.

Giving the pre-shift was her responsibility, but she had transferred the duty over to Gryffy. Speaking to a large group was not something Lyra looked forward to.

"This week's schedule is changed again as Lyra is back," began Gryffy. "By the way, Lyra, a guest left you a ginormous tip while you were away. He kept singing songs about the pilaf you prepared."

Lyra nodded.

"No one ever leaves us big tips," Gryffy complained. "We have things to buy too."

"You are not in my kitchen for financial validation," said Balin.

"Of course." Gryffy bent at her waist and bobbed her head. "Anyway, Kora is back from her break too; so she can resume her night shift and Wan can go back to working mornings. But that poor man needs a break. He hasn't taken an off in seven days! His snoring face was on the floor when I came. He looks like a week-old zucchini."

"No metaphors!" instructed Balin.

Lyra debated in her mind, with her eyes veering from side to side, whether Gryffy's statement was a simile or a metaphor, and if all similes were indeed metaphors.

"Sorry, Chef. Well, nothing else is new. It's a slow day." Gryffy closed her notepad. "Darn it, I forgot. We have a new apprentice. He will be training with us for six months. This guy!" She pulled a short, lanky nineteen-year-old culinary student in front of her.

The apprentice's face visibly relaxed when the executive chef took her eyes away from him to talk to the hotel's manager who had just walked in.

Gryffy took the opportunity to break the ice with the apprentice. She rested her arm on his nervous shoulder and said, "Let me introduce you to everyone. It's a wholesome kitchen. That guy over there is Per; he is our Garde Manger. He'll rip your chef coat and make roses out of it if you don't listen to him." Gryffy pointed at a big guy who frowned at her from the corner.

"This blonde guy, he is an apprentice like you. He joined last month and hasn't slept since then... That worn-out old man is Wan. You can call him Mr. Zucchini. Ooh, he makes the best jewelry! Contact him if you need a nose ring... That tiny woman hiding in the corner is Lyra. She is our Station Chef. She is the kind of girl your mother would want you to marry, but ask you to keep a hundred-yard distance after she sees what goes on in that head of hers. And, lo and behold, I am Gryffy, the pastry chef." She curtsied. "I am cool. As opposed to our hot-headed Chef. That's her, Balin. She will skin you alive if you are late, right before she makes you sit on a hot pan until you—"

"Gryffy!" Balin shouted. "Stop scaring the boy!" The manager had dispersed.

"Sorry, Chef."

"You, new boy," Balin addressed the new apprentice. "Get your ass in the walk-in freezer and clean that hell hole. It's nasty. I want every inch of the freezer cleaned, all spills gone, all rotten food disposed of. It's minus four degrees inside; you'll freeze to death if you think you can sneak in a nap there. Go now."

The apprentice's face turned into what looked like a week-old zucchini.

"The manager just informed me—two unplanned shuttles are arriving from Earth today. The sun is still broiling those vermin; so they'll be flocking to Zenith this week. Sadly, our economy runs on this tragedy. Two shuttles worth of inconsiderate Earthler tourists who will find faults in our cooking, no matter what. Don't fret. Do what you do every day—the best. You, old apprentice! I want every pot and pan scrubbed and shined. But, before that, grab the inventory list for me. Let's cancel black garlic rice from today's menu. The delicate little guts of Earthlers can't digest garlic, the most exquisite spice in this universe." Her red, glossy lips puckered as she thought of garlic.

"Per," she continued, "make those ugly carrots pretty. I don't care how! I need them for the buffet presentation. Gryffy, stop sprinkling sugar syrup on everything. It doesn't make your cakes moist. It makes them soggy, like your sense of humor. And Lyra..." Balin turned her face towards her. "Stop biting nails in my kitchen. Wait... why are you twenty-five days early?"

"Chef, I—"

"Not now. We are late, already. Line check, everybody. Come on, chop-chop!" Balin clapped again.

On the way back home, Lyra evaluated everything she had lost recently. She had been deported before reaching Earth. She was out of thousands of ferrics that she had spent on Earth tickets and visas. All her important documents were lost, leaving her with a temporary badge. And she had lost her tablet, on which she had stored her whole life. The one person who could help had had nothing but a jeer to offer. She had not even begun to dissect the mysterious disappearance of her folder yet.

When she got off the bus, instead of walking home, she found herself heading towards the William Herschel Observatory.

She climbed the observatory tower, the highest building on the asteroid, while pressuring her brain to come up with new ideas for leaving Zenith again. Her brows met each other as she harassed herself to think of different means to go to Earth once more. She would do anything, she told herself.

When she reached the top, Lyra glanced over the world she was born and raised in. From above, Zenith's crescent colony looked like a cozy cradle, twinkling with streetlights and harmony. Her world that looked like the inside of a horizontal barrel was occupied by over seven thousand Zenithers. She pictured them sitting in their houses with their families, content and satisfied.

Straight in the distance, she saw the farthest point of the asteroid thirty miles away. Its reflection glistened in her eyes under the dim lights of the observatory dome.

"Earthrise in one minute," said Rahi, one of the astronomers at the observatory.

Lyra turned around and placed her wet eye against the telescope's eyepiece. In the distance, the transit station flicked like a candle flame. It wounded her.

She peered into the dark, lonely depths of space as a giant blue marble emerged from beneath.

CHAPTER 4

Watching the numbers ascend and descend on the elevator screen always unnerved Aryabh. That made living on the 94th floor a mental battle. He distracted himself by reading the black-market book-

After three successful human probes, on July 26, 2050, the first batch of 48 Earthlers was sent to colonize the asteroid. Over two years, Earth transported twenty more batches. Why these specific people? We'll never know. The people of those batches, according to Zenither history, came to be called the 'Terraformers'. They were comprised of people from all fields—doctors, farmers, scientists and researchers, builders, technicians, teachers, entertainers, artists, and even children. Along with Earthler astronauts, they were able to terraform the asteroid by building its infrastructure and ecosystem. On January 26, 2052, one and a half years after the Pacamounts officially took over Earth, the

Terraformers formed their own constitution and wrote their laws and regulations. With a celebratory ceremony, they raised a toast and named their nation Zenith.

No one knows the two words the Pacamounts had uttered that day. The two words that might answer the question—why did they allow a group of people to form their own colony on an asteroid?

Seventy-five years later, asteroid Zenith operates today as an independent nation, populated by 7,262 Zenithers.

The elevator doors retracted. Aryabh walked along the lobby and entered a password to unit number 9413.

As he opened the door, he froze at the sight of his studio apartment. For a moment, he thought the Pacamounts had conducted a raid.

He rushed to the kitchen. It was empty; his secret library safe behind the cabinet. He advanced towards the bathroom and twisted the doorknob. It was locked from inside.

Aryabh glanced at the room once again, his hand still pulling at the knob. The wall that concealed the kitchen had a painting of a Trunk landscape hung on it. Thick clouds moved within its frame above stony mountains. On the back of the main door was another frame. The words 'Home Sweet Home' flashed and sparkled on it. But it was the frame on the wall behind his desk that pushed him over the edge.

It was a picture of a man in a green suit posing in front of a busy, Head street. His right leg was mounted on a bench and his hand volleyed from under his chin to his waist. Aryabh wanted to smack the picture and wipe the grin off his face, and he would have done that had not the entire floor been jammed with bags and boxes.

It was his new roommate. He had sent him the apartment password because even in his wildest dreams, Aryabh had not presumed that he would barge in and litter the house in his absence.

He banged the bathroom door.

"A minute," came a melodic reply.

Hearing a strange voice in his apartment turned on a switch in Aryabh. His reflex kicked in. He ran to his bed and sucked in a breath of relief. The paperback he was reading last night and the folder were safe under his pillow.

He popped two AwakeTabs to stop himself from assaulting his new roommate and sat on the edge of his bed, one foot by his hip. Guilt struck him. He grabbed the folder and pressed it to his chest. By being reckless, he had invalidated his lifelong struggle.

Aryabh removed a metal badge from the folder; the face of the woman he had robbed stared back at him. After months of tiring work, this was his first successful attempt in acquiring a badge. A Zenither badge was a unique identity card designed and given to every Zenither when they are born. It's a symbol of pride for them. The badge not only gave them access to various infrastructure on Zenith, such as the public gates, public transportation, schools, college, and their bank accounts, but it carried personal details like their lineage that tracked back to the Terraformer of their family.

For Aryabh, however, only two things were important—the badge's unique code and its material.

Despite his expertise, he was neither able to forge the code, because of how old-school it was, nor was he able to scour the metal from which the badges are made. They had been constructed from the alloys mined from the asteroid.

Therefore, he needed a Zenither.

Once a tourist Zenither landed on Earth, they were always under PacaEyes. The only place where he could access them was the PacaSpace Transit Station. The station, however, was only open to a certain class of Earthlers. To have the privilege to travel to outer space, an Earthler had to be in the inner circle of the Pacamounts, the elite circle called the Cream, and to be a Cream, one must either be born in that class or be approved after rigorous testing.

Aryabh had lost hope. Until he walked past a café and saw a barista.

He had hacked into a list of all the station's businesses and their employees. Among dozens of names, Shiaya's name had embossed the most. A few days of research had led Aryabh to the conclusion that she, like most NonCreamers, was a slave to fame, wealth, and power. That had made things easier.

Meeting her, however, wasn't as easy. Shiaya had a talent—she only ran into people she wanted to meet. Aryabh was not in that category. Weeks later, he had solved that problem too.

When Shiaya made Aryabh confess the real reason behind the theft, she had mocked him.

"So, you voluntarily want to go back to the Stone Age?" And then she laughed. "*Stone* age. Get it? Because it's an asteroid."

"Zenith is predominantly nickel-iron."

"Aha…That's why everyone calls it a tin-can. Doesn't make it better, dude. Do you know they sweep their floors and hang their clothes to dry? Buncha fuddy-duddies! No one leaves here and goes to a Third World that dangles in space. Not even people like us who hate the Rodents."

"Earth dangles in space too. How ignorant are you!"

"Ignorant enough to allow you to pay in gold!" Shiaya was furious because she was not getting money in return for her work. Wiring money to her would leave a trail. Every single monetary transaction was monitored. Even with his mastery in being discreet, Aryabh could not take chances. Many a time, when he read old books, he wished it was the 21st century. He could just give her a sack of paper money and call it a deal.

One of Aryabh's clients was a gold merchant. He had learned that working for gold and using it to bribe people was the safest way to get things done.

His mission was successful. He would give the remaining gold to Shiaya and forge his own identity on Lyra's badge. After a couple of months' work, he would be packing his bags to leave this planet behind.

The possibility of this dream had been Aryabh's sole comfort throughout the worthless monstrosity that had been his life. He was relieved that the hardest part was over.

"The roommate, finally!" said the same soft-spoken, melodic voice.

Aryabh sneaked the folder back into its hidden place and stayed stuck to his bed.

"I am Kenai." The man pointed at his own photo. "Kenai from Dvedi. It's a small Trunk in the 2nd Stratum. That's Dvedi." He knocked on the painting with the mountains.

Never in a million years had Aryabh imagined a sight like that in his apartment.

The man stood half-naked with a towel wrapped around his waist. Drops of water dripped from his tightly coiled, jet-black hair and glistened on his shoulders. If it was not for his over-expressive face, his hunched, skinny body would have resembled a shriveled palm tree.

"You took a shower?" Aryabh didn't bring the shock in his voice to his face. The filth lying around the house was no longer the reason for his wrath.

"Hah...yes." Kenai pushed his glasses up his wrinkled nose bridge. "You see, I was out of a job. Homeless for two months. I cannot meet my new roommate for the first time smelling like a dumpster now, could I?" His eyes, mouth, and limbs moved more than what Aryabh was comfortable with.

He was taken over by so much rage that the only safe way to deal with it was to suppress it. It was not like he could kick the guy out and afford to live alone; he needed money now more than ever. Besides, after the line of roommates who had refused to live with him or left within a week, Aryabh had to tolerate the new creature.

"Never shower..." Aryabh stopped midsentence and typed in the air by his wrist.

"Ooh, you have a widget! All I have is a dingy, old phone. My ex-girlfriend's boyfriend had a widget."

"Check your message," Aryabh ordered.

"You sent me a message? I am right here."

"Check your message!"

Aryabh's towel-clad roommate ran to his bag and pulled out an old, flat gadget. He read the message on its widescreen-

Never shower without a schedule.

Never interrogate me about my work or personal life.

Stay away from me and my things.

Aryabh needed this quiet time to inspect him. He observed his face. The first thing he noticed were the golden-framed glasses on Kenai's eyes. He had never seen an Earthler with eyeglasses.

The sunlight from the window cast a glare on them. It bothered Aryabh because he couldn't read his eyes.

But when Kenai turned away from the glare, Aryabh saw two big hazel eyes, one not aligning with the other. He had strabismus.

"This is reasonable. I can follow these rules, but I have a lot of questions."

Aryabh's silence forced Kenai to speak again.

"I brought a sleeping bag." He gestured at a bundle by Aryabh's bed. "Just tell me where to sleep. I won't need a bed, but I do have a lot of questions."

Aryabh calculated that not answering his questions right now meant random questions in the future at unexpected times. So he got up to give his roommate a tour. He noticed that Kenai was at least four inches taller than him. It irked him.

"That's a meal slot machine." Aryabh walked to the kitchen and placed his hand on a bulky appliance with an elongated lever on the side. "Ten recipes on its menu. Menu." He pointed at a list pasted on the machine. "Those are the slot refills." He motioned his head towards four sacks in the corner. "You pay half, more if you're a hog. I buy them in bulk every six months. Don't wait for my announcement. Refill the machine when nothing comes out."

"All these dishes look the same," Kenai whined as he read the list.

"You can mix and match."

"But they all have one basic sauce! And how are we going to get all the nutrients?"

Aryabh showed him another list that displayed four nutrients—Protein, Carbohydrates, Vitamins, and Minerals. He pressed the button next to Protein and pulled the lever. An inch-sized capsule dropped in the slot. He split the shell and shoved it under Kenai's face.

"Here! Sprinkle your way to nutritious food."

Kenai smelled the capsule powder and crinkled his nose, hoping he didn't offend his roommate. Luckily for him, Aryabh wasn't watching. He was glancing towards his secret room. Its door was hidden well behind the two sets of cabinets which stored dishes and bowls.

"A question," said Kenai. "Why so much clutter when you can make everything that comes out of this machine on one single stove?"

"Did you just fuckin' drop from the sky?"

"Sorry, Aryabh, I just moved to Sonmanto. I've only lived in Trunks before. This is my first time in a Head, and Sonmanto is like the master of Heads. Everything here is a bit too much for me, to be honest. I promise I will get used to it."

Kenai spoke in a tone so soft that Aryabh calmed down. He did, after all, know Kenai's history from his Pacaprofile.

From life to death, the Pacamounts recorded every single detail about a NonCreamer into their profiles. This invasion of privacy had helped Aryabh a great deal. Being a hacker had its privileges and gaining access to everyone's PacaProfile was one of them. He had scurried every little detail about Kenai before deciding to choose him as his roommate. His history was a bit jumbled, but it was established that this naïve Trunker was not a red flag.

"I know you Head folks don't like wasting time. But I love cooking!" Kenai went on. "It's therapeutic to me, you see. I can even cook for you. Hey, I can teach you! It'd be a great way to, you know, bond with each other. What do you think?" His eyes twinkled below his thick brows.

Aryabh draped his chest with his arms and changed the subject.

"That's the fresh-water tank." He gestured at the kitchen ceiling. "Water comes every Sunday for fifteen minutes and fills the tank. Two faucets are affixed to it, this one and the other in the bathroom. Treat this water like your blood." He walked out of the kitchen and headed to the bathroom. "This one behind the toilet collects urine and used water." Aryabh's eyes darted at a black tank larger than the one in the kitchen. "It has faucets in the kitchen and bathroom too. They have black knobs on them. Here." He threw a plastic jar at Kenai. "These are FilterBots. Drop them in the black tank every night. It recycles and purifies the wastewater."

"We have to drink our pee?" Kenai said, repulsed.

"A wise rule would be to use the fresh-water for drinking and the black tank water for everything else. But if an ignorant invades the apartment without notice and empties the whole fresh-water tank to shower, you drink your pee for the rest of the week," Aryabh said and left the bathroom.

Ridden with guilt and shame, Kenai dressed quietly in the bathroom and pondered over his immature actions. He rehearsed a speech and walked up to Aryabh in a fresh, pastel pink shirt, tucked inside black dress pants.

"I take this opportunity to apologize for my inconsiderate behavior and will, henceforth, live by all the standards set by this apartment. Please give me a chance to make a second first impression," Kenai recited and offered his hand.

"Listen," Aryabh spoke without looking at him or his hand. "I've already conversed more than I'd like, and that was the most I'll ever speak with you. Anytime you feel the need to talk, read my message. Cram it, memorize it, follow it. Now, do you mind?" He signaled at the space in front of his eyes and asked Kenai to leave him alone, hereby having the most polite conversation of his life.

If Kenai was disappointed, he didn't express it. Although, it excited him when he noticed the electric blue in Aryabh's eyes. He had heard about powerful people, like the Cream, who used lenses, but he had never watched someone using it up close.

He decided those were important retinas, that his roommate wasn't a regular person, and that thrilled him.

From a worn-out duffel bag, he grabbed a small metal device and shoved it in his pants pocket. Then he muttered something under his breath and punched the device. It made a clicking sound. Before Aryabh could ask him to keep it down, he was out of the apartment for his first job in Sonmanto.

The week that followed was filled with Kenai's numerous attempts at scoring another job after being fired from the first one. He went from employer to employer interviewing for a bottom-wage job. All he gained in return were harsh insults, sore feet, and painful hunger.

Aryabh spent that week in similar agony after listening to the loud clicks of Kenai's device and even louder snores that arose from his sleeping bag.

Kenai also thanked him every hour for letting him eat the slot machine meals without paying his share. "I will never forget this. Not until I die!" His thick glasses didn't hide the wetness in his eyes. "I am broke. I don't have a penny. I'd be starved right now if it weren't for you. Because of you, a person like me has the privilege to sit on the floor of a Sonmanto apartment and eat food for free. Thank you, buddy. I will never, ever forget this." He said as he ate a slice of vitamin-coated pizza. The lump in his throat moistened the hard bread. "My mother used to say if you want to help someone, feed them and—"

"You want to thank me?" Aryabh cut in. "Then sign this. I've put the apartment in your name. Your credit is stronger than mine," he lied. "It's just on paper; we'll split the rent." He brought his wrist close to Kenai so that he could sign on the projected lease.

With his chest out and chin elevated, Kenai agreed.

His hand wavered as he tried to sign mid-air. When he finished, he accidentally opened a minimized document. It was Aryabh's identity card with his picture on it and the word 'PacaChild' written above it.

Kenai observed that it was different from his own Earthler ID. Below Aryabh's picture, the ID read:

NAME: 171-2098-1102-8A
BORN: November 2, 2098
BIRTHPLACE: Sonmanto, 1st Stratum
BATCH: 8
HEIGHT: 5'10"
WEIGHT: 152 lbs
OCCUPATION: Web Designer
PARENTS: The Pacamounts

CHAPTER 5

Zenith

July 22, 2125

It was a regular Sunday morning. Zenith's market on Borlaug Street bustled with delighted shoppers who cut through the aroma of fresh vegetables and vibrant fruits. Next to a berries stand, an old Terraformer was arguing with a young boy over the lack of animal milk in the market.

"We once raised cows here, we can raise them again too. What are you farmers waiting for? Another century? I need Earth milk! I need my calcium!" She pointed her finger.

The boy mentioned how Zenith's resources like water and land were limited, that the asteroid's confined habitat was not suitable for raising livestock, and neither the scientists nor the farmers could do anything about it. When he explained why they stopped animal agriculture in the mid-80s, the old woman muttered curses under her breath.

The boy gave up and offered to walk her to an Earthler store to help her find imported animal products.

"I am taking this issue to the Terraformers Union, lad. They are going to hear about this."

As she turned around, her small, hunched body slammed into Lyra.

"Blind girl! Can't you see and walk?" The old Terraformer scowled at her and left.

Lyra gritted her teeth as she lugged a hefty tote bag of groceries which left an indent on her bony shoulder. As if some déjà vu had hit her, she remembered one of the other times when she had been in the Borlaug market, the time when she had received the first message from her Earthler friend. Only, he was a stranger then-

Hey, Dawn, I want to discuss something. Call me when you are free.

Over the years, Lyra had tried communicating with random Earthlers, including the guests who visited the hotel. She had also surfed all Earthler websites and portals that were accessible to Zenithers. There weren't many.

It was hard for her to reach out to strangers, but there was no harm in gaining an Earthler's perspective about her big trip, and if someone could answer even one of her thousand questions about the planet, that would be golden.

But Earthlers had mostly ignored her. That was why, even though she was not a punctual communicator, she responded to that message instantly. She drafted her response a dozen times before sending a reply-

This is not Dawn. If you are trying to contact someone on Zenith, you have reached the right place but not the right person.

The sender had apologized for the error and made small talk. He was also kind enough to send Lyra a free app, which she installed on her phone to message him without getting charged. Within a week, several messages began to transmit between Earth and Zenith.

Lyra: What's your name?

Aryabh: Aryabh, yours?

Lyra: Interesting name. What does it mean? I am Lyra.

Aryabh: It doesn't serve any meaning. What does Lyra mean?

Lyra: My father named me after one of the brightest constellations seen from Earth, probably because his father named him after a star.

Lyra had bonded with Aryabh over their shared interests in books and music. Their fondness for each other's habitat gave them endless topics to talk about. Aryabh was the most distinct person Lyra had ever known. His unique perspective on everything under the stars intrigued Lyra. The fact that he was a stranger and she didn't have to physically face him made it easier for her to speak her mind. Moreover, Aryabh had a hint of darkness that she related to. Unlike her fellow citizens, he didn't shy away from talking about morbid realities.

Before she knew it, she was sharing things that were only meant to perish in the cluttered corners of her head.

On the fourth day of talking to him, she spent the whole evening learning about Earth thunder, storms, earthquakes, and tsunamis. The pictures of those disasters left her speechless. Lyra cherished the fact that each conversation with Aryabh was like an Earth-education class.

In six weeks of knowing him, she had grown to consider the Earthler her close friend, which was an unlikely event in her life.

Lyra's past had made her conclude the bitter truth that she was incapable of making and keeping friends. Her need for space and keeping her world extremely private had repelled every friend she had made since childhood. That was why Aryabh now held a special place in her life. By talking to him every day, she had unearthed a side of her personality that she didn't know existed.

She was fascinated by the fact that Zenith, her entire world, was as tiny to Aryabh's city as an apple seed is to the whole apple. The population of his Head alone was a thousand times higher than the entire population of Zenith. What surprised her further was learning that Aryabh had never seen or tasted an apple.

Lyra's newfound friendship was so rewarding that she never felt the need to hear his voice or see his face.

Between the chats, she had once searched about him on all the Earthler websites. She did not admit it to herself but something didn't quite fit in. Upon finding no information on him, she had decided to go with the flow.

Lyra sat on the dusty pavement of Borlaug market to catch a breath and recalled the last decent conversation she had had with Aryabh.

Aryabh: I am excited to meet you, Lyra. I hope you like my gift. It should be big enough to carry all your paperwork.

Aryabh had sent her a 3D model file as a good luck present, which she had printed out a day before her journey. It was a blue envelope-shaped folder with a map of Earth printed on it.

Aryabh: By the way, get Estlechino from Spacebucks while you are at the Transit Station. Don't forget or you'll regret it.

Lyra had imagined Aryabh to be disappointed too. He had mocked her for wanting to move to Earth but had also helped her through a lot of the prep work.

She glanced at her watch. It was 10 a.m., which meant it was ten in Sonmanto too.

Because Zenith didn't have natural light, they had adopted Earth's 24-hour clock system to keep things simple. The simulated lights on the asteroid's roof were turned off at 6 p.m. and turned back on at 6 a.m. to mimic Earth's morning and evening. When the first colony settled on Zenith, the Pacamounts had set the Zenith Standard Time (ZST) the same as Sonmanto, the capital of Earth.

Lyra grabbed her phone from the pants pocket and stared at its screen, hesitating.

In another corner, Aryabh stared through his lenses, hoping to get an update from Lyra.

Communication between Earth and Zenith was monitored by the Pacamounts, and so Aryabh had built his own encrypted instant message client, which he had named Tunnel. He had tricked Lyra into installing Tunnel on her device to keep their communication off the Clearnet.

He had planned to cut off communication with Lyra after acquiring her badge. Once he was on Zenith, she couldn't interrupt his life. She had never seen his face and he would be using a different name.

But his need to see Lyra's reaction to the theft proved stronger than his need to be safe. In his own twisted way, he wanted to check the emotional damage he had wrought on the person who took him for a friend.

Aryabh squirmed on his bed like the lid on a boiling pot.

Along with other needless baggage, Kenai had brought along with him an old, outdated TV bot. To Aryabh's indifference, he had recently expressed that TV was his favorite stress-buster. His new ten-hour shift as a busser was his recent stress.

Kenai had ordered his robot to play a comedy movie, which he had been watching for an hour, sitting on the floor beside Aryabh's bed. He was cracking up at every scene that the TV bot projected on the kitchen wall.

Aryabh glanced at the projection. The character was attempting to climb the walls of a tall building and was falling on his back, repeatedly. The same scenario looped over and over. The more times it happened, the more Kenai giggled. When the actor finally reached the top, he belched, looked at the camera, and said, "Didn't see *that* coming!" Then he winked at the audience and the movie ended.

Kenai burst into a fit of laughter and fell on the floor, holding his stomach.

"Is this for real?" muttered Aryabh, even though the demise of art and entertainment was not news to him. He pushed the pods in his ears and turned on his lenses again.

Aryabh: I was only being honest. What happened to your documents?

After picking Lyra as his target, Aryabh had been confounded. She was a Zenither, a human without a PacaProfile. He couldn't study her. He had to build the profile himself after learning her likes, dislikes, and things that affected her and her decisions.

Making small talk was not difficult; it was his most effective shield. It took Aryabh fewer than three messages to conclude that Lyra was hopelessly obsessed with Earth. She was so blinded by her desire to talk to an Earthler that she had not even inquired about Dawn, the Zenither she thought he had been trying to reach.

He did admit that Lyra was clever and inquisitive. It would be a challenge to get her to do something without showing her sense and logic. But like everyone else, she had a weakness.

Aryabh knew that Lyra would use a folder that had an Earth's map printed on it. She was wearing an Earth pendant on her neck. He knew that Lyra would drink an Earthler beverage he recommended. She had shared her curiosity about Earthler cuisine. He knew that she would cross paths with Shiaya. All Shiaya had to do, after verifying her identity, was nab the folder from her bag.

Aryabh's wrist vibrated.

Lyra: Lost them at the transit station. I've filed a complaint with our Head of Law Enforcement. How can they just disappear? The more I think about this, the more it stops looking like an accident.

Bad news. That was not what he wanted to read.

Aryabh: Paranoia has taken over you. To be honest, it's great you lost them. Don't fight your fate. It sucks that you got deported, but if I were you, I'd be thanking my stars instead of moping.

Her reply was quick.

Lyra: What's with the sudden change in attitude? Please don't hurl fate and stars at me. I am responsible for my own life and where it leads. Let's also keep your honesty to yourself.

Aryabh: You live in a bubble that you've tailored to amuse yourself. There is nothing to adore about Earth. The grass is always greener.

Lyra: That's rich coming from someone who hates where he is and wants to live on Zenith.

Aryabh regretted sharing that.

Aryabh: Don't you dare compare your fantasies to my aspirations. You are some nature-obsessed dunce who is chasing beauty, some bucolic utopia. I want to leave this shithole because I deserve a dignified life. And while we are at it, Earth is not beautiful. It's a world of slot machines where everything has been disposed of but freedom. So don't tell me we are the same.

Aryabh was relieved to finally vomit his feelings. He was sick of sugarcoating his words for her badge.

His widget got a response after a minute.

Lyra: While not feeling free on the fourth biggest planet of our star system is justified, something I would never invalidate, my feeling of being trapped on this diminutive boulder is not a subject of your mockery. Freedom is subjective. For you, it's an escape from your oppressed world. For me, it's liberation from monotony, from a society that does not take into account an individual like me. You can sit in the freest state and still feel the shackles on your feet. Sometimes it's more than your political rights that liberate you. Imposing your customized self-righteous definition on everyone is what I define as a dunce. Don't talk like you know me. If nature-obsessed is the best adjective you can come up with for me, I feel foolish for even communicating with you.

It was not every day that someone shut Aryabh up. It did not settle well with him. Before he could respond, he received another message.

Lyra: If I am living in a bubble, you are walking in a tunnel, refusing to see things that are not aligned with your path. There are billions of people, the result of billions of years of evolution, and you want to box them all into set categories, too stubborn to accept that not everyone is going to fit in your tiny boxes. Look around, humans are the best example of variety and complexity.

Aryabh did look around. His eyes fell on Kenai whose phone

was by his mouth.

"Groovy animated posters," Kenai commanded his phone. When he noticed Aryabh's eyes on him, he asked, "Do you know a good seller in Sonmanto who'd make me customized photo frames, just like that one?" He pointed at his photo on the wall.

"Yes. He lives in the 21st century."

After the satisfying taunt, Aryabh got back to Lyra's messages. He pushed his left knee up to his chest and left the other dangling from his bed. When he thought about it, Kenai was the one person he could not fit in any of his boxes.

If there was a name for that stubborn bit of food stuck in your molars, the one that refuses to come out no matter how much you wiggle it with your tongue, it would be Kenai.
He was just different.

But Aryabh didn't care if Lyra was right. All he wanted to do was to give her a befitting reply. His fingers hung in the air, trying to come up with a proper comeback.

He failed.

On the empty pavement of Zenith's market, Lyra whirled a ruby red apple in her hand and smiled. For the first time since she was back, she felt lighter. Saying what the opposite person wants to hear was her native language. It was new, standing up for herself and speaking without a filter.

An incomplete thought pressed at her.

Lyra: What's "bucolic"? I've never heard of that word.

Then she took a bite of the crisp apple.

It tasted like determination.

Chapter 6

THE EARTHLER NEWS

July 24, 2125

23 CYBERCRIMINALS DISSOLVED IN CYMENS, 2ND STRATUM

After escaping The Pacamounts' dragnet for two years, a group of twenty-three cybercriminals were nabbed by the PacaCyber Force from a 2nd Stratum foxhole. The prisoners were dissolved last evening in the presence of 200 citizens who were summoned for Onlooker Duty.

Aryabh had procured all his books from a woman in the black market, whose face he had never seen. It was months since he had visited his bootlegger. His mind yearned for new words to read. Books were his only hobby, his sole entertainment. The ones that were shelved in his secret room were read so many times that he could recite every single one of them.

He sucked on an AwakeTab and lay on his back, hearing the hustle and bustle of Sonmanto even on the 94th floor.

Kenai, for once, was silent and writing something on his phone, a ritual he religiously followed every night. On some days, he would recite the journal entry to his phone as if he were talking to a person. Aryabh hated those days.

But right now, the quiet apartment felt like four spiked walls closing in on him. A familiar feeling resurfaced

Ever since he was a child, Aryabh experienced a noxious hollowness inside. A fear that something would drain all the life out of him one day. He tried to push the feeling away by thinking about his life on Zenith, his sunken eyes staring at the ceiling. It reminded him of a message Lyra had once sent – "When I have dark thoughts, I make up stories. They aren't readable. Or psychologically healthy. But there is an indescribable pleasure in writing about places and people that don't exist."

Aryabh grabbed Lyra's ancient tablet from under his pillow and tapped on the folder named Short-Stories. Multiple nuggets of Lyra's imagination appeared on the screen.

There was a story of a lonely old woman who discovered a time machine. She traveled to the past to befriend her child version so that she could accompany and comfort herself throughout her life. Another story was about a girl who was forced to choose between a lifetime of nightmares and the death of a loved one. Upon choosing a lifetime of nightmares, she was made to dream of the death of every single person she loved. Yet another story was of an inattentive, workaholic father who was deprived of all biological functions like aging, hunger, and sleep. When he finally went home from work, everyone he knew, including his friends and family, was long dead due to old age. The last story was about a girl who had her memory wiped clean due to an unbearable trauma and spent the rest of her life wondering the reason behind her grief.

In a strange way, Aryabh felt understood. Lyra's words sounded like the echo of his deranged thoughts. Her stories spoke of the demons inside her that weren't so different from his.

> A myriad of questions crossed my mind that day. How can someone so credulous be so insightful? How can someone so simple be so demented? Did I even know Lyra? How can someone so idiosyncratic survive in a conventional society? What kind of strength does one need to function and stay sane without concealing their demons? Do they have a

portal to sanity? How else can you endure such hollowness? I didn't, however, think of the privilege I had, the privilege to be able to live without masking my monsters.

Aryabh reached for his widget and typed a genuine message.
Aryabh: I misunderstood you.
He cringed with regret the next second.
Lyra: It's okay. It's not the first time someone has mocked me for wanting something they didn't.
Aryabh felt a crack in his soul. Different faces reeled around his head. They all had similar peals of laughter, each one mocking him for wanting to move to Zenith.
They were not that different, after all.

Three months ago

"Why are you following us?"
Aryabh worked evening shifts as a busser in downtown Sonmanto. He was disposing of trash bags in the restaurant's back alley when a seven-foot, beefy man poked his shoulder.
"Who are you?" Aryabh asked.
"Don't bullshit me. We've been watching you. You are everywhere."
"I don't have time for this. I am working. Do you mind?" Aryabh tried to walk past him.
"You fess up and I only break your nose. You lie, I dispose of your body along with your trash," threatened the man. He appeared to be in his early forties, his bulldogish face as immense

as his stature, but eyes small and kind.

"Look, dude, I've never followed you or anyone. I've never even seen you before. I need to get back to work. My boss will bust my balls and send me home without pay if I don't report my slavery to him in the next two minutes." Aryabh stepped away.

The man grabbed his collar and hauled him forward.

"So, you've never followed a small group to a bar last week? Never snooped into our network?"

"How did you—"

"What? Know what you did? You think you are the only talented hacker in Sonmanto...Aryabh?"

Aryabh's face was stunned.

"We know everything," the man said. "Where you were born, your history, what you are, where you stay, what you eat... So drop this act and start talking," he added in a calm but authoritative tone.

"If I talk and you turn out to be the wrong person, I am dead," Aryabh said as fear clouded his face.

The man spat. "I am not with the Rodents. Don't insult me."

"Rodents?"

"You know who. The government, the CEOs."

"Okay. Are you...with the Farm?"

"How did you find out about the Farm? What exactly do you know?" The man came up closer to Aryabh, the veins in his neck bulging.

"I was just curious."

"What do you know?" he enunciated.

"Look... all I know is, you are a group of activists fighting against The Pacamou...umm...the Rodents." Aryabh looked around. "I was looking for people, people like me, who are done taking their shit. I cannot live like this, not anymore. I want to fight. I want The Pacamo...the Rodents down. That was when I found The Farm. I don't know much, but I know that you and I...we are not that different."

"Activists?" The cords in the man's neck relaxed. "What kind of flimsy shit is that?"

"Then, what are you?"

The big guy sat on the pavement and took out a pack of cigarettes. He offered one to Aryabh, who pulled one and sat next to him.

"Dima." The man offered his hand.

"You know my name."

"We've been eyeing you for a long time. We were almost ready to break into your house to blackmail you out of Sonmanto. You've got some really good stuff on you, man. You definitely would have left, trust me." Dima lit Aryabh's cigarette with the ember of his. Puffs of smoke overpowered the wet smell of garbage. It brought Aryabh a world of agonizing memories.

"Then we dug into your insane background," he went on. "It's sad. I'd rip the world in two if I were you. So I convinced everyone that you didn't deserve to be shooed away; you should be one of us." He inspected the alley's PacaEyes.

"We're good," said Aryabh.

"I know. It's why I came here." Dima took a puff. "We need someone like you. You've got talent. Snooping into our network? Not that easy. I wanted to make sure you were Farm material."

Aryabh tilted his head backward and looked up at Dima. "What do you need me for?"

"Not here. Take this." Dima slid a small booklet into Aryabh's hand. "Decoding script. I'll send you a message. Use this to decode the address. Be there on time. Don't bother showing up if you are hoping to join a group of *activists*." He stood, trampled the cigarette, walked to the main street, and got inside a waiting car.

"Blackmail me out of Sonmanto..." Aryabh sneered to himself. "That's cute."

He took one last puff of the cigarette, looked at its ember, and flicked the bud in the garbage. He stroked the tiny booklet and pocketed it.

Aryabh's plan had gone exactly as he had hoped.

He had discovered the Farm not long ago. It was impossible to reach them, let alone get in. Which was why he brought them to him. He had hacked into their network in such a way that they would know. Then he let them snoop into all the right details about his life. He also took up a daily job at a restaurant to provide them with a predictable routine. When they still didn't act on it, he provoked them by following some of their members. And then, he waited.

Three days later, Dima was tailing him. Based on his PacaProfile, Aryabh had determined that he was a sheep in wolf's clothing. It was his favorite kind to manipulate, because he could provoke them physically as well as control them emotionally. With Dima, he decided to wear the mask of the 'enlightened, rebellious citizen' and speak a bunch of nonsense that would strike a chord with Dima's revolutionary mindset.

They were no activists, he knew. The Farm was a hardcore underground anti-Paca group, probably the biggest rebel group in the 1st Stratum, which had done vast damage to the Pacamounts. "To take back what's ours", was their motto and they had meant that.

Besides using the Farm for his intended purpose, what attracted Aryabh to them the most was their suspicious connection to Zenith.

He untied the restaurant's apron and tossed it in the garbage. He was now in the right circle. He was in The Farm.

A message beeped on his widget as soon as he reached his empty apartment. It was Dima. He had sent a couple of lines from the Pacamounts' anthem-

The shark's Head is out, and it smells the anti-Pacas' blood. In it, we will soak our flag. To the Dissolution chamber, their bodies we'll drag.

Aryabh used the script to decode the message—Tomorrow. 1530 hours. Café Sobak, at the corner of Hagat Street.

He left the house at two.

When he entered Sobak, he understood it was a foxhole, a breeding ground for anti-Pacas. The smell of cigarettes and alcohol had emulsified into the café's air. Like all public dining places, it had single occupants in all booths, except for one big table in the dark corner where Dima's huge bald head grabbed his attention.

Aryabh sucked on an AwakeTab and navigated through the café booths at a slow pace. He needed time to study each occupant at the big table before he spoke to them. Besides Dima, there were four other people.

The woman sitting on Dima's right looked different from the others. She wore a royal blue floor-length dress whose intricate embroidery merged with the art on her skin. Her silver pixie hair glossed over her foxlike face that looked not a day older than twenty.

As Aryabh approached, he observed the two men and one woman who sat on the opposite side.

Dima gestured at a seat next to him.

Aryabh sat and looked around the table again. The man in front of him was at least a foot and a half shorter than Dima. His odd features and complexion troubled Aryabh. He had pale skin and a set of green eyes that stared at everything and everyone suspiciously. Aryabh liked him the least. Next to him was a portly man who behaved as if he took pleasure in making others laugh. His eyes seemed constantly distracted and in search of anecdotes.

"We have more people joining in, but meet them first," said Dima. "Everyone, this is Aryabh. He'll be joining our Cyber Wing. Aryabh, she's Caspian."

The pixie-haired woman offered a fist to bump. When Dima sensed Aryabh's uneasiness, he spoke again, "You are a hound! Yes, she is Cream. Caspian has been with us for four years."

Aryabh relooked at her. He wanted to rub off the glint of wellbeing on her face.

"This is Arkas."

Aryabh's least favorite guy nodded.

"That's Dev."

The portly man greeted Aryabh with a casual salute.

"And that's Shiaya."

"'sup!" She winked with an expressionless face. The pointy teal tips of her metallic hair brushed against the table as she sipped vodka from a tumbler, her aqua lips looking like they had just kissed an ocean.

Finally, Aryabh thought. He had finally managed to be in the category of people Shiaya would voluntarily meet and trust. He wore the mask again and greeted everyone with a nod.

"Why a public place?" he asked Dima.

"The owner is a member. Three cameras here," Dima gestured with his head, "are tampered. They play pre-recorded footage. When in Sonmanto, public places are always safer than private, remember that. They are so crowded that it's easy to blend in."

Aryabh was impressed. It was his rule too, which was why three months later when he closed a deal with the woman sitting across him, he chose the busiest area of Sonmanto.

In the one-hour meeting, Aryabh had met six more Farm members who visited the café at different time slots. The Farm had branched into various wings. Aryabh was put in the Cyber wing, whose main purpose was to infiltrate the Pacamounts's network and seek classified information about them and the Cream circle. The information was used against them by other branches, like the Ground wing who damaged their infrastructure, and hence their operation, or the Direct wing who confronted weaker Cream directly to take them out. Or, to Aryabh's amusement, the Production Wing who built taste profiles based on Cyber Wing's data and manufactured items that were delectable and yet injurious to the consumer's health. The price margin of said items was set higher to keep them inaccessible to NonCreamers. Over the years, the Production Wing had gotten the Pacamounts and Cream circle addicted to their brand of wine, cheese, and chocolates, all of which had traces of toxic chemicals that sickened and slowly poisoned their consumers.

Aryabh learned that they all reported to a man called Master Snowball, a man they would never meet and who only communicated through messages.

When most members had left and only five of them remained, Aryabh's most awaited topic came into discussion.

"Here's a good one," said Dev. "How many Zenithers does it take to change a light bulb?" When no one spoke, he answered, "All seven thousand of 'em. One to change the bulb and the others to discuss it."

A fit of tittering arose from the table. Aryabh's face remained unchanged, the heat inside his chest not rising to the surface.

"One more, one more." Dev tapped the table. "Why can't a Zenither buy a new pair of shoes?"

No response.

"Because their neighbor hasn't thrown out their pair yet."

The table cackled again. Aryabh wanted to shut them up and tell how they could not even begin to understand the powerful mechanics of Zenith's Recycling Center. It had helped the colony reuse clothes, shoes, furniture, equipment, and appliances over and over for decades without creating an ocean of landfills.

"Yuckity eww, Dev," said Shiaya. "At least you don't have to deal with those fossils on regular basis. The other day, a Zenither walked up to me at the transit station and bothered me about my earrings. Yapped for ten minutes about how she had never seen gold before. I'm not paid enough to deal with those fusspots!"

"They don't have gold on Zenith," Aryabh said in a monotone. Everyone turned their heads at him. "All their jewelry is carved from either bamboo, recycled materials, or the metals harvested from the asteroid. They don't treasure jewelry, anyway. For them, it's merely a form of art."

"Whoa, who called a Zenith encyclopedia to the meeting!" Shiaya ridiculed.

Aryabh's least favorite guy squinted at him.

"Hey Dima, what's wrong?" Shiaya said, noticing Dima staring at his own lap, upset and distracted.

"Nothing. Just my brother. He is signing an annual contract with a girl he likes."

"What?!" everyone except Aryabh exclaimed in unison.

Aryabh thought about a conversation that had surprised Lyra. He had explained to her how the concept of marriage had turned into bi-monthly and yearly contracts, and now those too were becoming extinct. Earthlers were too exhausted to maintain relationships.

"My brother is a sheep," said Dima. "When we were kids, he once found me tampering with our building cameras. He almost reported me to the Rodents."

> NonCreamers were more comfortable reporting their own families than dealing with the Pacamounts if they are caught. There was a deadly fear of being reported for not reporting someone.

"The girl works directly for a Cream. It's just going to make things worse for me."

"Cut your brother out," Arkas advised.

Everyone else also instructed Dima to boycott his brother. He responded with slouched shoulders and fake nods. Then the members went back to cracking jokes on Zenithers.

The meeting adjourned when a woman signaled from the entrance. Everyone dispersed one by one reciting the Farm's motto—to take back what's ours.

On his way home, Aryabh couldn't help but feel like a frog in a well. He was not the only one breathing fire for the Pacamounts. Each member of the Farm had the same immense hatred for them. The only difference was that they didn't want to run away and leave the planet to rot. They wanted to stay in and bring change.

Not Aryabh. He wanted to get out at the first chance, to a

place even the Farm thought was the last place to go.

Two weeks later, Aryabh's beliefs were confirmed when he sat with Shiaya at Café Sobak.

She was nursing a tumbler of vodka as Aryabh sipped on an energy drink. The familiar stench of alcohol and cigarettes lingered in the dimly lit café.

"Trying to make a secret deal with a member in the Farm's own hood? You've got balls; gotta give you that." Shiaya said, impressed. "So that I don't waste your time, and more importantly mine, get this...I am not doing anything until I know why I am doing it."

"It's not your business," said Aryabh.

"It *is* my business!" She banged her fist on the table. "I am stealing from the fuckin' space transit station. I am betraying the Farm, the only people I trust on this planet. So, yes, jackass, it is my business. Am putting my neck on the line for you."

"For gold."

"Fuck you!" Shiaya polished off her drink and stood. "I don't have to do this."

"Don't make a scene." Aryabh looked around. Everyone was overly busy at their tables, some moving hands and talking in the air. "What do you want to know?"

"Everything." Shiaya sat and ordered another drink on her widget.

Aryabh explained to her the big picture of his plan.

"Don't see how it can work. If anyone who has a strong history with the Rodents, it's you, given your... history. NonCreamers are not even allowed to travel to the tin-can. I don't see how you can comfortably dream to settle there."

"I got hold of some old Rodents' data and found a list of Zenithers who traveled here."

"Holy fuckity fuck!" Shiaya's lips, which looked like she had just sipped at a bowl of fresh blood, parted, almost touching the tribal ring on her septum.

Before continuing, Aryabh stopped for a moment to consider

if he wasn't making the biggest mistake of his life. He was sharing his life's plan with a stranger. A part of him, however, did want to tell it to someone to check if it had a loophole.

Once Shiaya stole the badge for him, she would be equally involved in the crime. No way would she risk her life by snitching on him. Besides, Aryabh had unbreakable faith in his people-reading skills. As impulsive and greedy as Shiaya was, she was the kind of person who would die before dishonoring her words. Unless she was betrayed.

He had no intention to do that.

"In the last seventy-five years," Aryabh said, "out of the many Zenithers who visited Earth, forty-three never returned to Zenith. Thirty-six of those tourists died while they were on Earth. There were valid reasons behind their death, but I believe most of them were caught by the Rodents doing things they shouldn't have. The remaining seven are still missing."

"Okay, so?" Shiaya's fist was under her chin. Aryabh noticed her wrist tattoo. It looked like the logo of a corporation. He jeered inwardly and continued.

"I went through the background of those seven visitors. Among them, there was a family of three—a couple and a five-year-old kid. They visited Earth in 2103. That was when I turned five."

"What's that got to do with it?"

"They are still missing. If the Rodents' records have reported them missing, it means they are either the smartest hiders on this planet and don't want to be found, or they probably died in a remote area and their bodies were never discovered. For all we know, they are fossils now."

"Again, what has that got to do with you turning five in 2103?"

"I...experimented," Aryabh toyed with the bottle in front of him. "I can erase my complete identity. It would mean an Aryabh never existed. Once that's done, I can take the identity of the five-year-old boy who came with the couple. All I'd need would be a compelling story as to how my adults died, where I was raised, and why I waited so long to report myself. I have plans for that too. But my story wouldn't work without any concrete proof. Neither Zenith nor the Rodents would allow me to migrate based on just a story. This is why I need a Zenither badge. They are made out of the metals harvested from the asteroid and have old-school coding on them. I can't duplicate them here; I need a real badge. Once I have it, I can forge my identity with the kid's name on it.

"No way are the Rodents letting a twenty-seven-year-old Earthler lift off the planet with all the knowledge about them and settle in a world where they don't want to be exposed," Shiaya argued. "Everything those cavepeople know about us and this planet is what the Rodents want them to know."

Aryabh knew that, but he was stuck on the part where Shiaya was able to calculate his age so fast.

"I know. That was my biggest hurdle. So, I went over the Zenith Settlement Agreement. When the Terraformers were sent off to the asteroid, they were given many sweet promises. One of them was to keep the asteroid populated. So far, the Rodents have done their best to keep them happy on every front. They don't want unhappy Zenithers. When people are unhappy, they will find ways to get to you. It's still a risk, but I think it's going to work. I'll come up with a convincing story. I'll also make sure the Zenither officials know about this before it reaches the Rodents, and so it will be they who'll be asking for me."

"You are a genius!" said Shiaya. "An assholic genius, but a genius, nonetheless. You must be really desperate, huh?"

"So it'll work then," Aryabh concluded, but in his tone was a question. He wanted to know Shiaya's opinion.

"Don't know, dude. Sounds too risky, too complex to me. But if you are this serious, I am going to get that badge for you, of course for the payment we discussed."

"But, first, I need to get hold of a Zenither who is visiting Earth, preferably someone born in the late 90s, so that the design of their badge would match with the kid's. I have to know whose badge we are stealing so that we don't make any errors."

"You are just dying to make me rich, aren't you?" Shiaya smiled.

"What do you mean?"

"Thirty percent extra, and I solve that puzzle too."

Shiaya's greed disgusted Aryabh. "Only if it makes sense."

"I know someone from the Farm who always has a list of Zenither passengers and their dates of travel. And guess what. The list comes fresh from Zenith."

Despite himself, Aryabh's eyes widened. "How? Why? Who gets the list?"

"Thirty percent?"

"Yes."

"Arkas. Don't know why or how. Dev once told me the Farm smuggles things back and forth to Zenith. Not sure how true that is. "

Out of all the members, why does it has to be Arkas, Aryabh thought. "Arkas would rather lynch me than give me the list."

"Who says he has to *give* it? You are the wizarding invader of privacy; you can take it. He always carries the list on his widget."

"Why is this okay with you, doing this to a member?"

"That tiny turd once called me a bimbo. I won't lose sleep over making him feel like one. Plus, I'll have that extra gold sleeping next to me. It's a win-win. " She winked.

"Deal." Aryabh finished his energy drink. "See you at the next meeting."

"Why don't you drink alcohol? You didn't take a single sip of beer from your bottle that day."

"I don't like not being in control."

"Oh, with the kind of crazy shit you do, you should never give up abstinence."

When Aryabh left the bar, he was intoxicated with excitement. He knew his plan would work.

And it did.

Given how Arkas mostly worked as a hound for the Farm and was daft about technology, accessing his widget had been easy. Aryabh, in fact, found pleasure in doing it. During one of the Farm meetings, he sat next to him and transmitted malware to his widget. Within minutes, all of Arkas's data was on his wrist.

After he went through the passenger lists, he found one visitor a perfect fit. His next step was to befriend the Zenither who was not only born in the late 90s but was also visiting Earth soon.

Aryabh plotted ideas to befriend a Zenither named Lyra.

CHAPTER 7

Zenith

July 26, 2125

Lyra crushed cloves of garlic under a knife with the heel of her palm. Her head pounded, exhausted from the thoughts of her disappeared documents.

Ever since her mother had died due to, what Lyra believed, her daughter's apathy, she had trouble falling asleep. As soon as she would start to doze off, she found herself nauseated and out of breath. An inkling of danger would swaddle her and her head would throb. According to the doctor, she suffered from mild hypnophobia—an irrational fear of falling asleep, but Lyra had always denied its treatment.

Before she even turned sixteen, she was raising an infant, maintaining the household, and helping her father with his depression. She didn't have the mental capacity for treatment. At least, that was what she told herself. A part of her was afraid to lose control of her mind over psychotherapy.

To combat stress, she was advised to meditate, play a sport, or hang out with friends. But to Lyra, handling a dangerous metal object and slicing with its sharp blade was the most calming feeling in the universe.

She stood at the hotel's kitchen counter and enjoyed how the knife's blade fell on a mushroom at the same distance with the same impetus. Every time the knife finished a cut and landed on the cutting board, it generated a rhythmic sound. It was music to Lyra's ears.

She wiped the knife on her apron and cleaned the stray mushroom fragments from the cutting board. Then she pulled a crate of onions and began working on them. The pungent smell of the bulbs replaced the mealy odor of the portobellos.

The gurgle of the sauce drew her attention. She walked to the stove and dropped roasted potatoes in the bubbling tomato sauce. It splashed on her already stained chef coat.

She grinned.

Lyra relished the mess and chaos of the hotel's kitchen, something that she couldn't experience in the kitchen of her home.

"Come on, chop-chop!" barked Balin. "One hour to the lunch buffet."

The kitchen staff loved their chef's mama-bear loyalty towards them; however, they had grown to dislike her impudence. According to the rumors that circulated in the hotel, Balin suffered from a bad marriage. Some said she was a victim of domestic abuse, while others were sure that her husband had cheated on her. There were stories of her husband planning to elope with an Earthler tourist, while some whispered about her inability to conceive a child.

Lyra cared for none of those rumors. She didn't appreciate her autocratic ways but Balin's strength inspired her.

"What's today's special, Chef?" she asked.

"Handle the range today; I am busy" Balin replied as she sniffed at a bunch of thyme. "Pick whatever you want, honey."

"Umm..." Lyra pretended to think, but she had the perfect recipe in mind for an opportunity like this. "Garden vegetables in green coconut curry?"

"Stop asking. Get on with it."

"Cool." The harassment inside Lyra's head stopped. Her eyes veered from side to side as she dived into her mind's cookbook.

"I'll use ginger instead of garlic." She grabbed a pan. Behind the counter, her feet did a dance routine that she had memorized when in school. "And I'll add bok choy!" Her head bounced. "We received fresh shipment tod—"

"No. We have never served bok choy with a coconut sauce," said Balin.

"But that's exactly why—"

"And throw away that bottle of rice wine vinegar. I have smelled you experimenting with it." Balin stopped ruffling through cilantro as she fully committed to deciphering Lyra's suggestion. "You know what, just make the vegetables in black bean sauce. It's safer. That's what people like to eat."

Lyra wanted to tell the executive chef how the slightly bitter mineral flavor of bok choy would pair wonderfully with the sweetness of the vegetables and coconut. She wanted to state how the fermented sugars in the rice vinegar bring out a better, delicate flavor to certain dishes than the more acidic white vinegar. The scientist in her wanted to explain how certain chemicals in food reacted differently to different ingredients and how switching simple ingredients could elevate a normal dish. She wanted to inform that new ingredients had been invented and imported since she, Balin, had started working at the hotel, and just because they have been doing something for a long time didn't mean they couldn't try new things.

"Okay," Lyra replied and let out a breath. Then she emptied her handmade rice wine vinegar into the sink.

Balin grabbed a carrot from a crate and bit into it. The sound of its crispness amplified as she walked around the kitchen like a lioness strolling in her den. She devoured raw vegetables and fruits. No one had ever seen her sit for a meal.

"Wan, get the rice boiling for pilaf. Rice, not risotto. I want every grain of rice upright and independent. Like Zenithers."

"Aye, Chef!"

"Guess, who never needs simple instructions, chef?" Gryffy came out of the pastry kitchen, nearly hopping. "Already set up the dessert counter for the buffet."

Her vivaciousness was so infectious that even Balin had suc-
cumbed to her spirit on some days. "Good girl!" the executive
chef said.

"That I am." Gryffy bowed and saw Lyra. Her thick, mas-
cara-coated lashes fluttered. She walked up to her and started
peeling the onions.

"You don't have to," said Lyra.

"No one in the history has ever denied help with peeling
onions," Gryffy responded, making Lyra smile.

"Thanks."

"Sure. Sooo...what's up? It feels like I haven't talked to you in
ages. You've been skipping michaiyo ever since you are back."

When the Terraformers had first inhabited Zenith, one of
the leaders advised getting together twice a day to discuss the
progress of their respective tasks. Everyone would get together
and work out ways to make the asteroid more homely. Even after
the developmental stage of Zenith, people continued their usual
meetings. They gathered twice a day, once during the afternoon
at around four and once in the evening at around nine, to talk
about their Earth stories or celebrate a discovery, or sometimes
just to share a hot beverage. The tradition continued to be a vital
part of the Zenither culture.

Unlike old times when everyone gathered in one place,
Zenithers now came outside of their workplaces and homes and
sat with anyone who was around. They spent fifteen to thirty
minutes talking about their day over a cup of hot beverage.
No one knew how the term came into use but they called it
michaiyo.

Lyra had always despised the social obligation of spending
almost an hour of her day with people who barely knew her,
however she had skipped recent michaiyos for a different reason.

"I know you don't like mingling. Or answering Mr. Jag's
questions about your trip. But it's good to get out. You should
come with us next weekend. We are going to the club," Gryffy

said as she wept onion tears along with Lyra. "By the way, I know this falls into the topic you want to avoid, but did you report your lost passport and badge? Ren lost her badge after our divorce and reported it two weeks later. Ms. Clia gave her a hard time."

"The transit station authorities reported me to Ms. Clia before I even came back." Lyra gritted teeth.

"Ahh...why do you do this peasant work when we have two apprentices?" Gryffy rushed to the sink and splashed her eyes with cold water. "These sodding onions burn like betrayed little sons of bitches."

"Don't speak ill of the onions," Balin spoke from a distant table. "They are your crutches, brave little soldiers carrying all the weight on their shoulders... And if you ask me again what soldiers are, I am going to smack you with those onions. Now stop defaming my ingredients and get back to work."

Once the buffet was set, the kitchen staff headed towards the banquet hall. It was Zenith's Migration Day, a holiday Zenithers warmly celebrated every year on July 26.

Exactly seventy-five years ago on this day, the first batch of Terraformers had occupied the asteroid. One of the traditions was an invitation to an important Earthler who would visit Zenith and give a speech.

Lyra, Gryffy, Balin, Per, and the new apprentice stood by the entrance door of the hotel's biggest banquet hall along with the staff from other departments. The hall was packed with an excited audience, including children who occupied the first few rows. Sitting importantly between Mr. Zaif, Zenith's Head of Earth Relations and Ms. Clia, Zenith's Head of Law Enforcement was the spokesperson from Earth.

The hall went silent as Zenith's award-winning actor got on the stage. He greeted everyone. Lyra looked at him and mumbled to Gryffy, "It'd have made more sense to have a Terraformer host this instead of a celebrity." Only her lips moved. "And why do they always call a political puppet from Earth who has no substantial information to share?"

"It's all PR, baby. You think these little chumps would come to listen to a 90-year-old Terraformer?" Gryffy lifted her chin to point at the high-schoolers in a corner who were giggling away at the sight of their favorite actor. "And if you think the speaker is here for our benefit, you couldn't be more wrong. Earthlers don't even defecate without getting something out of it."

"What does that tell about us?" Lyra argued. "Knowing that and still inviting and listening to them on a day like this? We are just as fatuous."

A round of loud applause interrupted their conversation. The Earthler spokesperson arrived at the podium and nodded at the crowd with a forced smile. He wrinkled his nose at a piece of paper and started reading from it.

"Good afternoon, Zenithers. What energy! It is my first time in this foreign land, but it feels familiar already. I have always wanted to visit this simple nation, see its rich culture, and meet its humble people."

The audience cheered.

"That's one heck of a tall man," Gryffy commented, her arm resting on Lyra's shoulder. "Too bad none of us are as tall. We can't verify if that's a toupee."

The spokesperson wiggled the knot of his tie and continued, "Nearly a century ago, when we ping-ponged this tiny asteroid in our orbit, we had options. The Pacamounts could have mined the entire rock and made the planet richer. But instead..." he emphasized "...they decided to give future to a group of lucky people by devising a whole new world for them and their future generations. Our government busted their bottoms and spent a gazillion PacaDollars to train the Terraformers and make this place as comfortable as possible."

"Dude is not even blinking!" spoke Gryffy again.

"Many of you might not know but the Pacamounts had also offered Zenith its high-tech weapons as a sign of benevolence. Our latest model of Shark would blow your mind. But your

Head of Law Enforcement refused the offer. That's impressive. She told me…" the spokesperson attempted Zenither accent in a feminine voice and jiggled his eyes and mouth "…I don't need weapons. My population is manageable without pointing guns at them."

Ms. Clia shot a stern look at him.

"If that's true," the spokesperson went on, "I should applaud you. I am sure the Pacamounts will share my sentiment. This is indeed a peaceful place." He eyed and dusted a strand of lint off his suit's lapel. "I wish I could stay here forever."

"Unbelievable!" Balin said and left the hall.

"But I have to go back and tell our dear Earthlers about your four-days-a-week, six-hours-a-day work model. They'll laugh in my face. I will try to convince them it's not laziness; it's enjoying the essence of life."

"Did we sign up for an ass this year?" Gryffy spoke to her colleagues. Even Lyra shook her head this time.

"I thank the Council of Zenith for inviting me to this nation. For relentless power, we strive and ride." The spokesperson narrated the Pacamounts's official slogan and cupped his right hand like a shark's mouth and placed it across his chest. "Thank you!"

Then he crumpled his speech and threw it on the floor.

Once the event was over, the staff headed back to hand over their shift. When they reached the kitchen, they found Balin huffing at a counter.

"Yo, Chef, why did you leave?" Gryffy asked.

"I can't stand there listening to the pile of shit spewing out of that Earthler's mouth," Balin untied her apron and folded it into a neat square in aggression.

"I wish I could stay here forever…it so peaceful…so calm, no buildings, no traffic," Balin mocked the spokesperson. "Bull crap! They come here every year and tell us how they wish to stay here, how they love our culture, and nonsense baloney like that. None of those parroting Earthlers want to stay here. They will start missing their fancy little gadgets before they know. They'll be upset their toilets aren't giving them urinalysis and their food isn't instant. They say they want this. It makes them appear more human, more tender." She gestured with her hands. "They want to come here so that they can go back and be pretentious about the enlightening transformation they had here. It's all bull crap!"

Everyone stood still. No one dared to interrupt.

"Talking about offering weapons, as if they were going to arm us if we would have said yes. Do you know what one of these Earthler guests did to our housekeeper last month?"

"That turned out to be a rumor, chef." Everyone's head turned towards Lyra. "The housekeeper said it himself that nothing of that sort happened."

Lyra regretted that instantly. She knew how this conversation was going to evolve.

"Girl, I didn't ask for your opinion," said Balin. "I know how you feel about these people."

There it is, Lyra thought.

"You will defend them even if they explode this asteroid someday."

Lyra wanted to nod and leave.

"I wasn't defending! I was stating a fact," she said, her body unmoved. The faces of the kitchen staff swung from Balin to Lyra, agape.

"Everyone is obsessed with the fake housekeeper's story because an Earthler was at fault. We never talk about misconduct when our people are involved. We ignore those events until we forget them." Lyra looked into Balin's eyes and said in a firmer tone, "We dwell among rumors because we don't like the truth."

Balin stared at Lyra for a brief moment, cleared her throat, and then looked away as if she were ignoring a child throwing a tantrum.

"Enough chitter-chatter for today. Get out now and let the next shift get to work." She headed to her office, which was located between the kitchen and the restaurant.

Five minutes later, she called for Lyra.

Lyra walked into the office and sat on a stool placed on the other side of Balin's desk.

"It's your lucky day today. I am going to make you one of my special teas," Balin announced as she plugged in an electric kettle. "Oat milk or maple syrup?"

"Just the tea is fine," Lyra replied and twisted the hair-tie around her wrist.

"That's my girl!"

Balin grabbed a few tin cans from her desk drawer. She filled two muslin cloths with scoops of what looked like tea, dried flowers, and spices.

Lyra smelled hibiscus and cloves.

Balin tied the cloths with strings and dropped them in the cups. When she noticed Lyra's curious eyes, she spoke.

"Very much like bouquet-garni. This is black tea with dried hibiscus, ginger, and a few whole cloves, straight from my garden. Oy, oy, oy..." Balin gushed as she sniffed her concoction. "Smells like a slice of heaven." She put away the tin cans and sat straight to talk. "So...violent marriage, unfaithful husband, infertility...which one did you believe?"

The sudden question startled Lyra. She swallowed and thought about the right thing to say.

"Come on," Balin nudged, "I won't bite."

"I don't cater to rumors."

"What if they were true?"

Lyra considered it for a moment.

"I still don't care. It's not my business."

"You know what? I trust you on that," said Balin. "But not everyone thinks the same way. They see me as this insufferable, tough, lonely woman. They see me as a victim or a survivor of something tragic. Why else would a woman be so rough all the time, right? She can't be authoritative and strict and call it a day."

She grabbed a ring from her desk drawer and placed it on her finger.

"I don't like wearing it in the kitchen."

If Lyra wasn't mistaken, the executive chef was blushing.

"I have a loving and faithful husband. I am a fantastic wife too. We are a normal couple; we do normal things. Nico had a rough childhood. He mostly keeps it to himself and you know very well, Lyra, what they think of people here who don't engage with the society. But he is lovely. I am lucky." Lyra wanted to ask her to not explain herself. "I go home, and he cooks me a nice dinner. Mostly, we fall asleep on the couch, drinking wine and chatting. It's a good life, Lyra." She paused. The light in her eyes dimmed. "Nico had a younger brother whom I raised as my own kid. After he...left us, we both didn't want children. Not because I can't conceive. You must know, it doesn't settle well with the simpletons of Zenith, women not wanting kids. I was already an outcast. The tag of child-hater pushed me further away from everyone."

Lyra shifted in her chair. As much affection as she felt towards Balin, she couldn't accumulate words to comfort her. "Why didn't you stop people from spreading the rumors?" she asked. "Especially here, at the hotel." In her head, a person like Balin would rip people to shreds for uttering a wrong word against them.

"That's just me. I like keeping my two lives separate. People take you less seriously when they know what you are made of, especially in our work, and especially when you are a woman. They obey tough people." She balled up her fist. "Even if they hate them. I am not here to be liked or to share about my personal life."

"Of course," Lyra agreed.

"I am telling you this because I want you to know that our conduct is not going to change who we are. By stating your opinion openly, you are not going to turn cruel. I have seen you hide in your corner because you don't want to speak your mind and confront anyone. You probably think no one is going to understand. That's insulting. And too much thinking. My god, Lyra, you think a lot!" Balin shook her head.

She leaned forward and extended her hand towards Lyra. Lyra did not reciprocate.

"But Lyra, honey, you need to stop thinking and start talking, start doing. Or, one day, you will completely lose your voice. You are smart! Own your intellect." Balin slapped the table. "Speak more as you did back there. Even if it's against me. I am not saying I am going to love it, but, at least, I'll be arguing with an honest person. You are chef de partie; stop acting like an apprentice. Take authority. Behave like you are in charge because you are. Evoke that iron inside you, the iron of Zenith. We all have it in us. You have so much to give to this world, Lyra. So many people live their lives wishing for the kind of wisdom you have."

Lyra felt a clog in her throat. She gave a weak nod.

"No one gets just one shot." Balin retracted her hand. "Look at me. I have grabbed all sorts of shots in life. Now I may not get your obsession with Earth, but no one has the right to tell you what you should and shouldn't do. Not even I."

"I know." Lyra's voice came out wet.

"Oh, I don't want you to dehydrate in my office. We need that tea." Balin unplugged the kettle and poured hot water into their mugs. The tea bundles swam up to the brim.

"Look at this beautiful cup of tea," she said. "Looks like dropping a slice of lemon in it will solve all problems of humanity, don't you think?"

Lyra slipped a quiet giggle.

She wanted to confront Balin about the morning, about how she had stifled her recipe without giving it a chance, how it was one of the reasons she did not speak her mind. But she didn't.

She understood that Balin's beliefs stemmed from her own distinct experiences that were different from hers, that Balin believed in her tried and tested methods just like she herself believed in innovation.

"Chatting time is over. I am going home. Nico is making rainbow sorbet today, the food version of Gryffy...if you know what I mean."

Lyra took her cup and got up from the stool to leave. She stopped midway and spoke, "It doesn't matter, but people like you more than you think they do."

Balin nodded with pride.

With Balin's words still undulating inside her head, Lyra took a bus to the Council of Zenith, a two-storied building that operated as the head office for Zenith's government.

She entered the office of the Head of Law Enforcement and asked an upfront question, "Ms. Clia, do we have a citizen named Dawn living here on Zenith?"

CHAPTER 8

Zenith

July 29, 2125

"Whoa, that's one hot Earthler!" Gryffy commented on a guest exiting the hotel's 24-hour café.

Lyra, Gryffy, and Donea were sitting by the back entrance of the hotel, having michaiyo. The guest leaped towards her car in five-inch heels, carrying the poise of a swan.

"Check out the suit with her." Donea, Lyra's classmate from school and the hotel's front desk supervisor, motioned her chin towards a tall, silver-haired Earthler walking alongside the woman.

Lyra leaned forward to gaze at the man's face.

"Now, Lyra, don't drool in broad daylight!" Gryffy poked her elbow into Lyra's ribs.

"Not drooling. I think he is the guy who sat next to me in the shuttle to the transit station."

"Aah...So you've been in close quarters with this muscle man. Did something happen? Some nudging, some accidental touching?"

"Why?" Lyra asked with an uncertainty that made Gryffy and Donea exchange a look.

"Can I ask you a personal question, Lyra?" said Gryffy.

Lyra was not sure but she nodded.

"Have you ever...been with someone?" Gryffy asked with a face ready for disappointment.

Donea pulled her chair closer. Lyra found her round face like that of a cat that is approaching catnip. It made her uncomfortable. She wondered if Donea had told Gryffy about the school incident.

When Lyra was sixteen, she had once been asked out on a date by Kaymin, a boy who had liked her for a while. Puberty and its following years were a perplexing time for Lyra. Every time her friends brought up the subject of sex in a conversation, she had no input. She had learned to agree and give fake nods whenever they talked about a hot classmate or showed her pictures of attractive celebrities, but in reality, she had never found anyone sexually attractive.

As if to prove something to herself, she had agreed to go out with Kaymin. But, after three good dates, the fourth one came with an ordeal that Lyra had feared. Kaymin attempted to kiss her, and even though she didn't yearn to do the same, she gave in and pretended to kiss him back. It didn't stop there. He wanted more.

Then, instead of pretending, she confessed the truth. She expressed her disinterest in a sexual relationship. Kaymin took offense and described Lyra as 'unnatural' and 'abnormal' to everyone at school.

It affected Lyra for a long time, but she came to accept that nothing about her was unnatural. With time, she had come to embrace her asexuality. Loneliness and alienation was better than comprising on that aspect of her identity.

However, she knew that she lived in a society formed by species which functioned according to the biological imperative to have sex or reproduce. A social construct that made Zenith more unappetizing to Lyra.

"Back to Zenith," Gryffy waved her hand in front of Lyra's eyes. "I don't mean to pry. I am just worried for you."

Lyra swigged hot coffee from her cup. "No, I haven't been with anyone. Maybe someday when I'll find someone to whom I'll suffice," she said with a sentiment she believed in.

"High standards. I respect that." Gryffy ended the conversation, leaving Donea's thirst for a spicy snippet unquenched. "Fudge?" She offered her plate. "Ty got it for everyone."

"No, thanks," said Lyra. Her phone vibrated with a message. It was Sagan's teacher. She took a deep, frustrated breath.

"Can I take some for Sagan? He loves fudge."

"Sure."

Lyra pocketed a couple of fudge pieces and rushed to the Galileo School of Zenith.

"Why did you refuse to turn in your Earth History paper?" Lyra interrogated Sagan after they sat on the bus. Still in her uniform, she rested her tired back on the windowpane and faced her brother.

Sagan's huge backpack occupied most of the seat, and so he perched at its edge. He wore a brown buttoned-down shirt over black pleated pants. Its ironed hem brushed against a pair of polished oxford shoes.

Before Sagan could respond, a man called out from behind their seat. "Lyra!"

"Hey, Mr. Cany," Lyra greeted from the gap between the seats.

"What have you been up to? How is the..." Mr. Cany moved his wrist as if he were flipping a pancake in a pan "...cheffing going?"

Sagan raised his eyebrows at his sister.

"It's..."

"Did Rahi give you the good news?" Mr. Cany interrupted Lyra. "She is pregnant! My little girl is pregnant!"

Sagan leaned forward to avoid the screams.

Lyra glanced at him and then back at Mr. Cany. "That's great. I didn't…"

"Oh, what a wonderful feeling to be a grandfather! I am just returning from the observatory. Took her some fresh snacks for michaiyo."

"Please congratulate her on my behalf," said Lyra.

"Of course, I will."

Lyra turned back in her seat and waited for a few seconds. "So…you wanna tell me about the paper?" she asked her brother.

"I…"

"What's Keid up to? I haven't seen him in forever," Mr. Cany interrupted Sagan this time.

Lyra saw annoyance on the tip of her brother's nose. She shut her eyes, sighed, and looked behind through the gap again. "He is fine. I will give him your regards," she said in a kind yet flat tone.

"Oh, good."

Lyra swallowed another breath, hoping that the conversation had ended. But Mr. Cany leaned forward and whispered, "Lyra, I heard an Earthler who came for—"

Sagan stood from his seat and faced Mr. Cany. "Would you please excuse us, sir?" he dictated. "My sister and I are attempting to have a private conversation and you seem exceedingly determined to turn it into a public forum."

"Sagan!" Lyra hissed at her brother and pulled his sleeve, forcing him to sit. "I am sorry Mr. Cany. He just had a rough—"

"Is this how you talk with an elder?" Mr. Cany scowled.

"Is this how you make a conversation? Ask a question and then blow your own trumpet before the person answers?" said Sagan.

"Poor Keid!" Mr. Cany concluded, and then got up and took a seat five rows behind.

Sagan sat back on his seat and looked at his sister. She stared at him for a moment and then smiled.

"Thanks," she said.

"Anytime."

"Forget the paper." Lyra removed fudge from her pocket and offered it to Sagan. He made a face at the sight of unwrapped candy and the thought of Lyra's pocket but accepted it. "Your teacher said you used abusive words. Why?"

"I didn't. I addressed them as benighted," Sagan clarified and dusted the piece of fudge with his handkerchief.

"We have been through this. You can't uplift yourself or your opinion by putting people down. Going for name-calling is lazy or, in your words, benighted."

"You cannot comprehend the discontent that comes from pretending to learn things you already know."

"I do know; trust me."

"It's tiring to water down your intellect to appease the crowd."

Lyra lost her patience. "Sagan, return the trumpet to Mr. Cany and tell me what happened?"

"I'd like to stay mum until we are home."

"Fine."

Lyra pulled her tired legs up on the seat and kneaded her feet, avoiding Sagan's judgmental looks. She slid open the window and looked outside. The bus was gliding along the Main Street of Zenith. She stared far at the horizon where an outline of bamboo houses was pressed against the gray asteroid walls that curved like a saucer.

She didn't know what it was that drove her to Ms. Clia's office that day to ask about Dawn. The conversations with the new Earthler friend had been so enriching that she had been ignoring the rational part of her, the part that didn't believe in instant friendships. Fragments of doubt had settled in her mind ever since Aryabh had first messaged her and she wanted to evacuate them.

Ms. Clia had informed that there was no Zenither registered under that name, but a Dawn had stayed at her hotel, Faraway Paradise, for almost a week during April. She was an Earthler.

It relieved Lyra that her skepticism was defeated. April was the month Aryabh had messaged her for the first time. He was trying to reach the Earthler guest. Why? She didn't care.

A gush of warm air combed through Lyra's hair as the bus passed along the commercial district of Zenith. When it halted at a stop, she saw a group of friends sauntering towards the movie theater. One of the boys playfully punched the girl's shoulder. In return, she took the boy's neck in her arm's grip and pretended to punch him too. Their friends joined in the mischief. The cackling laughter of their friendship pricked Lyra. She turned her eyes away from the happy group.

A toddler standing on the front seat stared at her through the gap. Lyra scrunched her face and stuck her tongue out at him. The child cooed and giggled.

"Drat, I forgot!" Lyra exclaimed, turning to Sagan. "Dad's ex-colleagues from the botanical department are visiting him today. They'll still be at home. Do you want me to take you somewhere else?"

"Home is fine."

"Okay."

"You'll be there," Sagan said without looking at his sister and ate the fudge he had been holding in his fist all this time.

Lyra's stress melted under her sore feet. "I'll be there." She clutched Sagan in a half-hug.

Half a dozen people greeted Lyra and Sagan when they reached home. They all sat in the living room in a semicircle next to Keid. He was out of his usual clothes and had dressed up. It made Lyra happy.

"Lai, Sai, why are you home early?" Keid asked as he stared at the sauce stains on Lyra's chef coat. "Come and meet my old colleagues."

The siblings stood beside the coffee table which was stacked with items everyone had gotten for their father—homemade pickles, homegrown produce, and flowers. A Zenither's way of saying, 'I care for you'.

"Everyone, this is Lyra," Keid spoke. "You might know her. She worked in Ms. Merra's lab for four years. She is starting her master's this year."

Lyra flashed a fake smile and nodded.

"And that's my little prodigy, Sagan. He is in the seventh grade."

One of the men in a knitted blazer said, "I know Sagan. My daughter is in his class." He turned towards Sagan. "She always complain about how you won't let her top the class."

Everyone laughed.

"He is one gifted child, Keid," the man in blazer added.

"I beg your pardon." Sagan stepped forward. "I am not gifted. I toil for attaining knowledge. When I feel the rooflight on my skin, I think about the solar simulators that absorb the sun's energy to approximate natural sunlight. When I drink a glass of water, I attempt to understand the complex mechanism of Zenith's Regenerative Life Support System which transforms even the droplets from my sneeze into drinking water. When I place my feet on the ground in the morning, I wonder about the optimum centrifugal force of our asteroid that produces gravity and keeps us rooted to the surface. Every day, I think of the composition of our asteroid shell that protects us from harmful space radiation. When I plug in my computer to charge it, I try to imagine the texture of the thousands of purified chunks of silicon on the solar arrays that convert solar energy into electricity...And I am aware of this information because I am curious. I am always curious. I read a lot. My mind is always struggling to grasp information. It doesn't materialize in my head when I snooze. Calling me gifted is an insult to my self-acquired intellect. Now, if you'll excuse me, I have a horde of insects to feed." He turned to leave but stopped. "Just in case you are curious, the process that converts solar energy into electricity is called photovoltaics. I just memorized its spelling last week."

Sagan finally turned around on his heels and rushed upstairs leaving a group of uncomfortable grownups behind.

Lyra, dumbfounded, stared at the back of Sagan's teensy head that bobbled upwards. Her brother had been a difficult child growing up. The ghost of his tantrums rested on Lyra's arms and face in the form of nail scars. Then, without a warning, he evolved into a composed and mature child when he joined school. He started keeping to himself, reading, and playing Jal Tarang all day. Lyra couldn't remember the last time Sagan was so vocally aggressive.

Once the cluster of adults cleared, Keid handed Lyra the wedding invitation card of one of his colleagues' son and asked her to attend. The event occupied a space in Lyra's head, ready to mentally harass her until the date arrived. Then he inquired why Lyra had to visit Sagan's school.

"Just some silly banter with other kids," Lyra explained as she rearranged the living room furniture.

"He doesn't behave like a child, I tell you."

"He is fine, Dad. You can't force someone to be juvenile."

"You can if a twelve-year-old juvenile acts like he is thirty."

Keid shook his head and began to sort other pending invitations for his daughter to attend.

"Did you turn in your resignation at the hotel? The university will start soon."

Lyra froze midway while lifting a chair and peeped into the corner of her head where the decision to tell the truth to her father lay hidden. "I never applied to the university," she said.

"What?"

"I don't enjoy food science, Dad," she said, avoiding eye contact.

"I can't believe this!" Keid dropped on the couch with his head in his hand. "I have a pair of failures for children."

The aggravation that had been inside Lyra for more than a decade came out of hibernation and sprung like wildfire. "We are not failures. You are mad because you failed Mom by not giving us the life you think we deserve." Her hands shook as her bluntness punctured the fabric of niceness she had woven between her and her father. "But no one failed us. We turned out exactly how we were supposed to. We wouldn't have been any different if she was here. Maybe, a little supported and respected."

Keid started at Lyra, wide-eyed.

"Sagan would still have been an isolated, asocial kid," she went on. "I would still have been a quitter who gave up being a scientist to cook for people. I am sorry she died. I stew in that regret every miserable minute of my life. But what's worse is to be in your presence every day. We can't carry that burden all our lives. At least, Sagan shouldn't."

"Lai, you must have had a bad day at work," Keid said. "You should go change and rest for a while. This is exactly why I don't want you to work in that hot kitchen. It—"

"Are you even listening? I was leaving!" Lyra interrupted, her body still stiff as stone. "I wasn't going for a vacation; I was leaving Zenith forever. To settle there, on Earth. I wanted that for Sagan, too."

"What?" Keid's brows narrowed with pain. "You both were leaving me?"

"I am twenty-seven. I shouldn't be staying with you in the first place."

"Wow."

Lyra watched her father from the side, his back more curved than she remembered. It reminded her of the time when he had the gallbladder surgery and couldn't walk straight for days. When he had moaned each night in sleep, dreaming about his dead wife.

She badly wished for her father to walk away, so she won't have to spit more poison.

"Lai," Keid's voice came weak. "Your mother would have never thought in a million years that you'd turn out to be so self-centered."

"Self-centered?" Lyra couldn't stop herself. "Is it selfish to wish a life for myself that I really want? To live independently? To escape the place where my mother died?" She realized she was standing on the same exact spot where her mom had taken her last breath calling her name. She rubbed her stomach and went on. "Self-centeredness is not living with my father and taking care of him while people my age left their parents' home ten years ago. You are selfish."

Lyra felt slapped by her own words. Her body trembled and her nails dug into her palms. A bitter dryness parched her mouth and she lost grip on her breathing. She raced up the stairs and cooped herself inside her bedroom.

The resentment and fury took form of words which she spewed into her computer all evening. She wrote stories she would never read.

The next morning, when she opened her bedroom door, she found Sagan sitting across the hall on the floor of his room, reading a book. The most soothing sight to her eyes.

In a perfect world, Sagan would have been her biggest confidant. They had always been on the same wavelength. But he was almost a functional adult. She didn't want to burden the innocence of a twelve-year-old with her complexities.

Lyra wanted to go back to isolation, but instead, she knocked on the open door of Sagan's room and said in a fake, formal voice, "Excuse me, sir. Is this where they sell self-acquired intellect?"

Sagan looked up from his book and saw his sister standing by the door with her disarrayed hair, pajamas flowing over her ankles, and T-shirt sleeves running over her palms.

"And Dad says *I* have a low EQ."

"Sorry." Lyra grinned and perched next to her brother. For

minutes, they sat in silence. Sagan read his book and Lyra tried to solve her brother's Rubik's cube for the nth time.

"Stop! It's exasperating." Sagan snatched the cube and placed it by his side. "I told you one cannot solve it that way. You have to learn the algorithm."

Lyra shrugged.

Sagan faced his book and spoke again, "I am sorry for yesterday. I will apologize to Dad too."

"It's okay. I wasn't at my best either."

"I heard. In all its honesty, it was satisfying." Sagan nodded thrice. "I've never seen you so volcanic before."

Lyra gave her brother a look.

"Sorry, but it is galling to never see you losing your calm. How do you manage to stay nice all the time?" Sagan tried hard to not make it sound like he was asking for help.

"Hmm... I am quick to identify when I am at fault, and then I keep my mouth shut. When it's someone else's fault, I ask 'why'. I try to analyze, find out what makes them channel their thoughts and emotions in that manner. You have to think of humans as machines." Lyra instantly regretted saying that to a twelve-year-old. But she continued, knowing how nothing would make better sense to Sagan than such an analogy. "Machines run in a particular manner because they are designed that way. Or used or kept a certain way. Some are oiled and maintained well, some rust due to lack of care, some adapt, and some crash in the face of apathy. Just like machines, we are all wired and treated differently too which eventually decides how we react. Most often, there is a cause behind someone's actions. With practice and maturity, it becomes easier to acknowledge those causes. When this becomes your default process, it's easier to stay calm. Plus, I find undeniable bliss in not confronting someone." Lyra beamed a foolish grin. "Of course, this hack doesn't work every time. It didn't yesterday, even though I knew where Dad was coming from."

"Being understanding is exhausting," Sagan said.

"It is. But this cycle of analysis keeps you kind."

"I refuse to believe that everyone is that insightful."

"Well, most people don't have to go through this process," explained Lyra. "In human terms, it's called being empathetic. Most people use their emotions to be that. For others, for us, it doesn't come naturally, and so we have to use logic to formulate it."

Sagan looked at his book blankly and tried to draft his customized plan.

"Do you want to talk about what happened at school yesterday?" Lyra asked. "I have never seen you so indignant before, either."

"I loathe going to school."

"Why?" Lyra unconsciously read random words from Sagan's book as she said, "You used to love school."

"You know my classmate, Sipa, the one who always comes up with an assortment of ideas to do things together?"

"Yeah?"

"He asked me yesterday if I wanted to play vintage video games at his home. My refusal provoked everyone to make fun of me, including Sipa."

"Why did you refuse?"

"Because I don't like it," Sagan said like he was stating a fact. "Video games were an epidemic that seduced the 21st century Earthlers into idiocy and obesity. It retracted them from everything real. I was honest and told them exactly that."

"Oh, Sagan!"

He shrugged.

"You know, I was a video game addict before you were born. Does that make me shallow?"

Sagan raised his book-sized torso with surprise. "Why did you stop?"

"I had to play with you." Lyra twisted her lips. "It seems like Sipa wanted to befriend you."

"He did not want to befriend me. No one wants to. He invited me because no one talks to him, either."

"Either? No one talks with you?"

"Not unless they think they want to hear something funny."

"I am sorry. I will talk to your teacher, okay?"

"I am fine with not being talked to. I am smart enough to know that my perceived arrogance is the cause of my ill-treatment. I like my space anyway. Even if they talked, we wouldn't have anything in common to converse."

"Sagan, not everyone except you is dumb. I am sure at least a few of your classmates are worth talking to. It's not healthy to view everyone as inferior. You have every right to have an opinion. What makes you wiser is the way you let your opinions drive your behavior. Cleverness is great—I am a sap for it—but you should always strive to be kind. And you can't refuse. I just gave you the empathy formula for it."

"I don't see anyone as my inferior. I just feel I am not on the same spectrum as they are. I experience a fire inside me to learn and evolve. That's my definition of playtime. In that process, I've driven myself so far from everyone else that I cannot relate. Not in a superior-inferior way..."

"In an alienated way," Lyra mumbled. "Like you are always in the wrong room."

"Exactly! You can formulate as many formulas as your mind desires, but I know you experience that alienation too."

Lyra did not respond.

"I would be exhilarated to have someone challenge or defeat me," Sagan went on. "You know, I don't thrive on narcissism. It's exhausting being vacuous to fit in." He drooped his shoulders and blankly flipped pages of *Science of Percussion Instruments* with wrists narrower than the spine of the book.

Lyra related to everything he said but she had to play the adult here. "How did you get so clever?" She wished her father saw Sagan the way she saw him. "I get your point, but don't you think Sipa wants your company despite knowing you? There is nothing wrong with making friends or playing a video game once in a while. Who knows? Maybe that's one place where he might challenge or defeat you."

"*You* don't make friends."

"That's... different."

"We are both the same, sister. The only difference between us is that you try to conceal and suppress what you are, while I don't."

"Lord Sagacious, we are not talking about me right now." Lyra changed the topic. "Forget friends; you also offended your teacher, Sagan. He told me that you are always contradicting his teaching process."

"Can I show you something exceedingly interesting?" Sagan's face lit up.

"Oka-ay."

He walked Lyra to his balcony, which she knew was filled with his pet insects—some in cages, some roaming freely. Soft light pierced through the neighbor's tree and smeared the balcony walls. On it, a colony of ants, half a dozen spiders, three lizards, a few phasmids, and a couple of praying mantises were relishing their daily dose of rooflight.

Lyra folded her arms as she saw her brother reach a cage and grab his pet tarantula from it with careful hands. A maternal beam radiated on his face. "Sagan, I've never been thrilled to come here, you know that," she said.

"Amica is a lot like you." Sagan stroked the tarantula's orange abdomen. Thick prickly hair coated its electric blue body. Lyra watched the spider rub its two pedipalps against each other and thought of human palms in front of a delicious meal.

"She won't hurt you," her brother said. "The pretense of friendliness and the docility in her nature keeps her subdued all the time."

"Stop assessing me," Lyra said and walked inside. She noticed the entire room for the first time since she had walked in. On the left corner, by Sagan's bookshelf, were bowls of water laid in a semicircle on a rug, and the floor by the side of his bed was lined with books arranged in a maze-like form.

Sagan grabbed dried crickets from a container and placed them at every corner in the maze.

"What are you doing?" Lyra asked.

"I was going to show you something interesting, remember? Now." He placed Amica at the beginning of the maze. "Observe."

The tarantula lingered at the entrance of the maze for a couple of seconds. Then it took a right turn and ate a dried cricket. When it reached a fork, it took another right turn to eat the treat, avoiding a similar treat on the left. After navigating the whole maze and enjoying the treats, it reached the endpoint.

Sagan took Amica back in his hands and faced Lyra. "So?" he inquired.

"What am I looking for?"

"You know how humans are either left or right-handed? I believe spiders are too. I dropped equal amounts of similar treats in every corner of the maze, but Amica always turned right to eat those treats instead of left, proving that she's right-handed."

"That's right, she did!" Lyra was fascinated. "But it's just one spider. There are too many variables."

"I'll be glad to share one more tale if you vow to not tell anyone."

"Tell what?"

"I've been visiting Goodall Sanctuary every week to bring home different spiders."

"You...what?"

"But I've been switching my spiders with theirs so that they don't notice. All the spiders that iwent through this maze took right turns, every single one of them." When Sagan noticed the undisturbed shock on Lyra's face, he consoled her, "Don't fret. I have returned all the spiders to the sanctuary. They were well-fed and entertained in my care."

"Oh, Sagan!"

"I was curious."

Lyra's shock subdued. "Yeah, we always are."

"So?"

"You do know that you are misusing Mom's goodwill by stealing spiders from a public sanctuary, right? You were already getting partial treatment because of her. No one has pet insects at home."

"That's because no one wants to bring insects home."

Lyra visualized her little brother pretending to play with the spiders at the sanctuary and switching them when no one was watching. It made her chuckle. "I never took you for a trouble-maker."

"Not my intention," Sagan clarified. "Now, what about this discovery?"

"It's incredible. Impressive. But I don't know anything about entomology to give you proper feedback."

"I've read all Zenither books on arachnids, even the ones we got from Earth. None of those talk about the laterality in spiders."

"I can take you to some of Mom's old friends at the university. They might know more about this."

"That was all I wanted to hear from my teacher, because this is what I want to do when I grow up. Entomology research that hasn't been conducted on Zenith yet. But, instead, he termed this as a time-wasting experiment. He said Zenith would never have too many spiders to worry about their brain dominance. That was the reason I didn't submit my test papers. I despise these boundaries. I am tired of learning the same thing repeatedly. But no one reciprocates my concerns...are you listening to me?" Sagan found Lyra staring at the space above his head. He shook her. "Sister!"

"Sagan!" Lyra's mouth and eyes were wide open. "This is crazy. Extraordinarily crazy." She rattled her brother just like he had shaken her. "But I have an idea."

"About the laterality of spiders?"

"No, something bigger. But I can't just blurt out something

so huge. I need to do a lot of research before I can tell another soul."

"You know where to go."

After a quick shower and breakfast, the siblings were on their way to Orwell Library—a small two-storied building where all the books donated by Earth during the colonization and the books the Terraformers brought along with them were shelved. Unlike Zenither bookstores, where one could buy books penned by Zenithers, one could only read books at the library.

Lyra entered the library and like every time her heart ached for all the books she would never be able to read. She picked half a dozen books from different shelves and sat at a corner table. She read until her eyes turned raw. At another table, Sagan gloriously enjoyed the books of his choice. When the rooflight dimmed, Lyra pulled herself and Sagan out of the library to head home.

On their way, they stopped at Kish's bookstore, a place where Lyra had worked before. She bought the book named *Future of Zenith*.

When Kish handed the remaining change, Sagan carefully counted the ferrics. Lyra nudged him with her elbow. Mr. Kish, as she had known him, was one of the nicest people on the asteroid and she did not want to offend him.

"Please don't be offended," Sagan addressed Kish, still counting the change. "I do not doubt your intentions; I only doubt your math."

Kish gave out a full belly laugh.

"I am sorry, Mr. Kish. Good night." Lyra dragged Sagan away.

She spent the next two days reading and evaluating her idea. Then, she made up her mind—a perfect solution to Sagan's frustration and all the other concerns regarding Zenith.

Aryabh was the one with whom she wanted to share the news

first. She picked up her phone and typed a message with hasty fingers-

I am not coming to Earth alone, Aryabh. I am bringing Zenith with me.

CHAPTER 9

THE EARTHLER NEWS

August 3, 2125

LIFE EXPECTANCY IMPROVES FOR THE CITIZENS OF 1ST STRATUM

According to the study conducted by Dr Fesoj Elegnem of PacaBaylor University, the lifespan of 1st Stratum citizens has increased from 51.7 to 52.2 years. Global health conditions continue to improve as The Pacamounts...

Switch

'The Pacamounts introduced a new—'

Switch...

'Pain and suffering are always inevitable for a large intelligence and a deep heart. The really great men must, I think, have great sadness on earth.'

Aryabh tried hard to concentrate on the words he was reading in a bootlegged book, but his throat didn't let him; it felt like a brick was rubbing against it.

He argued with himself—the Pacamounts, in their right mind, would never let a whole civilization that was not bred in their factory, mix with the controlled population of Earth. But they had twisted psychology. Who knows what they might use seven thousand Zenithers for... But the Zenithers were not going to listen to Lyra, an imprudent woman with insane ideas.

Aryabh read people like he read his books; however, with Lyra, he had been inaccurate. She was not as compliant as he had anticipated. He had expected steadiness, but she was a cyclone that stormed his dreams in a whirlpool of disaster.

In his ears buzzed a two-hundred-year-old song that he had found on the dark web—*Dark Was the Night, Cold Was the Ground*. Its moaning stirred his emotions. His eyelids drooped and fatigue lulled him into a deep sleep.

When his eyes opened, he was standing in the middle of Chase Street. It was deserted, except for the depressive dimness of the street which had never been this empty before. Kenai had asked him to wait there for him.

Aryabh looked around. All the PacaEyes pointed in his direction. When he blinked, he saw a small cottage. He blinked again and noticed a lush green garden surrounding the house. Colorful flowers sprouted in it.

A chilly wind howled and rode through like the upper-level traffic, leaving a burning sensation on Aryabh's skin. He noticed scrapes and cuts all over his body. Blood oozed out of fresh wounds, while crusty scabs covered other gashes.

He blinked. A cozy wooden chair rocked him back and forth on the house's patio. He rubbed his cold palms and wrapped his arms around his chest.

Blink. House. Garden. Warm breeze.

Aryabh noticed that he was turning old. His skin wrinkled and his back arched. The hair on his arm grayed and he grew weaker. He couldn't be old, not here on Earth.

He was trying to escape and hide when a cheerful voice spoke from behind. He tried to turn around but he couldn't.

"Aryabh! I've been looking everywhere for you."

It was Kenai. To Aryabh's surprise, his voice made him feel safer. When he heard Kenai's footsteps approaching from behind, he asked, "Where is everyone?"

"When have you ever needed anyone, Aryabh?" said his roommate.

Kenai stood so close, Aryabh felt his breath on his nape.

"Don't speak from behind. Talk to my face! Where is everyone? Why can't I move?" He struggled.

Blink. House. Garden. Craters. His smile.

Kenai walked to the front and flashed his teeth at Aryabh. He was not wearing his glasses, and instead of black, his pupils were red. They zoomed in and out like camera lenses.

"Why are your eyes red?" Aryabh wiggled. "I can't move. Drag me to the apartment."

Kenai cachinnated in a manner that frightened Aryabh.

Blink. House. Craters. His smile. Rooflight.

"For relentless power, we strive and ride!" his roommate roared and laid a cupped palm on his chest.

Hundreds of uniformed guards in gear crawled towards him. Each of them fought to grab a piece of Aryabh.

"My work here is done." Kenai bowed to the PacaMilitary and left.

Aryabh shut his eyes intending to never open them. There was no house, no garden.

Blink. Blink. Blink.

But all he saw were the guards lynching him.

Aryabh felt like he was being pushed under cold water. Before he lost his breath, he woke up, shaking violently.

Sweat pooled around his body. He removed his wet T-shirt and threw it away. A shiver ran through him. He wrapped a blanket around his body and lay in a fetal position. When he looked around, he found red, blurry shapes in the air. His fever, which he could smell, had congealed with the darkness of the room. It made the apartment reek like an abandoned factory.

This is it, he thought. I am dying.

Something beeped outside. He heard movement by the main door.

"I am home!"

Aryabh turned on the night vision on his lenses.

Kenai's green face appeared by the entrance. His glossy eyes brought Aryabh a frightening realization.

He had cracked and studied PacaProfiles of people before merely talking to them, but he had decided to stay with a stranger based on his profile's minimal history. He didn't even know where exactly Kenai had been before he moved in. How could he be so reckless? What if Kenai was a PacaSpy? What if he was hired by the Farm to keep an eye on him? What if he was a Cream?

Aryabh wanted to throw him out of the house but he could barely move.

Kenai turned on the lights. He saw his roommate half-naked, squatting in a corner of his bed, staring at him like a wounded animal.

"Oh my god!" He dropped his bags. "What happened? You look terrible. You are shaking. Oh god."

He rushed to Aryabh and placed his hand on his forehead. Aryabh whisked it away with the last bit of energy he could muster.

"You are burning!" Kenai exclaimed. "Why didn't you call me?" He darted to the bathroom.

Aryabh watched him return with two bottles of liquid in one hand and a glass of fresh-tank water in another. He recalled how Kenai had been drinking the black tank water for four straight days to save enough fresh-water for a recipe he had been babbling about ever since he moved in.

Kenai gave him the medicines. Aryabh rejected them with a weak shake of his head.

"Take it. Come on, buddy. You are too smart to refuse medicines. Mind you, these are not some trashy Sonmanto pills that will shake you with a burst of energy and make you feel worse after a while. These are good medicines. Scored them from a Trunk. I promise they will make you feel better. Take it."

Aryabh grudgingly drank the fluids along with a whole glass of water. As they passed down his throat, he felt the frayed tissues resting back in their places.

Kenai opened the window. The purple of dusk entered the room. Despite the musty smell, the outside air livened the decaying ambiance of the apartment. He hummed, the noise of Sonmanto melding with it.

The house took a life of its own.

Kenai whistled and sang a chirpy jingle as he unpacked the two bags he had dropped at the door.

"You are in for a treat, my friend. I got my pay today. Look what I got...some real food!" He showed every single item to Aryabh from across the room. "Well, not real but edible," he went on. "I'd been craving the crunch of a vegetable for months. These are canned. I still can't afford fresh ones but, hey, they are still better than powdered ones, right? Thank goodness, I didn't have the willpower to save all my pay, because now I can cook you something that will make you better. You are not eating that garbage from the slot machine. Not until you heal." His voice rose. "And this, my friend, is the magic machine! Life as we know, Aryabh, will never be the same again."

He rushed to Aryabh's bed and showed him a thin black plate with a red circle in the center.

"That's a freaking hot plate! I got it from Mazona. They had it on sale. It's still a splurge, but you can't imagine the things I can make using this...Hey, what's that?" Kenai pointed at an elongated scar on Aryabh's waist. The scar stretched from his malnourished abdomen to the back.

Aryabh covered his bare upper body with the blanket. He was miserable and in no mood to share about the time when he was seventeen and had messed with the wrong people, and how he was drugged and had opened his eyes to mind-numbing pain and a few stitches over a missing kidney.

Kenai sensed Aryabh's discomfort. "Okay, some other day." He whistled again as he jaunted to the kitchen with his haul.

Aryabh heard a cacophony of beeps and bangs from the kitchen along with the clicking of Kenai's little device. On a regular day, it would have antagonized him. But, strangely, it palliated his pain.

As Kenai's medicine started to work, his physical torment was replaced by unbearable hunger. His stomach contracted and he felt dizzy. The last he had eaten was a day and a half ago when he had received Lyra's message.

This was the second time he had experienced hunger as merciless as this. It reminded him of the first time.

He was ten and had just escaped from the PacaOrphanage. A dusty nook by a forty-storied parking structure became his refuge. The alley that fronted his spot was lined with more cars. It was his third day without food and water. All he had were three bites of a stale protein bar that he had found in the trash and a can of soda he had managed to steal from a child on the street.

In this corner, he had lain like a crumpled can for nine hours, shaking with cold and hunger. He regretted running away and wanted to go back to the abusive orphanage only so that he could have a hot meal. Covered in dust, he had chewed on the collar of his uniform all night.

Aryabh could never forget the dryness of his skin, the taste of grime on his collar, and the hallucinations he had endured that night. He could still smell the soot of the vehicles zooming up and down the parking structure.

Similar hunger gnawed at his gut right now. He decided to pop half a dozen AwakeTabs to feel some weight in his stomach. That was what he had done in the past.

But before he could reach for his drug, Kenai emerged from the kitchen with a plate in his hand. On it was a steaming bowl of liquid. An unfamiliar aroma overwhelmed Aryabh's senses.

"If this is not the best remedy for cold and fever, I don't know what is." Kenai pulled the desk by Aryabh's bed and placed the plate on it. "It's a lemon-garlic broth with chicken in it, my mother's recipe. She always made this when I was sick. I used to call it liquid-love." Aryabh cringed. "However, she would use fresh garlic and a dash of real lemon juice. For now, what I had will work just fine. I've also added some carrots, celery, and mushrooms from the can, and it's made in fresh water. Here, I got this big spoon. Eat while it's hot."

Aryabh watched Kenai clean around him and then shifted his gaze to the clear soup. He wanted to retaliate, just for the sake of it, but instead, he reached straight for the spoon. He slurped the hot liquid. Warmth he could not have imagined embraced him. The broth was sour and spicy, the chicken juicy, and the vegetables had a bite to them.

In the dusty nook that night many years ago, someone had seen him in the orphanage uniform and reported him. They had dragged his unconscious body the next morning. The first thing he had eaten after gaining consciousness was a plate of hot brown slurry at the orphanage canteen. He had eaten seven plates of it and felt stronger and better with each plate. Aryabh never found out what was in that slurry that made him strong instantly, and yet it was mold compared to Kenai's soup, which he now slurped at a meteoric speed.

Kenai watched him with kind eyes. "Slow down, buddy. There is more."

It was by the last slurp of the third bowl that Aryabh remembered how Kenai had wanted to make something with the water. A feeling of gratitude fluttered inside him, but instead of thanking him, he did the next best thing his demeanor could manage.

"The place is too small for two beds. We can get a bunkbed so that you don't have to snore in my face from the floor."

"We can? That's awesome!" The idea of bunking with his roommate excited Kenai more than having an actual bed to sleep on. With newfound excitement, he took Aryabh's utensils and placed them in the dishwasher. A blasting gush of heat burnt the food particles and sanitized the dishes. In twenty seconds, the washer opened and Kenai grabbed the warm plate for his own dinner. He went to the slot machine and clicked the options.

Aryabh knew but he still asked, "Weren't you cooking that...thing?"

"Some other day. We aren't dying tomorrow. You should sleep now." He bobbed his head out of the kitchen. "Life can be tough and can stretch you too thin sometimes, but you don't have to keep fighting all the time. Sometimes you just quit and take a nap."

Aryabh wished he could but he had no room for sleep in his eyes. He was sick and he craved the comfort of familiar words. Ever since Kenai had moved in, he hadn't read any of his books. After giving it some thought, he brushed past Kenai in the kitchen and slid the cabinets.

Kenai's jaw dropped at the sight of a hidden door.

Aryabh went inside and emerged with a book in his hand.

"You have a book! How did you get that? Why is that room hidden?" Kenai seemed more impressed than scared or surprised.

"I've been collecting them from here and there ever since I have moved to this place. It's just books in there," Aryabh answered.

"But you can read on your lenses too, right?"

"Not without sharing them with the Pacamounts. They discarded all hard copies and digitalized them so that they could keep track of what people are reading. I can throw them off but it's an unparalleled feeling to hold a real book." Aryabh sniffed and stroked the cover of his book. "It's like holding an era from the past, like a time machine. It carries me to a time when things were all right. It makes me..." Aryabh stopped when it occurred to him that he had said too much.

"That's beautiful. But isn't it a punishable crime? Aren't you scared?"

"No. Now, do you mind?" Aryabh pretended to be bothered and went back to his bed.

"Oh, carry on."

Kenai built his dinner and sat on the floor by Aryabh's bed.

"Hey Aryabh, not today, but maybe when you are not sick, I'd love if you could read me something from your books. It's how you know big words, right? I have not met anyone who speaks like you." Kenai said and took a bite of elastic meat. "And, I love listening to stories."

Aryabh glanced at his book and considered how it was not meant to be read by someone like Kenai, someone so unworldly.

He opened a bookmarked page and read a sentence—'Tragedy, he perceived, belonged to the ancient time, to a time when there were still privacy, love, and friendship, and when the members of a family stood by one another without needing to know the reason.'

Behind his book, he saw his roommate on the floor, finishing an odious dinner.

After twenty-seven years of reading about it in old books, Aryabh had finally caught the first glimpse of sacrifice.

CHAPTER 10

August 5, 2125

Lyra: I know you hate my guts right now, but I don't expect you to be my cheerleader, Aryabh.

Aryabh: That's right. I don't endorse lunacy.

Lyra: Yeah, because wanting to settle on Zenith is endorsing sanity.

Aryabh: You won't get it.

Lyra: Out of four billion people, you are the only Earthler who wants to move to Zenith. I am the only one out of 7,262 Zenithers who wants to move to Earth. We both want something our society doesn't. We should be the only two people in the universe who should understand each other.

Aryabh: Don't compare yourself to me. Your world lacks nothing.

Lyra: Imagine waking up every day to see a boundary at the horizon, knowing this is where your world stops. Imagine living within that restricted boundary until the day you die.

Aryabh: Other Zenithers don't find an issue with that.

Lyra: I wish I was them. Trust me. What I feel every day is torture.

Aryabh: Stop overreacting.

Lyra: You want to settle on Zenith because you don't see anything beyond yourself. This asteroid has its limitations. I am thinking about the future Zenithers.

Aryabh: They'll grow up just like you not knowing or seeing what lies beyond the asteroid.

Lyra: I didn't grow up that way. I knew exactly what lay beyond my world. I grew up with resentment. Think what the resentment of hundreds of people will do to a world that is as small as Zenith is.

Aryabh: The Pacamounts would never allow you to migrate back here. You don't even know why they colonized Zenith in the first place.

Lyra: I am not disguising my ignorance over this matter. It's why I am still talking to you, to learn more.

Aryabh: Zenith was colonized by people who were against the Pacamounts, but couldn't be taken down like the billions of other powerless Earthlers, because the Terraformers were as influential, if not as powerful as the Pacamounts. These people had to either fight a powerful giant or leave the rotting planet behind to create a new world in space. It was a no-brainer. They chose the latter, picked people who shared the same moral reasoning, and left. The only reason you are there while others suffer here is that you probably had ethical ancestors who were privileged. You are letting them down.

Lyra: That's not what we are taught in history class. The colonization is one of the biggest outer space expeditions for us. A great exploration voyage. I didn't know this. Are you sure?

Aryabh: You don't know a lot of things.

Kenai throned on the top of his new bunkbed and dictated his daily journal on his phone. Every once in a while he would glance down at Aryabh who sat at his desk. He found it theatrical to watch Aryabh stare into nothingness, punch his fingers on the bare table, and move his hands in the air like a maestro. He enjoyed how Aryabh's face moved and crinkled, for it was only when he talked with Lyra that Kenai would get to see him emote.

CHAPTER 11

Zenith

August 6, 2125

"No, no..." Lyra muttered as she flipped her messenger bag inside out. She had not touched it ever since she had been back. It was like her personal vendetta against it for swallowing her dreams.

In all the chaos, she had not noticed that her great-grandma's diary was also missing along with her folder. She thought of the last time she had seen the diary. It was when she was in Trac's auto, heading towards the spaceport. She had placed it next to her folder.

Lyra collapsed on the floor in the middle of her rummage with her hand kneading her head.

The diary had been with her ever since she was sixteen. It was her first birthday after her mother had passed away and it wasn't until the evening that Lyra had remembered it. When she had placed a bawling Sagan in his bassinet after swinging him in her arms for an hour, she had noticed a note that had been slipped under her bedroom door.

Dear Lai,

I am sorry, I forgot your birthday. You turned sixteen today! I am so proud of the strong woman you are turning into. We have been through a lot as a family, but you alone have fought against all odds. I wish I had your strength.

Every day I wake up thinking I'd do something or be someone better today, and every day I lose. It is only because of your perennial support that I am alive today.

I wish I can make you as happy as you were when your mom was here, but today I merely have a small gift for you. Your mother wanted to pass it down to you. It's outside your door.

I hope you will forgive your father for forgetting your birthday. I'll always love you.

Dad

At her door, Lyra had found an old, worn-out diary of her great-grandmother. Poona's mother had brought her mother's diary when she had migrated to Zenith seventy-five years ago. She had wanted to pass it down to the women of their family as a memento of their ancestor's life on Earth, for it contained words of power and hope.

Poona's mother had had to leave her parents behind on Earth because they didn't want to be plucked out from the life they had worked so hard to build in that world. They had refused to spend their short remaining life on an alien asteroid.

After a decade of Zenith's colonization, Lyra's great-grandparents had died of old age on Earth without ever meeting their daughter again. When Lyra was a kid, she had heard surreal stories about them and their life on Earth. Her grandmother used to often talk about how her parents were the epitome of love. They were so intertwined with each other that they had died hours apart.

Lyra still remembered the day she held the diary. Its cover had lost its color over the years, but the pages were still intact. The year 2011-2012 was embossed on its hardcover, while its first page was covered with her great-grandmother's name and insightful messages and quotes. The remaining space was crammed with drawings of tiny butterflies, elephants, stars, planets, and various other shapes that Lyra didn't understand. On the top right corner was her great-grandfather's name written inside a star.

The first time, Lyra had thought the diary smelled like her father's desk. On the second sniff, it exuded the scent of old books, like the Earth books in the Orwell library. It exhilarated her to think of all the times and places the diary had been.

Lyra had felt like she was holding a time-traveling device. Every page of the diary had transported her to Earth. Her great-grandma's life was an adventurous thrill ride. The journal entries were written for around a year, but in that one year, she had lived a life worth a dozen lifetimes. Four difficult months into the diary, she had met her great-grandfather. It was a magical story, a tale of the kind that Lyra had only read in old books.

Her Indian great-grandmother had met her future husband in a foreign land where she was only a traveler. They were strangers who had stumbled upon each other in an Earthler city called Paris. Her great-grandfather, an Indian descendent, was local to Paris, and had shown her around the city on their first date.

They had sat and strolled by a river called the Seine, walked on the winding cobblestone streets of Saint Michel, gazed at the flower-adorned balconies of the city, drank delicious coffee, commuted on extensive metro trains, sat in the historic Jardin du Luxembourg, and talked ceaselessly for the whole day like they had known each other forever. On their third date, they went strolling in a forest called Forêt de Fontainebleau. When they sat to rest on a small wooden bench, surrounded by lush summer trees, her great-grandfather declared his feelings and she reciprocated them.

They were married six months later.

According to Lyra's grandmother, her parents had traveled all around the globe, fulfilled their dreams, and had worked towards the betterment of Earthlers until the day they died.

Lyra had spent her remaining birthday reading the diary. Through the words of her great-grandmother, she had learned more about Earth's food, its sun, its forests, the sky, and the oceans; about Earth's diversity and adversity. She had witnessed the thrill of the unknown and what meeting someone from another part of the world meant. She had learned how it was possible to turn one's life around. The stories of her great-grand-mother taught her strength, courage, and love for they were things that didn't come naturally to her.

It was the diary that spoke of the compassion and kindness of Earthlers, something she had never heard or read before. It was because of the diary, Lyra refused to believe that humanity on Earth could expire in a century.

On that night, she had decided that she would visit Forêt de Fontainebleau at least once. But, upon searching, Lyra was unable to find the places mentioned in the diary on Earth's map, not even the city of Paris.

The loss of her most precious possession finally made her accept the uncomfortable truth—the disappearance of her documents and her diary was not a coincidence.

The only place that could give her answers was Ms. Clia's office.

Beside Zenith's Museum, which flaunted replicas of various monuments of Earth, stood the Council of Zenith. Lyra stared at a board affixed outside, while she contemplated questions that volleyed from her documents and diary to everything she had learned in the past few days. The board read, "APPROACH WITH A PROBLEM, LEAVE WITH A SOLUTION - Our heads are not only highly qualified but are immensely driven by their passion for their respective fields. Each official strives to maintain an innovative and efficient government. The Brain Trust at the Council of Zenith believes in an open-door policy. Every complaint, suggestion, and doubt will be received with the utmost respect at this building."

When the Terraformers first moved to Zenith, they appointed a handful of efficient people from every field. This panel of ex-perts would analyze the problem and put forward their suggestions to the public to vote. Most often, everyone would be on the same side, which made putting decisions into motion easy. This little system seemed favorable and fair to the next generation as well. Hence, the first-generation Zenithers, or, as they were called, the 1st G, came up with an official group of experts called the Brain Trust.

As Zenith was a new world on a small asteroid, away from Earth, Zenithers were extremely careful with their habitat. It would only take one wrong decision to put them in danger, which was why they knew they could not risk choosing incapable people in charge of their newly born world.

The Head of Law Enforcement, Ms. Clia, a fierce 47-year-old woman, had played a vital role in introducing new criminal laws on Zenith and enforcing them. Everyone understood that Ms. Clia was a stern official who would fight alone for Zenith if needed. But, beneath those layers of the hard exterior, Lyra had discovered a well of kindness in Ms. Clia. Her habit of lending a patient ear to every Zenither made it easy for Lyra to approach her for something as small as a diary.

"Your case has been keeping me awake at night. Earth has the sole rights to the recorded footage of the station, and so we cannot even track you. My experience says that it's theft. It's evident. What baffles me is why a folder of unimportant documents gets stolen while your money and other valuables stay untouched."

"And a diary."

"Yes, now a diary too." Ms. Clia jotted something in her notepad and rocked back and forth in her chair. "Baffling. I checked." She pulled a register from her drawer and pushed it across the table towards Lyra. Her stocky finger pointed to a list of names. "There were only two Zenither passengers that day, besides you. An elderly couple heading to Earth for vacation. You might know them—Mr. Anton and Ms. Fani."

"Yes, I know Mr. Anton. He worked at the bank."

"Right. Apart from them, everyone at the transit station was an Earthler. Your hard documents are as useless to them as their

PacaProfile database to us. Then why the theft?" She rocked again. "Baffling." Her hair, the same length as Lyra's, fell flat and limp on her blazer's shoulder pads.

Lyra looked at the big, thoughtful face of Ms. Clia. It reminded her of a blue cartoon bird she watched as a kid.

"May I ask something? It's unrelated to my case." She hesitated.

"Shoot."

Lyra switched and interwove her serpentine legs again. "I recently learned about some of the atrocities of Earth's government, the Pacamounts, and the cold mentality of Earthlers. It's insane how much of their world is shielded from us," she said. "Darwin said that human emotions are universal, and so are the reactions to those emotions. Then why don't we have a similar political climate on Zenith? Why aren't we as apathetic as the citizens of Earth?"

"I am glad to know someone on this asteroid thinks about this." Ms. Clia said, impressed.

Lyra thought of her great-grandmother, for it was her words that had compelled her to think about it in the first place.

"How can I be of the same species as the ones who used humans as slaves, chained and tortured them, species that burned children alive?" The words in the diary had read.

"I know you are looking for a psychological explanation here," said the Head of Law Enforcement. "My answers might not satisfy your appetite."

"I am not a picky eater when it comes to learning something," Lyra said in a heartbeat.

"Fair enough. See, Lyra, our world is small." Ms. Clia placed her hands on the table. "Nearly no one alive here right now has known or seen the world our ancestors were once a part of. When our foreparents came here, they were not only professionally diverse but physically and culturally too. There were people sent of various nationalities, religions, ethnicities, races, and cultures. It might have been history's biggest blunder, sending a bunch of mixed people on a rock, away from the civilization. But it wasn't." She leaned forward. "Why? Because there was no way out. Their priority was to survive. They were too busy worrying about how to grow proper food to think about fighting. It happens in our old literature and movies, but in real life, when you are on a newly formed colony in space, committing a crime takes the backseat, if you know what I mean."

Lyra gave out a soft chuckle, but she remembered Aryabh's message about how the Terraformers were a rare combo of the privileged and ethical.

"Not that we are all saints. We do have our own shenanigans, for which our citizens are either sent to therapy, made to do community service, or put on probation or rehabilitated, as you might know. Nothing big, just someone having a bad day, couldn't stand the TV noise of the next-door neighbor, and hurls a rock at their window...or a silly barfight or some reckless drivers breaking traffic rules and causing accidents. Which is why I am here. Enforcing law and regulation is not too difficult here, unlike on Earth. Ever since Zenith's colonization, there has been only one assault as far as serious crimes are concerned."

Ms. Clia watched as Lyra's thirsty brain processed everything. She took the moment to sip water from her glass.

"For us, Lyra," she continued, "there is no escape. This is what we have. There is nothing to be greedy about. There is nothing here in abundance, and nothing you can do with abundance."

"Isn't it the same with Earth? That their planet is all they have?" Lyra argued, only her lips moving on her face. "I think they don't get this because Earth is so vast and there are too many Earthlers. Maybe we would behave the same way if we were in a society as expansive as Earth."

"Or maybe they have reached their peak. When humans get too comfortable, they find a reason to create chaos. Violence is the act of an idle mind. Zenith is a challenging society and we will never be too comfortable, not in the near future at least."

"I see," said Lyra even though she believed that a part of Zenith has already gotten too comfortable.

"Plus, unlike Earthlers, we don't have to live through multiple generations to see the outcome of our destruction. Zenith is so minute that people see the impact of their apathy and errors firsthand. For example, if you start throwing a can instead of recycling it, you will see the mountain of landfill forming right in front of your eyes. Or if you create a fog of hatred, you will live to see your children and grandchildren breathing in the same society. Since this is all we have, I guess, we have learned to let go of our ego and do what's needed to be done. Every Zenither wants to give a better world to their children, even though we get petty at times."

"So it all comes down to the size of the society we live in..." Lyra speculated aloud. "That means, if Zenithers were on Earth, we would be as heinous as them."

"Maybe, maybe not. Zenith is a prime example that humans have the ability to live in peace, that if they are provided with basic needs, security, dignity, and a supportive society, most humans would not need to get them by hurting others. Then they pass the same values to the next generation. I cannot tell what they would do in the absence of those needs. Humans are unpredictable, Lyra. You..." Ms. Clia stopped talking and her eyes narrowed. "Why are you asking so many questions today? The last time I tried to chat with you, I think it was your hotel's anniversary party. You barely mumbled four words. Did your brother send you?"

"No." Lyra smiled. "These questions have been troubling me. I am sorry, but may I ask one last question?"

Ms. Clia nodded.

"In all the time that you've been here, did you see any changes in the behavior or attitude of Zenithers, like a split in psychology? Are people behaving the same way they used to?"

"Hmm..." Ms. Clia rested her chin on her fingers. "That's a tough one. Let's see. The last I arrested someone for a crime was two months ago. The Zen Mavericks were having a small event in the park, when two teenagers got into an aggressive fight. Now, I have seen barfights, but I have never seen kids fighting like that before. It seems like the 3rd G has gotten impatient, especially the teens."

Zen Mavericks was Zenith's youth club.

"Ms. Clia, have you read the book *Future of Zenith*? It was written by Mr. Asres in the year 2101."

"I've heard of him. The renowned psychologist."

"Yes."

"He seems to have contributed some great books to Zenither literature. But I have not read his book, no. Not much of a reader, you see. Haven't got the patience to sit for hours and stare at a book."

"In his book, he has mentioned that he sees psychological tension on Zenith in the future, especially in the Terraformers and the later generations. The Terraformers will start to yearn for Earth in their old age as they'll struggle to find meaning in an idle life, while the teens will feel suffocated because of Zenith's limits."

Ms. Clia dropped the register and her notepad in the drawer and looked Lyra straight in the eye. "Humans will always find a way to feel suffocated in the world they live. We are designed to believe there is always a better place than the one we are in. There isn't."

"I see. So, you think the Terraformers shouldn't have moved here to Zenith. Right?"

The Head of Law Enforcement threw a wordless stare at Lyra, and took a moment. Then, she checked her watch.

"You should study your history books for that," she said. "You'll know we moved here to explore outer space. Is there anything else, Lyra? I am afraid I have to go visit my sister at the hospital."

"No. Thank you. Please let me know if you find something about my documents and diary."

"Absolutely."

"Lyra! We thought we'll never see ya."

Trac yelled as he noticed Lyra entering the gates of Goodall Sanctuary. He sprinted up to her and panted for half a minute.

"Hey," Lyra said and waited.

Trac wiped his hands and face with a towel. His tired face reminded Lyra of the time when he had wept and shared about his violent family history with the volunteer group. Her heart ached for him.

"Hey, ya shoestrings are loose!" Trac pointed while dabbing his temple. "Tie 'em up. You don't want to flip over them."

Lyra lifted her foot one after the other and tied the laces with all her strength. It almost changed the width of her shoe.

"These bats," Trac said, dusting his shoulder with the towel. "I'd send them on the shuttle to Earth tomorrow if I could. I'll never understand why bats have to come here. Deranged little creatures."

"Deranged and consenting." Lyra loved bats.

"Eh?"

"How are you?"

"Runnin' around like always. Hey, I heard about the deportation. Good for ya! Told you, not that good a place to visit. Sorry." He wrinkled his huge forehead in pity.

"Thanks."

"Alright, I needta run... auto time!" Trac pulled up his socks and rolled down the hem of his pants. "Remind me to give you my homegrown tomatoes. This harvest was perfect if I must say. Everyone loved it."

"Sure. Hey, Trac, did I leave a diary in your auto when you dropped me at the spaceport?"

"Nah...na. I would have run after ya to give it back. I always check my auto after I drop ma passengers. You shouldn't give any chance to the troublemakers."

"I see."

"Go now. The crazy animal world misses ya. Go, meet ya friends."

For days, Lyra had dreaded visiting the sanctuary. The animals along with the sanctuary's tiny forest and the little Alvariño pond—Zenith's only water body—in its corner were Lyra's most visited spots on the asteroid. She didn't want her grudge to ruin one of the few things she loved about Zenith.

When she entered the sanctuary, she saw a few farmers and volunteers. They were working near a fruiting chamber of mushrooms—one of the most used ingredients in the Zenither diet because of its high yield in small spaces. She plucked a couple of straw mushrooms from a straw bale below, wiped them on her pants, and munched on them. Then she picked some wild celery from a bucket and tiptoed through small spaces to avoid the workers.

When she turned inwards, a huge patch of bamboo trees embraced her. The forest emanated a damp mossy scent. A wave of calmness swept through Lyra as she entered the crisp green paradise.

She scanned the thicket of bamboo and heard slapping on the ground.

Besides a small grass hut, she noticed a huge, dark creature, almost twice her size, staring at her. She cheered.

"T. rex!"

The mountain gorilla grunted and started walking away from her. He shook his head in disagreement as Lyra paced towards him.

"I am sorry."

She pulled wild celery out of her pocket and paced some more. When she finally caught the gorilla, she pulled him in a tight embrace. Her head was buried in a coat of thick black hair that smelled familiar—pungent and musky.

"I am sorry I left."

T. rex grunted again. He jerked the celery off her hand, and pulled himself away. He walked quietly to a bamboo bench and sat on the ground beside it. Lyra followed him and took a seat on the bench. She stroked his crest and offered him another stalk of wild celery. T. rex accepted it without hesitation.

After he finished his snack, he looked up at Lyra.

She saw the grief of his mate's demise, still fresh in his dark brown eyes. "I felt too guilty to see you." She wiped a smudge of dirt off T. rex's shiny nose. "Because I left."

The gorilla sighed.

"I know how you feel. This is not a sanctuary; it's a zoo. Mom's heart was in the right place in bringing all of you here but this is a prison. You are here for our benefit, not yours. I know you want to run wild and free, groom under the warm sun...munch on tree barks in some giant forest, and feel the rain like your ancestors have...right?" She looked into T. rex's eyes again and saw the emptiness of her eyes mirrored in his. "I don't want you to feel trapped as I do. I thought I couldn't do anything about it before, but now I can. I am going to take you home, T. rex."

The gorilla listened like it had been waiting to hear that voice for days. He gently stroked Lyra's arm and dragged his body closer to the bench. Lyra got down and sat on the ground, resting her back on his side. She propped her head up on T. rex's arm and stared into the wide forest.

A sparrow chirped as it flew above them; the green foliage around it still steady and soundless due to the absence of wind.

Lyra held her knees and gazed at the distant pond without noticing it. "They mock me for wanting to visit Earth. I can't even imagine what they'll say when I tell them I want everyone to leave Zenith."

She turned her face to the side. "You'd love to go to Earth, right, dude? Roam with your kind?"

T. rex hooted.

"Mwahhhh...Mwaahhhh...haa..."

"You'll be home soon. We'll both be home soon."

CHAPTER 12

THE EARTHLER NEWS

August 25, 2125

EARTH TO BE OFFICIALLY RENAMED 'UNITED STRATUMS OF EARTH' ON EMERGENCE DAY

The grand Emergence Day celebrations will take off with the renaming ceremony of Earth, followed by the Pacalympics event. Children from PacaOrphanages will be given the opportunity to participate in all categories...

"I can't believe this is my life now," Aryabh lashed out in his head.

Beside him, Kenai sat with a face that looked as if he was heading for an adventure. It didn't take too long for Aryabh to regret his decision of getting a bunkbed.

To save money, they had gotten a cheap bed that wobbled and creaked every time Kenai tossed and turned, which was frequent. After sleeping most nights on his desk chair, Aryabh decided to exchange their bunkbed for a sturdier one.

They both sat in the waiting area of Mazona Furniture, which was suspended above ground level like a theater balcony. On the ground level was an enormous hangar filled with furniture of all kinds. Shoppers were gathered around each piece in huge numbers. All four walls of the warehouse, each as tall as a three-storied building, played loud advertisements of products not sold at that store.

Aryabh wouldn't have stepped foot in a Mazona store, but he wanted to make sure the new bed was unshakable even during the strongest quakes.

They sat on a plastic bench lined against the wall and waited for a whistle that would signal that the hangar had enough space and air to accommodate more shoppers.

Kenai punched his device over and over again while muttering unrecognizable words. It infuriated Aryabh. Each punch creaked gratingly in his ear, like the sounds of ancient typewriters. But what had annoyed him the most was Kenai offering a PacaDime to Neslo on their way to the store. The old guy had thrown the ten cents back at them.

"Just look at the energy there, Aryabh." Kenai was up from his seat, on his toes, trying to get the view of the hangar below where people were pushing and jostling each other to navigate. A commotion similar to the screeching of faulty machinery soared up to the waiting area.

"I don't remember the last time I looked at so many people at the same time. There must be hundreds of them!" To Aryabh, the warehouse looked like a nasty pigsty crammed with hungry pigs, pushing each other to the ground that was equally vile and filthy. Kenai, as usual, had failed at reading Aryabh's state of mind.

"Shut up. And stop that!" Aryabh barked.

"I don't have anything else to do. We've been here for an hour."

"Then read. Think. Or just be. Stop disturbing me," Aryabh said without looking up from his widget.

"Can I borrow one of your books?"

Aryabh's head darted towards Kenai like a lightning bolt. He peered into his glasses, wanting to gouge his eyes out.

"No...no," Kenai leaned and whispered, "Not those."

Aryabh didn't whisper. "I will kill you."

"That face...you will crack your teeth someday. I meant I want to read on my phone, but I don't know how."

Aryabh snatched his phone. He struggled to hold the giant device with one hand.

"What kind?" he asked.

"Umm...something inspiring but also funny. But it should also have some suspense to keep me hooked..."

Aryabh opened PacaLibrary on Kenai's phone. He typed 'funny', 'inspiring', and 'mystery' under the 'Create Book' option, and entered '5,000' under 'Number of Words'. When Kenai tried to shove his head between him and the phone, he changed the number to 50,000 words.

The website generated a story on its own.

He gave the phone back to Kenai. "Now if I hear a single word out of you, you are back to sleeping on the floor."

"Who wrote this?" Kenai slid his middle finger up his crinkled nose bridge to lift his glasses and gaped at a book on his phone. It was titled *The Hilarious Mystery*.

"No one. It just got written right now. You can build your own songs too. Same method."

"Wow!"

Aryabh titled his head backward.

"Nothing is impressive about it," he said.

> Real art and literature were only available to the Pacamounts and Cream. All we had was tepid, auto art. The NonCreamers didn't want to waste time reading a book or painting or singing, anyway. A few chosen people, talented in those fields, were plucked by the Pacamounts to make a career in PacaEntertainments, an industry specifically created to entertain them and the Cream. Everyone else was content with controlled mediocrity.

When anything that empowers, liberates, or pro-
vokes people is prohibited for years, a generation is
soon born without thoughts of their own, hungry
to digest any junk that's fed to them. Art, music,
and literature had that kind of power, and hence, it
was a fragment of bygone days.
But, like always, I had found my way around that
too. I was not here to follow.

Three kids from different families, aged between nine and
twelve, paced in the waiting room, staring at their watches. Their
nostrils flared and heads shook. Now and then, they would walk
to their respective adults and demand to be taken to the hangar
to shop. Every single time, they were ignored with an even bigger
tantrum from the adults.

One of the kids bumped into the tallest among them. The big
kid grabbed him by his shirt collar and peered into his eyes with
a kind of wrath Kenai didn't believe children could exhibit. His
throbbing veins fueled the fury on his face. Both kids clenched
their fists and started throwing punches at one another. The
third kid joined in with a sly smile.

Kenai looked around, anxious, and found himself to be the
only one watching the children.

There was spitting, scratching, biting, and more punching.
One of the kids tripped by Aryabh's feet and his bony elbow
jabbed into Aryabh's shoe. Kenai sprung from his seat to hold
the boy, but before that, Aryabh flung the kid with his foot as
if he were a dirty rag. The boy tumbled a foot away and was
grabbed by the other kids. The fight resumed.

"Aryabh!"

"I was too occupied to slap him." Aryabh dusted his shoe and
got back to his widget as if nothing had happened.

"That is not what I am complaining about. They are children.
They'll get hurt. Stop them."

Aryabh signaled at the cameras. "Someone eventually will."

"It's unbelievable. These kids. I can't..." The energy on Kenai's face dropped. "I don't feel good. Can we talk about something nice?" Without waiting for Aryabh's response, he went on, "When I was a kid, I loved the other kids. I enjoyed playing with them. That was when I was in Dvedi, my homeTrunk, a small but pleasant place that I had to leave...anyway, that's a story for another day." He snickered. "I have lived in so many places since then, I can't even keep count. For someone who has lived in two Stratums, you'd think I have interesting tales to tell. But I don't. It's all the same, just running and surviving. Life here in Sonmanto is interesting, though." He glanced around in wonderment. "I have never lived in a Head before. Well, for a short while in Ancome, in the 2nd Stratum, but that's it."

Aryabh was still mum, but his ears were open.

"What about you? Where else have you lived? I don't even know where you were born," Kenai asked hesitantly and giggled the next second. "I am sorry. For some reason, I cannot imagine you as a child. It feels like you were born just like this—an adult, straight out of the womb." His bony chest shook with a chortle.

That would have been great, Aryabh thought. He did wish he hadn't been a child at all, for his childhood was filled with terror. Although, he was not sure about the womb.

His womb had been an egg-shaped incubator in the Pacamounts' lab.

After a long day, Aryabh was relieved to stand by his window and smoke. He stared at the cold city, a murky nebula behind the smoke of his cigarette.

Amid the arguments in his head, he heard mumbles from the top of the new bunkbed.

"No! Don't! I will leave...No!"

Kenai was having a nightmare. Aryabh waited to hear more, but he kept moaning.

After a while, Aryabh amplified a piece of music on his widget. The loud beats roused Kenai and he sat straight on his bed.

"No...Don't hurt them," Kenai mumbled. Then he opened his eyes and looked around the dark room. He saw Aryabh at the window. "Aryabh." He rubbed his eyes. "I think I was dreaming something ugly. Did I wake you up?" He grabbed his eyeglasses from under his pillow and moved towards the window side of the bed. "Oh, you are smoking." He laid flat on his stomach and rested his chin on his palms. "It's beautiful outside, isn't it? I like standing there at night too."

Kenai tried to sound upbeat, but in the silver light from outside, Aryabh recognized the ghost of past terror on his illuminated face. He turned to look at the city again and before he could follow his usual protocol for sharing anything personal, he was speaking to the cigarette smoke, "I was born here in Sonmanto, in the PacaLabs."

"Labs?"

"I am a PacaChild."

"That thing written on your ID, I remember that. What does it mean?" Kenai pulled himself closer to the window with his elbows.

The new, sturdy bunkbed creaked.

"The world population was at an all-time low after the Political Fumigation. Due to the wars that preceded and followed the Pacamounts' takeover, people stopped birthing children too. The Pacamounts were in desperate need of numbers, especially the kind on which they can have full control. So, in the 2070s, they started experimenting with human exowombs for extrauterine fetal incubation."

"What?"

"Artificial wombs. They succeeded in less than a decade." Aryabh took a puff, blew smoke, and spoke again. "Development is rapid when morality and ethics are not in the picture. They introduced PacaBirths in the late 80s. They'd pick a Head neighborhood and make it mandatory for everyone living there to donate their eggs and sperm. The donation camps hopped from one area to another. Then they took it a step further." His lips curved. "They started screening the donors, made them take various tests to find special people that matched their criteria. I was from the first ten batches that were manufactured after those screenings."

Kenai had never heard more than two sentences out of Aryabh's mouth without provoking him, but more than his generosity with words right now, he was stunned by his roommate's history. He sat upright and folded his legs under him.

"So you...don't have parents?" he asked.

"I do. A highly sterilized petri-dish and a warm glass incubator." Aryabh flicked the cigarette butt out of the window and twisted his lips to form a half-smile.

"Then, who named you?"

"A rigamarole for another day."

"Huh?"

"Long story."

"Where did you live as a kid? Who raised you?" Kenai lowered his voice, embarrassed that he was not saying the right things. "Sorry, I don't understand this."

"Kids born in the PacaLabs are raised in the PacaOrphanage."

> When I think of my childhood, all I remember is walking in straight lines with other PacaChildren and chanting, 'Yes, Mx' at the top of my voice.
> Even though I understood I was an orphan, it wasn't until I was seven that I understood the meaning of PacaBirth. What bothered me more than that, more than the torturous institution, were the little things that happened around me

while growing up.

One day, a girl fell from her bunkbed and broke her leg. I felt an odd sadness for her. Then she bawled and screamed, which made me despise her the very next minute, because I couldn't figure out why or how she cried. My tear ducts were barren land. Maybe Kenai was right; I was never a child.

They explored my skills and talent throughout my childhood, just like they did with every other PacaChild. My tests showed that I was good at computer science, and so that was all I learned ever since I turned thirteen. According to the law, as soon we turn twenty-one, we have to work for the Pacamounts in our field of expertise. In return, we get an apartment, a brimming bank account, and a steady income.

But before I turned twenty-one, I knew enough. I didn't want a good house or a hefty bank account. I wanted to escape. The only option was Zenith. I lied on all my tests and scored 'below average' for all the jobs I was assigned. I was also a kidney short to work for the PacaMilitary. That way, I turned myself into a good-for-nothing liability, and that was how I landed myself a less complex job of designing websites for the Pacamounts. It's ironic that no one doubted my intentions, because a PacaChild would offer their limbs to score a great position with their 'parents'.

I spent the rest of my life learning and mastering the skills I needed to plot my escape. I was neither born nor raised as a regular human. I was a product, manufactured and maintained to fuel this despotic land. I was produced to serve as a devoting machine to one of the most nefarious entities in Earth's history. Proving myself to be a malfunctioning one was my first act of rebelliousness.

When too many old memories crowded Aryabh's mind, he pulled himself away from the chilly night and looked at the teary eyes of his roommate who had not spoken in a while. Aryabh tried to avoid him by searching for a fresh piece of AwakeTab.

Kenai got down from the bed and pulled Aryabh into a tight hug.

It startled Aryabh. He had always thought human bodies were cold and rigid. But Kenai was warm and comforting. His hands fell limply and awkwardly by his sides. He wanted to shove Kenai away, but the first hug of his life dissolved him into a state of solace.

"I am so sorry." Kenai pulled himself off Aryabh. "I am your family now, okay? You are not alone."

Aryabh tinkered with his widget for a while. Then he stretched his arm towards Kenai and displayed his wrist, not knowing if it was to erase the unease or something else.

"Is that your birth certificate?!" Kenai's eyes widened.

The document projected beside Aryabh's arm read 'Production Certificate'.

Aryabh assumed Kenai would erupt after reading his first name, which was '171-2098-1102-8A', or shed a few tears at his last name which was the model number of the incubator in which his fetus was raised. He thought Kenai would ask questions about 'batch number 8', which was mentioned under 'Family'. But he was surprised by what impacted his roommate.

"It's your birthday!" Kenai yelled.

"What?"

"It's your birthday next month!"

"Birth...day?"

"Don't tell me you don't understand birthday. It's the day you were born. So we celebrate that day."

"Why?"

Kenai tried to think of an answer. "I don't know. It's like...a rule. You eat cake, you get gifts..." His voice grew quieter with each word but regained its energy when an idea struck him. "You might have not done it before, but I am here now. We have to celebrate! How old are you? Oh, wait..." He pulled Aryabh's wrist and read. "You'll turn twenty-eight! This will be your best birthday ever! I need to plan." He rushed to the kitchen, talking to himself.

Aryabh really didn't believe this was his life now.

CHAPTER 13

Zenith

August 26, 2125

"What's up, renegade?" said Eeyan.

"Hey." Lyra ignored his jibe.

"To what do I owe this pleasure?" He bowed and faked a sophisticated tone.

Eeyan was Lyra's classmate from school and a mechanical engineer at the Zenith Regenerative Life Support System, also called the ZRLSS. Everything Lyra had researched in the past few weeks had led her here. Before she asked more than seven thousand people to move to a foreign planet, she wanted to be prepared.

The strongest factor, she thought, that would motivate Zenithers to move to Earth was water—a humble combination of two hydrogen and one oxygen atoms that turns itself into the most basic necessity of every living being in the universe.

"I am here for the educational tour." She pulled at the ends of her roomy black sweater.

"Isn't this your fourth tour here?"

"Sorry to bother you again."

"No, it's my privilege!" Eeyan folded his hands and crossed his ankles. "What else would I do besides enlightening the mass? It's not like I have a job here!"

"Your alacrity hasn't betrayed you yet."

"There's that pent-up, trademark Lyra-snark!" He pointed and guffawed. "Okay, let's go. I am content now."

Years ago, Lyra had come home from school distraught. Eeyan, who sat next to her in class, had called her the most boring person he had ever met. She had refused to participate in the school's annual spitting-on-the-ground tradition. When she explained how the ritual made no practical sense in the present, Eeyan had called her a sedative and pretended to snore amid her explanation. Their classmates had laughed.

A hurt, thirteen-year-old Lyra had asked her mother to help her improve her flat speech and be more interesting. Instead of doing that, Poona had assured her that she was anything but boring.

"Raising you was a walk in the park, Lai. You were never bored. You always had something to do, something to learn, something fascinating to imagine. A lot of interesting things spark within you. That was why you never bothered to make your outer world interesting, and that's okay. If that's boring, I am proud that you are boring," her mother had told her.

Fueled by an unquenchable curiosity, Lyra had familiarized herself with Zenith's mechanism at an early age. She visualized it as a complicated nervous system of a living body.

ZRLSS was one such vital mechanic of Zenith that she was familiar with. She had indeed been there thrice before intending to get a better understanding each time. It was the system that recycled water; the hardware responsible for keeping Zenithers alive. It created the ecosystem and atmosphere that Zenith didn't naturally have. In the initial years, it was called the 'Base'. Located on the far north-west corner of the asteroid, it was set away from the residential and commercial districts.

Every Zenither, as a child, was taught where their water came from so that they learned its value. The ZRLSS was inscribed in school textbooks every year. The higher the school grade, the more detailed and scientific it got. But today, Lyra was here to ask questions that no one had ever asked before.

Prior to doing that, she had to humor her old acquaintance by asking him questions she already knew the answers to.

"Let's start with the water recycling system. We currently have around sixty-three million gallons of water. Some of it was excavated from the water ice on this asteroid when it was being carved. A lot of it was transported from Earth over the first ten years. We haven't needed a single drop after that!" Eeyan boasted.

They stood at the entrance of a huge room whose ceiling was thirty feet above. On its floor, complex machines were stacked one after the other.

Lyra gazed around. She was looking at the lifeline of 7,262 Zenithers.

"Sixty-three million gallons...that's a lot of water," she said.

"Yes and no. Yes, because our water recycling system keeps this number stagnant. Our system is highly efficient." Eeyan strolled on a long narrow path that was sandwiched between operating plants. Lyra followed his clicking, shiny shoes.

"Every drop of liquid on Zenith, whether it's the water from your bathroom or your body, or an animal's body, passes through these bad boys." Eeyan signaled at three giant blue cylinders, which to Lyra looked like beakers in a chemistry lab. They were interconnected with pipes.

"These are filtration beds." He walked closer to the cylinders. "Once the system draws the humidity from the air, it strains the condensed liquid to remove particles and debris. The water then passes through these beds. They remove all the organic and non-organic impurities. This here." He pointed his gloved hand at a large capsule attached to the beds. "It's the catalytic oxidation reactor. It removes volatile organic compounds and kills all bacteria and viruses. Star of the show, isn't it?"

"Very much like on Earth." Lyra pointed out. "Where water that passes through animals is made fresh again by natural processes. Microbes in the soil break down urea and convert it to a...to a form that plants can absorb and use to build new plant tissue." Her eyes were on Eeyan but they were contemplating a different visual. "The granular soil on Earth also acts as a physical filter. Bits of clay cling to nutrients in urine electrostatically, purifying the water, and providing nutrients for plants, and that whole process happens without the interference of humans. It's phenomenal."

"Say, what now?" Eeyan's brows creased.

Lyra, however, continued voicing her thought process, "Some of the animal waste also evaporates into Earth's atmosphere and rains back to Earth, a natural method of distillation, if you may. In the absence of air pollution, nearly pure water falls back to the ground. We, here at Zenith, although partly, mimic the same process."

"Look, dude, do you really need this tour? I can use a long lunch break."

"I do." Lyra shook her head. "I am sorry. Please continue."

"To put it in simple terms, the air that Zenithers exhaled yesterday, the water they used to wash their bodies, and the liquid they secreted through their glands will be caught and passed through these cylinders after being strained for debris. These babies will get rid of needless compounds and harmful bacteria, and water will be at your faucet tomorrow in its freshest, purest form. Purer than water found in Earth's rivers or their plastic bottles. You hear me, patron of Earth?"

"Yeah."

"So to come back to your question, is sixty-three million gallons a lot of water? Yes, because the efficiency of our recycling system is 99.8%. That means, if we use, say, a hundred gallons of water today, this machine will recycle it and give us 99.8 gallons of fresh water back! That's how we have been using and reusing the same water for seventy-five years. Any questions?"

"Novel full of."

"Of course."

"You said no too. Why?"

"No, because no amount of water is a lot of water when it comes to human consumption."

"And there will come a day," Lyra added, "when all the sixty-three million gallons of water will be gone, because even if the recycling efficiency is 99.8%, we are losing 0.2% every time we recycle, right?"

"Correct."

Lyra grabbed one pen out of the two lying in her messenger bag, pulled out her notepad, and pretended to do the calculations. She had already done the math.

"Our current population is seven thousand, two hundred, and sixty-two. An average Zenither uses about seventy gallons of water per day including for oxygen. That comes to a total of 508,340 gallons of water per day. Agriculture and other infrastructural and industrial needs account for the usage of about 250,000 gallons. That's 758,340 gallons of water usage per day in total. Let's also take into account our annual 0.3% population growth rate, which will bloat our asteroid to a whopping population of almost 10,000 Zenithers in a century." Lyra checked Eeyan's face to see if he was still listening. Surprisingly, he was.

"Just tell me your agenda," he said. "What do you want?"

"According to this math, I believe we will run out of water in ninety-eight years." Lyra waited for a reaction.

"So?"

"So, what do we plan on doing when we are out of all the water we have?"

"Well, that's a century away!" The indifference returned to Eeyan's tone. "We are humans, renegade. Survival is our basic instinct. We'll find a way when the time comes. Besides, we have a contract with the Pacamounts. In the event that Zenith runs out of water, they would be responsible for transporting water here."

"Right. I just needed to confirm that," Lyra mumbled.

"Are we done yet?"

"Last question, please?"

"Here to serve you."

"What happens if something malfunctions in this room?" Lyra asked.

"Backups. We have emergency protocols set up for every major and minor malfunction. We even have a control room on Earth, just in case ours goes nutso."

"Can someone override the system in this room from the Earth's control room?"

"Dude, it's just a room. Why are you so obsessed with it?" Eeyan's hands were on his waist. "What kind of mutiny are you scheming today?"

"This is not just a room. It provides us with oxygen to breathe. It gives us water to drink, to wash, and to grow food." Lyra's voice went up several decibels as her eyes veered from side to side. "It's our sole ecosystem, our lifeline. It terraforms our entire asteroid. How can this just be a room?"

"Ah...that's what I needed after an advanced degree in this field. A lesson from a chef. I need to go check an item off my bucket list. Tell my parents I made it."

Lyra ignored his remark. "You know what happens if this ecosystem is disturbed or destroyed somehow?"

"Surprise me."

She stared into Eeyan's green eyes. "We all drop dead like flies."

CHAPTER 14

Zenith

September 9, 2125

Alongside thousands of satellites, Zenith orbited the Earth at its own pace, wombing a fragile colony. Its crescent topography sat inside luminescently, under the hushed night lights. Between the quiet clusters of bamboo houses of the Archimedes district, one window was lit brightly like a lonely star. Lyra's head silhouetted against its pane, swaying to Beethoven's *Fidelio Chorus of Prisoners*.

She had sat at her desk for hours and jotted down all of her findings, including the summary of her meeting with Eeyan two weeks ago. Finally, she formulated an action plan and watched as the light from the asteroid's roof touched its iron ground.

"You are definitely a paradigmatic of Amica," Sagan complained as Lyra dragged him to their garden.

He wore a black night-suit whose lapels were ironed so well that it looked like a blazer.

"Why?" Lyra asked.

"When she doesn't want to get out of her cage, she acts out."

Lyra grabbed garden tools from their patio cabinet and said, "I am not acting out."

"Why else would you make fresh stock at seven in the morning on a Sunday, or force me to consume lavender tea when you clearly know my preferences? I drink Centella. Lavender is too fragrant to be in a tea," Sagan dictated with his head held high. He pocketed his one hand in his pajama bottoms and held the teacup with the other.

"I am not forcing you. I am instructing you to have it. It will help calm your nerves. You've been straining your mind a lot."

"That's not a novel discovery."

"Lavender tea is exactly what you need right now, not something that will accelerate your brain."

"Gotu Kola, which is present in my regular tea, does not just boost brainpower but it is also an adaptogen. Meaning, it lowers stress," Sagan explained.

"If an herb is adaptogenic, it doesn't lower your stress; it makes your body adaptable to *resist* stress. You might be the cleverest Zenither there is, but I taught you to read," Lyra stated matter-of-factly.

Sagan looked at the ground, his face flushed. He knew his sister was right about adaptogens.

"In a nutshell, I win," said Lyra. "Now, finish your tea and grab that shovel. I need to transplant these plants. This garden is dying. Dad doesn't even care about it anymore. One needs discipline in life."

"Sister, you had tooth cavities as an adult."

"Once."

"We'll see."

Lyra glared at her brother and tied her hair above her nape. Numerous strands escaped the tiny bun within seconds and braced her sharp jaw. "Start digging here." She pointed at a spot next to her.

"That is browbeating at its peak. I do not appreciate that."

Sagan finished the remaining tea and entered the garden.

"You become such a child when you are proved wrong."

"I *am* a child."

Under the shade of their cozy bamboo house, the siblings heard Ms. Tara's voice as it tore through the street. She was teaching someone how to pickle raw mangoes.

Sagan cringed, and then rolled the hem of his pants in neat pleats. His pristine white socks were protected by garden slippers and his hands by a pair of gloves. Next to him, Lyra knelt in soiled shorts with her naked feet and knees sunk deep in wet soil.

Lyra glanced over Sagan as they transferred a potted plant into the ground. She knew that her brother regarded gardening as punishment for his ignorance of adaptogens.

"Okay, fine. I am procrastinating. I don't think I can do it." Lyra dropped the shovel.

"I do not doubt that. For you to convince people, you have to interact with them, speak your mind, and if the situation calls for it, manipulate them. You are a proven disaster in all three domains."

"Thanks." Lyra crossed her legs and sat on the wet ground. Sagan sprang in disgust and placed a big napkin under her.

"You probably don't remember this," Lyra said. "Until seven years ago, the Terraformers Union held this bi-monthly meet, a social assemblage to maintain harmony and get hermits out of their houses. Not only was the presence mandatory but a couple of people from every district had to also perform during each meetup."

"No! That should not be legal."

"Tell me about it. The culture here have always worked against people who didn't socialize or talk much. Or sat in corners." Lyra looked down. "My social anxiety was even worse then. The thought of getting on stage in front of hundreds of people horrified me. I couldn't sleep or eat or relax for days just thinking about it. Our district didn't help either. They even, sort of, threatened Dad that my behavior would cut us off from the community. It's why," she whispered, "Ms. Tara hates me. I've said no to her more than she likes."

Lyra paused and then took a deep breath.

"So, on one of the meetups, I…" She looked at Sagan. "I took you to the hospital an hour before my performance. I lied that you had a bad stomachache."

Sagan's face turned into a child's.

A grin pulled at Lyra's mouth. "You know what the best part was? I asked you to lie for me and you did just that. You even pointed on the left side of your belly to show the doctor where it hurt."

"Why don't I remember this?"

"You must be four or five. Then something big happened one time, a shameful spat, as they called it." Lyra snorted. "So the TU gave up and canceled the whole thing."

"How unsurprising!" Sagan said.

"Not only do I suck at this but I have also nuked bridges with these people. How do I convince them now?"

"Do you remember the analogy you made up when you first told me about Earth?" Sagan asked. "We were transplanting that morning too. Right here."

"I remember. A plant needs to be repotted from a small pot to wider and deeper ground if it needs to grow bigger." Lyra swung her brow. "It was a rad one, brother, wasn't it?"

"Very. Now, remember that. Do you want to grow bigger or not?"

"I do."

Sagan stood and orated, "Then you can roost on this itchy mud and question yourself all day, or stand up and do what you are supposed to."

"It's easy for you. You have never had trouble speaking your mind," said Lyra.

"That's because I am not the least bit concerned about being misconstrued. Opinions do not matter where facts reside. Tell your truth and leave the room."

"You really think I can do it?"

"If I can finish a cup of lavender tea."

Lyra had to put her father first on her list of people she wanted to approach with her idea. The proposal was going to cause a ripple across the asteroid and she did not want her father to hear it from someone else.

As expected, Keid's response was negative. What Lyra didn't expect was her own ramble. Instead of stating clear facts and reasons, she had circled around how his parents had died early because they had felt trapped on Zenith towards the end of their life.

Keid had argued that her grandparents had felt that way because they had been Terraformers, and that he or his children wouldn't face the same problem as they were 1st and 2nd G Zenithers. He concluded the argument with, "Play out this fantasy too. It's not going to work."

The next person on Lyra's list was Mr. Zaif, Head of Earth Relations. All official communication between Zenith and Earth transpired through him. If she somehow managed to convince all Zenithers to move to Earth, it would be Mr. Zaif's job to put the proposal across to the Pacamounts.

Lyra entered his office carrying a purple box. The stout man in his late fifties with whom she had never spoken occupied the chair behind a huge desk. She placed the box on the desk and offered her hand.

Mr. Zaif, surprised by the greeting, stood from his seat. "Ah, a firm one," he said as he shook Lyra's hand.

Lyra took her seat and breathed in the fruity smell of Gryffy's pastries from the box.

"I'd be naïve to assume this treat comes without any special requests, wouldn't I?" Mr. Zaif said. His chevron mustache puckered above his salivating mouth.

"It was the treat that tagged along with the special request," replied Lyra as she fidgeted and tried to adapt to the new environment.

Mr. Zaif gave out a throaty laugh. It reminded Lyra of her hotel's faulty food processor. "I am nothing without the ideas and requests of our fellow citizens," he said. "Go ahead."

Lyra swallowed and spoke in a tone as firm as she could manage. "I don't think it's sensible to live in an asteroid colony when a habitable planet is available so close to us. I...believe it's time for us to migrate back to Earth. I've studied various..."

"Wait a minute, Ms. Lyra!" Mr. Zaif interrupted. "I want to make sure I heard that right. Did you say all Zenithers should move back to Earth?"

"I did."

"Is this a joke?" He squirmed in his chair.

Lyra pulled away from the table, intimidated. She didn't want to be in Mr. Zaif's bad books. What if he warned everyone against her? What if he banned her from visiting Earth?

She began to consult herself if she should run back home, when Sagan's words trickled in her head—'Tell your truth and leave the room.'

Lyra blocked her anxieties and let her mental faculties take control. "I know it's hard to see this as a sane idea, but please...let me finish."

Mr. Zaif nodded.

"I've been going through various aspects of Zenith and studies conducted by Zenither scientists. They indicate that the path forward is not safe and bright." Lyra waited for him to speak, but when he didn't, she continued, "Let's start with the future of Zenith, the children. We haven't fostered any major advancement in scientific, technological, or academic fields in decades. So we are teaching them the same lessons again and again. There is no new knowledge for them to explore."

"Maybe our goal should not be to always achieve newer things but be content with what we have."

"When has a civilization succeeded by being averse to change and growth? As wholesome as our system is, which I can debate it's not," said Lyra without changing her pitch, "there will come a time when it will not be enough. We might not want change, but the universe around us is changing constantly. We either match its pace or we cease to exist. And how can you say that our goal shouldn't be to learn new things when the foundation of Zenith was solely built on the pursuit of new knowledge?"

Mr. Zaif raised one of his brows and nodded. "So, Ms. Lyra, how do you think you can make this happen? By taking everyone to Earth?"

Lyra heard the jibe in his question. "If the majority of Zenithers agree, it's you who could make this happen. You could put across a proposal to the Pacamounts, and see if they would let us emigrate. In return, they can have a whole asteroid at their disposal which they could use as they like. They will have over seven thousand people to contribute to their economy. They like that."

"And you believe they'll just take us back with open arms? Give us jobs and homes?" He mocked more.

"Most probably not, but we'll never know without asking."

Mr. Zaif got up from his seat, closed the doors of his office, and scanned the surroundings.

"I am going to tell you a few things that I wouldn't share with a soul here." He took his seat again and spoke in a hushed tone, "But you are scaring me with this crazy idea of yours, Ms. Lyra. So I have to."

He leaned forward.

"I've been talking, negotiating, and dealing with the Pacamounts all my adult life. They are shielded and mysterious. No wonder the Terraformers moved here. I have visited them more than a dozen times and every time I've returned home puzzled and stressed. They make us believe we are on our own. But I could smell the thick veil that is cloaked around our freedom—freedom that they want us to believe we have. It seems like we are some Earthler cattle to them that they want happy, fed, and afar. They scare me. So, I swallow my doubts and try my best to keep our relationship positive. That's my job, to keep us safe. Are you understanding me, Ms. Lyra? I don't want to speak about things I might later regret. I have already said enough."

"I am a bit—"

"This is not a wise idea, Ms. Lyra." He relaxed back in his chair.

"Mr. Zaif, I understand the caution, but I don't get the logic. If what you are saying is correct, how is staying here safer than my idea? If you were the Pacamounts wanting to control or get rid of a group of people, would it be easier to do that on a crowded two-hundred-million-square-miles planet or a small, isolated space colony?" Lyra lost her patience. "Everyone keeps talking about how dangerous they are, yet why am I the only one seeing this? We have no weapons to fight them and we have nowhere to hide or escape. We even rely on them for our basic survival needs. You just said they make us believe we are on our own. Then how is it rational to pretend that we are?"

Lyra's palms were balled into fists and they almost reached Mr. Zaif's side of the table. She retracted her arms and sat back with her legs entwined around each other like snakes.

"I am sorry," she said.

"You know," Mr. Zaif intertwined his fingers on his stomach, "If I disclose this to our people, that you are questioning our well-established colony and our well-admired prosperous constitution, you would be labeled as a disloyal citizen of our asteroid."

Lyra huffed. "Loyalty is in identifying and questioning the cracks in the system. It proves you intend the betterment of the society," she said with a face lacking any expression. "Favoring allegiance rather than objectivity and honesty is wrong. That's blind loyalty and is as harmful to society as intentional treachery." She stopped and inhaled some much-needed air.

Mr. Zaif's face dove deep into thought as he stared at his table. He looked at Lyra's face and spoke after a while, "Okay. Silencing your voice is against everything I stand for. That is not who we are. We are a democracy. I won't stop you. If you can bring me enough signatures, I will announce this proposal to the Brain Trust and in public. I will then do my job of making everyone see how this is a horrible idea."

Despite Mr. Zaif's personal opinion, Lyra's spirits soared. She finally had a tangible next step towards her goal. Signatures.

"And I would appreciate if you do not talk about this to anyone, about what I told regarding the Pacamounts. I don't want to create panic and make Zenithers feel unsafe." Mr. Zaif sat up straight and buttoned his suit's jacket.

"It won't go outside this office, I promise. I hope you enjoy the pastries." Lyra got up and left Mr. Zaif's office to head to work.

The mere thought of talking to the last person on her list crippled her. Lyra rehearsed the speech in her head as she took the bus to the hotel. She was to talk to her executive chef. Balin held the reins on some important people; having their support would make a huge difference.

Lyra was glad to find Balin in a chirpier mood.

When she saw Lyra, she vigorously waved towards her. A half-eaten, pearly white radish stained with pink lipstick jutted out of her chef coat's pocket. "Come here. Fast!" she said.

"Morning, Chef," greeted Lyra.

Balin looked around and carefully removed a bouquet of fresh herbs from her herb chest. "Chew on this. The pearls, not the whole twig."

Lyra observed and smelled the herb. It had a strong fragrance. She popped the upper part of the stem in her mouth without a second thought. Her molars bit into soft, fibrous pearls. Within seconds, an intense flavor coated her tongue. She took another bite of the green, rice-like pearls and chewed.

"How is it?" asked Balin.

"Delicate and tender, yet intense," said Lyra, looking in the air. "Such a unique flavor. I haven't tasted anything like this before. What is it?"

"Now drink water." Balin handed her a glass.

Lyra chugged half a glass to dislodge the fibers from her teeth. It amplified the taste. The amusement on her face thoroughly satisfied Balin. "Yes?" Her eyes danced.

"The water tastes...sweet. What is it?"

"It's wild fennel buds!" Balin smelled another bouquet. "Good for digestion, excellent at infusing flavors, and refreshes your mouth better than toothpaste does!" she squealed. "But, oh, Lyra, nothing beats the tea made out of it. Here." She handed a steaming cup to Lyra. "I've been brewing this for you. Drink while it's hot. Lukewarm tea is an offense to the senses. *And* the tea."

"Where did you get this herb from?"

"Why, I grew it! In my garden." The pride in Balin's voice matched her face.

"But where did you get the seeds from? I have never seen this plant here." Lyra recalled all the botany books of her father that she had read.

"I have a forest of things you haven't seen before," Balin scolded and then waved her herb again. "I've heard that even most Earthlers don't know this grows on their land. Pity, isn't it?" She sipped her tea. "It needs warmer soil. Took us a long time to get it right. But now I can grow it as much as I want. Ooh...I am going to try mixing this in my eye masks!"

Balin's euphoria overwhelmed Lyra. But she knew she could not procrastinate anymore, and so she spoke, "There are so many Earthler things whose existence we are unaware of. Wouldn't you like it better if you were right there...on Earth?"

Balin's delight vanished in a blink. "Why are you asking me this?"

"Just curious." Lyra leaned her back against the kitchen

counter. "You love growing your herbs and vegetables and making your own beauty products. I know you have always wanted to run your own business. Wouldn't you want to do that without any inhibitions?" Before Balin could answer, Lyra spoke again, struggling to pull one word after the other, "I have just returned from Mr. Zaif's office. We talked about the idea of Zenithers emigrating back to Earth."

Balin's nostrils flared. She started packing her chest of herbs.

"I think we should," Lyra added. "It would be great for the future generations to..."

"Look at this Pied Piper, everyone!" the executive chef slammed her precious possession on the table and pointed at Lyra.

Everyone looked in her direction.

Lyra flexed one body muscle after the other until she turned into a log. She fantasized a different timeline where she hadn't talked to Balin and stayed home instead, drinking tea in her bedroom.

"You want to talk about future generations?" Balin placed her hands on her hip. "My father used to talk about that. He once told me that every once in a while there comes a generation which fights hard to bring something the world needs—freedom, equality, voting rights, or something as simple as drinking water. They fight and they fight without worrying about their lives."

She bent and jabbed her head towards Lyra.

"What happens next? As history is the witness, the true fighters win," she stated. "But like everything on a big scale, it doesn't happen overnight. It takes time. It takes lifetimes, generations. By the time it is achieved, the generation which is reaping its benefits has forgotten its importance. They don't respect it because they have never experienced its absence. All of you here..." Balin pointed at everyone. "None of you understand what it means to be standing free and liberated on this iron ground today." She shook with anger. "I have seen my share of fools, but you, Lyra, you are one of a kind. You should be ashamed for even thinking something like that."

Balin packed her things and exited the kitchen, leaving the echo of her wrath behind.

Lyra stared at the floor hoping everyone around would vanish.

They did, in a while.

During michaiyo, instead of joining everyone outside the kitchen, she walked to her thinking-place.

To the east of the hotel, on the slopped side of the asteroid's wall, was Zenith's Ángeles Alvariño pond. It was right next to the sanctuary. After colonization, the Terraformers and then the 1st G had filled a huge crater with soil, water, and aquatic creatures and built an ecosystem within it. A string of blue jacaranda trees and a variety of shrubs outlined its 550-feet diameter like a lace. The surrounding area was lined with wildflower meadow upon which small rocks hauled from the initial carving of the asteroid were placed at random places as seats.

Lyra's usual spot was a huge boulder at the opposite side of the entrance. Growing up, she had sat there to read books or recharge. She loved the corner spot because it gave her a beautiful view of the pond, the forest, and the Goodall Sanctuary.

She sat on the boulder and stared at a nebulous burn surrounding the nail of her middle finger, amused by how different a steam burn looked than a regular burn.

Trac's chest-bouncing laughter rang in her ears. The sanctuary's staff were having michaiyo by a cabin outside the forest.

Lyra moved her eyes towards the entrance. She saw Gryffy walking towards her in a chocolate-stained chef uniform. The gleam of the rooflight threw a golden sheen over her bouncy hair, her contoured face, and the steam that wafted from the two mugs she carried.

"When you don't go to michaiyo, michaiyo comes to you." Gryffy handed Lyra one mug and looked for a safe spot on the boulder to sit. Her eyes landed on Lyra's feet. "Your shoes are untied."

Lyra hid her feet beneath her thighs, making a mental note to tie the laces later. She carefully whisked away a bit when Gryffy sat next to her—a reflex to reestablish her personal space. People standing or sitting in close proximity to her had always made her uncomfortable.

"I know this drink is not your thing but just taste it," said Gryffy. "There is more than chocolate in it."

Lyra took a careful sip of the hot liquid. Gryffy was right. There were multiple spices in the drink that hit her nose and tastebuds.

Gryffy interrupted her analysis. "Just heard the whole spiel."

"Super."

"What's going on with you? I don't see you as a person who cares about what happens to the people here. I mean, you won't mean any harm to us, but it's just that...ever since I know you, you've only minded your own business. Then what's with the sudden...revolutionary mode? Is it just your ploy to get out of here?"

Lyra wanted to tell Gryffy that it was a selfless idea, but in her heart she knew it was not. She had acknowledged her self-serving motive behind this plan long before today. It was next to impossible for her to save enough ferrics again and move to Earth, at least not until she was forty or fifty. But if the whole asteroid moved there, she would not only accomplish her goal but could also take Sagan with her.

She also knew Gryffy well. If she was investing her time, she deserved the truth.

So Lyra supplied her half-honesty. "It's not a ploy. But...yes. It will make things easier for me. I do believe that our future here is bleak. It doesn't make sense to live in a space colony when we revolve around a habitable planet. We don't know exactly why our ancestors moved here. I don't have patience to unearth that truth. But staying here..." Lyra looked afar. "At the mercy of Earth's government, doesn't sit right with me."

"I see," Gryffy said. "I can't believe I am saying this, but that noisy vessel in our kitchen is right. I don't know squat about Earthler issues, but even I know their shit stinks. They can't even create a dough mixer worth investing in. Why would I invest my future in them? Make me understand."

Lyra had never understood why Gryffy wasted so much time and energy after her. She had never provided anything in return. Guilt struck her. "I am going to be extremely disreputable soon. You don't want to be on my side." she said, partly paying attention to the trilling of a frog inside the pond.

"You..." Gryffy broke eye contact and stayed quiet. "It's best not to say much," she said as she looked at Lyra again, "when you know the outcome." Her face had a vulnerability that Lyra had never seen before.

Then it struck Lyra. She had been so daft. "I am sorry. I..." She struggled to find the appropriate words. "I didn't know."

"Come on. Don't apologize. You don't owe me anything because I like you." Gryffy looked at the pond. "Took me a while to figure it out too."

Lyra looked at Gryffy's face again and ground her teeth, wondering if it was wise to say what she was thinking. But she had already made enough adversaries; she didn't need another one. So she spoke her mind. "Gryffy, as far as I am concerned, I am...not going to change my mind...I am not..."

"I know. I know. You are straight."

"No, it's not that. I am...asexual."

"Oh..."

"I still don't know where I stand on romantic relationships...with anyone. I've never found myself in that spot. But that's a different topic. What I was trying to say was, I don't want you to feel disappointed later. I know how situations like these usually end. I don't want you to feel like you got nothing in return for helping me. I won't be able to reciprocate…this." Lyra ground her teeth again. "I don't want to take advantage of your feelings."

"What the fuck, Lyra!" Gryffy spun towards her. Lyra leaned backward, intimidated. "Do you think I am that vain, that entitled?" The vulnerability vanished from her face. "This is not a business deal. I am a freakin' adult. I know when to cut ties and when not to. My kindness is not for sale. Don't think you can buy it by giving me something in return. I am helping because I want to. Don't insult me!"

"I am sorry." Lyra scratched her hand even though there wasn't an itch. "It's just that I am not good with getting out of such situations without cutting ties."

"This is not a situation, Lyra."

"Uhh…" Lyra wanted to smash her own head. She took a deep breath. "Your constant kindness means a lot to me even though I don't say it. I don't want to hurt you later when I still have nothing to give but my friendship."

Gryffy sighed. "I know. I am sorry for the dramatic outburst." She smiled. "It's funny. I had not felt this in a long time. You used to get on my nerves exactly like this. I used to think you were self-centered and incredibly tedious. No offense."

"None taken," said Lyra, without moving her face muscles, even though the sudden remark stirred her.

"It hurt how indifferent you were to me and everyone who cared about you. I mean, you probably like those animals better than us." Gryffy pointed her chin towards the sanctuary.

"It's not like—"

"Remember when Wan's wife died?" Gryffy interrupted. "We were at her funeral. Everyone was in tears, even Balin. I mean, his wife was only forty. Wan was shaking her dead body, trying to wake her up."

Lyra looked far away to remember.

"He had stashed some ferrics, his wife's favorite purse, and some other belongings around her body. They were about to suspend her outside the walls when you started mumbling how he shouldn't freeze those items. That it was a waste of resources or space or something like that." Gryffy shook her head. "God, I wanted to punch you. How could someone think like that when their friend is heartbreakingly weeping over their dead wife? I thought you were the most arrogant person ever."

"Wow." Lyra raised her brows. "I know that's despicable. It's just that those things could have been put to good use by giving them to people who needed them. So many of us do that, put belongings with the dead. Freezing and powdering such items with the bodies harm our ecosystem greatly. Those items are not biodegradable like the human body."

"See? Exactly this!" Gryffy pointed as she laughed. "Who cares, Lyra? The dude's young wife just died. And you thought that her funeral was the right place to bring that up?"

"It was not." In her head, Lyra thought she would have said it sooner if she knew it beforehand, and there was no point in saying it later because the harm would already be done.

"Okay, good. At least you agree."

Lyra did not share how thinking about facts and logistics was one of the ways she had learned to compartmentalize grief. She had always dealt with pain by blocking the actual event and concentrating on things that demanded her judgement and reasoning. She understood well that she was not capable of sorting emotions within, and so she survived by sorting feelings into files and stowing them away.

"So," Gryffy continued, "I kept my distance from that day onward. I knew I couldn't be friends with someone like you. Then one day I saw a different side of you. Everyone in the kitchen was debating about what goes in...Shallambi Bombe, I guess? They said that a splash of vinegar goes in it before the frying. You were dead set that it doesn't. You kept insisting how it was against the food chemistry or something."

"I remember that." It surprised Lyra how Gryffy remembered so many things about her.

"I had never seen you so talkative before. You were all fired up. Then Per called his Terraformer grandmother to ask the authentic recipe. You, unfortunately, were proved wrong."

"Yup." Lyra twisted her lips.

"If I were you, I'd have gone into hiding or kept arguing... No one likes losing face. I was sure you wouldn't believe his grandmother; you were that passionate about it. But, instead, you didn't care you were wrong. You were, in fact, thrilled, sort of. You admitted your mistake like you were saying your name. I had never seen someone like that before. Everyone here wants to be right, but no one is interested in finding the truth."

Gryffy swallowed and spoke again.

"That was when I realized how wrong I was in understanding you. You preferred truth to social niceties. I don't endorse that but I get it." She paused. "So I...started to like you. More and more. Even though I knew nothing good was going to come out of it."

"I am sorry," said Lyra.

"Me too." Gryffy forced a smile. "But that is why I trust you and want to help you. If you say, it's going to be dangerous here, I believe you."

Lyra struggled again to find words. It didn't sit right with her that someone thought about her to this extent. She felt exposed.

Then she felt grateful. She stowed her discomfort away and did her best to explain her viewpoint, even the things she should have mentioned to Mr. Zaif and Balin. She talked about the issues that Zenithers might face in future like the water shortage, ZRLSS, and overpopulation, and she talked about the psychological effects on the older and younger generation. She also shared about her meeting with Mr. Zaif without disclosing the sensitive details he had shared with her.

Gryffy threw her hands in the air. "Why didn't you say all that in the kitchen?"

"I don't do well in emotionally charged conversations." Lyra thought of Balin's loud voice and theatrical body-language. "Besides, I don't want to use fear as motivation."

"You can't afford to have rules when you are dealing with an issue as sensitive as this." Gryffy paused for a moment as a foreign thought distracted her. "Hmm...Now that I think about it, it all makes sense. All the old folks at Holding Hands are always cranky and miserable." Holding Hands was the care center where Gryffy had volunteered most of her life. "Everyone tells me that old people are supposed to be like that, but that's not just what it is. It's like they are angry and upset about something they don't even know. I wish we had more funding. I want to do more for them."

Her comments made Lyra think of both sets of her grandparents. They had all died earlier than they should have.

"This place gets to you after a while, doesn't it?" Gryffy said.

"I think so. There is nothing sadder than not having anything new to know. Or learn or see."

"That's actually my comfort zone, not having to worry about the unknown, although I can see why you feel that way. But, Lyra, I don't believe the Earth government is going to mess with our water. People are watching; people will say something. They can't just do that. It's not going to happen."

"That's what everyone throughout history said right before rulers and governments did exactly what people said they wouldn't do," stated Lyra. "It can happen."

"Okay, you are frightening me now. So, what's your next move? Mr. Zaif won't help. Balin showed you the middle finger. Who's next in line?"

"The people. I plan to go door to door to talk about this and collect signatures...see what they think."

"You suck at talking, and door to door?" Gryffy got down from the boulder and paced back and forth... "You'd give up before you reach the third door."

Her involvement confused Lyra. "You are going to help me with this?" she asked.

"Look, I don't know how feasible this idea is, but I believe in freedom of speech more than anything. Even though I can't stand her on most days, I always thought Balin was cool. But repressing your voice like that, that's not cool." Gryffy picked her cup from the rock and sipped her hot chocolate. "As I said, I trust you. No way would you intentionally hurt so many people. So, to answer your question—yes, I will help you."

"Thank you!"

"Magic of michaiyo, you see?" Gryffy raised her cup. "It does solve your problems at times."

Lyra understood her teasing. She smiled again.

"And I'll get to annoy a huge chunk of Zenithers at the same time. That's what I live for," Gryffy added. "Let's meet next Sunday." She collected Lyra's half-full mug and straightened her apron. "Meanwhile, brush up on the 3rd G lingo."

"Why?" asked Lyra.

"We are sucking up to Zen Mavericks."

Chapter 15

"Look at this crooked-eyed slime! Who do you think you are, giving away free stuff like that?" the manager barked at Kenai in front of all the employees.

Kenai's head hung low as he stared at the chili-sauce that was seeping inside his shoes through the eyelets.

"I should never hire you Trunkers! Bloody, uncivilized bunch of turds."

"I...uh...I spilled water on her and was just trying to make nice with her. I didn't want her to be upset," explained Kenai.

"Well, then you shouldn't have given her a quick shower! You can see straight with at least one eye, can't you? These muffins you keep giving away don't grow on trees!"

Kenai's eyebrows twitched as the chili from the sauce burned a two-day-old blister on his feet. He jiggled his toes inside his cheap shoes to avoid the temptation to scratch. It was not polite to lose his composure in front of his boss, an important Sonmanto lesson he had learned that week besides 'greeting or smiling at strangers on the street is considered offensive'.

"Last week he put aside an order and ran to hold an old man because he was tripping," commented one of the staff members standing in the corner. Kenai couldn't see who it was, but he heard the giggle that followed the complaint.

"Just get out of my office!" the manager yelled. "If I wasn't short on staff for the Pacalympics, I'd be firing your ass left, right, and center. Consider this your last warning. Now, get out!"

Aryabh had avoided Lyra's messages and her proposal to meet for weeks. But he was desperate to know what she was up to.

Aryabh: Okay, what do you want?

Lyra: Do you want to get to Zenith?

Aryabh: Excuse me?

Lyra: Not physically but virtually. How about Ángeles Alvariño, our pond?

Aryabh: And how do you think you can do that? Your technology is more ancient than our bedsheets.

Aryabh looked up at the upper bunk. The side of Kenai's bedsheet blinked "You will be happy today, Kenai." in big, neon letters. He wrinkled his nose.

Lyra: Maybe our brainpower is more advanced than your widgets.

Aryabh looked outside the window and wondered what Lyra meant. She would not say something so grave just to joke. Of that, he was sure.

If there was a mirror in the sky, he would have seen a silly smile on his face.

Kenai erupted from the front door and startled his daydream. "The fuck!" Aryabh grumbled.

Kenai flung his shoes and rushed to the kitchen. The water level in both tanks was low, and so he wiped the sauce off his feet with wet paper napkins. He tore an IngredientSac, grabbed a handful of flour from it, and pressed it on his blister. His eyes watered as he moaned in pain.

Aryabh got back to his desk and continued communicating with Dima using the Farm's script. A huge Farm mission was to take place during the Pacalympics and Dima needed Aryabh's help to retrieve the Cream guest list. On the second screen, Aryabh wrote the code for the Pacalympics website—an official PacaChild job for which he would be paid by the Pacamounts. Neither of those tasks was as important as working on his Zenither badge, which was taking more time than he had imagined.

Something fell in the kitchen.

"What the fuck are you doing?!" Aryabh yelled.

"Fuck you!" Kenai replied in a loud, harassed voice. "Don't treat me like the garbage you all are."

Aryabh froze, not knowing what to say. He heard a louder thud this time and rushed to the kitchen.

The floor was carpeted with flour and oil. On it, Kenai lay on his back, his hands by his side. His eyeglasses were flung around in the corner by the pile of IngredientSacs.

Aryabh walked closer to inspect Kenai's face. His eyes were blinking and his chest, heaving. "Alive, are we?" he said, as if to conceal his relief.

Kenai pressed his palms on the floor to move towards the kitchen counter. His hair and clothes were covered in flour and oil. He rested his back on one of the cabinets and buried his face in his hands. "I am sorry. I slipped on the oil I spilled. I'll clean this up in a...bit."

Aryabh heard a sob.

"Oh, god...I can't do this. I can't live like this," Kenai spoke again as his hunch cradled his quivering body.

It bothered Aryabh to see him in that state. It was not sympathy, of that he was sure. It's because he had thought it was humanly impossible for Kenai to be upset, let alone this miserable. There were days when he had wished misery upon him just so that he would shut up and leave him alone, but right now Aryabh didn't like the sight he was looking at.

"Don't stare at me like that," said Kenai when he noticed a blurry Aryabh looking in his direction.

Without his glasses, Aryabh observed, Kenai looked different. He didn't understand why Kenai was embarrassed about his eyes. To him, the brown in his eyes shone like artistically formed granite. Their nonalignment made them less mechanical, more real.

Kenai wiped his cheeks. "I am so ashamed of myself. I apologize." He looked around for his glasses.

Aryabh grabbed it from the floor and handed it to him.

"Thank you." Kenai paused. "Two weeks back on my way to work, I saw an old lady fiddling with her wheelchair. When I saw a bunch of plastic bags tangled in her wheels, I helped her get them out. But I accidentally pulled the handle of her bag and cracked it. She got so angry. I apologized but she wouldn't listen. She kept raising her voice. I was scared. I didn't want to be in trouble. I told her I would buy her a new bag and deliver it to her if she gave her address..."

Aryabh's face wrinkled with disgust but he kept quiet.

"She wouldn't trust me. So I had to take her to the nearest store and buy her a bag. It cost me three weeks of pay. I didn't even get paid that day because I reached work late." Kenai's voice grew quieter. "And you know what the old lady gave me in return? She threw those plastic bags at me, called me a Trunker, and left."

Aryabh was so exasperated with Kenai's actions that if he wasn't miserable already, Aryabh would have made him. "So you avenged by soiling the kitchen?" he commented.

"My boss humiliated me in front of everyone today. He told me to grow a pair," Kenai stressed the last three words to mock his manager's Sonmanto accent, "or I was going to the hellhole I came from." His eyes watered again. "I thought life would be easy here compared to the Trunks. It kind of is. It won't take two minutes to clean this mess." He eyed the kitchen floor. "But all these gadgets can't clean the ugliness of the Heads."

"Why are you even here?" Aryabh couldn't help but ask.

"You'd think I am a fool if I tell you." Kenai looked at Aryabh. His face was unaltered. So he continued, "I...came here to find my parents."

Kenai folded his legs under him and his eyes searched for a memory. "I grew up in a small 2nd Stratum Trunk called Dvedi. That was where my whole life was, my parents, my home, my friends, my school. It was my fifteenth birthday when we all got the notice. We had to vacate our homes in twenty-four hours. They were merging our Trunk with the Tail next to us to set up some labs. We all panicked. No one had anywhere else to go." He looked at Aryabh. "Can you imagine packing your whole life in twenty-four hours and leaving for strange lands? It's so scary. It wasn't like here. We had an actual home; a bed I had slept in since I was four, a desk I did my schoolwork on, utensils we had our food in, the swing outside our front door that my mother loved, my baba's...umm, my father's, workshop in the backyard that earned our daily bread, the huge oak tree I played around with my friends, my books, my clothes, my childhood toys...How can you fit all that in one bag? When you leave home, you don't just leave your shelter; you leave all that is familiar. You leave a place where you know just how hot the sun is going to be or where to stroll after a heavy dinner or whom to call for help..."

He sniffed.

"The older people were promised camps in nearby Trunks, but everyone between the ages of fifteen to thirty-five was ordered to move to the Heads. Anyone who protested was sent for dissolution right then. They..." Kenai tried to smother his sob but it came out as a loud, convulsive gasp. "They sharked and shot dozens of people right in front of my eyes. I saw them die.

Their eyes were open but they didn't move or breathe."

He wiped the snot with his sleeve.

"My friends were excited about the cool jobs in Heads where they would earn the kind of money they could never earn in Dvedi. But I feared it. Ever since I was a child, I was scared of living alone. I didn't want to leave my family, my home. But my baba and mama insisted that I move to the nearest Head, get a good job, and a house so that they could move in with me. I had to agree because the camps were not permanent; we needed a house. I packed whatever I could and left Dvedi and my family. I remember walking through a pile of bodies scattered around like garbage bags. Bodies with holes bigger than our hearts, bodies of people I knew and cared about. I don't think I will ever forget that sight, not even in my grave."

Kenai winced and wiped his face again.

"I moved to the nearest Head, Saasol, where I barely stayed for a month. I found out that my parents had been taken to three different camps in three different Trunks. It was okay because I was at least able to track them. But...but when I called them during the second month, their numbers were disconnected. I tried reaching my friends' parents, but they were unreachable too. In the three years that I spent in Trunks around Saasol, I did several odd jobs to survive, and I continued tracking everyone from Dvedi. But they were all just gone, like some kind of evil magic. One day...I met this girl I went to school with. She advised me to stop looking for them. She had given up too. 'Finding our family is a luxury we can't afford,' she said. I spent that night weeping and splitting half a sandwich with her for dinner."

Aryabh switched legs and placed his chin on his right knee.

"That's what I've been doing for the past fourteen years, wandering in different Trunks and looking for my parents. I've reached out to so many Pacamounts's offices, but no luck. They threw me out every time. Then one day in Ancome's office, I met this nice lady who advised me to come to Sonmanto. She told me this city was the heart of the planet, and if there was a way to find them, it was here. So here I was, knocking on your door. I got lucky I found this apartment, and you. I was living on the streets for three weeks before that happened. You know, in all these years, I've seen so many horrible things, Aryabh—hunger, poverty, homelessness, and death. Scary things. But this feels worse. I came here to find my parents, to find a purpose in my life, but I am more lost than I ever was. I...even keep forgetting that I am here to look for them. So shameful, don't you think?"

He looked at Aryabh with a face wet with guilt and tears.

"I was afraid I would not fit in this city," he spoke again, "but it is this city that is not fitting into me. A few weeks ago, I was feeling sorry for you for eating this food." He looked over at the slot machine. "And now, even affording that is a dream. I don't know what to do."

The apartment turned quiet as Kenai buried his head in his palms and smooshed his glasses against his temples.

Aryabh lifted his chin from his knee and began toying with his widget to pretend he wasn't listening. But he wanted to hear more.

"I lost my old phone. I don't even have my parents' picture," Kenai said. "Every night when I lay on the bed, I try to remember their faces. Sometimes, I forget what they looked like. I try hard to remember how they talked, how my father rested his arms while sitting on his chair, and how my mother smelled. I wish I had something of theirs to remember them. My father gave me this." He removed the device he punched on every day from his pants pocket. "It helps me remember him, but I don't have anything of my mother."

"What does it smell like?" Aryabh asked.

"What?"

"What do mothers smell like? You said something about their smell?"

"Mothers are not *it*." Kenai could not deny himself a giggle.

"Answer."

"Um...I don't know. They smell like home. But it's not the

same with all mothers. What does your..." Kenai gasped. "I am so sorry. Look at me, feeling sorry about my life while you weren't even—"

"Our house smells like shit." Aryabh interrupted. "Why would one miss that?"

"Not house, home. There is a difference. But my mama? She smelled like cinnamon, and so did our home. All day, she would chew on pieces of its bark. She used to even simmer cinnamon water every evening to ward off the chemical smell from the nearby Tail factories. If there is a paradise, it was my home at sunset. The familiar cinnamon scent in the air, Baba coming back from his workshop, washing, changing, and setting up our dining table." Kenai smiled at the air, trying to recall a visual. "You know that feeling of comfort when you come back home after a long time? I felt like that every day in Dvedi. Do you think we'll ever be able to feel that here?"

Aryabh yearned for the feeling without ever having experienced how it felt. When he sensed the discomfort his thoughts brought him, he got up and went back to his desk.

Kenai got up too as if he had ended a conversation with himself and started to clean his mess.

The NanoCleaner that he had lifted from the building's maintenance room hummed in the kitchen. Numerous water pearls dispersed from underneath it and scattered around the floor. The giant water droplets attracted the flour and oil and got sucked back into the cleaner to filter themselves. Once the dirt was extracted, the clean water was collected in the water chamber ready to be reused.

"Kenai!" came a frightening yell.

Kenai dropped his precious cleaner and darted towards the sound. "Aryabh. You okay?"

He found his roommate standing against the corner wall, sweating and holding his breath. His eyes were pointing at the leg of his desk.

"Maggot...a fuckin' maggot." Aryabh yelled. "Get it out. Get it out!”

Kenai walked to the desk. “Maggot? Here?”

“Get it out!”

“Aah, what do you know, a maggot it is!”

Kenai found a giant, pasty worm crawling below Aryabh’s desk. Under its thick translucent skin, its body, almost as big as Kenai’s index finger, wriggled like a soft lump. “Hello, there, little buddy.” He knelt on the floor and bent to converse with the maggot. “What are you up to?”

“If you don’t get rid of it right away…” Aryabh yelled again.

Kenai looked at Aryabh and found his body trembling with fear and disgust. “Okay, okay. Calm down,” he said. “I didn’t know you were so scared of maggots.” He pushed the worm on a paper napkin and turned towards the main door to set it free.

“No, kill it. Squish it,” Aryabh ordered.

“What? No. I won’t.”

“Kill it now! See what’s inside. Check if it’s real.” Aryabh was standing on the tip of his toes, his palms still pressed against the wall.

“What do you mean real?” Kenai’s scratched his cheek. “It’s moving and everything.”

“Do as I say!”

“Sorry, Aryabh. I can’t kill an innocent worm.” Kenai paced to the window before Aryabh could stop him and gently descended the maggot out in the open.

“How the fuck is that not killing it?” Aryabh screamed, then ran to the window as if the wall had demagnetized him.

“He might live; we don’t know. I can’t kill him.”

“You could have flushed him down the toilet.”

“Do you want to drink him the next day?”

“You…” Aryabh opened his mouth to curse at Kenai but a suspicion stopped him midsentence. What was a worm doing in the middle of their apartment on the 94th floor? He switched his thought because even the mental image of the maggot nauseated him. He turned toward Kenai and said, “I am broke. I need money. Because you did that, you are going to help me now. I know your manager hires temp-workers for special events. Refer me. He'll need more workers for Pacalympics."

Aryabh had been looking for cracks to slip this topic. Now he had found one.

As if an adrenaline shot had taken its effect, Kenai's face glowed. "Sure, sure. It would be a pleasure to help you, my friend. What..."

"Let me know when it's done." Aryabh ended the chat. Then he grabbed a disinfectant mist from the bathroom and soaked the floor beneath his desk with it. As if that wasn't enough, he spent the entire evening scrubbing the same spot.

On the upper bunkbed, Kenai dozed off to the sight of his dear roommate trying to clean and re-clean his doubts and fear.

> As I watched Kenai drool on his pillow that day, I wondered if I would ever have that privilege — to be able to unload all my fear and suffering in the noon and nestle into the arms of comfort and sleep by nighttime. I didn't even know humans could do that. My torment lingered within me as some sort of maggot infestation that I could neither scrub nor clean. My pain was the permanent myiasis for which I had no remedy.

When Aryabh bent to lie down on his bed, his arm brushed Kenai's cold foot that dangled from the upper bunk. In his peripheral vision, his lenses displayed the cold October evening weather—40 Fahrenheit.

"Cover yourself," Aryabh muttered in his face. "Come on; sleep like a human."

Kenai responded with a snore.

After he moved to and fro for a while, Aryabh finally lifted Kenai's leg and tucked it inside his blanket. Then he rushed to his own bed as if he was fleeing from a crime and closed his eyes.

CHAPTER 16

Zenith

October 20, 2125

A month ago, thanks to Gryffy, Lyra had met her ardent supporters—Zen Mavericks, Zenith's only youth club.

There were 886 Zenither youths between the ages of fifteen and twenty-four, and Zen Mavericks was a whopping 622-member strong. They were not known for their amiability, and Lyra had her doubts about their intentions, but they had what she needed the most. A different opinion from the rest.

"We need more freedom and advancement," the president of the club had told Lyra during their meeting. "We can't keep acting like a product on a well-oiled conveyor belt."

Lyra had had a hard time agreeing with their point of view. She deduced that their problem with Zenith and its authority came from a state of rebelliousness more than from any principles of validity. They were brainy and perceptive, no doubt. That was why she enjoyed conversing with them. But if it wasn't for Gryffy's plea, she would have bid adieu to the Mavericks without discussing the issue.

At the end of the meeting, they had shaken hands and agreed to support Lyra's mission.

Out of the six meetings they had had since then, Lyra had

skipped four, partly because of indolence, but mainly because she had already made up her mind. Zen Mavericks's endorsement was not going to help her cause. They were too abrasive and juvenile for Zenithers to take them seriously.

However, their vice-president, Hawk, a seventeen-year-old, self-professed tech-wizard, had something that Lyra wanted.

She was in his house, walking around his room, and looking at his unique inventions with fervent curiosity, asking, "What's this?" every few minutes.

Hawk, like the other members, was infuriated with the colony for their lack of advancement in his field. But, unlike others, he was more focused on asking what he wanted rather than showing Zenithers their place. What surprised Lyra the most about him was how much he enjoyed her company. He had once called her the dopest Zenither on the asteroid.

"Are you going to the rally next week?" Hawk asked.

They both stood at an elongated table in the middle of his room.

"No. It's as unnecessary an event as Earthless Day," replied Lyra.

"Thank you!" Hawk bowed. "All he did was to say a dozen vague, sentiment-harvesting sentences some fifty years ago."

Lyra shook her head in agreement. Hawk's response made her cut the awkward gap between her and the table. "Exactly," she said. "He shouldn't be celebrated as a hero. No one should. It puts people on a pedestal. It's not the right vantage point for anyone to see their defected side."

"Ha! Correct. They have to stop turning people into god!"

"That's what I say!" Lyra leaned on the table with bright eyes. "Nothing stagnates us like worshiping the past."

"I only asked because you volunteer at Goodall. Didn't this guy make volunteering mandatory for a while in the 90s or something?"

"It's why I don't like him," Lyra said as she observed one of Hawk's latest cellphone models. "When you make a selfless act a compulsion, its altruism vanishes. It makes people despise the very thing they enjoyed. He turned away so many people who liked working with the Goodall animals. Without choice, we are just meat and bones."

Hawk stopped moving his fingers around the device he held. "Where can I find a legal version of you?"

Lyra gave out a half-suppressed laugh. Relieved from not being judged for her opinion, she even joked, "At your eighteenth birthday."

The seventeen-year-old snorted a laugh, too.

"So, where are we on those devices?" Lyra asked, looking at the table full of wires, batteries, capacitors, circuits, transistors, and other materials she did not recognize. She imagined the table to be the inside of a giant cell phone.

"Here." Hawk presented a wristband, a camera, and a pair of goggles. "These will work with your phone. I have modeled them after the design your Earthler friend sent. I had to print some parts. It's disappointing, though. I imagined they'd be more advanced than this, the Earthlers."

"Only their government and their inner circle...they call them Cream. Only they have access to advanced technology," said Lyra.

"I wouldn't know. I do know that their toilets whisper to them if they are sick. It's smart, but that's where I draw the line. I like my toilets without mouths."

Lyra flashed a genuine smile. She was happy Hawk didn't respond to her Earth-trivia with scorn like everyone else.

"Now, don't flaunt this around," Hawk advised. "You know how it is with one of these things. If one has it, everyone wants it even if it's a piece of crap."

"I won't. But as discussed, you too can't make more of this. You know the Council would frown."

"Don't worry. Mass-producing it would be an insult to my art. It's not my style. Besides, everyone we want to see is closer than thirty minutes away. No one would need this."

"But people can use it to communicate with the Earthlers," Lyra said.

"Do you know anyone else who wants to communicate with someone on Earth?"

"Touché."

"Anyway, see here?" Hawk showed a feature on the wristband. "This enables space roaming. I need not mention that it's illegal; we are stealing the observatory's network."

"Got it." Lyra pocketed the device.

"You have to admit, though, Lyra, Earthlers are not as smart as everyone here describes them," Hawk said without looking up from his next project. "What they make there with limitless technology, I can design in my bedroom here. That's exactly why all of us at Zen Mavericks think we can excel on Earth. We can easily beat those nerds. Don't tell your hacker friend that, though." He winked at Lyra.

"Hacker?" Lyra's stomach churned.

"You think a non-suicidal layperson can send a blueprint of a gadget like this from Earth? They'd butcher him. Even I know that. This guy is a genius. Firstly, for figuring this out and secondly, for sending it to us without getting tracked."

Lyra re-asphyxiated a lingering thought. "Thank you for doing this," she said.

"Tickets?" Hawk offered his empty hand.

"Not just the band, but even the organizers are Earthlers. Don't get me fired." Lyra handed him tickets for a concert that was going to take place at her hotel, Faraway Paradise.

"They will talk about our manners for ages to come," Hawk replied.

Lyra: I've placed the camera where you asked me to. You want to switch on yours?

At the other end, Aryabh juggled a dilemma. Was he really doing this? He never wanted Lyra to see his face. She would recognize him when he moved to Zenith. He'd see Zenith's pond soon, anyway. Why the recklessness?

Aryabh: Okay.

He placed his camera on the kitchen wall and pulled his desk right in front of it before the window. With the camera turned on behind him, he sat on the desk and faced Sonmanto.

By Zenith's Alvariño pond, Lyra sat on her boulder, put on a thick pair of goggles, and turned on the camera that she had placed on the rock behind her.

Aryabh turned on his lenses, straightened his T-shirt, and inhaled. Then he made the call.

Lyra brushed her hair with her fingers. Her hand got stuck in one of the knots. She untangled it using her forefinger and thumb like a pair of tongs. Then she took a deep breath and answered.

To Aryabh's right, on a wobbly plastic desk, a girl whose face he had only seen in pictures materialized. He flinched as Lyra's holographic image became clearer.

Lyra, however, stared straight through.

Once Aryabh realized what she was seeing, he looked ahead as well.

"Is this Zen—"

"Is this Ear—"

Lyra and Aryabh muttered together and stopped each other midsentence.

Neither of them would ever forget this moment, the time when their dreams virtually transpired in front of their eyes.

On Earth, a small portion of Zenith replaced Aryabh's window. He opened his eyes wider to gape at all the corners with his peripheral vision.

Straight ahead, where the Sonmanto lights should have glimmered, he saw a dark water body with the surrounding trees reflecting their silhouettes on its stillness. In the left corner, he saw a distant ghostly forest. A shrill static chirped from it at irregular intervals. His ears swung in that direction.

"What's that sound?" he asked.

"From the forest? Crickets."

"Crickets?"

"You've never heard crickets? There must be trillions of them on Earth. They are little insects with antennas. Male crickets create that sound by rubbing their wings together. It's called stridulating."

If Aryabh was amused, he didn't express it. But his ears were still pressed in that direction.

Beyond the pond, Aryabh saw a wide green space, its fences draped in night lights. Tiny houses and small buildings surrounded the rest of the area. He observed that it all stood calm, as if the people inside were soundly asleep without a care in the world.

What accelerated his heartbeat was the inner side of the asteroid, which gave a backdrop to everything around. The cratered, metallic wall of Zenith curved upward at the far distance like the inside of a bowl.

His heart ached and fluttered at the same time. The sense of wonderment that children deserve in their childhood had finally arrived on Aryabh's face.

At last, he looked above. He saw the line that subtracted Zenith from his reality. It was the ceiling of his own house.

He turned towards Lyra again, who stirred next to him.

Through her goggles, Lyra saw in front of her a wide city skyline instead of Zenith's pond. She swayed her face from left to right like an enchanted child.

Lyra looked so real. Aryabh could see the sharp, scratchy texture of her oversized black sweater and the faint blue ink lines on her black tapered pants.

Throughout his life, Aryabh had surfed random pictures of Zenithers. Apart from the paleness of their skin, slightly shorter average height, and a cheerful liveliness on their faces, he could not make out any difference between them and the Earthlers.

He failed to find the trademark Zenither liveliness on the face of the person he had robbed three months ago. Lyra looked like a battered tree that had been withered too many times by strong winds.

Aryabh forgot how angry he was with her and her silly antics. He tried to get a closer look at her when her face turned towards him.

"Can you see me?" she spoke in a voice that was deeper than the brittle voice Aryabh had imagined.

"Yea. Can you?"

"Yes. I can't believe this. This looks so real... Impressive!" Lyra complimented Aryabh and removed her goggles to check. She was indeed still sitting on Zenith. With hasty hands, she wore the goggles back as if she would lose Earth if she did not.

She looked at Aryabh again.

"And that's you."

Lyra wanted to turn away quickly for saying something as silly as that, but she couldn't. She lost her voice when she noticed his face for the first time. A harrowing mirror. His eyes, although different in shape and color, looked the same as hers. Two sunken potholes on each side of the nose bridge.

"What are those blue outlines?" she asked when she noticed his irises.

"Lenses. I am watching you through them."

"Interesting."

A frog croaked from around the pond during their moment of silence. Aryabh ignored the sound, assuming it was static.

"I am sorry. I am being awkward," Lyra said. "It just seems so..."

"Awkward?"

They both chuckled.

"Where is your roommate?"

Aryabh had mentioned Kenai once or twice in their chats

before.

"Work."

"Your voice..."

"What's with it?" said Aryabh, afraid.

"It sounds different. So does your language, even though we are speaking the same."

"You sound familiar."

"I do?"

"Somehow...yes. Why did you bring me here?"

"I am going live on our radio in a few days to talk about moving back to Earth. I could have just messaged you but I learned about this glorious thing." She touched her goggles. "So, I thought, why not use some felonious technology while we are at it?"

Aryabh ignored the news about radio and listened to crickets again for a while. Then he spoke without looking at Lyra.

"What's that mark below your goggles?"

Lyra touched the tear-shaped scar below her eye.

"Sagan. He was three. I was taking him to the doctor and he didn't want to go."

"I thought only Earthler children scratched and bit."

"It's not his standard behavior. He grew out of it."

Another minute of silence.

"It's your first time seeing Zenith, right?" Lyra asked. "Happy?"

Aryabh couldn't silence his answer. "I don't know. I don't understand 'happy'. Even on my best days, I feel...less angry but not happy. Are you?"

"I imagined to be exhilarated, but somehow all this is doing is reminding me how far-fetched a dream this is."

Aryabh stared at the ripples in the pond. "We are too dysfunctional to see things as they are."

"We are, aren't we?"

"How can you be upset? You have everything. Zenith gives you everything."

It was not until then that Lyra sensed genuine curiosity behind Aryabh's cynicism. She opted for an honest reply. "Not everything. This place feels…" she tried hard to express exactly how she felt, "…lonelier than solitude."

"Zenithers cannot be lonely."

"How totalitarian of you," Lyra said with a smile.

Aryabh felt as if a blade just cut him.

"If you can feel lonely on a planet packed with billions of people…" she said.

"I am not."

"You don't have to lie. It makes sense. It's why you desperately want to escape from there. People create a sense of belonging when loneliness prospers inside them for too long. Been lonely for long?" Lyra asked in an effort to decode Aryabh.

"No. I have been lonely for a long time *because* I haven't escaped," Aryabh said. "I am lonely because on Earth even a person in the most crowded room feels alone." The Earthler in him had surfaced. "And I didn't meet for you to study me."

"Sorry." Lyra looked down.

Her choice to not defend herself made Aryabh feel defeated. He stared at an isolated lotus in the water and asked, "Why do *you* feel lonely?"

Lyra took a moment.

"My loneliness is partly voluntary. I keep people at a distance because I am afraid my half-hearted closeness will hurt them more." She paused, and then let her words flow. "All my life, I've felt like I am decaying inside this claustrophobic rock. They teach you to be afraid of the dark. They never tell you of the dark things that can happen in the light. You know, my biggest fear is turning into a completely different person than I really am, which will definitely happen if I grow old here on Zenith." Lyra looked at the twinkling lights of Sonmanto. "I already feel like I am always wearing someone else's personality. The only thing that kept me going all these years was the blue marble in space." She spoke her mind, feeling invisible. "It was my sense of belonging, a byproduct of loneliness. My dream kept me sane. But all of that is gone, and now, even a small leap of faith feels like I am falling down a frightening..." She searched for the right word.

"Rabbit hole," Aryabh finished her sentence.

"You've read *Alice's Adventures in Wonderland*?!" Lyra's eyes grew big and bright and her teeth appeared between her lips.

"One of my favorites. Almost got me arrested."

"Mine too!" A childlike excitement filled Lyra. "What else do you read?"

"Haven't read a good story in a while. You have any?" Aryabh asked remembering Lyra's stories on her tablet. "Something Earthlers might not have heard before?"

"Nothing like a good story, right?"

"Nothing like a good story," he agreed.

"Okay, let's see..." Lyra pressed her eyes. "Alright, it's not from a book. My mother told me this fable when I was younger. There once was a rare black-and-white tiger locked in a cage. People from faraway places would travel to see this unique animal. One day, a painter who was famous for painting in the air without paint or canvas announced—"

"Canvas?"

"Oh, it's a kind of cloth people paint on."

Aryabh liked that Lyra answered all his questions with enthusiasm instead of mocking his ignorance, which was something he always did when people came to him with questions.

"Continue..." he said.

"So this crazy painter announced he could paint colors on the tiger without touching it. People turned him into a joke. One fine day, he visited the tiger's cage, flicked his paintbrush in the air, and whispered something into the tiger's ear. To everyone's surprise, vibrant colors appeared on the animal's skin. When people asked him how he did it, he said he kept repeating a phrase into the tiger's ears."

"What phrase?"

"In just a few days, you will be free again." Lyra completed the story.

Aryabh gulped something heavy down his throat.

"Can I do something to help you come to Zenith?" Lyra asked, wanting to give a hacker that option.

The generosity surprised Aryabh but he did not show. "Nothing you can do," he hissed through his teeth to quiet his guilt. "And don't expect me to offer you the same help."

"I don't."

"Because I will never ever understand how someone as smart as you would want to settle on Earth."

Lyra did not respond.

"Is it some kind of savior complex?" Aryabh tilted his head towards Lyra. "You want to come here and change the planet, make people realize what they are missing, or some similar kind of crap?"

This time, Lyra let out a mocking chuckle.

"Trust me, I am not a savior. I know what I am. I've spent twenty-seven years thinking about it," she stated. "I don't care what happens on Earth or what Earthlers do with their lives. All I wanted was to find a corner on your enormous planet where I can keep to myself and make a living. If things seemed better, I would have traveled a bit, discovered the unknown. It fascinates me, the ability to travel around a world so big and the possibility of coming across places and people you didn't even know existed...but that was it. I don't know everything that is to be known about Earth, but I know me, and I am sure I can do all that without getting into trouble. Things are astronomically worse on Earth than here. I understand that. But I find it easier to deal with strangers than struggling and fighting with people I know."

It annoyed Aryabh that he could see the point in Lyra's reasoning. "You think a lot," he concluded.

"Why wouldn't I? It's free," she said in a flat tone.

Aryabh couldn't stifle his laugh.

"What's that?" Lyra pointed towards Earth's sky.

Aryabh turned off his lenses to check. "Mazona's SpaceAd, a giant banner orbiting Earth."

"That's abominable!"

Aryabh agreed with a huff.

"I've read the countryside is still as beautiful as it was a century ago," said Lyra. "That they still have natural landscapes and old-Earth houses."

"Countryside?"

"Trunks and Tails, as you all call it."

"Some corners do, but it's changing at a fast pace. The erasing of the Trunks and Tails, and replacing them with skylines and industries, has not stopped since the Political Fumigation. You think of Earth and picture a green haven, but nothing about this place is raw or earthy. What's in front of you right now is a colorful well-framed painting, while the wood behind it rots and gets infested with bugs of rapacity and tyranny." With Lyra, Aryabh talked the same way he talked to himself, and that scary fact creeped up to him.

"That's a good word. Rapacity," said Lyra. Aryabh's revelations influenced her even though they were distressing. She thought of other things she had planned to ask Aryabh. "Have you ever heard of a place called Forêt de Fontainebleau? It's a small town...a Trunk in a country called France?"

"I don't think so. All old-Earth places were renamed before I was even born. There is no record of them."

"I see."

"What's in that place?" Aryabh asked, even though he knew. He had read Lyra's great-grandmother's diary many times. It offended him that Lyra had not shared about it before he stole her documents.

"That was where my great-grandparents expressed their love for each other. My great-grandmother, my mom's mom, had described that place majestically. Her words had compelled me to see that spot, to confirm if something as surreal even existed."

Lyra's voice grew quieter. "Guess I'll never know."

"Could it be that she was just a good writer?" Aryabh's head tilted back.

Lyra shrugged.

"It was just one of the things on my list, things I wanted to do on…whoa, something smells like bad coffee."

Aryabh remembered he had turned on the 'olfactory' feature on his widget.

"AwakeTab, my candy," he explained. "I had sent the scent-blend to the guy who assembled your device.

"I am smelling your surroundings?!" Lyra's voice amplified. "How? What else can I smell?"

Aryabh cranked the feature to the highest. His widget registered nearby scents and transmitted an electrical simulation of those odors. It triggered the scent-blend, which emitted smells through the perforation on the bridge of Lyra's goggles.

A medley of half a dozen scents stormed Lyra's heightened olfactory sense.

Chemicals

Metal

Smoke

Chilly night air

Coffee

Cigarettes

The lingering musky scent of Kenai's cologne

She took a deep breath.

"I smell it!" Lyra's back shot upright. "This is unreal. I love technology!"

The excitement on her face troubled Aryabh. He had to ask, "Why aren't you angry enough?"

"What?"

"If I were you, I'd be smashing every tangible thing in my sight. You almost boarded the elevator when your documents disappeared. Why aren't you angry?"

Lyra chewed her inner lip and asked herself the same question.

Once she got the answer, she relayed, "I was. At least angry in my own way. Anger has always metamorphosed inside me into frustration and pain. I don't know who taught me to suppress anger, but I have mastered it well."

She looked at a restaurant's laser ad on the tallest skyscraper in her sight and a part of her wondered about its menu. "I wish it wasn't this way. Anger is healthy. Pain leaves you drifting help-lessly in a void." She inhaled again and smelled mold. "After I returned from the transit station, I was mad at everything and everyone. I thought I didn't deserve that. But aren't we all the most entitled advocates of ourselves? We all believe the universe should provide us with everything we desire. But no one owes us anything. If I lost my folder, I lost it. I should have kept it safer if it meant that much to me, right?"

"And you really believe that?"

"On most days."

"Don't you get tired?"

"Of?"

"Pretending?" Aryabh thought again of stories Lyra had writ-ten on her tablet, which lay under his pillow less than two feet away from her holographic image.

"What do you mean?"

"I see your mask. You are fake as they come. If we are doing this heart-to-heart, let's be honest."

"Heart?" Lyra smirked. "I am sure the thing that pumps blood inside my body is a landfill." She spoke as if those words had been in her head for a long time. She remembered how she had learned about Earth's landfill from Sagan. "How about that for honesty?" She hesitated from speaking further, but she was curious herself to listen to the thoughts she had never given voice to.

"More honesty? Let's see." She pulled the hair-tie on her wrist. "There have been days when I had lain in bed thinking about my father's funeral."

Behind the goggles, a tear rolled down Lyra's cheek.

"I hated myself for it. Not just because I imagined it, but because the thought made me feel lighter." The hot lump in her throat scorched her voice. "When I was leaving for Earth, I was sad not because I would miss my brother but because how much he would miss me or needed me."

Lyra did not like how the truth tasted on her tongue, but she carried on.

"You want to hear something even richer? I didn't tell my brother, the only person I am humanly attached to, that I was leaving Zenith forever until the last moment because I didn't want to deal with the emotional baggage that would come with the confession. A twelve-year-old boy who struggles with understanding small emotions every day must have cried alone in his room because a twenty-seven-year-old is not emotionally intelligent enough to have an intimate conversation with her brother. How fucked up is that?" She held her head, as if to hide.

Aryabh was stunned. He had never heard such unfiltered words before.

"It's like...an evil monster grows inside me every time I suppress myself," Lyra said, her face nested in her hands. "I am fake. I do wear a mask because my apathy had...cost a life."

She didn't wait for Aryabh's reaction.

"But that is not how I want to live. I want to wake up in the morning not thinking about things expected of me. I want the liberty to say no without feeling horrendous about it. That's what I meant when I told you freedom is subjective. I just want to be free."

The explosion of her words shook Lyra. She composed herself and spoke in a calmer voice.

"You must be gloating, seeing how I asked you to be considerate, while I am...this."

"I will never judge the monster in you." The words spilled out of Aryabh like liquid.

Lyra looked at him. She saw kindness she had never received from him before.

"You don't get to be heartless so easily," Aryabh said, struggling to find consoling words for the first time in his life. "That's my badge of honor. You are not apathetic. You do care for your brother, right?"

"Sagan?" Lyra's eyes shone again. "I do. But that's solely his doing. He's one of a kind. The only person who makes me feel sane. You know, he despised me till he was four. Maybe I did too, and he just reciprocated it. I wasn't ready to raise a child, a difficult child at that." She smiled as she remembered something. "He used to think I wasn't his real sister. That's why he hated me."

"Why?"

"We are mixed race. I look a lot like my mother." Lyra rubbed her wrist. "She had brown skin, brown hair, deep features. Sagan picked up my Dad's genes. He is white. We don't exactly look like siblings."

Aryabh stared at his own brown skin, which was a lot more tanned than Lyra's. He had never thought about the genes and identities of his donors before. He couldn't even imagine them as humans.

"What changed? With your brother?" he asked.

Lyra verbalized a memory. "Years ago, a Goodall Sanctuary program used to air on TV every day. The show would feature T. rex and his mate, who, sadly, is not alive anymore."

Aryabh glanced at her at the sound of 'T. rex'.

"Oh, T. rex is a mountain gorilla."

"A monkey named T. rex? What's next, a cat named Dog?"

"I named him. I was barely two years old."

Aryabh raised an eyebrow. "That's your defense?"

"No, I was bragging. I was aware of an extinct reptile species of a foreign planet before I learned to climb stairs," Lyra said as a subtle fierceness erupted on her face.

It made Aryabh smile again.

"Anyway, every time that program would come on television, Sagan would run away and hide. He would peep from behind the couch to see if T. rex was gone." Lyra exhaled a gleeful laugh. "Then he would throw tantrums all day! So, one day, I decided to take him to the sanctuary and introduce him to T. rex. I knew he'd either end up loving him or hating me more than he already did. It took some hiding and some crying, but once he saw T. rex eating a banana, he walked up to him with another banana."

Aryabh got used to Lyra's smile.

"They played for hours! Sagan finally took a tour of the entire sanctuary and fell in love with wildlife. He started trusting me more after that day. Has never left my side since then."

"That could easily have gone the other way."

"I know. But he was my brother, after all." Lyra shrugged. She reflected on the incident for a moment and spoke again, "I don't know why I did that. For years, I only did what I was supposed to do, or what made Sagan happy. Maybe I had had enough, or maybe I trusted my instinct. I don't know."

"You have a lot of maybes in your life," Aryabh commented.

"Maybe." Lyra smiled. "It's like I have two minds. One is being itself. It's feeling, reacting, thinking, and sending signals to my body to act naturally, while the other mind is constantly judging, criticizing, correcting, and commanding my first mind. And I am the spectator of this constant battle between the two. Hardly have I ever made concrete decisions in my life, but one of those rare ones was coming to Earth."

Aryabh wanted to deride her, but he couldn't.

"That's not who I wanted to be," Lyra continued without pausing to wonder why she was speaking a year's worth of words in a day. "I wanted to be sure of all my decisions and declare them without filters. I wanted to be invincible, like Earth's sunlight, which travels millions of miles to give warmth and life but is still strong enough to pierce your cornea. I..."

She halted her words as if she was out of a trance when she felt Aryabh's presence next to her. She removed her goggles, hoping it would make her invisible.

It didn't. It only gave Aryabh a chance to look at her full face.

Lyra's eyes beamed with adrenaline.

He drew a breath of gladness that he had gotten to know her. "Well, that's not the only thing that pierces corneas on Earth." He changed the subject to stop Lyra from being embarrassed.

"What?" She wore the goggles again.

"Sun is not the only thing that burns your eyes here." Aryabh pointed at his blue iris.

"The lenses? Are they that bad?"

"They are. Or it's just me, because everyone says I am the only one who finds them and the widgets abrasive."

"Maybe since you are more observant of their side-effects, you notice them more than others."

"Exactly! Hah..." Aryabh's voice reached its highest decibel. He was almost on his feet, but he pushed himself to sit back on the table. "That's exactly what I always say. But less nicely."

No, Aryabh wasn't glad. He was thrilled to know someone like Lyra.

CHAPTER 17

THE EARTHLER NEWS

October 25, 2125

THE 74TH EMERGENCE DAY TO TAKE OFF GRANDLY AT SONMANTO'S ROBUST STADIUM

PacaLab announces the inauguration of 160 newly built humanoid bots engineered to compete with human Olympiads this year. No limits...

Emergence Day was more important for the Farm than the Pacamounts. It was the only day of the year when the Rodents were out in the open and crammed together at one, less restrictive venue. Over the years, the Farm had created tiny cracks, but this time they were prepping for long-lasting damage.

"We want to change the meaning of this day," they had said at the meeting. "The Rodents celebrate it as the day they took over Earth. We want to make it the day they lost like the little fucks they are!"

To have an upper hand, Aryabh had broken the news of his roommate's connection to the caterers of the after-Pacalympics party. Kenai's restaurant manager was one of the hundreds of restaurateurs who would serve food at the event.

The PacaProfile of Kenai's manager reflected that his MO was taking the cheapest route. As a result, Aryabh had infiltrated himself as well as five other Farm members into his workforce. He needed a reference from a current employee of the restaurant, and Kenai had given that wholeheartedly.

"How did you do it?"

"Manipulating our PacaProfile is impossible," Aryabh had lied to Dima; he didn't want the Farm to know what he was capable of. "So, I created our fake flash profiles. It's only visible on the manager's database for a short period. A cautious person would have hired background verifiers, but he is cheap. I put minimum pay in 'expected wages' and he pounced on it."

Aryabh had been comparing his incomplete badge with Lyra's when his bunkbed shook.

Kenai got down and went to the bathroom, rubbing the sleep in his eyes. Fifteen minutes later, he was back, looking like a mass-produced Earthler.

"Get ready," he said. "You don't want to be late to my manager's job. He doesn't pay latecomers." He hovered over Aryabh as he buttoned his cuffs.

"Would it kill you to maintain normal proximity?" Aryabh lashed out when Kenai's elbow grazed his shoulder.

"That usually gets you out of the bed. But it made your sentences longer. Not bad." Kenai nodded, smiled, and got back to his cuffs.

Aryabh exhaled and got up. "I am ready," he said, his eyes on his widget.

"You can't wear this. You need to wear a white shirt like this one." Kenai lifted his collar.

"Don't have one."

"What are roomies for! I have three." Kenai pranced to the bathroom cabinet and returned with a similar shirt in his hand.

Knowing that an argument would be futile, Aryabh snatched the shirt, went to the bathroom, and put it on.

His reflection in the mirror looked like a stranger as he fidgeted, feeling uncomfortable in his skin. He had never worn anything so bright. And the shirt smelled like Kenai. It wasn't an unpleasant smell, but strong enough to make him uneasy. As if someone was touching him.

"Whoa!" Kenai came from behind. "Have you ever noticed that you are an unconventionally handsome man?"

"There are two kinds of handsome. Right-in-your-face handsome and the unusual, grows-on-you handsome, which I now see you are," Kenai continued to compliment Aryabh as they took big steps on the sidewalk of Chase Street.

"Quit being a creep," Aryabh snarled.

"Oh, Aryabh, there is nothing wrong with an adult man uplifting and complimenting another adult man. You should try it sometimes," said Kenai, lifting the waistband of his beltless pants.

He walked in front of Aryabh and took a picture of them.

"The fuck?!" Aryabh pushed him out of the way.

Kenai ignored his scowl and checked the picture. "Argh! This acne!"

Aryabh's hand went to his own cheek.

"Not yours, Aryabh. Your face is full of it; they give you character. I am talking about this one." Kenai broke Aryabh's stride again and stood in front of him, pointing at a pimple on his cheekbone. "It looks like a whole other person."

As if Kenai wasn't enough, Aryabh had to find Neslo at his usual place. He was singing the goblin song and throwing pebbles at the homeless sitting on the ground.

"Go stuff your fat faces!" he yelled at a woman entering the PacaMarket. "I can't stand your hideous faces. Oh lookit! Mr Grumpet is here." He pointed at Aryabh. "Hisis the most hideous face."

Aryabh's hand reached for his cheek again.

"Ugly. Filthy! Bleghh..." Neslo spat and chugged some liquid from his chipped, stained glass.

Luckily, for Aryabh, his voice faded as they raced past him.

Locals and tourists had crowded the Café Sobak neighborhood to watch the Pacalympics on aerial screens. The café, as a result, was full and the members stood outside, split into groups.

The first person Aryabh saw was Caspian. She was standing alone, moving authoritative hands in the hair. Her foxlike face radiated the vigor that came with being a Cream. She donned a sparkly coat over a black suit and gloved hands. A labyrinth-like design was painted on her lips and her silver pixie hair was coiffed into a side mohawk.

Aryabh and Kenai joined Shiaya, Arkas, and Dev, who stood a few feet away from Caspian.

"Hey, man!" Dev greeted Aryabh with a fist-bump.

Aryabh looked around and above, then nodded.

Kenai, feeling bad for Dev and his cheerful, kind face, pushed his own fist to bump.

"While you mofos earn peanuts, I'll be making top-tier salary for ruining the Rodents," Shiaya teased everyone. She was already a server at the PacaSpace Transit Station and that had earned her a higher position at the event than the rest.

"Look at that fool. Terrified up to the balls," Dev said, looking at the Pacalympics host who was announcing something on one of the screens. "He's probably going to get dissolved today for messing up."

"Bitch!" Shiaya mumbled, dispensing a whiff of vodka.

Aryabh turned towards her and found her staring at a woman behind Kenai. She was about the same age as Shiaya but dressed more like Caspian.

Shiaya's eyes flinched and her jaw clenched as she gazed at her.

"Worked with me about half a decade ago at a casino," she told Aryabh in cold whispers. "Managed to score a Cream; devil knows how. Now she goes and flaunts her Creamness everywhere she had worked before...bosses and bullies her old colleagues."

Aryabh saw fury raging inside Shiaya's lavender-colored eyes.

"Came to the transit station once. Spilled two cups of coffee on the floor and asked me to clean it. Stared and smiled at me the whole time, that gold-fucking sadist slurry!"

It wasn't fury, Aryabh realized; it was envy that fumed in Shiaya's eyes.

Shiaya saw a remark coming and spoke before he could, "Na...uh. Don't you dare judge me! You can't walk past a group of people without using every single one of them, and you talk about fair-treatment all day. We are all pretentious cunts. So zip it!"

Aryabh turned away and buried his hands into his coat's pocket to thaw his fingertips.

"That's the manager's employee?" He heard a hushed voice behind him. It was Dima. He followed his eyes and found Kenai staring at Shiaya.

"Yup."

"Is he safe?"

"He keeps a journal."

"Okay, Benjamin." Dima winked.

Aryabh understood the reference, for he had read the Orwell book numerous times.

"Now, look!" Dima spoke again and whisked Aryabh aside. "The atmosphere is tense. Some foolish anti-Pacas set seven Mazonas on fire. Security is tight. Stay alert."

Shiaya and Dev left as soon as he finished his sentence.

"Caspian has bought off some of the security guards, so we should be okay. We are driving in pairs. You and the dork leave twenty minutes after us."

Aryabh nodded.

"Good luck," Dima leaned towards Aryabh and whispered, "to take back what's ours."

When Aryabh didn't respond, Dima looked into his eyes for the first time since the conversation started and recited the Farm's motto again. "To take back what's ours."

"To take back what's ours," said Aryabh.

Dima and Arkas left. Caspian left her corner too and followed them.

Kenai, who had been busy looking around and watching the event, filled in the big space that Dima occupied.

"I think I am in love," he spoke as he thought of Shiaya's lavender lips. "What's her name, that tall beautiful woman who was here?"

"Sign this." Aryabh pushed his hand in front of him.

"What's this?"

"I've rented a car in your name. I don't have a steady job like yours, so they wouldn't rent me one," Aryabh flattered Kenai. He found it safer to rent the car under Kenai's name as he was in the process of deleting his PacaProfile one detail at a time.

"We are going in a car?! I've never sat in a car in a Head before!" Kenai signed with an inflated chest.

As they waited, the temperature dropped and even the warm stench from Café Sobak didn't win against the bone-cracking cold. Aryabh struggled to compose his body but it quivered. It annoyed him that Kenai didn't shake as much.

"Why aren't you cold?" he asked.

"I am wearing a heated jacket." Kenai sprung his brows with pride. "Oh, you are shaking. Take my jacket."

Sacrifice, Aryabh thought. "No, it's okay," he said in a grateful tone and checked time.

"Let's go."

They walked up to the rental car parking structure, picked up their car, and drove off in the ground-level traffic towards Robust Stadium.

"Why are you driving if you rented the car under my name?"

asked Kenai.

"To reach there alive," Aryabh mumbled as he kept checking the car's rear camera through his lenses.

"I have no complaints. I thought I'll never get to use my driver's license. Anyway..." Kenai shrugged. "I just want to look outside. I've never been in this part of the Head...Oh my lord!" He jumped from his seat. "Look at that banner! It's me. My face. I am putting on a suit!"

Aryabh looked at a similar ad on his side. It reflected his own face. He was putting on the same suit.

"I look like a hero." Kenai said. "I have to buy that suit, Aryabh."

An auto-announcement interrupted Kenai's amazement.

'Happy 74th Emergence Day, Earthlers! On this day, vow to protect your Stratum and its curators. You hear foul plans, call 666. Report people with facial hair, dial 666. You hear anti-Pacas, call 666. You hear banned languages, dial 666. Do your job. Much praised the Pacamounts. God bless the Pacamounts.'

Kenai's wide grin vanished and he slid back in his seat.

"What now?" Aryabh asked.

"Just thinking about my family." He took the punching device out of his pocket and stared at it. "When they declared all non-English languages illegal on the first Emergence Day—it was 2051, I think—my grandparents faced the hardest time. They lived in a backward Tail and didn't speak English. Both got fired from their jobs. They would keep mum all day and talk in sign language. Even inside the house. One day when they were walking back home, my grandmother fell and scraped her knee. She accidentally moaned in our native language. My grandfather got so scared, he hit her to shut her up. They didn't use the bank much, and so they lost most of their wealth too when they banned paper money. I can't even imagine how they survived."

Aryabh had read history in black-market books and had imagined some of the horrors of the Political Fumigation, but hearing it firsthand from someone he knew made the past even grimmer.

"What language did they speak before?" he asked.

"I don't know. My baba wouldn't tell me. He said I'd tell everyone," said Kenai in a muzzled tone. Something clicked inside his head. He turned towards Aryabh. "Hey, who are all these people? You don't know my manager. He is dangerous. You don't want to fool him."

"Not fooling anyone."

"I am not stupid, Aryabh. I might not understand your ways, but I know they were not regular people. You work with them." Kenai mustered some courage. "I know many things, okay? Are you...planning to do something?"

Aryabh didn't respond.

"I am scared. Just tell me, is it good or bad?"

"Something bad for the greater good," Aryabh supplied a gibberish answer.

"If only I were wise enough to understand what it means."

"You're privileged. Wisdom is poison," he said and checked the stream of his rear camera. "Okay, listen. Stick with me. Do as I say. Try not to be...you."

"Okay."

They drove for an hour.

When they parked the car, a gut feeling overtook Aryabh that he was being followed. He checked his surroundings again but found no one in sight. His paranoia was not a pressing matter right now, he thought. He had too much on his mind. Besides, Kenai wasn't catching a breath. He loudly recited the rules from the employees' manual that his restaurant had given for the event.

"Wear gloves all the time. Do not take pictures. Do not make eye contact with the guests. Do not touch them. Do not greet, speak, or talk with them. Do not smile... Wait, what? How can you serve a guest without smiling? That's Hospitality 101."

When they entered the stadium gates, a sea of workers engulfed them. They pushed and grumbled as they headed to their assigned jobs.

Aryabh felt as if he were trapped in a jungle of gloom and desperation.

On the left, he saw the rotating stadium that was filled with the Pacamounts and Cream. They were attending the Pacalympics ceremony. Their faces were not visible because of the stadium's humongous walls, but he felt their sadistic presence within them. He could smell the cheer that came from watching humans being defeated by the PacaAndroids.

On his right, the workers hired to serve the Pacalympics guests were being herded like cattle. They walked in a line to pass through the security gates with their heads turned towards the stadium, their mouths salivating at the privilege.

Aryabh and Kenai joined the line. As they waited, a blaring horn blasted from the rotating stadium. An announcement echoed through the enormous ground.

"Lively parade, 2nd Stratum. But now, it's time! With great honor, I invite the Pacamounts of all three Stratums to come up on stage and start the Earth-renaming ceremony. Today, on the 74th Emergence day, we rename Earth to United Stratums of Earth. U-S-E. U-S-E," he started chanting. "U-S-E, USE! USE!"

The Pacamounts and Cream joined the chant.

"USE! USE! USE!"

"Everyone," the voice continued. "Rise from your seats for the anthem."

Every single person in Aryabh's eyesight turned into a sculpture. They cupped their palms like a shark's jaw, laid it across their chest, and joined the anthem that played on the speaker. In dutiful voices, they sang along-

"Much praised the Pacamounts!
God bless the Pacamounts!

They granted eternal wealth and glory
To NonCreamers and PacaChildren.
They granted eternal seclusion and indifference,

To NonCreamers and PacaChildren.

Much praised the Pacamounts!
God bless the Pacamounts!

They destroyed the haters,
They fought the traitors.
And their greatness shall live in the memory of Earthlers.
The shark's Head is out,
And it smells the anti-Pacas' blood.
In it, we will soak our flag.
To the Dissolution chamber, their bodies we'll drag
And march ahead to the beat of their irradiating bones.

Much praised the Pacamounts!
God bless the Pacamounts!

Rid us of our old-Earth ways,
O PacaEyes, guide us where loyalty lays,
Clothe us with the paraphernalia of your partners,
O teach us the dangers of PacaMilitary's armors.
Protect our Stratums, our profits, and our Cream,
May the deadly shark live long, and so its regime!

Much praised the Pacamounts!
God bless the Pacamounts!"

A humongous Pacamounts flag emerged at the center of the stadium. The left half was black, the other half yellow, and in between was a red, toothy silhouette of a shark head.

> It's not an anthem. It's the mission statement of
> the biggest corporation in the universe.

Aryabh and Kenai entered the security gates and walked to their assigned work area where they saw all the other Farm members.

"Hey!" Kenai waved and walked towards Dima.

Aryabh grabbed him by the arm and pulled him back. "Stop! You don't know them here."

"But we just—"

"If you make this hard for me, I am going to kill you," Aryabh spoke under his breath as he looked around.

"You say that a lot. I don't like it. I—"

A big guy interrupted Kenai and threw aprons on their faces.

"Put them on," he said. "Party starts in two hours. Read the instruction manual again. You mess up, you die. Get to your assigned work."

Aryabh and Kenai joined some of the Farm members who headed towards the kitchen area. They carried food from the kitchen and prepped trays until guests arrived.

When the Pacalympics after-party started, Aryabh and Kenai, along with hundreds of other servers, entered the venue—a lush green lot covered with dozens of black, round tables. Twinkling lights draped the area like walls. Next to each table stood a cluster of Cream in their elaborate garb and equanimous mannerism. They talked in assertive voices with faces devoid of the weariness that the workers wore.

While Aryabh hated every moment, the rest of the servers raced past him, stomping each other to be the first ones to serve from their trays. An opportunity of a lifetime.

Aryabh was not sure what made him angrier, the towering water fountain in the center or the endless platter of fresh food, or that an open ground like this was warmer than their tiny 350-square-feet apartment.

> They didn't just anger me that day; they saddened
> me. Those healthy faces with blood flowing freely

in their cheeks juxtaposed against the cold, malnourished faces of the people I had known.

But it doesn't matter how much you hate them.
They will take everything you have and deprive
you of everything you need until you are helpless.
They'll make you work for them, envy and admire
them, and before you know it, you'll become the
part of the same evil you had hated all along.

"To weaken their power, we have to fracture their unity," Dima had said at one of the Farm meetings. "We have drafted a few fake email communication between a dozen high-ranking Cream and some anti-Paca groups. At the party, Aryabh will not only transfer the Rodents' data to his widget but will also implant these fabricated emails into the Cream's devices. The Ground Wing will carry out some of the tasks mentioned in the said emails to make the messages seem real. Let the Rodents thin their own herd for us."

Aryabh had been impressed with the plan but he was not going through so much trouble and risking his safety for the benefit of the Farm.

The Pacalympics after-party was a golden opportunity for him to come in close quarters with the Zenith Relations Officer, a person solely appointed by the Pacamounts to deal with the matters of Zenith. Aryabh was sure that the Zenither child whose identity he would steal was still missing, but he wanted to have as much information as possible on him and his family. In the sea of data, he might also find clues that would make his transfer to Zenith smoother.

Aryabh looked around the party ground, knowing well that at least a dozen PacaEyes were watching him. He searched for Caspian and found her sitting at one of the tables. When she gave him a slight nod, he turned on his lenses.

The workers were not allowed to carry devices, but the Farm

had carried them in their pockets, thanks to Caspian. She had also lent Aryabh lenses of Cream technology. They didn't change the color of his irises.

In his peripheral vision, Aryabh saw darts pinned over a few party guests. Caspian had tagged the Cream whose devices were to be implanted with the messages.

Aryabh picked a tray of synthetic caviar from the serving station and headed to an important-looking table. The darts were pinned on its two occupants. When he was less than three feet away from the table, the emails transferred from his widget to the Cream's devices—a centimeter-long widgets set under their fingernails. The data from the table's occupants also transferred to his widget by the time he finished serving the table.

He was about to reach the next dart when he heard a commotion. It came from a table near Caspian's.

A Cream was yelling. Other guests had gathered around her. Aryabh saw four heavily armed guards rush to the scene. In the middle of the flamboyant, glittering crowd, he saw a glimpse of a hunched white shirt and shiny eyeglasses.

Aryabh's heart sank in a way he didn't know it could.

CHAPTER 18

"His skin touched my dress! I felt it and...then he smiled, that psychopath!" Aryabh heard the frantic yells of the Cream. He rushed towards the commotion.

In the center of the opulent circle formed by gaped mouths and disgusted faces was Kenai. He was on his knees with his hands behind him and two guns pointed at his head.

Aryabh clicked a button on his widget. Should anything happen, a member was supposed to send an emergency signal, indicating everyone to leave the venue immediately. Then he wandered around the ground's entrance to locate one of Caspian's security guards.

When he found a guard with a green dot above his head, he paced towards him, the serving tray still lifted above his shoulder. "Help us get out of here or you get dissolved with us," he said.

The guard flared his nostrils and clutched his gun, and then dropped his gaze when fear caught up to him. "Okay. But if I get caught in this..."

"Spill." Aryabh cut him off.

"The second gate in the back is open. No PacaEyes in that section. I will inform my people. They'll let you leave," the guard said, shaking. "But fast and never show your face again."

When he turned to leave, Aryabh placed his foot before him.

"Not so soon. There..." he signaled towards the ruckus in the distance. "You see that server on his knees? Get him out too."

"I am not doing that," the guard said through gritted teeth.

"I have heard they slice you open before they fry you with radia—"

"Okay, okay. I'll bring him to the back gate. Give me some time."

Aryabh moved away from the guard and clicked the button on his widget again.

"Back entrance, second gate." He sent the message to the members. "I'll get Kenai."

He was about to leave but he walked behind the guard instead and whispered in his ear, "I know people. If something happens to that server, I'll make sure they fry you extra crisp."

The members who were scattered around the ground walked towards the back gate one by one. Aryabh followed them and waited for Kenai at the exit.

He hugged his arms and paced near the gate, with his eyes glued to the ground's direction. Pain arose in his chest as he fought the fear of not seeing the dumbest person on Earth again.

From a dark passage on the side, the guard approached. Kenai slouched behind him.

Aryabh let out a deep breath and walked up to them. The guard looked around and freed Kenai's hands. "Get away from here before they figure it out," he said, his body still shaking with fear and exhaustion.

Aryabh glanced at his roommate. Kenai stood frozen with terror, his arms still on his stomach as if they were cuffed, and eyes staring at the ground, not blinking.

"Run!" the guard yelled.

Kenai didn't move.

Aryabh grabbed his shirt's sleeve and sprinted towards the main road. He exited the gate and entered an extensive parking lot. The stadium's floodlights that swept across the ground helped him navigate the jungle of cars.

They ran for minutes without stopping to breathe. When they crossed the middle of the lot, Aryabh heard a sound.

Footsteps.

But they didn't come from behind them.

He looked to his left. In a parallel aisle, he saw two heads gliding above the roof of parked cars, their footsteps as quick and frightened as theirs.

"It's not the Rodents," Aryabh mumbled as if to console Kenai. "Probably members. Come on, this way!" They diverted from the runners and entered another lane.

"Pick up your fuckin' pace!" Aryabh yelled when he felt Kenai's limp hand.

Kenai snatched his hand from his grasp and halted behind a limo. He held his waist and took deep, loud breaths. Sweat and tears dripped from his agonized face.

"You are mistaken if you think I wouldn't leave you here," Aryabh said. "I am not dying because of you." He turned and ran towards the street.

Kenai leaped and ran behind him, his lungs screaming. His fisted hands swung back and forth as he wiped his face and pushed his glasses to keep them from falling.

When they reached an open space, Aryabh heard the footsteps again. So did Kenai. They turned around.

Two people were running towards them. They were wearing white shirts.

"Dev and Gany," Aryabh recognized.

Kenai squinted. In the distance, behind Dev and Gany, he saw three people emerge from the parked cars. Air escaped his lungs. His mouth went dry. A chill ran down his sweaty spine.

"Aryabh...the guards!" he yelped. "They are after your friends. They have weapons!"

"They will not shoot. They want us alive. Come on..."

A sound like a whiplash echoed in the air.

One guard had fired a Shark. A wire ejaculated from his widget. At the wire's end, a sharp claw spread its mouth open and locked onto Gany's Achilles tendon. The second guard fired another Shark. It clawed at Gany's nape. She dropped to the ground.

The third guard Sharked Dev.

Loud moans reverberated through the parking lot.

"Oh god!" Kenai moaned too. He leaned to run towards the members.

"The fuck are you doing!" Aryabh pulled his shirt.

"The guards are far away. I don't think they can see us. We can carry Dev. Look, he is still walking."

Aryabh observed the guards. Kenai was right. They had not seen them. All three guards were busy de-clawing Gany and ridiculing Dev, who was trying to limp away from them.

"Shove your messiah complex somewhere else," he said.

Then he grabbed Kenai's elbow and started running again. Kenai ran too, but stared behind. He didn't stop looking until he saw Dev getting Sharked again, not until he saw his silhouetted body drop to the ground.

Dev's screams earthed in Kenai's ears forever.

When they reached the outside perimeters, Aryabh stopped. Without moving his head, he gazed in all directions to look for PacaEyes. He pretended to crack his neck to look above him. No Eyes were watching them.

"They'll sweep the entire area in a while. We'll have to hide here someplace until then," Aryabh said.

He led Kenai towards a string of cars parked alongside the street. An older car grabbed his attention. He cracked the password on the driver's door and got inside. Kenai followed him to the back seat.

The car reeked of cigar and overpriced cologne. Aryabh crouched on the floorboard behind the passenger's seat. Once he felt safe in his spot, he let out a quiet, tired breath. Next to him, Kenai breathed like a broken engine.

Aryabh scooched towards Kenai when he felt exposed to the streetlight, his shoulder pressing into Kenai's knees.

Kenai pushed him away.

"The fuck!" Aryabh grumbled and crouched again.

"Don't touch me. You are horrible! We...we could have saved them," Kenai cried, his face covered in sweat, tears, and snot.

Aryabh ignored him and turned on his lenses. The headline of *The Earthler News* popped up in his vision. Sadistic bastards, he cursed at the PacaDiscipliners.

"You are the most heartless person I have ever met."

Aryabh switched to maps to figure out a safe route to Café Sobak.

"They were your friends. We were just standing with them this morning," said Kenai as he remembered Dev's kind smile when he had fist-bumped him a few hours ago. "How do you sleep at night?"

Aryabh shot towards him and grabbed his collar. "I sleep at night just fine. You know who shouldn't be sleeping? You! If you had leashed your tomfoolery, I wouldn't be crouching here like a rat and they wouldn't be dead. *You* are the fuckin' problem. Your life must be a fantasy land with lemon soups and cooking-is-therapy and journaling every single day. Mine is not. I have sliced myself raw all my life to survive. I won't risk it because of an ignorant airhead like you. You think you get a higher moral ground because you wanted to save them? You just came back from serving wine to a bunch of people whose most thrilling form of entertainment is to watch people get irradiated. You work for a man who makes a living off of slavery and exploitation. So you don't get to sit here and judge me. Get your head out of your ass!"

Aryabh released Kenai's shirt and trashed him towards the

door. He sat back and looked outside the window on tiptoe.

Still empty and cold.

They stayed in silence in the car for an hour before leaving. By four in the morning, they reached Café Sobak.

"Can I go home?" Kenai asked, his eyes red with pain and fatigue.

"You can't. Follow me."

They walked into an alley next to the café. Aryabh knocked on the wall at the end of it. Two slow knocks followed by three fast ones.

A door opened through the wall.

"Good. Two more to go," Dima spoke to the room inside and let Aryabh and Kenai in.

More than a dozen Farm members filled the restaurant, all sitting in silence in different corners. Caspian paced towards Kenai as soon as she saw him, her hair disheveled, her suit creased.

"No talking to the guests!" She stood a foot shorter than Kenai, even with her heels. "How hard is it to get that inside your thick skull?"

Kenai dropped on a chair and stared at his lap. He slid his glasses back to their place. He was miserable and scared before, but Aryabh's words had overwhelmed him with guilt too.

"Messed up the whole plan," said another member from a corner. "We worked for months on this. Something needs to be done about him."

"He didn't just talk to her; he started complimenting her," Caspian added. "He was smiling! I saw him. I was at the next table."

Her attire, her Cream accent, and her audacity got on Aryabh's nerves. "Cut him some slack," he said. "If it wasn't for your unreliable source, this wouldn't have gone so far. You said that security won't be a problem." He couldn't believe he was defending Kenai because he was as mad at him as everyone else.

"I bought a few guards, not the whole fuckin' army!"

"You bragged like you did," said Aryabh.

"What the hell is your problem with me?"

"Will you all shut the fuck up and get an update on Dev and Gany?!" Shiaya screamed. Dev, who had been Shiaya's roommate for years, was her closest and only friend.

"I cannot track them, Shiaya," Dima said, "but I have wiped off their widgets, just in case. Arkas is also looking for them. Don't worry. Master Snowball has asked some members to rake the venue. They'll be here any minute."

Aryabh knew no one was returning, but he kept mum and hoped Kenai did too.

He had never seen the Master before, nor had a lot of members. Was it safe to be in that room when he came? Why was he risking everything by working with the Farm when he was so close to his own plan? He should get out before it was too late.

Caspian's nail played a notification. She read the message and cupped her mouth.

A few seconds later, all the widgets in the room buzzed. It was the Pacamounts. Dima read the message aloud.

"Two homicidal anti-Pacas arrested at the Pacalympics event. Weapons and explosives found on them. Both terrorists to be dissolved this morning at 1000 hours. Citizens appointed for this week's Onlooker Duty to report at 0900 hours."

Dev and Gany's pictures were published below the lie about ammunition.

Everyone froze in shock. The Farm had not lost a single member since most of the current members had joined. Kenai showered fat tears on his shirt. Shiaya sniffed in her chair with her face buried in her knees.

> The Pacamounts prided themselves on having zero prisons on Earth in their realm. That's because they dissolve everyone who's arrested for a crime, small or big. It is exactly what it sounds like. Perpetrators are enclosed in a glass coffin and fried with radia-

tion until they are disintegrated. It doesn't always start there, though. First comes the Pre-Dissolution routine. If they think the arrestee holds important information, they are carved and tortured before they are executed. They dissolve people for crimes as trivial as touching a Cream or breaking a signal. The accused are picked up from their homes in the darkness of the night, first Sharked and chained, and then tortured until radiation and death take away their pain.

"Why are we letting a non-member who got two of us killed sit here and listen to our conversation?" Caspian asked Dima. "Why is he even alive?"

"Spoken like a true Rodent," Aryabh commented.

"How dare you!" She leaped at Aryabh.

Dima put his towering body between them.

"How can you let him talk like that, Dima? Forget this cross-eyed idiot." She looked at Kenai. "We shouldn't even be trusting him." Now at Aryabh. "He is not one of us. I can feel it. I know he is going to be the death of us. Who knows...maybe he is the one handing our information to the Rodents."

"Sounds entertaining, coming from someone who was sitting at their table and breaking bread with them." Aryabh moved around Dima and spoke to her face.

"I am more a member of the Farm than you'll ever be." Caspian's eyes glistened with rage. "I put my life in danger every day," she said, more to herself than to Aryabh. "Every morning I wake up and watch them suck every drop of our blood. I have to witness that. My helplessness has more loyalty than your fake-ass efforts." She took a deep breath. "Talking about loyalty, you know whose blood runs deep with the Rodents? PacaChildren. I see your kind every day too, working like puppies for them, licking ass and wagging tails for an ounce of recognition. I have never seen a single PacaChild going against them. Ever! That's what you are—a PacaChild, and that's what you'll always be. Their baby."

Aryabh stepped in her direction, but Dima pushed him away. "Enough of this foolery. This is not the fight we live for!" he barked. "Everyone, take a seat and sit quietly. It's been a horrible night already."

Aryabh looked around. Most members were looking at Kenai, discussing his fate. Fear rose in his chest again. He spoke to the room. "Why is everyone shocked by something we all know can happen if we are up against the Rodents? Anti-Pacas die. That was what we signed up for. It's not a big deal. Move on. What's our next—"

Before he could finish, a hot punch hit his jaw. It was Shiaya.

"Say one more word about the dead," she said, "and I will kill you."

Caspian smirked.

"Bitch!" Aryabh turned to hit Shiaya, his eyes and nose watering from the punch.

"Stop. Right. Now!" Dima screamed. "I know you all are upset. So am I. But what we don't do here is disrespect our friends or be okay with their death. We do not question each other's loyalty. When we doubt each other, we create cracks, and that makes us weak and easy to break." His arms and jaw flexed with tension. "We don't move on..."

The burst of the backdoor opening interrupted Dima's speech. A short round man in a suit that didn't look like it was his rushed in. Two men followed him with a body in their arms.

"Master Snowball," Dima addressed the man in the suit.

Everyone got up from their seats and stood at attention.

"Gany!" Shiaya ran to the men with the body. "Is she alive?"

"Alive but wounded. Sharked at three places," said Master Snowball as he marched across the room without making eye contact with anyone. The muscles of his face moved as if he were processing a surfeit of information at the same time.

"Cameras?" His voice was shrill, a contrast to his face.

"All dead," Dima answered.

The two men placed Gany on the large corner table where Aryabh had had his first meeting with the Farm. She was unconscious, but her chest undulated gently. There were bruises on her face and body and her legs looked deformed.

"We can't take her to our doctors right now," the Master said. "It's bad outside. A Cream member informed me about her. They were being taken to the Dissolution Chamber when I rescued her."

"What about Dev, the other guy?" Shiaya asked.

Master Snowball shook his head.

Shiaya rubbed her temple and went back to her seat in the corner.

Caspian grabbed a solid glove from her purse and put it on. She traced her gloved hand over Gany's body from her battered head to her bloodied toes. When she noticed everyone's baffled faces, she said, "Cream technology. We'll know what's broken. Dima, there is a can in my purse. Spray it all over her wounds."

Dima obeyed.

Caspian removed the glove and read the results in her peripheral vision. "Her left ankle and right kneecap are fractured, multiple tendons and ligaments are ruptured, and her left shoulder is dislocated. They must have started the Pre-Dissolution routine on their way to the chamber. Master..." she turned towards the rotund man, "...if you permit, I can call one of my contacts. She can fix this. She is Cream but safe."

"Not here and not with us around. Send your contact here." Master Snowball sent an address to Caspian's widget. "I will have someone drop the girl there. Meanwhile, I want all of you to disappear for a few days."

"I can take everyone to my aerial house and we can fly to the North Atlantic," Caspian offered again. "I know a secluded spot above the water where I often go. The house is licensed by the Rodents, and so it won't be tracked or surveilled. I can bring it to the nearest landing site."

"Fine. I don't want everyone in the same place. Scatter." Master Snowball walked towards the door and spoke without looking back, "When this is over, I want to know exactly what happened." He adjusted his suit jacket. "To take back what's ours."

"To take back what's ours," said everyone.

Master Snowball left. Caspian followed him to bring her car around the backdoor. Murmurs filled the café again.

Dima sat at a table and allotted hiding spots to everyone. "Arkas will stay where he is. Aryabh, you are coming with us. And your friend..." He looked at Kenai.

"I know he is a dingbat, but you can trust him," said Aryabh. "What about her? We can't go with her."

"Not again, man," Dima shook her head. "I'd trust her with my life. There. Assured now? Now, go wait for her car. You can bring the dingbat. Can't leave him alone, anyway."

Seven members, including Dima, Shiaya, Aryabh, and Kenai, got into Caspian's car. Dima sat in the front with Caspian, Kenai sat in the middle seat between Aryabh and Shiaya, and the three remaining members took the rear seats.

Caspian dictated the address, and the car sped up. It hovered ten feet above the ground and merged with the street on the upper-level. Then it darted like a bullet above the sea of ground-level traffic.

Aryabh watched as Caspian messaged someone. He cursed Dima for looking outside the window instead of monitoring a Cream who was taking everyone to an unknown location.

A message of his own flashed in front of his eyes.

Lyra: Beat Sagan at chess today. Arabian mate! You should have seen his face.

Aryabh didn't have time to think about Sagan's face or what chess was. He was brainstorming ways to get rid of the group before Caspian boarded them on a Cream house. Who knew what awaited there!

He looked again in the front and glimpsed Kenai in the

rearview mirror. He remembered he was somehow now responsible for another being.

Next to him, Kenai's heart hovered like the car. He looked outside as if he were riding a scary yet fascinating rollercoaster. It was his first time riding the upper-level. His adrenaline shot up as his fear turned into excitement. It was, however, sitting next to Shiaya that thrilled him more than anything. His cheeks flushed as Shiaya's thighs touched his. He shuffled away to avoid offending her with his touch, even though he loved every moment of it.

The rush of the speeding car and the presence of a beautiful woman next to him tickled his stomach. A smile lit up his tormented face.

For one brief second, he forgot that the world was a dreadful valley of nightmares.

CHAPTER 19

It was almost four in the evening when they reached the landing site. Caspian's two-storied black aerial house was waiting for them.

Everyone watched in disbelief as an enormous drone, bigger than the house, ascended from its roof like a hat. It stood still twenty feet above. Four sturdy cables ejected from the corners of the house and met at the center of the drone. The drone clasped them with its bottom.

Caspian escorted the members inside the house.

"House, fly me to location D," she commanded.

"Flying to location D," said the house. The blades attached to the drone's four circular wings spun, and the house lifted from the ground. "Welcome home, Caspian. How are you on—"

Caspian muted the house. Behind her, the members gaped at

the interiors.

The glass walls of the house and its snowy white ceiling wombed a lavish living room and an elongated dining area. A four-foot black crystal chandelier hung from above. Thirty miniature chandeliers fixed around its oxidized silver body cast their lusty brilliance on the marbled floor. Connecting the floor to its high ceiling were four pilasters. Gourmand scents of coffee, white flowers, and vanilla emitted from the intricate art carved on them. At the center of everything was a flamboyant seating area filled with leather sofas and armchairs.

"Wow!" Kenai couldn't help himself as he looked at the massive dining table next to the living room. A great amount of colorful food lay on its transparent glass.

"I had messaged the servants to stock the house with food and drinks, told them I was having a party," Caspian said. She glanced at a camouflaged screen behind the dining table. It hid a black and yellow flag with a red shark on it. "Please make yourself comfortable. I'll be upstairs in my bedroom, making sure we are safe. You can open the curtains once we reach cruising altitude," she said and left.

The members stood stiffly at the main door, unable to move ahead, as if their very presence would stain the house. A visceral emotion stormed them as they watched the life of a Cream.

Once the house stabilized, Dima turned off the chandelier and opened the curtains. Bright but gentle light flooded the house.

Everyone scattered and sat in different corners. Dima walked to a velvet wingback chair and was lost in thoughts as soon as he sat in its plush seat. Two members stroked the fabric of a throw blanket and discussed its cost. Shiaya sat on the steps leading to Caspian's bedroom and rested her head on the glass wall. With vacant eyes she stared at the orange horizon that was ready to devour the sun.

Kenai sat on a dining chair and ogled the enormous amount of food on the table. There was bread, cheese, curries, roasted meat, stir-fried vegetables, fried potatoes, desserts, and many other items he didn't even recognize. Below each item the table reflected its nutritional value and calories. He wondered if this was all real—hovering cars, flying houses, the sights outside, and the surplus amount of fresh food.

His stomach screamed with hunger as he looked back at the spread. Everyone was already miffed with him. He didn't want to offend them by reaching for the food. So he sat there with a wet mouth and longing eyes, waiting for someone else to proceed first.

Still at the main door, Aryabh glanced at a small screen by the entrance. It read the altitude and displayed a map. They were flying at 10,000 feet. The house had flown past land and was now gliding over the ocean.

Aryabh popped two AwakeTabs and lit a cigarette. He took a puff and peered below at the blue water as the leftover sunrays turned it into a pot of gold. He had never seen an ocean before, let alone be in the middle of it. The panoramic view soothed him. He couldn't escape the group as he had planned, but he felt safer now in the air than he had on land.

"No smoking in the house," Caspian said as she came down from her room with a small drone in her hand. She entered her parents' address on it, attached a package, and sent the drone flying from a mail window.

No, it's not safe here, thought Aryabh. He had to get away from Caspian as soon as possible. Her voice rang in his head again, calling him 'Pacamounts's baby'.

"Letting my family know I am traveling," Caspian explained to Dima. "I told them I was stressed because of last night's event. Sent them souvenirs of VacaRealm. Hey...why is no one eating? Come on, I am famished!"

Kenai sprung from his seat.

Caspian sliced a raspberry tart for everyone and filled eight crystal flutes with champagne. Her table dictated her portion size. She obeyed the furniture.

"To Dev," she said, raising her glass.

Everyone except Aryabh and Shiaya joined the table, raised their glasses, and picked their plates.

"Three beds are ready upstairs," Caspian said. "Three of you can sleep on the sofas here. I'll turn them into beds. Shiaya, you may sleep in my room."

Kenai's gaze shifted from his plate to Shiaya and her swollen eyes. He took her plate of tart from the table and placed it next to her on the steps. "I am sorry for your loss," he said.

Shiaya's eyes stayed glued to the ocean.

He carried another plate to Aryabh. "Are you...still mad at me?"

"No."

"I am sorry. I didn't want that to happen."

Aryabh too stared at the ocean.

"A man lost his life because of me. I am terrible. And I was asking you to help them. The guards could have killed you too. I am so dumb." Kenai lost interest in his tart.

"Not your fault," said Aryabh.

"What?"

"You acted like a human among a bunch of people who are under the delusion they are one. Not your fault."

"You are really not angry with me?"

Aryabh replied with a cloud of cigarette smoke.

"You don't want to talk, that's fine, but eat this. This is not something you get to eat every day. Just look at this." Kenai looked at his plate and smacked his lips as his interest in the tart returned. "Do you know, these round red things on top, they are real fruit! It also smells like it was made today."

Aryabh tried to kill the tart scent with another puff of smoke.

"Please stop smoking, Aryabh!" Kenai whispered. "She will scold again. She scares me. At the café, I thought she was going to hit me." He reflected at the memory but the smell of the warm crust brought him back. "I am leaving this here. Eat." He placed Aryabh's plate on the nearby table and went back to the dining area to ravage the food.

Aryabh stood at the same spot and watched as a black sky replaced the dusk. A half moon hung just above the house. Under its silver light, he identified the outline of mountains on the horizon. The taste of nicotine dawdled on his parched tongue, evoking a haunting memory.

He was thirteen, living in the PacaOrphanage. One weekend, they took his batch to a Trunk on an educational trip. That was what they were called. It was a day of lessons. To see the privilege of being PacaChildren. To learn how inadequate and worthless life in Trunks was. How people who had to live there were deprived of the comforts that they enjoyed in Sonmanto. On such trips, the instructor would encourage the children to bully and make fun of the Trunkers.

Everyone did it gladly. Aryabh didn't. Not because he believed it was wrong, but because his loathing for the Pacamounts's authority prevailed over everything else.

One of the trip tasks was to live atop a mountain in flimsy tents. It was to teach PacaChildren about the horrors of a Trunker's life and their poverty.

At night, the orphans sat around the instructor. Each of them had to state how thankful they were to their parents, the Pacamounts. It was the oldest and the biggest boy's turn. He was known for bullying the younger PacaChildren.

"I am extremely obliged to our mighty saviors," he said. "When I grow up, I am going to spend every second of my life serving them. I will destroy anyone who hurt our parents!" He cupped his right palm and placed it across his chest. Then he howled, "For relentless power, we strive and ride."

Everyone mimicked his chant and applauded, except for Aryabh. By that age, his hatred for the Pacamounts had been instilled in his marrow.

When everybody was sleeping, Aryabh's legs were pulled from the door of his tent. Three PacaChildren dragged him to a cliff. The oldest boy waited there, smoking a cigarette. They laughed and then took turns to trash Aryabh. One punched him in the nose, while another smashed his ribs. A girl, smaller than Aryabh, pulled out a chunk of his hair and giggled.

Aryabh hissed through his teeth with watered eyes.

"That's for not clapping." The big boy blew the last smoke and rammed the cigarette butt into Aryabh's neck.

Aryabh coughed and clenched his jaw so hard that he thought he was going to crack his teeth.

They all laughed and joked again.

Once they were tired of tormenting him, they went to the instructor and complained about the boy who had not only refused to clap but was also smoking. The instructor punished Aryabh by not permitting him to sleep inside the tent. Aryabh didn't argue. Instead, he went to the same cliff and collected the cigarette butts that the group had left behind.

It wasn't fall yet but there was a nip in the air. Aryabh scooched to the edge of the cliff and wrapped his sleeping bag around him. From his uniform pocket, he grabbed the lighter he had stolen from the bullies. He lit one butt and sucked on it. Smoke clouded his mouth. A gagging burn flared up his throat and nostrils. He coughed and gasped for air.

Then he took another drag.

He smoked until it eradicated the foreign feeling in his mouth. His bruises and aches itched for comfort, but he suppressed those too.

As the fog cleared, he saw a few Trunks below, nestled between the mountains. They lit up like an unimportant constellation. Illuminated winged roads wound through them like fluorescent snakes.

Aryabh watched, thinking about nothing. He sat there staring into a merciless void, smoking and fighting the pain. If a fragment of innocence had survived in him at the PacaOrphanage, it had escaped that night. It was the day he had bid goodbye to the little part of him that believed he was not alone in this world.

Fourteen years later, cigarettes still nauseated him, but it reminded him of the fact that he walked alone on this planet, that he was strong and he resisted.

"Aryabh!" Kenai broke his reverie. "There is something in this house!" he whispered. "You'll faint on the floor if you see it."

Aryabh stood unmoved, deafened by the sight—a path of light tossed by the moon on the ocean's surface.

"Are you okay?" Kenai asked.

Words came out of Aryabh's mouth. "It's the twenty-second century but we are still living in the dark ages. We shouldn't be living like rodents in a box when some live like this."

Everyone had gone off to bed. Dima was sleeping on one of the sofa beds while the others were upstairs.

"You want to live like this?" said Kenai.

"No. You wouldn't understand."

"I do." Kenai stayed silent for a while. Then he grabbed the punching device from his pocket. "Do you know what this is?"

Aryabh shook his head.

"It's a tally counter. My father gave it to me. He got it from his father who got it from his. It's over two hundred years old. You know what its purpose was?"

"To antagonize people."

"You are funny," Kenai waved, "but no. It was made to keep a count of cattle before the invention of...whatever they use now. But that was not how they used this piece. My father said that for generations our foreparents worked as prison guards in one of the biggest prisons of our continent. This little device..." he rolled it between his fingers, "...was used to count prisoners. Every day, my ancestors used this to keep track of criminals. A machine I now use to take god's name."

Aryabh leaned closer with his ears opened wider. "Your father was a prison guard?" he asked.

"Not my father, my grandfather. My father was...is a carpenter. You see, there must be so many prisoners that they needed this to keep track of them. Do you think that was not a dark time? I don't think any time was a better time. People have been bad and good in every generation. I think it's about how we live *our* life. You and I."

Aryabh couldn't believe this was coming from the same man who had a special tool to scratch his back. 'No feeling is more satisfying than getting your back scratched. Wanna borrow?' he had said.

Aryabh almost smiled. He grabbed the tally counter from Kenai's hand and felt its cold metal. It was a rusty, walnut-sized, round device. The surrounding paint had faded, but the embossed numbers were still visible. The counter was at 7,262.

Holding a device from the old days brought an energy to Aryabh that he had always received from books. "Why do you keep track of how many times you repeat your deity's name?" he asked.

"I know you'll mock me, but I'll tell you because you asked. That never happens." Kenai rested his slouched back on the wall. He intertwined his fingers and rested them on his thighs. "My father built small parts of furniture in our backyard for a big Cream store. I would sit with him every day after school and ask a hundred questions. He would make me do menial tasks to keep me busy. He'd come up with these amazing stories related to those tasks to indulge me." Yearning glowed in Kenai's eyes. "One day, he told me he had built a machine that could take me anywhere in the past, present, or future."

Aryabh tucked his chin. "A time machine?"

"Yes, that. He gave me this tally counter and said that he had wired it to a time machine. When I will complete punching one million counts, the machine would be charged and activated and I could travel in time. I wasted not a single minute." Kenai beamed. "I took the counter and started clicking it day and night. I would jot down the total because it only goes up to 9999. Then one day, I lost the total count and slowly forgot all about this. Then something even worse happened. I grew up." He shrugged. "When the Pacamounts took over my Trunk and I had to leave..." His voice grew soft. "I took this with me. A few months later, I started punching the counter again. From the beginning. 0001."

When Aryabh didn't respond, he continued. "It's silly, I know. I don't believe in the time machine story anymore. But it's just something I look forward to every day. It's like a goal. Goals are good, right?"

"How far are you?" Aryabh's mocking tone had faded.

"Very close. I am nearing nine hundred thousand. I am so excited!"

"You are too tall for a five year old." The tone returned.

"I am old enough to not believe in magic, but young enough to wish for some."

"A realist."

"You won't get it."

"If you only had to finish the count somehow, why do you take your God's name?"

"That was my father's rule. He told me it had to be these exact words. Maybe he really wanted to keep me busy."

"I don't judge him."

Kenai tried to make a snarky face but failed.

"Where would you travel? If your wired machine is all charged and activated?" Aryabh asked with genuine curiosity, even though he mocked the words. Dima often talked about the happy childhood he had had with his brother. This was how Aryabh imagined they might have talked to each other.

"I'll go see my mama and baba," Kenai answered.

The concept of parents had always baffled Aryabh. He didn't understand how and why a child would be under the care of adults for years. He shook his head and felt the tally counter in his hand again.

"This is exquisite machinery." Aryabh rubbed his fingers on the numbers. It prompted him to punch the round switch in the center. With a clicking sound, the last number changed from 2 to 3.

Kenai gasped. "Oh good lord, you do not do that!" He closed his eyes and mumbled his deity's name. "Okay, you are good now."

Aryabh went for a jeering sniff but a chuckle escaped from the corner of his lips. He handed the counter back to Kenai.

"Do you know what this is? It's my Constant," Kenai stated.

"Like a control variable?"

"Huh?"

"When a scientist conducts experiments, they keep one or more elements constant throughout all trials so that they can figure out other variables. That's what a constant is," Aryabh explained to Kenai's puzzled face.

"Actually, yes," Kenai said when he understood. "Like that. It's the same with humans. A Constant is something that has been with you for a while, that reminds you of who you were yesterday and the years before that. Our life changes, people change, our world changes." He waved his hand around the house. "We change too. But to make sense of all that, or other vari...variables, we need at least one Constant. This counter is mine. When I stand in this flying house on a full stomach and look at it, it reminds me that I am the same person who was kicked out of his home. The person who begged for food in the 2nd Stratum. I keep pushing because it reminds me that things change. Everyone should have a Constant."

"Utter hogwash," said Aryabh. "That's called being stuck in the past. Anyway, I am tired; I'm hitting the hay. Night." He walked away.

"Good night," Kenai said in a dispirited tone and looked outside at the black sky.

Aryabh turned around. "I am..." he hesitated. "I don't always mean to be a jerk. Sorry."

Kenai's lips parted in disbelief. "It's all cool," he said. "I know you are a good man, Arya."

"What?" Aryabh's frown returned. "What in the world is wrong with you?"

"I thought we were sharing emotions. I..."

Aryabh didn't stay to listen. He went to the couch that Caspian had transformed into a giant, comfortable bed and lay down. He spent the rest of the night staring at the ceiling, trying to think about his Constant. He didn't have any.

The big bully from the educational trip was approaching his car. The menacing snarl magnified his face. His red pupils zoomed in and out. Aryabh yelled at Caspian to start the car. She jumped out of the window, scoffed at him, and waved goodbye. Aryabh recited his apartment's address to the car and commanded it to accelerate. The car picked up speed. So did the boy. Parts of his body, including half of his face, transformed into metal as he tailed the car. Aryabh stuck his face outside the window and asked him to leave him alone. It provoked the boy, and he leaped. He grabbed the trunk of the car and scratched the window. Aryabh watched as his mouth foamed like a rabid dog, before he turned wholly into metal. His robotic arms ejaculated a Shark and its claws locked into Aryabh's jaw.

Aryabh whimpered.

"Hey...it's okay. It's okay. It's me, Kenai. Your roommate."

Aryabh's upper body shot up from the bed. He looked around incoherently and released his breath when he figured out where he was. It was still dark outside, the moon now on the horizon.

"Are you okay?" Kenai asked.

It was three in the morning as per the clock in Aryabh's lenses. "What the hell were you doing hovering over my face?"

"Before, over there, I came to tell you about something I saw, but then you talked like never before. So I forgot about it. When I remembered again, you were already asleep," Kenai said without breathing. "I've been waiting for hours for you to wake up. Then you started crying in your sleep."

"I wasn't crying!" Aryabh grinded his teeth.

"Fine. I lied. But..." Kenai hopped on his toes. "I cannot hold in any longer. Come with me, please."

To his relief, Aryabh got up.

Kenai led him through the living room into a smaller room that looked like a recreation area. When they reached a closed door at its end, he placed his palm on the doorknob.

"You ready?"

"Why are you being a creep and snooping around in the middle—"

Before Aryabh could finish, Kenai opened the door. His eyes widened.

They entered a wide room lined with shelves, containers, and boxes. Each of those were stocked with so much food and drink that the room looked crowded. Kenai locked Aryabh's face between his palms and turned it towards the right side of the room. There, in the corner, was a tall shelf lined with bottled water. Hundreds of those bottles.

Kenai looked at Aryabh with a grin so wide that Aryabh could count his teeth. "Do you think she'll scold us if we eat some of this?" Kenai inquired.

"She wouldn't dare."

Aryabh walked to one container, grabbed chocolate bars, and chomped down on them. Kenai approached the fruit crate and gobbled one fruit after the other.

"Oh, good lord...oh god!" he chanted with every bite he took. "What is life without munching on midnight snacks in secret, am I right?" He gulped a grape without chewing it. "Aryabh, water...we forgot water!"

With stuffed mouths, they walked to the tall shelf and emptied bottles inside them.

"Why does this taste so different?" Kenai asked after drinking two bottles.

"Its main ingredient isn't urine."

Kenai laughed.

"Hey, can I make coffee with this?"

"Go nuts."

"And tea?! She has both in that box over—"

"Well, well, if it's not the hogs of Chase Street!" Caspian appeared on the door, her arms folded over a black silk nightrobe.

Kenai kicked the empty water bottles behind him. Fear layered over the face that had been full of joy and contentment.

"Great! The more the merrier," Aryabh spoke, making a teasing face. He walked past Caspian and announced loudly to the house, "Party in the storage room!"

"What the fuck are you doing?" Caspian asked him in hushed tones.

"Inviting the Farm to watch a Cream curdle."

"It's not who I am. I—"

"It'll be better if you shut up. Remember that you come from this before you pounce on me with your loyalty and heroism again. You and I will never have the same metrics," said Aryabh. "And next time, hide the flag better." He signaled towards the camouflaged screen and went to his old spot to smoke.

Kenai greeted the confused and sleepy members and took them to the storage room as if to show them a tourist site. Caspian took a deep breath, smiled, and offered to make everyone fresh breakfast.

When she came back with trays of freshly prepared food, her eyes had regained their fierceness but her cheeks were still damp. She realized it would be hard to break the wall that had now formed between her and her friends of years.

She looked at Dima. He was trying hard to shake the discomfort he now felt in her presence. So, she did what she thought she had to.

"I talked to my father while making breakfast. He had just gotten out of an emergency Rodents' meeting. I knew he was hiding something. I had to coax him a little but we've got a classified." Caspian was so desperate to prove her worth that she didn't realize a non-member was at the table. "Plan Z," she said.

"What's Plan Z?"

"The last alternative for Rodents. Plan Zenith. Their lifelong plan to take over the asteroid."

CHAPTER 20

Zenith

October 27, 2125

Lyra: You ready?

Aryabh remembered the meeting they had set up a few days ago. Amid the recent chaos, her message felt familiar and safe.

Aryabh: Give me two minutes.

He looked at the dining table. Kenai and the members were feasting on Caspian's repentance. He took the stairs and walked to an open room at the end of the top floor. At its entrance, he stood with suspicion.

It was a strange room, almost like a Pre-Dissolution routine chamber. There were mirrors over the walls and strange metal equipment all over the floor. He scanned the room with his lenses, terrified, but also partly excited. One more way to show Caspian her place.

The lenses told him they were fitness equipment used to exercise the body. Aryabh huffed at the regality.

He picked a corner away from the clutter and sat on the floor facing a floor-to-ceiling window, one leg pressed to his chest. When he reached for his widget to call Lyra, he wondered. How was it that the person he had once detested now made her way into his daily schedule? Why was he eager to share things with another human being?

He placed the call.

"Hey," he said in a flat voice.

"Hey," Lyra replied with the same monotony. "I am taking you to our observatory. The last time I rode a motorbike, I was sixteen." Her voice shook. "Fuck, my legs are shaking! I hope I don't crash. It's not even mine; it's Gryffy's. I won't be able to see you because I'll be riding, but you should be able to see my side."

"What are you blabbering? Where are you?"

Lyra slapped her head and turned on her camera. "Ah, sorry. I am nervous."

A dimly lit street appeared in Aryabh's sight. He observed all the corners of his peripheral vision and heard a slight buzzing that came from operating Zenith.

"I've hoisted my camera on a motorbike. I am going to drive. You ready to ride through Zenith?"

"Wait." Aryabh wanted to say that he was not ready to see the streets that had appeared in his dreams for years, to see the houses he longed for, to see the world that he didn't even know if he'd ever get to live in.

"We have an astronomical appointment." Lyra started the motorbike. "Can't wait."

Aryabh pressed his eyes, took a deep breath, and embarked on a journey he would remember until his end days.

Lyra rode through the convergence of dawn and morning while the Zenithers enjoyed their REM sleep. Her spirit took flight, and so did her loose sweater and hair, as she rode along the empty streets. With Aryabh by her side, she felt as if she were traveling on these roads for the first time.

"Wicked awesome!" she cheered as her body lifted above the seat.

Aryabh laughed.

Lyra showed him Kish's bookstore, the Borlaug market, and Balin's house in the distance. Zenith's O'Neill Hospital, its restaurants, and a small garden passed by. Aryabh read signs of Ammal, Daly, and Bose Streets and saw the cultural center he had read about. It resembled Earth's buildings of worship.

"It sucks that I can't show you the Orwell Library," said Lyra, almost screaming through the wind in her face. "It's on the other side."

"This is enough."

Despite knowing it was a virtual simulation, Aryabh's faced turned upward in desperation, trying to feel the air of Zenith. Soon, he said to himself and savored the remaining ride.

Lyra stopped in front of a tall building.

"Where are we?"

"William Herschel Observatory," she said and detached the camera from the motorbike. "It's not just Terra Perigee today; we'll also get to see Super Earth tonight."

"In English."

"Our orbit around Earth is elliptical. Because of it, the distance between Zenith and your planet varies throughout the year. Terra Perigee is when our orbit comes closest to Earth." The image in front of Aryabh shook as Lyra climbed the observatory tower. "Now, we see Earth like you see the moon. In phases. Today, Earth wouldn't just be closest but it'll also be full, the way you see a full moon. Okay, we are here," Lyra whispered in a breathy voice.

"I thought you were going to miss it," Rahi said without looking back at Lyra, her eyes glued to a computer.

Lyra wondered if Rahi's father had told her about Sagan's misconduct in the bus.

"I wouldn't," she said.

"Take left, second door. It's open."

The observatory staff had never allowed Lyra to visit their cupola before even though she had requested numerous times. Now that she was here, there was a spring in her step.

"I can't see anything, it's all black," Aryabh spoke in her earphones.

"Sorry. I had to put the camera in my pocket. People who don't work at the observatory are not permitted here, let alone a virtual Earthler."

"Then how did you get in?"

"Rahi, our astronomer here, is sort of a...friend. I promised her I'd cook lunch for her baby shower."

"I'd have never taken you for a briber," Aryabh said, but didn't bother to ask what a baby shower was.

"Or a smuggler," Lyra added.

"Zenith's upcoming mafia, everyone!" Aryabh chuckled at his own comment. So did Lyra.

She opened the door to a small space. It took her to the upper level through a ladder. Her head emerged into a round attic, around twenty feet in diameter. She climbed and crossed her legs under her in front of a curved wall. Rahi had asked her to find a black button, which she did, and pressed it. The blinds covering the cupola's windows rolled up, revealing the dark outer space.

"These window panes are composed of four separate panes." Lyra said, her gaze fixed on the windows. "Each of them is made from high-strength, bulletproof glasses. They protect against micrometeorites and orbital debris."

"Not interested."

Lyra pushed a strand of hair behind her ears and swallowed her excitement.

"How much longer?" asked Aryabh.

Lyra checked her watch. "Five more minutes."

She stood and placed her camera on a plank behind her. Her image materialized next to Aryabh. "Can I see your side?" she asked, wearing her goggles.

Aryabh turned on his widget's camera and hung it on a hook behind him. In the observatory cupola, he appeared on Lyra's left.

Lyra nodded at him and whisked away a little, despite knowing that the person next to her was a hologram. Then she looked straight ahead and gasped.

"Where are you?"

"Somewhere above the Atlantic ocean."

"Is that the moon? Is that...ocean water?"

"Yeh. The sky is brighter here than in Sonmanto."

"Curiouser and curiouser," she muttered and gazed with her chin on her knees.

Aryabh glanced at her with fondness.

"I thought I was making your day," Lyra said. "But all I did was show you the dark alleys of a far-flung asteroid while you were looking at this." Her shoulders slumped with embarrassment. "How can you be above an ocean? Are you on an airplane?"

"It's an aerial house."

"A flying house? For rock's sake. How does it work? Propellers?"

"Why did you assume I'd want to see the full Earth?" Aryabh changed the subject. He didn't want to talk more about the hideout or why he was in it. "I am not as obsessed with it as you are. I've already seen enough of it."

"Not like this."

"Whatever."

"Excellent comeback," Lyra said. After a few moments of silence, she spoke again, "I know, you and everyone here think of me as someone who woke up one day, found out about the pretty, blue planet, and turned it into an unreasonable fantasy." Lyra crossed her legs again. Her biggest fear of being misunderstood had been long dead, but with Aryabh it revived. "That's not what happened," she said. "I did initially see Earth as an escape, the only way to get away from here, but I didn't stop there. I did my research, found places where I could safely survive. I spent my entire adult life weighing the pros and cons of moving to Earth and worrying about its repercussions. It wasn't an impulse decision."

Aryabh took a breath.

"I...get it. Even if I don't want to. I... Oh look!" Aryabh tapped Lyra's knee but it cut through her holographic image and fell on the floor. He looked away, embarrassed.

Lyra removed her goggles.

A hazy sliver appeared on the horizon. Within seconds, it grew into a prominent blue crescent.

"Nothing like the pictures you ever saw, right?" Lyra asked.

"Right."

Aryabh had never seen pictures of Earth. Based on the planet's environmental health, he had always pictured the planet to look like a sooty ball of mess from outer space. "Never thought something that has gone through all that it has can still be strong enough to look like that," he said without censoring.

"The power of resistance," said Lyra.

They watched as Earth rose like an inflated balloon.

"Your planet has survived for more than four and a half billion years, taking all the pounding it could take," she added. "It's the grandest survivor of damage and brutality."

Lyra's words pulled Aryabh's head towards her. When he shifted his gaze back to the planet, it was out in full form—a prodigious, blue orb prominent against the pitch-black space.

Aryabh couldn't trace the green patches that he had read about in old books, but he saw the white spots scattered in random patterns.

"That's the 3rd Stratum, right?" Lyra asked.

"Yes. Sonmanto is on the far right in the 1st Stratum."

"My ancestors were from the 3rd Stratum, from a country called India."

It piqued Aryabh's curiosity.

"Do you have any stories of those times?" he asked.

"No. My maternal great-grandmother was born and raised there, but all I have...had was the account of a year of her life when she was living in the 2nd Stratum."

The diary, Aryabh thought.

"And my grandparents grew up in the 1st Stratum before they moved to Zenith. So no stories of India."

"They were all over the place!"

"That's what fascinates me, living with the knowledge that there are millions of unknown, unseen places where you can visit or live someday. My great-grandmother was born in one country, lived in other, and died in another."

"I keep getting confused between country and countryside."

"Countries are how Earth was divided before the Political Fumigation. Each of your Stratum had multiple countries. Each country had a separate government, culture, and language."

"Got it."

"My great-grandma spoke four languages. My grandmother spoke two when she migrated here. My mother spoke one and so did I, except for a handful of words we know of our native language. Zenithers pride on their diversity, but when it came to convenience, they opted for one colonial language even though a total of sixteen languages were spoken by the first colonizers."

"They had other important problems to solve," Aryabh argued.

"So it's worthy of attention when a language is suppressed by an authority, but not when common people ethnocentrically suppress other languages?"

"It was assimilation."

"Assimilation is when a minority culture acclimates to a majority group and English wasn't even among the top three Terraformer languages." Lyra stated. "Zenith isn't as perfect as you think."

Aryabh didn't know how to argue and not lose, so he changed the topic. "Do you still know those words of your native language?"

"Just a handful. I knew many growing up. I used to include them in my day-to-day life as a practice. But one day, my teacher sent a letter to my parents asking them to stop me. She said it made me a bad team player." Lyra huffed.

"Which ones do you remember?"

"Ah, let's see. Haa is yes. Naa means no. Kem cho means hello. Aajo... no, Aavjo is goodbye."

Aryabh was thrilled he was recording the call. He now had a small dictionary for a non-English language.

"What else... Ann can mean food or grain. Vruddhi—that was my mom's favorite. Difficult word to pronounce. It means growth. Then, Vanaspati is for either plants or vegetation. She found that word for my Dad. He is a botanist. Oh, Vignaan is my favorite. It means science. Oh, wait, the best one for the last. Bhaad ma jaa. Go to hell!" Lyra bent and laughed, her hair falling all over her face.

"I like that too," said Aryabh.

"I am sure I am saying these words incorrectly. I always wanted to visit there and verify these pronunciations."

"Did you look up the place? India?"

"All over the web. No trace of it. Strange how places disappear even though they still exist," Lyra said as she tried to find India on the globe outside the window. "Is the 3rd Stratum like Sonmanto?" she asked, feeling exhilarated about having someone to ask such questions to.

"Don't know. There aren't many updates from that part of the world even though it's governed by the Ro...the Pacamounts."

"We have a Terraformer here, Ms Tara. Our front-door neighbor. You know, the neighborhood kids think she is a witch. They talk about how she brews potions in her secret room and walks to our district's sacred fig tree every night to talk to the spirits."

Aryabh snorted. "You believe that?"

"As much as I believe in a god."

"And that is?"

"Not at all."

"Then, what about her?"

"Oh, yeah. Sorry. I think she is from the 3rd Stratum. I always wanted to ask her about it. But...she is a tough person to talk to." Lyra looked at Earth again and breathed in. "Oh, the things I've done just to be on that," she said with longing in her eyes. "I feel...like an asymptote."

Aryabh's head turned at the mention of an unknown word.

"What's that?"

"Asymptote?" Lyra's eyes livened up too as she tried to formulate a way to explain it. "In analytic geometry, when a straight line continually approaches a given curve," she placed her palms next to each other, one curved, one straight, "and yet does not meet it at any finite distance, it's called an asymptote." Satisfied with her explanation, she looked back at the blue planet. "Earth is my asymptotic dream. An unattainable goal."

Aryabh observed her face. This time, it pinched him.

Lyra wore her goggles again. "It's so strange how things turn out," she ruminated. "I am virtually sitting above an Earth's ocean and looking at the moon. I bribed my way into our observatory and I am talking to an Earthler I smuggled in my pocket."

They both dispensed suppressed laughs.

"And that's coming from someone who sat in a jammed walk-in freezer for forty-five minutes because she didn't want to ring the hotel's emergency alarm and draw everyone's attention." Lyra liked not being an editor of her words. She could get used to it.

"People often say I am a bad influence," said Aryabh.

A laugh arose from their bellies. To Aryabh, it felt like retrieving a long-lost object from a foggy hole.

"Your shoes," he said as his eyes fell on Lyra's feet.

"Yeah." Lyra waved her hand without looking at them. "I'll tie them later."

"No, they look painfully tight. That must hurt."

"I have to tie them tightly because the laces always come off."

"Maybe they come off because you tie them too tightly?" Aryabh said, looking at her tortured feet. "It doesn't matter how much you compress, your feet are going to relax and expand when you aren't actively flexing them."

"Right," Lyra mumbled and massaged her foot. Then she turned quiet until she heard beeps. "What's that sound?"

"Notification. A news headline."

"What does it say?"

Aryabh skimmed the piece. "Marriages will be illegal starting next year and some other nonsense about the relationship contracts."

"I read that the sexual urges of Earthlers have depleted exponentially. Is that true?"

Aryabh froze at the unanticipated question. "I don't know. Maybe. It's not been any different since...I remember. What about Zenith. You people still mingle and even marry, right?"

"Yes."

"Good for you."

"Not really."

"Why?"

Lyra looked at Aryabh and sensed he wouldn't judge. So she went ahead, unedited. "Zenith is a highly accepting society. I've read old Earthler books, heard many stories of prejudice that existed when the Terraformers left Earth. Compared to that, the settlers here have created...a fairly nurturing environment. Unfortunately, Zenith has only accepted allosexuality as of yet, a side effect of a community-driven society."

"Elaborate."

"It does not accept the other kind as easily. People who do not have romantic or carnal desires."

Aryabh thought about it for a while. "I am guessing you are talking about yourself," he said.

"And many like me."

"You hate love and sex. You'd fit perfectly on Earth."

"I don't hate love and sex. It's not a decision." Lyra peeled her thumb's cuticle. "I don't even know where I stand on the whole...love and romance spectrum. This place never gave me the chance to separate affection from sex to figure that out. But, yes, sex surely doesn't come naturally to me, and that fact doesn't fit in a society whose cultural values are love, union, and procreation."

Aryabh strained his mind again as the drone's blades whirred above the house. "At least, Zenithers move according to their design," he argued. "It's so messed up here, I don't even know what I am. They modify us. They even alter our urges."

"Yeah, that's worse."

Lyra's objectivity struck Aryabh again. She was not as tangled as he had assumed. In fact, he had not seen anyone move through their life with such clarity. She had her answers. Lyra was not lost; she was confined.

"Why did you do all this for me?" he asked the question that had been nagging him. "The ride, the sneaking." He was going through the same strange emotion he had experienced when Kenai had fed him the soup. "I thought you hated being responsible for others."

Lyra huffed at the oversimplification. Or maybe it wasn't. She had lived her life doing things she had had to without seeing the person she could have been if the fences around her were dismantled. Lyra liked that person; she seemed less monstrous.

"I did it because I wanted to. Not because I had to," she said.

Aryabh leaned in with a nod.

"I've lived for almost three decades," she spoke again, "and today is the first time I don't feel miserable and alone."

Aryabh glanced back at the blue marble, the world he had grown up hating, and tried to find him in it. He saw himself as a tiny mote on the globe, running away from monsters, sitting in a threatening house in a strange room, and watching the same world from outer space. That mote on the globe looked as lost as he had always been. But even then, he felt calm and existent. A voice inside him told him he would be okay.

"Me too," he said.

Under the observatory dome of a frigid asteroid, Lyra's head tilted to the left. Sixty thousand miles away over Earth's ocean, Aryabh didn't mind her holographic head on his shoulder.

Thanks to loneliness, deception, and technology, a Zenither and an Earthler had found a fitting society in each other.

CHAPTER 21

"What do you mean by takeover?" Dima asked Caspian about Plan Z.

"When the Rodents took over in the 2020s, Earth was already in shambles. Too destructed to sustain humans. They were desperate. That was when Zenith knocked on our door. The Rodents were powerful enough by then to colonize the asteroid themselves, but they didn't know if it was habitable, especially in the long run. Plus, they had other interests here on Earth as well."

"Yeah, who else would exploit the planet?" said a member who sat next to Kenai.

"So, instead of repairing the damage, they stalled doomsday by mining the asteroid. They used the wealth made from the mined metals and geoengineered the planet with short-term, band-aid solutions. For how long that will last, no one knows." Caspian leaned over and placed her arms on the table. "But the

Rodents know one thing for sure. If one fine day the planet runs out of resources or the Earthlers revolt, they'll have a well-oiled, super-functioning asteroid in space to colonize."

"But what about Zenithers?"

"Think of the tin-can as cattle that the Rodents are keeping happy and fed. So, when the time comes to slaughter it, they'll be guaranteed a big juicy steak." Caspian felt like herself again. "Tell me, how many Zenithers live on the asteroid?"

"Around seven thousand," Dima answered.

"What's the total headcount of Sonmanto Rodents and Cream?"

"Let's see," a member said. "Each Stratum has four Rodents and around five...six million Cream? So Sonmanto has..."

"Around seven thousand Cream and one Rodent CEO," Dima answered without doing the math as his lips parted in shock.

"Eureka!"

"They are ditching all the others?"

"Most likely. They have been having issues with 3rd Stratum, anyway."

"How are they going to get rid of all the Zenithers?"

"Dad said they talked about the ZLSS switch or something...too technical. Besides, with Zenither cremation technology, it'll be a cinch to discard seven thousand bodies."

Everyone at the table reflected the horror in Dima's eyes.

"Unbelievable!"

"Who cares? They fled instead of fighting. They are not one of us," Caspian said. "But, Dima, we can't share this with Arkas yet. Let's keep him out of the loop for a while. And...the PacaChild too, okay?"

Dima didn't agree, but he nodded.

"Isn't this great news? It's win-win for us."

"It kind of is," said Dima. "We can not only use this to create..." His eyes fell on Kenai, who was peeling an orange. "Kenai, can you please check where Aryabh is?"

"Sure."

Kenai searched the house as he relished his orange, poking his protruding belly and laughing at it. He found his roommate dozing on the floor of one of the upstairs rooms. "Aryabh, why are you sleeping like a child? These windows are ice-cold. You'll freeze. Get up. Sleep on the bed."

"Stop touching me with those sticky hands!" Aryabh grumbled in his sleep.

"Okay, fine. I'll bring you fresh breakfast in a while." Kenai grabbed towels from a cabinet and spread them over Aryabh. Then he went downstairs to enjoy the luxuries of a Cream's house.

If he didn't have childhood memories, this would have been the happiest day of his life. He had profited from a thirty-minute hot shower and danced to the music coming out of a place he couldn't find. He had exhaled on the bathroom mirror as requested by the vanity counter, and was told that his oral health was critical. After emptying his bowels, the toilet had given him a health report too, which dampened his mood for a while. Then he had spent the next few days in a sumptuous robe as he watched snippets of his favorite movie on the guestroom wall. The picture was so immersive, he kept walking into it, thinking it was all happening in the next room.

To his surprise, Caspian had showed him how to download food ingredients from a complicated machine she owned. He had thanked her by giving her his mother's lemon-garlic soup recipe.

Five days later, they were back at their apartment on Chase Street. The Farm had said they were not in danger anymore, but Aryabh knew exactly why they got off easily. Caspian probably had had someone else arrested. He thought of worrying about it later, because for now he was shocked to find himself glad to be home.

Kenai, meanwhile, had been quiet.

Fearing that it was the calm before the storm, Aryabh inquired.

"What now?"

"You are my time machine, Aryabh. My tally counter worked." Kenai spoke as he placed their slot-machine dinner on the desk.

"Elaborate."

"I am a simple man from a simple land. I have never had big ambitions. I would have died content knowing that I had survived this world. But you changed my life." He sat on Aryabh's desk chair and didn't worry about its repercussions. "I have lived a better life in the last five days than all the years before," he continued. "Saw some horrible things which I will not forget until I die. I still hear Dev's screams in my mind." He teared up. "But you gave me great memories too. You took me to a house that flew above an ocean and was filled with water. I ate things I wouldn't have in my wildest dreams. I met people who were important and brave. I met Shiaya." He blushed. "All because of you. I was just a lost boy and you are my Peter Pan."

Aryabh turned away from the window and looked at him. "You know Peter Pan?" His hand went to his hip, despite him.

"Everyone in my Trunk does. It was a popular fable there. Someone's great-great-grandparents would tell stories like those and they would pass along generations."

> I had never thought of a family chain as a medium to pass on stories of the old years. My family chain was the black market that stocked my shelf with ample books and countless stories. It would have been nice to enjoy stories without fearing execution.

"That's nice," said Aryabh.

"Thank you for taking me into your world. You also saved my life, even though I messed up."

"I didn't save you."

"You did and I know why. If I get caught, I would spill everything about you and your friends. I heard from Dima that they torture until they get the information. I am sure I would crack. They scare me to death. So even though you saved me for a reason, I am thankful."

"I am hungry." Aryabh walked to his desk and grabbed a spoonful of rubbery meatballs from his plate. He tried to convince himself he had saved Kenai for the reasons he had just mentioned.

"Explain this, though," he said with a mouth full of chewed meat. "Why do you like Shiaya? You have zero things in common."

"Who wouldn't like her? She is so beautiful. And brave. Have you seen her handle things? She is so strong."

"Isn't."

"Well, she punched you."

Aryabh threw Kenai a bitter glare, his nose still sore from the punch.

"Go lick her then," he scowled. "Or maybe you already did at the house."

"What? No, no. " Kenai leaned towards Aryabh. "She was hurting, mourning for her friend. She didn't need people hitting on her."

Aryabh nodded and ate his dinner. Once he was full, he went to bed, and after days, slept without worrying about his environment.

"Aryabh!" Kenai shook him from sleep.

"I am not liking this pattern."

"Happy birthday!" Kenai yelled to the room. "It's midnight. Come on, I have something for you."

Aryabh had hated November 2 all his life. It was the day that reminded him he was a year older and still stuck on Earth.

"Later," he mumbled.

"Please. You will love it, I promise."

Aryabh breathed like a wild animal. Then he gave in. "Where are we going?"

"Grab your coat."

Kenai led Aryabh to the elevator and pressed button 125, the topmost floor of the building. "I am so happy," he bounced on his toes, "I can finally celebrate birthdays again. You are going to have the best birthdays from now on. Mark my words. Oh, on my birthday, we can go on a trip!"

Aryabh yawned and avoided the numbers on the elevator screen.

"Why aren't you excited?" Kenai asked.

"Nothing celebratory about a planet revolving around the sun and coming back to the same unimportant position."

"That's the most depressing way to describe birthdays." Kenai said without understanding Aryabh's statement. "It *is* celebratory. You circle back to the day you were born, having spent one whole year in this world. It's like a renewal."

The elevator opened. Kenai walked toward the only door on the floor and entered a password.

Aryabh looked around. "What are you doing? Residents aren't allowed here."

"I have permission," Kenai bragged, "don't worry."

As the door opened, the chilly wind slapped Aryabh's face. He embraced the open sky and looked up. A clear, waning gibbous moon stared back at him. In the corner, he saw two bottles of Pitaya liquor, his favorite, a covered plate, and a tall instrument. "Is that a telescope?" he asked.

"Yes, it is, my friend. Happy birthday again. It's yours."

"But..."

"No but. Come and see this." He led Aryabh to the telescope. "Don't move it. Just look through it."

Aryabh did.

For a second, his world stood still. He saw the one thing every inch of his being had yearned for. In the smoggy sky of Sonmanto, Aryabh looked at Earth's second moon, his sole purpose of living, and Lyra's home. It was his first time watching Zenith through a telescope.

A realization broke his trance. His insides churned. He cocked his head at Kenai. "What do you know?" he asked.

"If I snore in sleep, you talk in yours. Barely any night when you don't mumble about Zenith in your sleep." Kenai tilted his head to show how well he knew his roommate.

Aryabh felt naked. All this time, he had been giving away sensitive information about himself. What else had he spoken? Did Kenai know the things he had done?

"Stop worrying," Kenai shook his shoulder. "I don't understand half the words you say when you are awake. How am I going to understand your sleepy ramble? I remember Zenith because you have also talked about it before and then I heard it when we were in the flying house."

Aryabh inched forward. "What did you hear in that house?"

"Oh, come on. Stop acting like a PacaSpy all the time. Relax. Enjoy this moment. You have your whole life to interrogate me."

He didn't want to obey Kenai, but the view of Zenith was too tempting.

Aryabh looked through the telescope again. He saw Zenith's spaceport in one corner and its observatory cupola on the other. A few days ago, he was watching Earthrise with Lyra from it. He also saw the solar panels that were attached above the peanut-shaped asteroid.

Lyra will enjoy watching this, he thought. Just like he had liked watching Earth from their observatory. It's funny how distance makes the same place a little less loathsome.

Kenai tried to read Aryabh's emotions. "It looks like a broken piece of moon, doesn't it?"

"Yeh."

Aryabh got greedier and wished if he could see the inside of the asteroid too.

"Let me know when you have looked at it to your heart's content," Kenai said and sat in the corner, even though he was dying to ask Aryabh a million things.

How was it?

Is it what you had imagined it to be?

Are you going to live there?

Will you come back?

Why do you hate here so much?

It took a lot of self-restraint for him to not ask any of those questions. He didn't want to ruin it for Aryabh this time. Instead, he fetched a misshapen cake from the plate and readied a knife next to it.

Aryabh practiced self-restraint too and got away from the telescope. He joined Kenai on the floor and fell into a chain of thoughts. Then he said, looking in Zenith's direction, "How much did you spend on this? You don't even have a job now."

"Don't worry about that. It's a used telescope, not new. What an invention! In fact, once I save enough again, I am going to get one for myself too. Then I'll see you through it. You'll be all happy and busy with your life there on Zenith."

"That's not how telescopes work."

"You know what I mean. I'll see and just know that you are there, living your dream."

Aryabh didn't ask how Kenai had figured out so much. He didn't care. The little flake of contentment had reduced the noise in his head. He summoned the dignity to ask, "How do you do this?"

"Do what?"

"You've been through unimaginable shit. How do you not wake up with...infuriating pain and hatred? I had nothing to begin with and I still walk around like a spiteful hole of an ass. You lost everything you had."

Kenai chuckled.

"See, that's our problem. We are so calculative with pain. How much has he gone through? How much has she lost? I don't think it works that way. It all depends on how much trauma those experiences give us. Someone loses their family and still wakes up the next day feeling fine, while someone loses a month's pay and is already planning to end their life. Everyone's pain matters. Besides, having something nice and losing it is less scary than having nothing at all. You were alone all this time, God knows, experiencing what horrors. No one was beside you. It can make anyone bitter."

Kenai shook his head to stop the conversation. "Let's not talk about sad things. Look here!"

Aryabh turned towards him.

Kenai was sitting dramatically with his hands pointing at what looked like a weird grayish cake. In childish font, was a bright blue greeting on the top.

Happy Birthday Aryabh!

Kenai handed him the knife.

"This is not an ordinary cake, Aryabh. I used the flour from our IngredientSac, but the rest of the ingredients...Caspian gave them to me! Eggs, butter, chocolate, everything. We misunderstood her. She behaves tough, but she is soft from the inside. You know, she has traveled all around the planet. She has even been to a place in the ocean. An entire city sits inside the water! Did you know that?"

Aryabh knew the PacaOcean World well. That was where the Pacamounts conducted human experiments in their secret labs.

"Anyway, the cake came out perfectly. I had a bit of a problem with the shape. It's hard to bake a cake without a mold."

Aryabh realized that the improper shape of the cake was intentional. "You made it in the shape of Zenith?"

"Yes, indeed. I found some pictures on my phone." Kenai beamed proudly.

Aryabh maintained a calm demeanor, but he was exploding from within. The habit of not expecting love and kindness had been etched so deep into his humanity that he felt guilty for feeling happy. A part of him wanted to allow himself to experience it, while the other part begged him to be cautious.

He took the knife and went for the cake like he was about to stab it.

"What are you doing? Hold it this way. Cut it like how you would slice my hand if I touched your books."

"This is exactly how I would slice your hand if you touched my books."

They stared at each other for a moment and broke into full laughter.

Aryabh cut the cake and ate it. Kenai, who expected to be fed the cake, cut one piece for himself.

"It's soft," Aryabh said with his mouth stuffed with cake.

"Ahn fuffy," replied Kenai with a mouth fuller than Aryabh's. "So, what are we watching next?"

Aryabh stood and arranged the telescope without consulting his widget. Kenai was impressed. It took him hours to figure out where to point.

"Here." Aryabh directed Kenai towards the mouth of the telescope. "That's Venus, the planet between Mercury and us." His usage of 'us' surprised him. "Check out its yellowish-white spectrum."

"Wow!" Kenai's mouth hung open. He looked at Aryabh. "You know, you are the first person who didn't make fun of my strabismus."

"Your eyes?"

"Yes. Everyone makes fun of it. Even my friends did because I couldn't read well. Or catch the ball. Sometimes, I have a hard time seeing things clearly, like when we were running from the guards. It's why I wear these glasses." He took his glasses off and wiped them with his shirt. "People call me names. They don't even hire me because of it. I have always been ashamed of this disability." He blinked. "It made me feel like I don't fit. But you never remind me about it. With you, I don't feel...abnormal."

Aryabh wanted to tell him he was not special for not making fun of his disability. That it was default; what others did was abnormal. But he heard Kenai and stayed mum. Instead, he said, "You have a very distinct eye color."

"Oh, thank you."

"Now watch this," Aryabh showed him a group of six stars that outlined a kite.

"What is it?"

"It's the constellation Lyra."

"Lyra. You know, that's another name you mumble a lot in your sleep." Kenai avoided eye contact, fearing Aryabh's explosion.

But Aryabh's face went pale. More because he was taking Lyra's name in sleep than of Kenai finding out about it.

"Who is Lyra?" Kenai tilted his head to tease. "The name sounds like my ex-girlfriend's." He thought of a girl who had lived next to him in Dvedi.

"Friend. She lives on Zenith."

"Up there?" He pointed at the sky. "On the asteroid?"

"Yes. She wants to move here."

"That's awesome! You need more friends here. Is she also like you? Clever? She must be. She is your friend. And if you are voluntarily addressing her as your friend, she must be special."

Aryabh looked at Kenai as if he were making sense. He wanted to tell him he was his friend, too.

"Everybody should have a friend."

Aryabh didn't respond.

Kenai returned to the telescope. "Okay, now let's see the moon."

For hours, they talked and gazed at the sky.

Two words floated up to Aryabh's throat. He tried harder to let them out. "Thank you...for this."

"No problem, roomie. More liquor?"

"Why not!"

They sat on the floor and drank.

"Who gave you the permission for the roof?" Aryabh asked.

"Oh, it's a great story. You remember, you taught me password combinations for our building's maintenance room so that we could borrow their NanoCleaner?"

"Steal."

"I place it back," Kenai justified. "Anyway, a few weeks ago, the maintenance guy was on our floor, fixing something on the ceiling, and his ladder cracked. He was holding on to the vents. I had to run to the maintenance room and hack the password."

"That's not hacking."

"I did everything you taught me," he boasted. "Then took the ladder from the room and held it for him until he got down. Oh, he must have been, like, three hundred pounds. I almost broke my back."

"I teach you to crack passwords and this is what you use for?"

"It was good I helped. That was why he gave me the roof password. He warned me to not to share it with anyone. Why would I, right?"

"What was the password?"

Kenai held his phone to Aryabh's face. Aryabh copied the password and saved it on his widget, just in case.

"You do know," he said, "we could have just cracked the roof's password too, don't you?"

Kenai's eyes grew big.

The next second, Aryabh's roaring cackle swaddled the desolate night of Sonmanto.

CHAPTER 22

THE EARTHLER NEWS

November 2, 2125

THE PACAMOUNTS CREATES ANOTHER SOURCE OF INCOME FOR EARTHLERS

The PacaLabs scientists revolutionize healthcare with FatEndow—a procedure where fat will be transferred from one body to another, beating obesity in Cream and malnourishment in NonCreamers with one stone. Along with healthy fat, NonCreamers will earn a hefty incentive. Five pounds of fat...

Kenai stared at Lyra. She was wearing goggles on a deadpan face. He couldn't decide what was crazier—meeting an alien or watching a lifelike image of a person who was sitting inside an asteroid in space. Lyra, on the other hand, looked around the house to avoid eye-contact with him.

Aryabh gazed at both and wondered why they were socializing in his apartment. How had he reached this point in his life?

While they were celebrating his birthday, he had received Lyra's message asking to meet urgently. Kenai had figured out the situation and insisted that he wanted to meet her, too. Aryabh had said yes, knowing that Lyra would never accept the proposal. But, to his dismay, she had agreed to meet his roommate.

His willingness to bring together two people he had cheated and lied to baffled him. Aryabh's rational part berated him for acting like a reckless fool, but he had long abandoned heeding to that side of him.

Lyra, I am sorry this letter has turned into a lengthy, weird memoir, but I have to tell you this—out of all my bizarre days here on Earth, the day you met Kenai was the strangest of all. I don't know why I agreed to Kenai's childish request. I pretended there was no escape, but I have gotten out of worse things. I guess I was happy. In my own sick way, I was proud that two people were willing to spend time with me. For once in my life, I wanted to be surrounded by people who didn't despise me. I was drunk on the promise of camaraderie.

This time, Lyra had materialized on Aryabh's desk chair in front of the bunkbed. Around her was a faded visual of her bedroom, its edges like an incomplete painting. A messy bed lay between her and the blue wall behind that was covered with pictures of Earth.

"Do you know it's Aryabh's birthday today?" Kenai initiated the conversation, pushing the fancy new glasses up his nose.

"No, I didn't," Lyra replied and looked at Aryabh. He stood at the window, hands folded on his chest.

Kenai had hoped she would convey birthday wishes. But her indifference that had disappointed him quickly turned into relief. He was happy that Aryabh had finally met someone very much like himself.

More minutes passed in awkward silence, peppered with Kenai's random remarks from the bunkbed. He made one last effort. "Let's play a game!"

"No," Aryabh said, thinking of a way to end the weird meeting.

"It will be fun. We used to do that, play group games on birthdays. What do you say, Lyra?"

"Okay."

"Then it's done!" Kenai stood from the bed. "Ooh, let's play Crap-a-Tat!"

"No." Lyra and Aryabh both spoke at the same time.

Kenai's eyes pendulated between the two. He leaked a naughty smile. "How about Truth or Dare? It's an old-Earth game we used to play in our Trunk."

"How does that work?" Aryabh's interest piqued at the mention of 'old-Earth'.

"You spin a bottle. Whomever the bottle points at must choose between Truth and Dare. If they select Truth, they have to answer a question honestly. If they choose Dare, they must do what we ask them to."

Kenai looked at Lyra with raised eyebrows. She nodded. Then he looked at Aryabh.

This is easy, Aryabh thought. He would choose the former option and use his natural talent to pass off anything as truth. Playing this was better than whatever game Kenai might suggest next.

"Fine."

Kenai fetched the empty pitaya bottle from the kitchen and kneeled on the floor. "Lyra, can you see this bottle?" he asked.

"Yes."

"Okay, it's spinning, people."

The bottle stopped and pointed its mouth at Kenai.

"Oh, no. Dare! No, Truth!" He squealed and tapped his thigh. "Come on. Ask me something."

Lyra gave in and asked, "What's something you have never told anyone?"

"There isn't anything," mocked Aryabh.

Kenai twisted his face like an important carrier of secrets. "No, my friend. We all carry secrets." He crossed his legs and sat on the floor. "Okay, ready? When I was twenty-four, I was married for two months."

"What?" Aryabh uttered as if he were cheated. He had not seen marriage in Kenai's PacaProfile.

"Not according to PacaLaws, but we had a small ceremony in the Trunk I was living in at the time." Kenai's face went pale. "She left me, telling me I was too emotional and naïve."

Lyra and Aryabh both expressed their concern by nodding and looking back at the bottle. Kenai spun it, and it pointed at Lyra.

"Me, me. I will ask." Kenai raised his hand. "Did you ever have a lover?"

Aryabh cringed at the sound of the last word.

"No," said Lyra. She tapped her feet and scratched her thumb. Despite the goggles, Aryabh felt her eyes peer at him.

"Even genuine friendships are hard to come by," said she.

Kenai raised his thick brows and spoke, "I truly hope you find someone." He looked at Aryabh to nudge him, but to his delight his roommate was already looking at Lyra with a kind of affection Kenai had never seen on his face before.

Aryabh had forgotten the sense of time and space. When he found Kenai looking at him, he cleared his throat and asked him to spin the bottle.

"Oh, look at that!" Kenai screamed as the bottle pointed at him again.

Aryabh wanted to dare him to complain about Neslo at the PacaMarket again, but before he could begin, Lyra and Kenai had already started their game.

"Okay, Truth again. I am too chicken for a Dare." Kenai giggled.

"Do you trust Aryabh?" Lyra asked.

Kenai looked at his roommate. He raised his chin and said, "With my life."

Aryabh hugged his arms as he scavenged his vocabulary for a response.

"I know who it's going to be now." Kenai relieved him and spun the bottle again. "Yes! I knew it."

The bottle pointed at Aryabh.

"Tell me..."

"May I?" Lyra interrupted Kenai.

"Oh, sure. Go ahead. Crack him!"

Lyra looked at Aryabh in the same distinct manner. Aryabh watched as she dug around her scabbed thumbnail. "Did the transit station server also bring you my diary along with my documents?" she said.

Aryabh's breathing stopped. He disconnected the call and Lyra's image extinguished.

"Shit," he mumbled.

"What happened? Why did you shut it off?" asked Kenai, baffled and disappointed.

"I need to sleep."

Aryabh turned off the lights and lay down on his bed.

"But what's wrong? What was she asking about?"

"I'll crack your skull open if you say another word," said the rediscovered rational part of Aryabh. It needed quiet to think and plan.

What do I do now? Would you report me to Zenith officials? What were you thinking about me? Would you stop hating me if I explained why I did it and apologized? — those were the thoughts running through my mind that night as I exploded from within. Had it been a few months ago, I would have turned on my autopilot mode and my survival instinct would have taken care of my problem. But that day, I struggled between wanting to save my ass and our friendship. Had I known it was the last time I was seeing you, I would have... I don't know what I would have done.

Aryabh wanted to smash his head on the headboard. His mind flared up with unnecessary questions—questions he would have never asked himself if he hadn't met Kenai and Lyra.

He switched off the side that caused him uncontainable fury

and got to work.

He knew Lyra would take days to decide if she should rat him out, but he had to be prepared. He identified all the people he had touched for his Zenith's plan. When he heard Kenai's snore, he went to the kitchen and called the first person.

Shiaya answered on the first ring.

"Did you tell anyone about our deal?"

"What?" Her voice wasn't sleepy at three a.m.

"About my plan and the documents? Don't you dare lie."

"Listen, you ungrateful asshole. I had told you if I get my gold, I wouldn't talk about it even if I was sliced in half. And I did get my gold."

"Then how did she find out?"

"Who did?"

"The girl...the Zenither."

"Fuck a luck!" Shiaya remembered something. "Dima told me the other day that Arkas was fussing about the Zenither passenger list. He was arguing with his contact on Zenith."

"Who is his Zenith contact?"

"The one who sends him the passenger list every time."

"Who. Is. It?" Aryabh grinded his teeth.

"Calm down, jackass. I don't know. Some big chef at a fancy hotel."

CHAPTER 23

Zenith

November 1, 2125

Lyra met Gryffy's frown when she reached Zenith's radio station.

"Sorry I am late," she said as she pulled her sweater and rearranged the strap of her messenger bag across her chest. In her head, she was still reliving the time she had virtually spent on an Earth's aerial house four days ago.

"That's for the best." Gryffy flashed a fake smile. "Shouldn't have relied on the ex-wife."

"What happened?"

"Ren is not letting us on her program." Gryffy placed her hands on her hips and chinned towards the station. "This is exactly why I hate monopoly. We need more radio stations."

"Why? She was excited to host us."

"She *was.*"

"Is she doing it because of you?" Lyra asked.

"No. We are great on that front. But she didn't know our content when she agreed to my request. When I showed her our 'Back to Earth' flyers right now, she lost it."

Lyra wanted to mention why that was one of the many reasons she didn't like Gryffy's idea of making flyers. They reduced their broad idea to a dozen vague words and made it unnecessarily controversial. But she kept mum.

"Get out of here, you sociopaths." Ren, the RJ, emerged from the entrance of her studio. "Had I known your foolish plans, I'd have scripted a satire on you."

"Had I known how close-minded you are, I'd have worn pointier heels." Gryffy pointed her foot at Ren. "Now stop polluting the air and go back to your cave."

Lyra threw her head back in shock.

"Wait," she whispered, and blocked Gryffy with her hand. "Look," she told Ren, "you don't have to agree with us. You can even debate with us on the show. Just let us have our say. Wasn't that the whole point of your program?"

"You, the master-planner!" The RJ walked a few steps towards them. "Stop explaining my own program to me. Shove your agenda somewhere else. Now, off you go, shoo!" She waved her hand and turned to leave. Then she stopped to speak again. "Don't forget to tune in to the first fifteen minutes of my show tonight. I am going to do a poll. Send A for Fuck Lyra. Send B for Fuck Lyra."

"You stubborn witch..." Gryffy rolled her sleeves and moved towards her ex-wife. Lyra stopped her again, her eyebrows almost hugging each other with amusement and frustration.

Ren gave them the finger and went inside.

"It's okay. Maybe this wasn't a good idea," said Lyra. "I knew this is how everyone was going to react."

"Oh, for god's sake, Lyra. I want to root for you but you have to fight too. How are people going to believe you when you don't believe in yourself?"

"I see their point too. There are so many lives at stake." Lyra let one of her mind-windows open. It showed her the repercussions of her hasty decision. "What if I am wrong?"

"Then pick a side even if it's wrong. You'll at least know you went down fighting for it."

"That sounds heroic in theory but is unreasonable and irresponsible."

"Well, then I don't know what else to do." Gryffy threw up her hands. "All I have is my loud mouth. I'll yell as much as I can, but it's you who has to change minds."

Lyra blew air, not knowing how to explain herself. She had to try. Gryffy deserved it.

"For now, all I need is a small chunk of rational people who are willing to discuss this with an open mind. Once they listen to what I have to say, and once I hear their opinion, I'll be more assured of my idea. I'll have a stronger voice."

"Oh-kay..." Gryffy squatted on the ground and scratched her nape. Lyra sat on the ground too. "You sure you don't want the Zen Mavericks to do the talk?"

"Yes."

Lyra's eyes wavered from side to side as an idea orbited her head. "I am going to regret this, but I have a plan."

"What do you need?" Gryffy asked.

Lyra twisted her mouth and bit her inner lip. She looked at the space where Ren had stood. "Courage," she said as her stomach fluttered.

And the will to manipulate, she thought to herself.

Lyra's hands went on autopilot, and her brain split into two as she stood in the hotel's kitchen. One part of her brain did the thinking while the other analyzed those thoughts. When it got too noisy in her head, she distracted herself by reducing the stock. Skimming always gave her a semblance of control.

Her eyes brightened as she scooped another ladle full of scum from the surface of the gurgling liquid.

She was enjoying the trance when she felt a presence behind her. She jumped. The ladle slipped from her hand and fell into the stock. "Oh, Chef!" She let out a breath and retrieved the ladle from the hot liquid with her bare hand and wiped it on the apron.

"I am sorry, Lyra. I am so sorry," Balin said and held Lyra's shoulders. Her own shoulders were drooped a few inches lower than usual, and so were her burgundy hair.

"For what?" Lyra wriggled out of her grip.

"It was me. You couldn't go to Earth because of me."

When Lyra didn't respond, Balin fell on the chair that often lay in the kitchen corner, dusty and ignored, her face disarrayed.

"I know you followed me to the Council of Zenith," she said. "Jevic told me you were asking him about me."

The fake pleasantness on Lyra's face disappeared.

A few weeks ago, she had gone to Balin's office to drop the buffet menu. On her table, she had found a paper that read 'Passenger List'. It was a list of people who were traveling to and from Earth. Lyra knew it was not an information that the Council distributed like a newspaper.

Firstly, because of curiosity and then suspicion, Lyra had traced Balin's relations with the officials at the Council. Jevic, the administrator, provided Balin with the list every two weeks.

Lyra had tried to come up with all the reasons why a chef might require a list like that. But she couldn't stop thinking about the disappearance of her own documents. There was a connection; she was sure of it but she couldn't see it. The fact that Ms Clia, despite her position, had failed to find out what had happened baffled her more.

She had tried many times to ask Balin about the list but she couldn't. There was a part of her that was a slave to authority and it disgusted her. She couldn't find the courage to confront her boss, especially in the matters of Earth. Then distractions came in her way and she kept postponing the conversation.

"I didn't follow you," Lyra told Balin. "I saw the passenger list on your desk. But thanks for coming to me so soon."

"Honey, I didn't know about the damage the list caused until yesterday. I swear—"

"Just," Lyra gritted her teeth, "tell me what's going on."

"You remember I told you about my brother-in-law? Nico's brother, Arkas? I can't get into how he moved to Earth because that would put Nico in trouble, but Arkas wanted to leave Zenith. He never fit in here. Always out of place, always makin' trouble. We didn't support his decision, he was only fourteen, but we also didn't oppose it. He was like my baby. Most people here don't know about him."

Lyra tried to connect the dots in her head. All she wanted to know was how this had anything to do with her trip. But, she leaned on the kitchen counter, folded her arms, and kept mum.

"Arkas is in a rebel group on Earth called The Farm. They...oh, you don't have to know what they do." Balin waved. "Nico, that little softie! He thinks Earth can change. That there is hope and all that fluffy idealism. But he can't run to Earth to fight as Arkas did, and so he does all that he can from here. He provides the group with his strategic guidance and I try to help them by giving insider information about Zenith. In return, Arkas smuggles Earthler ingredients, seeds, spices—"

"The wild fennel." Lyra knew Balin had lied about the fennel buds. She had even looked it up in her father's academic books. Fennel had never grown on Zenither land.

"Yes. Arkas sent me those."

"How is this related to me?" She formed a link but erased it.

"I give the passenger list to Nico and he forwards it to Arkas. Your name went on the list too. I don't even read it; I swear. I didn't know you would end up being deported because of it. I didn't—"

"How would a list lead to my deportation?" Lyra's chest grew warmer as she repressed another thought.

"I swear on my garden, honey. I meant no harm."

But she couldn't repress her temper. "The bush you are beating around is dead. Just tell me what I asked."

Balin's eyes grew wide. "Right...right. I think because of that list, someone knew you were visiting Earth. They were waiting for you at the transit station, and stole your documents."

"Why would your brother-in-law steal my documents?" Lyra straightened and leaned forward, her nail peeling her cuticles.

Balin stood from the chair and walked forward. She held Lyra's hands. "No...no, honey. Arkas might be a little disoriented, but he is the most honest person I know. He would never do that. He told me someone got hold of the passenger list, someone from their group."

"Who was it?"

"Arkas says he knows who did it and is going to catch him soon. He will solve this, I promise." Balin nodded repeatedly.

"Who is he?" Lyra's stomach churned, as if she were falling into a deep abyss after being cut off from a rope.

"I don't know, but we'll find him. He will pay for this, I promise. Do you forgive me, Lyra?"

"Is this guy...a hacker?"

"Maybe." Balin scratched her belly. "Oh wait, yes! He is a hacker. That's what Arkas said when he first told me about this."

"I need to go." Lyra removed her apron, placed it on the counter, and walked away.

"Honey, wait."

She turned around, looked Balin in the eye, and said, "All these years, I've not crushed a single lime before shifts."

Unaffected by Balin's frightened face, Lyra left the hotel and went to the Alvariño pond. She sat on her boulder and fought a violent wave of thoughts.

Aryabh had cheated and used her.

The second wave that hit her was of anger from feeling like a fool. Even in her lowest times, she had not allowed herself to feel obtuse. Because she knew she wasn't. Then how had a stranger managed to not only trick her and destroy her life but also become the sort of friend she never had? Why did he intrigue her? Why did she crave a connection so much that she had overlooked the obvious motives? Why did she ditch her gut instincts?

All her questions pointed to one answer—Zenith.

This place had made her lonely, obtuse, and desperate.

The skeptical side of her prevented her from sharing a few things with Aryabh, and for that she was glad, but she had shared enough. Her mind projected all the memories and conversations she had had with him since day one. It all became clearer to her, like wiping steam off a glass.

He had messaged her on purpose, pretending to be messaging someone else, and befriended her.

He had identified her weakness and taken advantage of it.

He had sent her a document-folder with a map of Earth on it, knowing that she would use it.

It must be the server at the Spacebucks. She had checked her id to confirm her identity because of a beverage that Aryabh had recommended.

He had stayed in touch to keep track of her.

He had always wanted to come to Zenith.

He wanted her documents, most likely her badge, to forge them.

Heat flared up within Lyra. It bled when she dug into an old scab around her fingertip. She was angry not just because Aryabh had conned her, but also because a part of her always knew that something was wrong. She had been sucked so deeply into his friendship that she hadn't even allowed herself to investigate.

This place had made her lonely, obtuse, and desperate.

She was done. The time for being nice had passed. Her vulnerability had been proven as useless as her shields. She needed to grab what she wanted. No more failures. Just two things. One—get out of here, out of this loneliness, obtuseness, and desperation, and for that if she had to use fear and manipulation, so be it. Two—she had to make it impossible for Aryabh to ever set his foot on Zenith.

On her way back home, as the rooflight of the asteroid dimmed, she thought of ways to confront Aryabh. She wanted to hear his justification, after which she would report him.

By the time she reached home, she had also worked out how

she was going to make every single person on Zenith listen to her.

Lyra entered her room and dropped her bag on the floor. She sat on the foot of her bed and looked around. The debris of her broken aspirations littered the walls. She remembered how she had felt when she had hung those Earth pictures—clever, ambitious, and alive.

This place has made her lonely, obtuse, and desperate.

She fell on the bed and lost the tight control she had had over her tear ducts. For hours, she bore the pain that she wanted to inflict on Aryabh.

When she finally got out of bed, she messaged him to meet urgently. He gave the excuse of his roommate, but he wasn't getting out of it. Lyra agreed to meet Kenai too. That way, she'd get to see the gullibility of one more person who trusted him. Either way, Aryabh would not live another day thinking that he had fooled her.

The meet, however, didn't go as planned. When she saw Aryabh, her anger turned into regret. His face reminded her of the last time they had talked, the most honest and fulfilling conversation she had ever had with anyone. She realized why she hadn't been cautious. In the daily dullness of life, he was a constant intellectual stimulation. Their views barely aligned, but it felt like they were on the same trajectory. He had triggered her to bare her demons. Ironically, Aryabh had been the safe space she had always searched.

Lyra deeply regretted losing his friendship.

She had wanted to ask him why he had done it, even though she knew why. She wanted to say, "You are a fraud who pretends to be self-righteous and now you are going to pay for it." That's what she had practiced. But Aryabh's roommate had started a game and that had led to a complicated moment.

She had blurted a combination of words she hadn't planned on saying. Her dramatic confrontation had amused her. Aryabh had understood her jibe and disconnected the call. Not that she had expected more from him. He would rather disconnect than apologize.

But she didn't know she might have seen the last of Aryabh.

CHAPTER 24

THE EARTHLER NEWS

November 5, 2125

HUMANITY TAKES A GIANT LEAP WITH THE BIGGEST SPACE BANNER EVER!

This just in—Swarms of 42,000 light-reflecting satellites will be used to create the biggest space banner yet. The Pacamounts flag will be broadcasted for its inauguration, after which the banner space will be open for bidding starting December 25, 21...

Kenai looked at Aryabh with concern and curiosity, his body seesawing on the upper bunk. Ever since their call with Lyra three days ago, Aryabh had not properly eaten or slept, let alone talked with him. He wanted to make sure his roommate was okay. But every time he tried, Aryabh scowled.

To get rid of Kenai's prying, Aryabh locked himself in his secret library. With careful hands, he opened an envelope he had fetched the previous night. From it, he pulled out a metal sheet the size of a wallet. It was disfigured on purpose to make it look old. He gazed at it like a weary wanderer looking at their home. His new name and a child's picture glossed on his brand-new Zenither badge. He imagined himself as a Zenither. It made him smile.

Outsourcing the badge's final embossing was a risk he had to take. He couldn't have figured it out himself in such a short time. Now that the badge was in his hand, he could start wrapping it up. Before Lyra took any action or the Farm figured out what he was up to, he had to get out of Earth. Besides, he had a nagging feeling that someone was watching and following him. In the last few days, his suspicion had only gotten stronger. He felt it in his gut—the red eyes and the lurking shadow that disappears when he turns around. It was impossible that there would be no repercussions after the Pacalympics escape.

Aryabh looked around the dusty shelves and created a mental check-list.

One—erase his identity from the Pacamounts's records. He had been wiping bits and pieces of his digital footprint ever since he had received Lyra's badge from Shiaya, but it was time to obliterate Aryabh from the PacaProfile completely. The job position he had worked for would be occupied by a dummy identity. Aryabh made sure that when the Pacamounts figured it out, it would lead them to an endless trail. It pleased him that the futile investigation was going to leave them confused and angry.

Two—leave no traces of his physical existence, including the library. The thought of leaving his closet full of books agonized him. The stories within those pages had made his life on Earth tolerable. An idea crossed his mind—to lend the books to Kenai. He rejected it that very next second. His roommate was too Kenai to handle contraband. Apart from books, people also had been a witness to his identity, but as far as the Pacamounts were concerned, if it was not in their database, it did not exist.

Three—pack and leave. He had rented a hotel capsule until he got on the space elevator to the transit station. It was not safe to live in his apartment after getting off the grid. He would check-in tonight and connect with the Zenither embassy the day after. He would tell them he was a lost Zenither kid who wanted to return home.

That was it. Aryabh would then expire.

"I'll be gone for a few days," he said as he got out of the

kitchen.

Kenai jumped from the upper bunk. "Where are you going?"

"Need to handle a few things."

Four—say goodbye to Kenai. He didn't know how.

But he wanted to make sure Kenai was taken care of after he left. He had transferred enough money to Kenai's account to cover two months' rent. Half a dozen IngredientSacs would be delivered to their apartment in a couple of days; so he would have food to eat. He documented everything under Kenai's name so that he had the authority to decide. Once he was on Zenith, he would find better ways to support him.

"I know you did something bad to Lyra," Kenai mumbled. "She sounded hurt. I am never wrong about such things. What did you do?"

Aryabh grabbed a backpack from underneath his desk. "Just told her something she didn't want to hear."

Kenai followed him around the house as he collected things to pack. "I don't think so. She was telling something about the transit station. Come on, you can tell me. You'll feel better."

"I told her that whatever happened on the station, with her documents being stolen and all, happened for the best," Aryabh said whatever crap his mind supplied to his mouth.

"But that's mean!" Kenai towered Aryabh, who was shoving six bottles of AwakeTabs in his bag. "That many bottles? Where are you going?"

Aryabh was not ready for the nightmare that would ensue if he told Kenai he was leaving for Zenith, and so he made up a story. "I...am going to find that place Lyra wanted to visit." He said the first thing he could think of and was surprised by his own words. He touched Lyra's great-grandmother's diary inside his bag. Within its pages rested his Zenither badge.

"What?" Kenai scratched his bushy head.

"That place where her old people met, the one she couldn't find on the map."

"Oh, my word! Really?! That's so thoughtful. She deserves

this. You have such a big heart." He shook Aryabh's shoulders.

Aryabh imagined doing something like that. Just the thought of it made him feel inauthentic. He retracted his shoulders from Kenai's grip.

"I am not sure how long it'll take, but listen carefully now." He turned towards Kenai. The jovial face of his roommate looked back at him. It was impossible, even for Aryabh, to miss the affliction that lay deep beneath the big, toothy smile.

Aryabh's chest tightened.

"To help Lyra," he said, "I have to leave my job and stop working with those people. The ones we stayed with after Pacalympics. You cannot tell anyone where I am going. This hunt might take days, weeks. Don't go looking for me, don't contact me. I will call you. You got that?"

"I won't. But I am so proud of you. Not many people in this world have the courage to correct their mistakes. You have my full support. I will keep your secret for as long as you want."

"Don't even ask about me to anyone, okay?"

"Yes, yes. I promise." Kenai raised his palm. "We have consumed each other's body wastes. That creates a special bond, you know? We are urine brothers."

"For fuck's sake, why do you have to put it that way?" Aryabh looked at the water bottle he had filled with the recycled water and now had second thoughts about taking it with him.

Kenai kept tailing him even after the discussion, and so Aryabh distracted him by clicking on a switch and turning their bunkbeds into a single bed. Kenai pushed his glasses up to his wide eyes as his upper bunk cascaded next to the bottom bed.

"We could do that? Why didn't you tell me?"

"You can use it this way while I'm gone."

Kenai jumped on the bed and spread his wiry arms wide. They no longer stretched outside the mattress.

Aryabh placed his bag by the door and went around the house again to make sure he hadn't forgotten anything. His eyes landed on the telescope sitting in the corner. His first birthday present.

If only he could take it with him! He hoped it would entertain Kenai on lonely days.

"You are leaving already?" Kenai shot up from the bed when he saw Aryabh tying his shoelaces.

"I am late."

Aryabh headed to the door and glanced at his apartment. There was no longing or remorse. It felt as if he were shedding a filthy, worn-out pair of clothes that he had worn for too long.

"You are coming back soon, right?"

"Yeh."

Aryabh imagined Kenai living alone in Sonmanto. The thought horrified him. Then he looked at the floor and mustered the courage to speak his mind. He owed it to the only person who cared for him in his drawn-out life. "Stay cautious...and alert," he said. "Always. Stay out of trouble. Be aware of your surroundings all the time. When you are walking, keep glancing at your shoes. It gives you a wider peripheral vision and hides your face from the PacaEyes too. Be unpredictable. Run to any-where but here if someone is following you. And act like you are being watched all the time, okay? And for heaven's sake, stop talking to everyone who crosses your path. Be careful. Stay out of trouble..."

"You already said that."

"I have messaged you an address. Go there next week. You'll have a job. And...don't let anyone treat you like that asshole manager of yours." Aryabh looked at his feet. "Not even me. You...don't deserve that. And be careful."

Aryabh forgot what to do with his hands or eyes or body. He shifted his weight from one leg to another with his thumb between his shoulder and the strap of his backpack.

"What a day!" Kenai said. "All this is coming from a man whose response to 'how are you?' is 'no.'"

A smile appeared on Aryabh's face. "I'll...I..."

"I'll miss you too," Kenai said and hugged him.

Aryabh touched his back with his arm for a brief second,

retracted himself, and rushed out of the house.

"It's called selflessness," said Kenai.

Aryabh turned around. "What?"

"The thing that's troubling you. You are doing something for someone else expecting nothing in return. Probably for the first time. It's called selflessness. This is going to be good for you, helping Lyra, I promise. Just don't cheat this time. Or be mean." Kenai pointed his head towards him. "Don't worry about me. You'll be back before you know it."

Aryabh nodded and walked towards the elevator.

"All the best, Arya." Kenai sing-sang. "See you soon." And swung by the door frame.

"Oh, for fuck's sake, go inside!" Aryabh said his last words to his roommate and entered the elevator.

Kenai shut the door. His chest pumped with pride as he looked at Aryabh's empty desk, not knowing that he, too, had had the last glimpse of his dear friend.

"Hotel Ranko, Shellec Street, by bus," he ordered his widget.

A map formed in front of his eyes and a voice hummed in his ears.

"Good evening, Alsy. Welcome to PacaMaps. Your destination, Kilpington Square, famously known as Sonmanto's Tech-Paradise, is a forty-eight-minute ride by Bus 82C and..."

He selected the bus route.

"While you wait for the PacaBus, select a product that interests you. Specially designed to enhance your bus experience. We have mind-boggling products such as ear pods, eye masks, eye blinkers..." He shut off his lenses and headed towards the bus stop.

Walking on the street was Alsy, a 27-year-old Zenither who had lost his parents to a wild accident on Earth and now wanted to go back to his homeland. Aryabh had finally erased every single trace of his identity from the Pacamounts's records. If they were to look into PacaProfiles or the list of PacaChildren or the past occupants of PacaOrphanage, his name would not be found.

He felt no loss in shedding his identity.

It was a day since he had left his apartment. The trip to his black-market book supplier thereafter had been worth it. She had agreed to take care of his secret library for a small fee. A room full of free contraband and a payment? She was ready to kill for it.

Aryabh used the remaining hours to work out a detailed plan. With Kenai in the house, he knew he would have missed a few things.

He indeed had.

There was no contingency plan for how he would deal with Lyra once he was on Zenith. From what he knew about her, he was sure she wouldn't create trouble for him. Or maybe she would; Lyra was unpredictable.

Aryabh decided to worry about it once he was on Zenith. It would have been easier if he hadn't acted like a fool and showed her his face.

> I have many regrets in life, especially after I left
> my apartment, but I will never regret one thing —
> meeting you. I was too arrogant to admit it, but on
> the bus that night, I missed you. It hurt me to think
> I'd never regain your friendship.

When Aryabh reached the bus stop, he stood in the corner and thought about the Farm. It wouldn't be long until Arkas figured out everything with the help of the chef. He was not one to be quiet about it. That was why Aryabh had kept his number and email active under an alias; to keep track of the development.

You must have realized by now that I worked with the Farm, one of the biggest anti-Pacas groups of 1st Stratum. What is the extent of their power and network, I still don't know. But in the short time that I pretended to be one of them, I learned that I had the potential to be something bigger and better. Maybe that was why I tagged along with them long after I was done using them. It was as if their purpose validated my indifferent existence. In a way, they showed me a side of me that I could have been if I didn't have Zenith.

The bus arrived. Aryabh scanned his widget at the door. An automated voice came from the driver's seat.

"Alsy, you are now on PacaBus. A manual has been sent to your number. Earthlers caught disobeying the laws will be PacaDisciplined or dissolved. Thank you, Alsy."

Aryabh deleted the manual without opening it. He quickly inspected the seats and took the one with the least number of people in its radius. Luckily for him, it was past midnight and the bus wasn't as packed as it was during the day.

It was a chilly night. He buttoned up his coat and looked outside the window. As the bus rolled through Chase Street, he glanced at the skyscrapers, the colossal stores, and the offices; all steeped in decay. He hoped it was his last time seeing them. To-morrow morning, he would visit the Zenither embassy and recite the whole spiel. If the emotionally charged email he had sent to Zenith's Head of Earth Relations, Mr Zaif, worked wonders, he would be on his way to Zenith next week.

Hope and optimism struck Aryabh. The nagging feeling that he was being followed was gone too. He leaned back on the seat, pulled his left foot to his hip, and looked outside again.

The bus approached his own building, a ginormous concrete

block perforated with hundreds of square windows.

Aryabh bent and looked up, hoping to catch a glimpse of Kenai by the window. Before he could identify the 94th floor, the bus had already passed.

A minute later, the neighborhood PacaMarket arrived. He saw the usual line of the homeless people sleeping on the street, their frigid, malnourished bodies covered in thin sheets. The same warmth fluttered in his gut. He pressed his arms and scanned the line. Neslo's stool was missing and so was he.

A few weeks ago, he had forced Kenai to complain about Neslo to the PacaMarket where the homeless sat. If Aryabh wasn't mistaken, it had pushed Kenai on the verge of tears.

"What has the poor fella done to you?" he had said.

Maybe they had taken the complaint seriously and thrown Neslo out. It didn't satisfy Aryabh as much as he had imagined.

He dragged his sight away from the outside and studied the inside of the bus. Most passengers were dozing off like tired dogs. The woman two seats in front in the opposite aisle was wearing blinkers on her eyes, while a suited man three rows behind him was staring at the roof of the bus like a dead body. The outline of his iris was blue.

All the faces made Aryabh feel as if he had stepped in fresh vomit. It was why he had always hated public transportation. They were a reminder that he was part of that crowd.

Once he felt secure inside his surroundings, he turned on his number. There were four missed calls from Kenai. He sighed with frustration. You can tell someone to act a certain way only so many times, he thought. When he called him back to threaten, Kenai didn't answer.

There were also eighteen missed calls from Dima.

The nineteenth call rang.

Aryabh had to answer it to know what they had on him.

"Where the hell are you? I've been trying to reach you since morning," Dima barked in a low voice.

"I was—"

"Have you been to your apartment recently?"

"No. Why?"

"I have some bad news. They...I am sorry...they took your roommate yesterday in the middle of the night."

"Who took my roommate?"

"The Rodents. They dissolved the boy this morning."

CHAPTER 25

His heartbeats ricocheted inside his chest. Did he hear that right?

"You sure?" Aryabh asked.

"Yes, we verified. He is not in the news yet because it was a raid Dissolution. I am sorry. He was a good lad."

"Why him?"

"That's what we're working on with Caspian. We think they were keeping tabs on him ever since they caught him at the Pacalympics. Caspian is sure they didn't follow us to her house because the rest of us are okay. But not for too long. Your friend saw us. He was even in Sobak. He didn't look like a person who could hold one's own against the Pre-Dissolution routine." Dima paused and spoke again, "Everyone is going into hiding again. I suggest you run too. I am just confused why they didn't take you."

Aryabh wasn't.

They were not just being tailed since the party; they were being followed way before that. He had noticed it for the first time when they were driving to the Pacalympics. All this time, he had thought someone was following him, but they were after Kenai. As far as he was concerned, his digital footprint was a ghost. He had always erased his tracks, but not Kenai's.

Their house and bills were under Kenai's name, and so was the car that they had rented during the Pacalympics. Looking at the apartment, no one could detect that it was housed by two residents. The walls were covered with Kenai's pictures. The closet had his clothes. There was one desk and one chair. It now had one bed, and the kitchen had a secret library.

A few days back Kenai had also...

"You there?" Dima said.

"What do you want me to do?"

"You've lost the right to ask that. You are not with the Farm anymore. I just wanted to tell you to stay away from your apartment." Aryabh heard the regret in Dima's voice. "Look, boy, we know everything. Arkas is hunting for you. Even I can't stop him. Just...stay away. You played us. So this is a big gentle fuck-you. Goodbye." Dima ended the call.

The next second, Aryabh's fingers, even though they shook, moved as if on their own accord. The devices of a dissolved prisoner are kept in custody for twenty-four hours for fingerprints and other investigation. They are then sent to the PacaCyber Force to dissect every single information on them.

Even with a faltering mind, Aryabh had accessed Kenai's phone, transferred all its data to his own widget, and wiped it clean within minutes. He had installed a spyware on Kenai's phone the day he had moved in. Just as he had done with all his past roommates.

When the bus stopped at the next stop, he alighted and walked towards no destination. The sticky Sonmanto smog pressed at his skin and the rowdy wind rattled in his ears. He shivered and entered a dark, landfill alley. Trash was mounted alongside the tall walls of the buildings. It reeked of fermented garbage and rotted waste.

Flashes of Kenai's face obstructed Aryabh's sight while his voice stormed in his ears. He hugged his arms, rubbed his chest, and forced his senses to go numb.

An incomplete thought clicked again.

For his birthday, Kenai had accessed the restricted roof of their building. He had borrowed the password from someone he had assumed was a good person trying to reciprocate his help. It had happened not long before the Pacalympics, where the Pacamounts might have followed him for the first time. The maintenance man must have ratted Kenai out.

His roommate's face flashed again.

That asshole, Aryabh thought. He had never been the best judge of character.

Aryabh's palms balled into fists and his breath grew heavier. He stopped and stood still in his spot. For the first time in his life, he didn't know what to do. The thought of going back to his suffocating underground hotel room traumatized him. There was no Farm.

Lyra would never talk to him.

He was alone.

Then his eyes fell on his wrist. He turned on his lenses and checked pending calls and messages. Among the multiple messages from Dima, Arkas, and his clients, there were two voice messages from Kenai.

His heart pounded as he selected the first message.

A familiar, over-excited voice whirred in Aryabh's ears.

"Did you find it? It would be nice for you to have it on your journey. Use it every time you cheat. Or when you are mean to someone, so that you realize how often you do it." Kenai giggled. "That will make you stop."

Did he find what?

Aryabh played the second message.

"Did you see it? Come on, answer the call. Are you not answering because I called you Arya? If you are mad about the urine-brothers comment, I am sorry."

Aryabh pushed the pods into his ears, hoping to hear more, but the message had ended. Those were his last words to him.

He replayed the messages and wondered what they meant. He grabbed his bag and went through its contents. Between the folds of his T-shirt, he felt a cold metal device. When he pulled it out, he had to make a conscious effort to breathe.

It was Kenai's tally counter. Its count was at 0000.

"What do you think of yourself?" Aryabh mumbled. "Why do you always have to cross boundaries? Why did you call and leave messages when I clearly asked you not to?"

He kicked the curb with sheer force, crushing his toes against the concrete. "Fuck!" He bent over with pain. The metal corners of the tally counter jammed in his fist. He was holding on to his foot when his wrist vibrated.

It was a message from Shiaya.

"1803 Golan Street, Apt. 712, if you need to crash. The Farm won't know. Sorry about your roommate."

No way could he trust Shiaya. For all he knew, they might all be waiting for him. Maybe they had caught Shiaya too.

Aryabh walked to the bus stop and took a bus to her apartment.

He stared at Kenai's tally counter throughout his ride. In return for getting him killed, his roommate had left him the one thing that had meant the most to him. His Constant.

That insufferable bastard.

CHAPTER 26

Zenith

November 8, 2125

All her life, Lyra had tried to stay away from attention. Growing up, she would occupy lonely corners of crowded rooms, walk in the shadows of objects and subjects bigger than her, and reach places on time, not because of punctuality but to avoid attracting eyeballs if she entered late. She took buses during off-peak hours, made an excuse of stage-fright when asked to give the graduation speech, and steered clear from asking questions even when she had many—all to avoid attention.

As if years' worth of avoided attention was out to avenge her, Lyra had become the most popular citizen on Zenith, and not for the right reasons.

The RJ, Ren, had not only made Lyra the talk of the asteroid but also turned her from an unknown chef to the 'Back-to-Earth Girl' overnight. Murmurs and despising looks followed her everywhere she went.

Her one escape, Aryabh, didn't exist anymore. She was tempted to go to Mr Zaif to file a complaint against him. But she wasn't getting her money back, nor the time she had lost. All it might do would get Aryabh arrested, or worse, executed. As much as she detested him, she didn't want that.

"You have been pretend-sleeping since six a.m. The Science Day event starts in an hour. You might want to get out of bed," Sagan spoke from Lyra's bedroom door.

To commemorate scientists and their contributions, the Terraformers had set November 8th as Science Day, a day to celebrate the field that had helped them establish a colony on an asteroid.

"Thanks. I couldn't have read the clock on my own," said Lyra.

Sagan tried to read her face but it was hidden under her blanket. "You are not obligated to attend. I have reminded you that every year," he said.

"And I'll be there on time, like every year."

Lyra got up and headed to the bathroom.

For the first few years of Sagan's life, Keid had conveyed that he was not ready to be a healthy parent. He had spent the remaining years without trying. Lyra never argued. She attended all of Sagan's events, including the parent meetings at his school.

When her brother was four and had refused to go to school on his first day, she had tried to pick him up and carry him to the waiting auto outside. She imagined that was what her mother would have done. Sagan had kicked her and pulled her hair with such strength that Lyra had tumbled to the ground. Her wrist still throbbed from the injury at times.

On that day, Lyra had yelled at her brother, raising her voice for the first time, and had come close to hitting him. Later, they had both cried in different corners of the room, despising each other.

Sagan was now in the seventh grade. As Lyra sat in the school park, surrounded by overzealous parents, she wondered how she had made it so far.

"She is the one who wants to take everyone to Earth," a man spoke behind Lyra.

"I know," whispered another. "I heard she is telling everyone we will die in fifty years. Such a negative woman, scaring everyone!"

Lyra took a deep breath, folded her arms, and stared at the stage with her thoughts in her sight. She pushed both shoes off her feet and clutched the ground with her toes. The damp green grass sent a sense of calm to her body.

Kids in various avatars appeared on stage one after the other. They performed skits and gave speeches. One student had dressed up as Lyra's mother and pretended to treat a sick, plushy gorilla on the stage. After him, a small girl walked up with long hair, round eyeglasses, and a full-sleeved knee-length dress. She stood next to a stack of books piled as high as her own height. In a fake adult tone, she recited.

"I fought to bring the software legitimacy so that it would be given due respect and thus I began to use the term 'Software Engineering' to distinguish it from hardware and other kinds of engineering, and yet, treat each type of engineering as part of the overall systems engineering process. When I first started using this phrase, it was considered quite amusing. It was an ongoing joke for a long time. They liked to kid me about my radical ideas. Software eventually and deservedly gained the same respect as any other discipline."

The girl curtsied and left the stage. Everyone applauded.

The faces of proud parents beamed at their dressed-up children as three more students played their parts.

It was Sagan's turn next. He got on the stage with his usual stoic face. Only Lyra could detect his unpleasantness that came from wearing someone else's clothes. He wore a red turtleneck sweater under a tan blazer. His hair was a few shades darker and his posture less stiff.

Sagan scanned the last few rows to locate his sister. He found her exactly there, in the corner.

As he spoke, Lyra realized he was going off track from the speech he had prepared.

"Imagination will often carry us to worlds that never were. But without it, we go nowhere. Somewhere, something incredible is waiting to be known." Sagan paused, straightened his blazer, and spoke again, "We can judge our progress by the courage of our questions and the depth of our answers, our willingness to embrace what is true rather than what feels good. You're an interesting species." He looked straight at his sister. "An interesting mix. You are capable of such beautiful dreams and such horrible nightmares. You feel so lost, so cut off, so alone; only you're not. See, in all our searching, the only thing we have found that makes the emptiness bearable is each other."

A stream of silent tears rolled down Lyra's cheeks.

To everyone else, Sagan had mixed different quotes to pay tribute to a prominent 20th century astronomer and scientist, but for Lyra, this was a tribute from her little brother who had struggled his whole life to express his love for her.

Lyra had hated being the mother that she had to be for Sagan, but the sister in her found herself lucky to have him.

"The nitrogen in our DNA, the calcium in our teeth, the iron in our blood, the carbon in our apple pies were made in the interiors of collapsing stars. We are made of star-stuff," Sagan continued in his flat tone. He shifted his eyes from Lyra and looked at the confused crowd with wrinkled brows. He took a moment and spoke again in a sterner voice, "If a human disagrees with you, let them live. In a hundred billion galaxies, you will not find another. You all get to live today. Much obliged."

Sagan bent in a manner that looked like a forced nod and left the stage with his hands in his pockets.

Lyra clapped the loudest.

Lyra was waiting at the school gate along with other parents. In the far distance, she spotted Sagan. He was walking towards the boy with whom he had argued about video games. A few other classmates joined Sagan and gathered around.

"Shit..." Lyra paced towards them.

To her surprise, everyone held hands. They formed a circle and sang a song. The video-game-boy, who was in the center, rubbed tears from his face.

Lyra squinted with confusion. Sagan was holding hands too. She stayed away and waited for her brother to solve the puzzle.

"What happened there?" she asked when Sagan finally joined her.

"Your laces, sister."

Lyra lifted her foot and shoved the shoestrings in the gaps of her shoe. Sagan made a face and held her arm to keep her from tripping.

"What was that?" Lyra asked again.

"We were singing *Life Lives* for Sipa."

"Why?"

"His mother passed away last week."

Lyra looked at the boy and saw a relatable sadness on his face. "What happened?"

"Dementia," Sagan said in a tone that comes from mastering the meaning of every disease.

"Why were you singing that song?"

"Whenever someone loses a loved one or goes through a traumatic occurrence, the SOP is to comfort them. We are supposed to do nice things for the sufferer. I gave my lunch to him yesterday. Two classmates are taking him to the arcade tonight. It's a long-established school tradition. Didn't you do it too?" Sagan asked as he wiped his hands with a neatly folded handkerchief.

"I don't think so. Or maybe I don't remember."

Lyra awakened both her minds and looked around. Children in costumes were running here and there, cutting through the cloud of playground dust, their faces full of joy and fulfillment. She looked back at Sagan as she recalled something. "You were holding hands!"

"Not something I would prefer on a regular day, especially hands as greasy as those. You don't want to know how much they sweat and how little they care about it. But..." Sagan looked at

Lyra. "I learned from you to do things you are supposed to even though you don't like them."

Lyra remembered their morning conversation. "I am so sorry for this morning."

"I know." Sagan nodded.

"Now you are truly Lord Sagacious. What you did for Sipa was very thoughtful."

"I know that too. I understand how it feels, not having a mother."

Lyra placed her hand on his shoulder.

"Not through my own experiences. My mind wasn't even capable of bundling information into complex neural patterns when Mom was alive. Or containing declarative memories," Sagan rambled. Then he spoke slowly. "I can imagine how it feels by looking at you."

Lyra grabbed him and pressed him to her sides. Sagan reciprocated by holding her. "Why are you so nice to be me today?" she asked. "I was awful to you."

"Because your capriciousness is only amusing when it's directed towards others."

Lyra burst into laughter. "You are my most favorite person in the universe!" She rubbed Sagan's forehead.

"That's nonsense. You don't know everyone in the universe."

They turned to walk towards the bus stop.

Lyra was not done satisfying her curiosity. "Weren't you upset with Sipa?"

"I still am. But he has endured something traumatic. He had to watch his mother deteriorate every day. Did you know dementia also leads to hallucinations?"

"No. In the later stage?"

"Most likely. He was hurting and when people don't equip themselves with healthy methods to handle pain, they use anger to channel it. That's just his amygdala doing its job. A lousy job, but still..."

"The brain compartment that also processes our emotions,"

Lyra interrupted, as if to talk to herself. She thought of the hot anger she had been feeling in her chest recently.

"Yes! I have started seeing humans as you do," Sagan said with his chin high. "The amygdala triggers the release of catecholamines. Hormones from this family increase our blood pressure and our body temperature, and accelerate our heart rate. These changes, when not understood or controlled, make a person lash out. That was all he was doing."

"Fight or flight."

"Correct. Sister, you belong in a lab. You are too clever to be a chef."

"Hey!" Lyra almost squealed. "Chefs can be clever, too. And artistic."

"I doubt that."

"Says the one who needs more than a dozen words to explain Infantile Amnesia."

Sagan scrunched his face at Lyra's jibe. "You get exceedingly mean, exceedingly fast."

They laughed and bantered until the bus arrived.

"I never told you something before," Sagan said when they took their seats. "I didn't want to upset you."

"Tell me."

"I was...thrilled when they sent you back from the transit station."

Lyra turned towards her brother. He was looking at his lap. "It's selfish and inconsiderate. I know."

"It's not." She played with his hair. "When I think of the time we spent together after I returned, I feel glad they deported me."

"You say that because that's what dutiful elder sisters are supposed to say."

Lyra reflected on her words. She felt victorious when she found them honest. The bond she had formed with Sagan in the last few weeks would not have happened if she hadn't returned.

She slid down her seat and placed her head on her brother's tiny shoulder. "It's the truest thing I've ever said to you."

Sagan patted her head and smiled, his pearly teeth showing.

The bus passed through familiar streets. Lyra looked outside and wondered about the power of Zenith, the power that influenced Sagan to hold hands and be considerate. How did a culture like that come into existence when a merciless world existed across space? What kind of adults these children would grow up to be when their childhood was filled with such compassion and reasoning. Would they be struggling like her, looking for a different world? Would they even need another world?

The dissonance didn't help. Lyra thought of the decision she had made at the lake. She still wanted to get out of here. She still didn't care how. That's good.

The bus stopped at Holding Hands, the tail of Bibha district. They got down and walked inside. A mélange of floral and medicinal scents greeted the siblings.

"I'll be out soon. You'll be okay?"

"Yes." Sagan pulled out a big book from his bag and took a seat. He placed his hand by his nose to block the smell of fresh lilies that were placed all around the waiting room.

"Hiya!" Gryffy walked up to them. "Hey, little dude."

"Hello," Sagan greeted her with a nod.

"Is she willing to talk?" asked Lyra.

"We'll find out. Let's go!"

Gryffy escorted Lyra to a room. Colorful vintage tapestry adorned its walls. Solid yellow marigolds, eccentric vases made by Zenither potters, an electric kettle, an ancient bamboo cabinet full of cups and saucers, and a small bed packed the rest of the space.

"Now what?" Ms Tara barked from a corner without turning her face towards the door. She was sitting in a wheelchair and untangling shreds of yarn from its wheel.

To compel everyone to listen to her, Lyra had made the hardest decision of her life—give a live speech in Curie Park, an important historical place. To deny someone a speech at that park was against Zenith's cultural code. By choosing that location, Lyra wanted to trap Zenithers in their own pointless cultural rules.

As a finishing touch, she needed the support of someone influential. Previously, she had been looking for a group of open-minded people to listen to her, but she was being a fool then. To make Zenithers listen, she had to speak their language. For that, she needed someone popular or reputable to trigger their emotions in a conformist manner. She had to provide fluff and chants, not logic and reasoning.

Ms Tara was a slightly disliked but respected citizen of Zenith. She was one of the few living Terraformers, and Lyra knew her opinion would matter to the masses.

The old woman had recently shifted to Holding Hands because of her deteriorating health. It was where people moved when they could no longer receive physical, medical, or familial support at home. The staff and volunteers of the facility provided free care for as long as it was needed.

"It's Lyra, Ms Tara. Your front-door neighbor. She is here to talk to you," Gryffy spoke in a tone so kind that Lyra couldn't have guessed it came out of her mouth.

"That snobbish twig?" said the old woman. "What does she want?"

Gryffy suppressed a giggle. Before Lyra could jab her elbow in her, a dog, one of Zenith's thirty canines, dashed from between them. It wagged its tail and hopped on Ms Tara's lap.

"Oh...Sweetums!" Ms Tara's voice switched to syrupy. She lifted the dog's left leg and stroked its abdomen. The dog licked her arm. "Your boobies are well now, Sweetums. They were hanging so red and dry yesterday."

"Yes, she is healing. Your coconut oil hack worked," Gryffy said. "Ms Tara, Lyra only needs a few minutes of your time. Please."

The old woman grunted.

"She is also curious about what makes your carrot pudding so rich."

"You can kiss my ass some other day, Gryffy," said Ms Tara.

When no one spoke, she continued, "Cream…nice, fluffy cream. For the pudding. Not the one you get in the stores. Homemade cream. You whippersnappers won't understand."

"Homemade cream, huh? Lyra, would you mind taking it from here? I need to go churn some." With that, Gryffy left the room. The dog skedaddled behind her.

"Always up to ruining my nap time, that one." Ms Tara grunted again and rolled her wheelchair to the window. "Here, girl. Give this to that chatterbox." She flung a bright yellow scarf that she had knitted towards Lyra.

"I will, and thanks for the tip, Ms Tara. Did you learn to make cream while you were on Earth?" Lyra asked.

"From Earth? Balderdash! They squeeze animal tits to make theirs. Nasty. It stinks. I make my own cream. From coconuts."

"I see." Taking it as a positive sign, Lyra walked to the window, leaned against it, and faced Ms Tara. She saw three incense sticks burning in a corner. Their rose-scented vapory smoke awakened her senses.

"Have you ever tasted their cream?" asked Ms. Tara. "They sell it at the Borlaug market. Heavily fattened plastic, that nasty thing." She clicked her tongue.

Lyra glanced at the small figure. Thick maroon-framed glasses covered a fierce, wrinkled face. Her short, curly hair, which was a mix of black and gray, gave Ms Tara a youthful look. She donned a bright orange cardigan over a flowy, baby pink nightgown. Its lacy seam brushed her fox slippers.

"I have heard the food there is really crappy," Lyra mirrored Ms Tara's language without wanting to.

"Crappy? Their food is what…crap shit after a sick stomach."

"There must be something that you miss from the old world, if not food. You spent a good twenty-three years of your life there, didn't you?"

"It's common math, girl. I am 98. We colonized Zenith seventy-five years ago. So, I've obviously spent twenty-three years on Earth. I am the oldest Terraformer alive!" Ms Tara patted her chest.

"You must be proud, having had the chance to live in both worlds."

"Proud-shmoud." She fanned her hand. "There is no pride in that. I had to live here and there. It wasn't my choice."

"So you'd still be on Earth if it was up to you?"

"Who knows? Maybe." Ms Tara looked outside the window and stared towards the asteroid's roof.

Lyra jotted something on her notepad and asked another question.

"Why would you say so? Was it better there?"

"I don't know, girl. You think of your childhood place not because it was better or worse, but because it belongs to a time that you'll never get back."

"Would you go back to Earth if given a chance?"

The Terraformer's face softened and her eyes brimmed.

"I didn't mean to upset you," said Lyra.

"I grew up in a small town on Earth. As a kid, it irritated me how much my mother adored and missed her childhood. She would talk about things they did growing up—playing on the streets, climbing trees, turning paper into boats, dancing in the rain. The golden 1990s, she used to say. It was annoying. Why would she be so proud of doing ridiculous things like that? But now...I understand. She wasn't proud; she was nostalgic. She missed the parts that were long gone and lost. I thought when I grew old, I'd annoy the hell out of someone too by telling my childhood stories. But I have no one. No children, no grandchildren." She paused and her shoulders sagged. "Not being able to tell your stories leaves you bitter."

A gush of regret swept over Lyra. She grew up craving stories of Earth, not knowing that they lived less than twenty feet away from her home. She despised her unwillingness to mingle with people and wished she had talked with Ms Tara before.

"I make carrot pudding because that's the only Earth-food I remember. My mother called it gajar halwa or somethin."

Lyra jotted down the foreign words.

"I don't know the authentic recipe. I make do with my memory. The pudding reminds me of all the times I spent there. It wasn't a perfect time or a perfect world, but it was my world. And when you get old, you yearn for your roots."

"What do the words mean? Gajar halwa?"

"Who the hell knows!" Ms Tara coughed and cleared her throat. To Lyra, it sounded like the belches of T. rex. "I am lucky I even remember them."

"How do you feel about going back to Earth, Ms Tara? All of us can go. I am working on it. It will..."

"Stop right there, you crazy girl!" Ms Tara interrupted, the power back in her voice box.

"You said—"

"Yes, because I am almost a hundred and one of my feet rests in the grave. But I would never do that to the kids, rascals as they may be. Do you even know how much trouble we Terraformers faced to make this place what it is? To make this world perfect for you little brats?"

"No world is perfect, Ms Tara."

"Well, this one is, young lady. And only I get to decide that, not you! Because I have lived in both worlds, not you!" She pointed her finger, which made Lyra lower her eyes. "They call it 3rd Stratum shitum somethin', but in my time, my country was called India."

"What?" Lyra straightened. "I am part Indian too! My mom's family was also from India." She wanted to ask Ms Tara why she had never mentioned this before, but she leaned against the window again. She remembered another pointless, contradictory Zenither cultural norm. The citizens were not supposed to speak too much of their heritage because it would not only place greater importance on the tyrannical Earth that they had left behind, but also create barriers in a culture they had worked so hard to build. Zenith was their world now, and talking about where they came from was considered disharmonious.

Lyra inhaled and found the mixed aroma of roses and marigolds strangely unpleasant.

"It wasn't like what we hear now." Ms Tara ignored Lyra's brief burst of excitement and continued in a soft voice again, "We had a humble but pleasant house, a wholesome family, great friends, and a comfortable life. People were nicer, places were brighter. But the rascal government..." She shook her head. "When we colonized Zenith, I left all that behind, just so people could have a better future here. We thought of it as humanity's second chance. We had seen so much on Earth by then. All we wanted was a better world for us and our children. That was what we did, and we did a darn good job, you hear me? I nursed and healed our people for almost fifty damn years!"

"Then why do you hate here so much? Why are you always so...angry?" Lyra fumbled, but let her words out.

"That's just who I am. I used to hurl profanities at patients before treating them. Smack them, even."

Lyra couldn't help but smile.

"Silly girl, I don't hate it here. I am old and shriveled. My limbs don't work like they used to. I helped the doctor who delivered the first birth of our colony. I carried patients all my life. And now, I am lying here like a lump myself. Every morning I wake up worrying about what I'll do to pass the day. A life like that will change anyone. But you are young. You have a life to live. You cannot walk into that jungle."

"But what about you?"

"You asked me what I miss about Earth." Ms Tara looked outside and stared at the rooflight again. "I have stood inside this asteroid for decades and have always felt...boxed in. On Earth, under that wide, magnificent sky, you can't help but feel free. Humbled. I miss feeling that." She squeezed her eyes and shook her head. "I miss that darn blue sky."

"Ms Tara, forget about the societal benefit." Lyra bent to face her. "If you alone had the chance to return to Earth, would you go back before you...?"

Lyra knew she was going to twist Ms Tara's words to get what she wanted, but she didn't stop herself.

"What? Before I turn into a tree-snack?"

Lyra nodded.

Ms Tara held her elbows with her palms and spoke warmly, "No, I wouldn't go. You see this place?" She looked around the vibrant room. Lyra did too. "This is what this tin-can gives. When your bones start to melt and you can't even walk, Zenith gives you legs." She rubbed the wheelchair's arm. "When you can't cook anymore, it gives you food." She pointed at the bedside table where several neighbors had dropped lunchboxes. "And when you have no family or are lonely, it gives you a babbling fool for whom you knit scarves every day. You don't get that on Earth, girl. This place has given me its seventy-five years. It has made me who I am. It deserves my ice-remains too."

On her way back, Lyra jotted down her thoughts to see what she felt. A part of her mind asked her not to introspect but to continue hunting for an influential citizen to back her up. But the other part kept holding on to the conversations she had had with Sagan and Ms Tara.

She opened the bus window and looked outside. It was 4.30 in the evening, michaiyo time. People were sitting or standing in groups, laughing, discussing, swapping stories, and sipping warm beverages. She had always assumed she hated michaiyo because it was a compulsion for her to sit and socialize. But that wasn't it. She had never warmed up to the idea because she didn't have a single person with whom she wanted to sit and talk, and for that she was solely responsible.

Her mind relayed an imagery of her, sitting with Ms Tara outside her home, sipping tea, eating warm carrot pudding, and listening to stories of India. Of Earth. An alternate universe where Ms Tara was less bitter and she less lonely.

As Lyra passed through the chattering streets, she thought about Zenither culture again. She imagined how helpful it would have been for Kenai and Aryabh if they had been Zenithers. They could have talked about their issues and received support.

She had despised Aryabh for exploiting her, but she was about to do the same to Zenithers. On a much bigger scale. She too was willing to cross limits and manipulate to get what she had always desired. The reason she couldn't take the next step was in front of her.

Lyra looked outside at her fellow citizens as she felt a sense of autocracy over her internal anarchy.

Zenith was the sole reason she was not an Aryabh.

CHAPTER 27

Shiaya's house was a misrepresentation of herself. Her studio apartment smelled of mold and the lamps hung dimly from its chipped ceiling. Where the light didn't reach, the whirring of the heater did. A stained couch was flopped in the middle of the room, hiding a thin bed perpendicular to its back. The only other furniture was a vanity table with a big mirror, a fridge, and a meal slot machine next to the bathroom. An empty IngredientSac lay atop the machine.

At the end of the room was a small balcony. Aryabh sat on its floor and placed his backpack behind him, making sure it touched his back. Shiaya grabbed two beer bottles from the broken refrigerator and perched across from him.

"It's cold tonight," she rubbed her legs, "but don't worry. You won't feel a thing after a while."

Aryabh buttoned his coat and looked at her out of the corner of his eye. She was barely recognizable in a worn-out, oversized T-shirt, her long hair tied in a bun, lips undrenched, face devoid of any piercings, and eyes natural and brown. The scar on her forehead was still as prominent under the bleached Sonmanto lights.

"Can only keep you for one night," said Shiaya. "Dima has set me up for another place." The grimy floor itched her bare legs, but she ignored. "I'll head out tomorrow evening. You can crash until then. Got no food. It's all I have." She rolled a beer to Aryabh. "It's flat and warm. Might taste like piss but I've chugged like four of these. You get used to it."

Aryabh washed down half the bottle in one big gulp.

"Thought you didn't like losing control over your mind."

Aryabh didn't respond, and so Shiaya spoke again, "Am not very proud of this shitty house, and so I don't invite people here."

More silence.

"You should leave Sonmanto. The Farm has a better reach than you'd like to give them credit for."

Aryabh gave the slightest nod.

"How are you so calm?" asked Shiaya.

Aryabh looked at her face, not quite understanding what she said.

"They just offed your roommate. How are you so fuckin' calm? Look, I am no wimp, but when the Rodents dissolved Dev, I lost it. Once I was back from Caspian's house, I smashed this entire place." She looked around the room. "Dev's things were lying around. Seeing them... If I were you, there'd be a chair flying through this balcony right now. And, mind you, my roommate was as much of an idiot as yours is. Was. But he was my friend. My only friend." She whispered, "I miss him."

Aryabh shifted in his spot, his fingers clutching the beer bottle with all their strength.

"Although, I see it. It's written all over your face—the anger, the shame." She exhaled a scorn. "Our lives are shitty, aren't they? I'm surprised we don't feel the need to take a machete and go on a night prowl to hunt." She chugged a sip of her beer and went on, "I ran away from my house when I was fourteen. Not a single belonging but bruises and scars over my body. Thanks to mommy dearest. She wanted to send me to our Trunk's labor camp. It was the new trend then, sending children to work to bring in some extra PacaDollars. I couldn't ruin my face and body doing labor. I wanted to be a PacaModel. You know, the ones they hire to sell their stuff?"

She thought of a memory and smiled at it.

"Used to cut mine and my sisters' clothes and redesign them. Then I'd pick any object from the house and try to sell it while cat-walking between the gaps of our beds. I called them ramps. They both hated it, my little sisters. The middle one, the prettiest girl I have ever seen. Had a better sense of fashion than I did. And the youngest, small and quiet like a mouse. Would rather play with a mouse than care about clothes. But I knew they were impressed. If only by my confidence. We knew I was good. Darn good. Even the leather of my mother's belt couldn't rip my dreams."

Aryabh took another look at Shiaya. Still unrecognizable.

"So I left. Waited for my sisters to join me. Assumed they'd hate the labor camps too. But they never came. I don't know if it was the fear of the unknown or my mother. I'll never know. But I ran. Knew I had to settle in a Head if I wanted to make it into modeling. But I had no ability to last even a week in a place like this. So, I started small. I lived in Trunks. Got odd jobs. Made beds, served coffee, stripped, rubbed feet, tested a Cream's meals for poison, brushed their teeth, and cleaned their ears. But I never stopped. I worked, and I ran. Ran until I was here, in Sonmanto, only to serve coffee again. You know, it was a sucky day when I learned I wasn't elite enough to be a PacaModel...almost jumped off a building." She sniggered. "To walk on the ramp, I had to be a Cream, and you know, you are born in that class or approved. All that hustling seemed pointless. My body, my hard work, my dreams, and I were nothing without money and privilege."

Aryabh held his silence, but he was listening.

"You know...where I come from, there is a special word for someone who hustles and makes it big in Sonmanto. Qori. It's not English, and so they say it in hush tones, the people in my homeTrunk in Southern 1st Stratum. It's what I always wanted to be. Qori."

"What does the word mean?" Aryabh spoke his first words.

Shiaya turned the corner of her lip upward. "Gold," she said and laughed with such a tremendous jolt that her hair came loose. She tucked the dangling lock of hair into her bun and spoke again without looking at Aryabh.

"Some nights when I can't fall asleep, I think about my sisters. Wonder how big, how beautiful they must be right now. Wonder if they are safe. But I just keep seeing them as kids, still in the same house, scared and abused. I keep thinking about the day I'd have enough money and power to pull them here. That fuckin' day never comes. Some days, all I want to do is go to my house and chop my mother's head off. It's crazy, isn't it? We can be so demented and yet we expect a sane world to live in."

The last words hit Aryabh like a hot brick.

"I don't know how to survive anymore," Shiaya said. "Misfortune is tattooed on my bones."

Aryabh glanced at Shiaya's wrist tattoo. This time, he understood what it meant. It wasn't a corporation's logo. It was a drawing of three sisters holding hands in a circle, as seen from above.

"There used to be a homeless old man," Aryabh said, "down on Chase Street near my apartment. He used to antagonize the other homeless. Most repulsive guy ever. I've seen him in that spot ever since I can remember. He wasn't there tonight. Just disappeared."

"Huh?" Shiaya leaned in.

"I bullied Kenai into filing a complaint against him, to get him kicked out. Kenai didn't want to. He said the homeless man reminded him of..." Aryabh revisited the conversation he had had with his roommate and was repulsed by himself. "Someone I know told me that not everyone on Earth can be as bad as the Rodents. She said the probability of that happening is too low. That never throughout history have all Earthlers ever been on one side. But, to me, good people were a myth. An oxymoron." He clenched his jaw. "Then I met Kenai. He was...good. Foolish but good."

"You think he snitched on us during the Pre-Dissolution routine?" Shiaya asked.

Aryabh didn't want to stop talking because each moment of silence forced him to imagine Kenai's last moments. He knew the PacaMilitary must have first bashed the door open. The sound would have terrified Kenai. Then they would have snatched his eyeglasses, blindfolded him with a gun to his head, and cuffed his hands. Most people are dissolved after this step, but Kenai probably was a mine of information. He was definitely taken and tortured before being tied and melted with radiation. Aryabh couldn't stop feeling the fear Kenai must have felt during the ordeal. Death must have been a relief.

"Aryabh! What do you think? He snitched on us?"

"No." He just knew.

A slight smile came upon Aryabh's face as he thought of something. "He liked you a lot. Kenai."

"He did? Ah, was that why he brought me food and water every day when we were at Caspian's?"

"He would have done that even if he didn't like you," Aryabh exhaled a short-lived laugh.

They both sat in silence for a while as they lamented the losses of their lost friends.

"Okay...off to bed." Shiaya said.

"What about you?" asked Aryabh. "The Farm must have gathered it was you who helped me."

"I think Dima knows, but he is trying to not go there. Let's see how fiery Arkas's ass gets. I'll figure something out."

"Okay."

"You can take the couch. I have to get ready early in the morning to go collect gold from a client. So I'll be noisy, but you can keep the apartment to yourself until noon."

They got up together and almost collided into each other. Their eyes met.

Without heels, Shiaya was still taller than Aryabh. Her big eyes pierced into his as she pretended to straighten the strands of her hair. Aryabh stared at her, frozen. Shiaya's recently licked lips glistened as she walked closer to him. She reached for Aryabh's arm and pressed herself against him.

As if the touch had broken a spell, Aryabh's body alerted. He turned around, picked up his backpack, and moved away.

"What the fuck!" Shiaya raised her hands in the air. "I was just trying to hug you, you ugly piece of shit... Do the human thing! Way to insult me in my own friggin' house. Jackass!"

"Stop pretending as if we are wired to do that," Aryabh said as he plopped on the couch.

"Speak for yourself. I have done plenty."

"At the Self-Pleasure Booths?"

"Jerk off!" Shiaya threw a cushion at him from her bed.

Aryabh almost laughed.

For minutes, they both lay staring at the ceiling, knowing that the other was awake.

"Do you have a Constant?" Aryabh asked out of the blue.

"A constant?" Shiaya spoke from her bed.

"Something you've had for a long time, something...constant."

"Have had this giant-ass scar on my forehead from when my mother threw a fuckin' pan at me. I was sick, and so she lost half a day of pay. I've had it since I was four. Does that count?"

"Don't know." He couldn't know. He would have had to consult Kenai to know the rules. "I am sorry for what I said about Dev that day at Sobak," Aryabh added. "After he was diss—"

"People die. It's no big deal. Move on," Shiaya recited in Aryabh's bitter tone. "I remember. How can I forget? It inspired the most badass punch out of me."

"You are welcome."

Aryabh lay for a while with his hands clasped on his chest. Then he spoke as if he were talking to himself, "In a normal world, what happened to Kenai and Dev would be called a murder. We should say they were killed. Instead, we say they were dissolved as if they deserved it. They also change our diction."

"That's the thing with thinking too much," said Shiaya. "You start to hate everything, including yourself. I can't do that. I have to sleep at night. Can't afford baggy eyes; my livelihood depends on it. So nighty night." She turned off the lamp, blanketing the apartment with darkness.

Aryabh closed his eyes and sneaked into the discomfort of his thoughts again.

If scars were a Constant, he had many.

When Shiaya woke up the next morning, Aryabh was gone.

"Where now, asshole?" she said as she stared at the empty couch.

> Every time, I had to cauterize my wounds before I could even feel the pain. Life didn't give me the luxury to lament over my losses. That night, I faced many horrors, but the one that stuck with me the most was my reflex to wipe Kenai's phone before I even let myself feel anything about the news. That

was when I smelled the rot inside me. Self-preserva-
tion came more naturally to me than my emotions.
I thought of your words. You told me once that I
was so preoccupied with seeing the bad in Earthlers
that I couldn't see the good around me. You were
right. I lived with good and I rejected it.

Kenai's goodness refuted my entire belief system
and that bothered me. I wanted Earthlers to be
evil and inhuman, and he kept proving me wrong.
I read in old books that as time passed, humans
were so exhausted with surviving that they had no
time for conversations or relationships. Somehow,
distancing from people got easier. Humans are a
creature of habit. If evolution can lead to big biological changes, social changes were a cakewalk.
We have forgotten the world where humans needed
intimacy. The Pacamounts only added fuel to the
fire that had already been burning brightly.

Kenai was lonely too. But he didn't punish people
around him for his misery. He made sure no one
went through what he had gone through.

In a world rampant with inhumanity, Kenai was
a ray of hope. The Farm and the likes plotted for
decades and worked tirelessly, whereas I mapped
my way out of Earth. But Kenai rebelled against
the Pacamounts just by being Kenai. If the government had as much brains as they had power,
they'd fear people like him more than any weapon
or rebel group, for they are the ones who'll remain
untouched by their branding and tempering.

A bus headed out of Sonmanto. The rays of the rising sun
stabbed its windows. On the last seat sat Aryabh, his fingers busy
around his wrist. He booked a ticket to VacaRealm as an internal

anarchy commandeered his lifelong autocracy.

CHAPTER 28

Zenith

November 12, 2125

"Stage is ready," Gryffy read to Lyra. "Zen Mavericks have set up the chairs. I've made some chocolate truffle bombs for the attendees. Some sweet bribe. Trac volunteered to bring tea after I ordered him to. *The Zenith Report* and *Iron TV* both will be here soon. I told you, there isn't a journalist who'd say no to a juicy news byte. Well, that's it!" She closed her notepad. "Everything is ready! I hope you are too."

They stood on the second-floor balcony of Gryffy's house that overlooked Curie Park. Lyra avoided looking below and gazed at the distant farms on Zenith's slanted wall.

Ever since she decided to do the speech, she had packed all her anxieties about it in a box and stowed it in the cluttered corner of her head. The speech wouldn't have happened otherwise. But now that she was less than an hour away from it, the box had popped open.

"Trac said some people were—"

"Stop thinking about others." Gryffy interrupted. "This is your final chance. Whether they like it or not, they are going to come today to hear you."

"What if no one comes?" A tiny part of Lyra wished for it.

"I doubt that." Gryffy pointed her chin at the park's entrance where a thick crowd was building up.

A hot rock spun inside Lyra's stomach.

"I'll see you downstairs," said Gryffy.

"Wait."

Lyra fidgeted for a few seconds and then hugged her. "Thank you," she said, jabbing her bony shoulders into Gryffy's. "I am sorry for putting you through this. You didn't sign up for it."

"It's okay. For what it's worth, the last few weeks have slayed all your appeal. Totally over you."

Lyra stood quiet, embarrassed. During their time working together for this mission, she had noticed the eye-rolls and sighs, and how much she had irked Gryffy with her fickle mind.

"I am kidding, Lyra!" Gryffy burst into laughter. "About the appeal part. You are..." she stopped laughing and looked intently, "...the most incredible person I have ever known. Your mental resilience astounds me. I have learnt a great deal from you, actually. So, thank *you* for taking me on this journey, however messy it was." She touched Lyra's arm. "You are going to do great things, Lyra. Don't change."

"I don't know what to say."

"You don't have to say anything. I'll see you on the other side." Gryffy grabbed a huge steel container full of chocolate bombs and left. Lyra watched from the balcony as she crossed the park below and walked up to a woman she had never seen before. They kissed and carried the container together towards the park's gate.

As if a heavy weight had been lifted off her chest, Lyra let out a breath and smiled. She watched as Gryffy climbed on an iron trashcan and screamed, waving their flyer.

"Come and hear the whole story. Misinformation is Satan's territory. Bring your ears and heart. A little knowledge is demon's fart."

Lyra giggled at her chants.

"She has taken quiet a liking to the dark spirits." A voice came from behind. It startled Lyra and she dropped the speech.

"Oh, Sagan." She picked up the paper and shoved it in her pocket

"You always jump like a guilty person caught mid-action."

"Well, no one likes to be caught red-minded." Lyra sat on Gryffy's couch and invited her brother. "Look at you, visiting a stranger's house."

"I am on social terms with Gryffy. She even let me in. I came to check on you."

It touched Lyra, but she didn't want to insult Sagan's affection by acting surprised. "Thank you. I am okay. Just a little nervous."

"I read your speech. I had no intention of prying. A copy was lying by the printer and I wanted to proofread—"

"It's okay. I would have read it too."

"You changed it."

"Yeah." Lyra twisted her mouth. "Following your footsteps, brother."

Sagan scooched his wee body towards her, his soft hair bobbling on his head. He patted her back with a grandfather-like mannerism.

"I have always been proud of your intellect and rationality, but your humility amazes me. It makes you even cleverer."

"Awh...you sycophant." Lyra squeezed Sagan in her arms and kissed his head. "Come, let's offend the masses."

A buzzing grumble charged the energy of Curie Park. The bright afternoon rooflight passed through the surrounding hackberry trees and cast skeletal patterns on the ground and the attendees sitting on it.

Lyra stood hidden by the side of the stage, her feet shaking and her chest thrumming. When she flexed her sweaty fingers, she realized she hadn't trimmed her nails, and then out of nowhere, a dozen other realizations hit her. Her shoelaces weren't tied properly, her sweater was too casual, her hair looked uncombed, and the speech was so crumpled in her pocket that she couldn't identify some of the words.

After a brief introduction, she heard Gryffy invite her on the stage.

"Open your ears wide for Lyra!"

Lyra combed her hair with her fingers and took a deep breath. She swallowed the dryness of her throat and went up on the stage. With the hot rock still spinning inside her stomach, she arrived at the podium.

Hundreds of faces stared at her, including her dad's and Ms Tara's, who were watching her live on their televisions. Among the packed park crowd were Sagan, Balin, Ms Clia, and the people she knew from the hotel and sanctuary. But even their familiarity blended with the foreign mass. The crowd, to Lyra, was one giant faceless cloud of disappointment and anger.

She inhaled a lungful of air and began.

"Good afternoon, everyone. I am Lyra." Her voice came out breathy and coarse. "I am the last person you want to listen to in this park, a historical place where important people have given life-altering messages. They were people who mattered. I don't. I am an ordinary chef at Faraway Paradise whose only big achievement is getting on this stage today."

She avoided looking at the faces and kept her attention focused on the edge of the park.

"It has taken me courage of enormous proportions to stand here and speak my mind. All I ask is for patient ears." She paused. "You heard it right. I want all Zenithers to migrate back to Earth."

Murmurs vaporized in the crowd.

Gryffy had asked her not to read the speech from the paper. It would make her robotic delivery more impersonal. Lyra was glad she didn't listen to her because the creased paper felt like a strong crutch right now. She unfolded the speech and read from it.

"My mother used to say that when she delivered me, she birthed twins. Me and my curiosity. I always had too many questions and I liked having the liberty of finding their answers. Zenith gave me that. But when I joined school, my whys became bigger. The answers, however, didn't. Then the school told me about this foreign world, a habitat a lot bigger than ours. Earth. I learned that even the most educated, the most curious, and the most capable minds had failed to fathom the depth of this planet. It gave me hope. In this foreign world, I found a place to seek answers to the bigger whys. Earth became a realistic fantasy. Its mysteries kept me awake and alive. The more I learned about it, the less rewarding Zenith became.

"As I grew older, I noticed my whys beginning to die. Doing the same things over and over again broke me. I felt trapped. That was when I arranged my entire life for one mission—to move to Earth. I wasn't planning to just travel there. I wanted to settle somewhere in its secluded corner."

Lyra was surprised she didn't hear a round of gasps.

"You all know how that turned out. I was deported from the transit station. I was hurt and angry with no money to travel again. Then, on one sully afternoon, in a casual conversation with my brother, I struck upon an idea. Why don't we all go back to Earth? The more I researched about Zenith, the better the idea seemed. I found it irrational to rely on machines for air and water when a perfectly habitable planet existed not too far from us. I believed it is pointless to live in a pond while an ocean awaited us inside our orbit. Given the political climate on Earth and the atrocities suffered by its citizens, I also felt it was foolish to stay put here. At least on Earth, we might have resources and space to escape. My logic told me it was safer to live among them than away from them at their mercy."

Silence.

"That was until four days ago." Lyra shifted her weight on one leg and scratched the podium. "These last few days, I talked to more people than I did in my entire lifetime. I was forced to stare deep into the core of Zenith. Under its fabric, I found its soul. Since childhood, we are taught that Zenith is a utopian world that we are privileged to inherit. That notion had always bothered me."

She looked at the confused faces and felt vulnerable.

"How can we declare something so bold? I still don't know if Zenith is an ideal paradise, but I have unearthed our asteroid enough to know that it comes close to it. We have created generations of kind and brave Zenithers. We have escaped hatred and brutality and created harmony in this dark void. I thought our habitat was just a leftover as all asteroids are, but we have created a whole new world inside this cosmic remains. The last few days taught me the importance of our world and its people. It used to frustrate me how Earthlers didn't appreciate what they had, and yet I lived my whole life ignoring and not appreciating everything Zenith offered me."

Faith emerged from Lyra's incoming words. She straightened her posture.

"There is strength in community. In tribes, in michaiyo, and in every shared meal and story. There is comfort in lending of supplies and borrowing of help, in sharing big events and small miseries. There is power in listening and in the selfless act of just being there for someone else. A community helps fight the demons that solitude often can't. When we look back and think about the most important and life-changing events of our lives, it often involves other people. There is only so much a person can do alone, I have learnt that. I am not one to shy away from admitting my mistakes, but it took me a while to recognize this one. That afternoon, while talking to my brother, I didn't get an idea; I found a shortcut, a last resort to escape. What I believed then was my prison. To fulfill it, I projected my own needs onto the people of Zenith. I was wrong. I always thought I was a seeker of truth, but when the truth presented itself, I ignored it because it didn't align with my goal. When I found out why we migrated here, I didn't dig deeper."

Ms Clia shifted in her seat.

"Like every Zenither, I believed we came here to explore. We didn't. We escaped. We ran away from Earth, its wars and genocides, the Political Fumigation, and the Pacamounts."

The crowd roared, but Lyra went on.

"And there is nothing wrong with that. I don't know if I would have laid the foundation of my dream had I known this growing up. But I do know that we, the children of Zenith, deserve this truth. You cannot shield us or expect loyalty by rewriting history. Patriotism will not obliterate our problems. We need freedom to talk about things and say the emperor has no clothes. We should have the right to question. I am still highly concerned about the issues mentioned in our flyer."

Everyone buried their heads in their leaflets.

"We have to think about our future, our water, and the Pacamounts. Pardon my impudence," Lyra grinded her teeth, "but our attitude has been myopic. Zenith *will* run out of water in ninety-eight years. Which means running out of oxygen. It seems far away, you'd say, but the Terraformers thrived on a haunted asteroid because they were visionaries. When they landed here seventy-five years ago, they thought of today. I also still stand by my belief that the Pacamounts don't have our best interests at heart. We cannot rely on them for our existence. We have to do something about it. Now."

Lyra realized that her fear was gone. Her feet weren't shaking anymore, and she had control over her body.

"Has this realization changed my plans?" She took a moment to rethink. "No. I am proud of my audacity to find flaws in things I admire and goodness in things I don't. I have come to respect this place, but I still need to find my place in this universe. The intimidation of the unforeseen is what has helped shape humans. I still want to leap into uncertainty, for the fear of limitations is far greater to me than the fear of the unknown. So…" She filled her lungs with air. "I don't know how and when, but I am going to travel to Earth. I volunteer to be an investigator for this cause and do my bit in this community. Not all of us have to migrate. Under Mr Zaif's and Ms Clia's guidance, if they agree, I will gauge the reality of the Pacamounts and Earth. It will help you all to determine our future. I promise I will seek nothing but the truth.

"A friend whose wits I dearly respect, someone who has seen Earth closer than any of us, has told me that their planet is a colorful, well-framed painting whose canvas is rotted and infested with bugs of rapacity and tyranny. From what little I know about Earth, it seems like a grim, rotted painting behind which, in tiny little corners, lies mishandled beauty.

"We teach our children to accept everyone with an open heart, and yet we have collectively hated the people of our ancestors' planet without ever knowing them. Right now as I speak, there might be someone like you on Earth, searching for an answer. There must be an Earthler Gryffy who holds hands of people in need. A Sagan whose nights are sleepless because there is too much to learn. An Earthler Balin growing bountiful herbs and running her business."

In the audience, Balin gloated with pride.

"There must be an Earthler Trac napping under thick tree foliage to get away from the crowd. A Ms Tara waking up to the darn blue sky she grew up watching. An Earthler Keid, who travels to unknown places to deal with his losses. An Earthler Poona marveling at the sight of thousands of unseen animal species. A T. rex roaming free in lush forests with his troops. A Ms Clia digging her feet in the sand after a long day. A Hawk sitting on the cutting edge of an invention. Right now as I speak, there must be an Earthler Lyra looking up and wondering about the little worlds in the sky."

Aryabh's dream echoed in her head.

"To form a better judgment, we have to stop pretending we are safe and investigate not just their government, but their people too. Not doing that is akin to believing you won't age if you throw away the calendar."

Lyra put away her speech and spoke again to the attentive crowd.

"I am Lyra, a second-generation Zenither. I dared to dream and wished for a world that lay beyond the sturdy walls of Zenith. It cost me a lot, but it taught me important things that I wouldn't have learnt otherwise. I am curious to know your opinion too. There are pens and papers at the gate. Please drop your views in the box. Thank you."

She looked at the crowd, and then back at the edge of the park. A familiar tall man in the far right corner caught her attention. His appearance stood out—an authoritative Earthler-like posture clothed in a crisp black suit and shiny shoes. He had silver hair coiffed over a head that looked like it demanded respect and attention. When he noticed Lyra looking in his direction, he left.

Lyra recognized him. He was the man who had sat next to her in the shuttle. The Earthler guest at her hotel. She shook her train of thoughts, looked back at the unresponsive audience, and left the stage.

A moment later, she heard Gryffy's yell.

"It's michaiyo time. Tea and chocolate bombs on the house!"

"Wait. Lyra!" Balin screamed from the audience when she saw Lyra leaving the park. She ran behind her, her apron in her hand.

Lyra halted when she heard her voice.

"That..." Balin was out of breath. She bent and held her hips. "That speech, Lyra! It was beautiful. You made me cry."

Lyra avoided eye contact. "Thanks."

"I am sorry, honey. I am the one responsible for all this. It—"

"No, it all happened for the best..." She searched for words. "We are good."

"Not just that, honey. I gave you a hard time for wanting to go to Earth. All my life, I called Earthlers destructive and cruel, but look at me. I am just like them. You are unhappy because of me. I destroyed your dream."

Lyra couldn't decide how she felt about Balin, but she knew something to be true. "It's okay, chef. You have also given me a lot. After Mom, you were the one woman I looked up to. Maybe it was your strength that influenced me to go on stage today," she said, earnestly.

"Oh, Lyra, honey! You are one precious little girl." Balin pulled Lyra into a hug. "And don't you worry a bit about that bastard. Arkas will find him. He'll pay for this!"

"No, please don't." Lyra pulled away. "That's what I wanted to ask."

"Why?"

"What he did was wrong but I don't want to punish him. I was doing the same thing."

"But you were thinking about our future. You don't have a selfish bone in your body, Lyra."

"That's what I told myself."

CHAPTER 29

THE EARTHLER NEWS

November 11, 2125

BREAKING NEWS: ANTI-PACAS HAVE CLAIMED A SMALL PART OF WESTERN 3RD STRATUM

3rd Stratum anti-Pacas continue to destroy the integrity of the planet. The CEO of the Stratum has deployed PacaMilitary to capture and dismantle the checkpoints and roadblocks held by the anti-Paca terrorists.

Aryabh stood strapped to an airplane plank like cattle. He tapped the wall next to him. A flash of daylight blinded his eyes. He stretched himself towards the window, as much as his seatbelt allowed, and looked outside.

An abundance of gray clouds was scattered over the Atlantic Ocean. Thin trails of cargo ships scarred its green water like comets. Aryabh watched as Sonmanto shrunk on the horizon.

Flying didn't suit him as he had suspected; however, he hadn't imagined it would make him so restless. VacaRealm was in the 2nd Stratum, only two hours by air, but a quarter day's journey by the PacaOcean train. He had neither the time nor the patience for it. Therefore, he was up in the air, strapped and crammed along with hundreds of other passengers.

In some measure, Aryabh was relieved. He had passed the airport security without trouble. With a fake name and forged ID, it was no less than walking towards his Dissolution. He didn't have to worry about visas, either. The first thing the Pacamounts had done after the Political Fumigation was to eliminate travel permits. They wanted people to move and migrate, to separate themselves from their communities.

Aryabh gasped for air in his congested Economy spot. The Economy Plus with chairs was not something he could splurge on. Next to him, a burly man snored whistles. A stench of stale wine emanated from his mouth. Behind him, two women bickered about a business deal. The kid in the front seat argued about children's rights with his adult. Above him, the rates of food, drinks, music, and other amenities flashed on the ceiling. His head throbbed from its light. He stirred in his seat as the thin, dry air cracked his lips and popped his ears.

He was trying to shut his eyes when a notification vibrated his wrist. The nausea that he was suppressing resurfaced. Kenai's picture was published in the Dissolution portal of *The Earthler News*. He unbuckled his seatbelt and rushed to the restroom.

The turbulence triggered his dizziness. He bolted the bathroom door and rubbed his stomach. Sweat covered his body. He unbuttoned his coat and dry-heaved. When he couldn't take it anymore, he dropped to his knees and emptied his guts into the toilet. The bowl swallowed the brown slurry of three AwakeTabs. He sat in the crammed space between the door and the commode, still tasting the remnants of the acidic bile.

Kenai's face from the news flashed in his mind. In the picture, he looked the same and yet different. Instead of the usual grin, his face was drenched in terror. Instead of his eyeglasses, a dreadful horror had layered his eyes, and instead of Kenai, there stood an empty shell with its soul sucked out of it.

Aryabh stabbed his knees into his hurting chest and hugged them. Tears brimmed in his eyes. He tried to leash what was coming, but he couldn't.

A sob exploded from his throat. He rocked back and forth and held his mouth to stifle his cry. Kenai's death had brought him guilt and anger before, but the pure grief that struck him was new.

A knock made him jump. He held the door as if to stop them from breaking in.

Another hard knock.

Aryabh banged the door harder and cried.

"Fuck you, gutter punk!" a man cursed outside and went away.

In twenty-eight years of his life, Aryabh had been pushed from the stairs as a child. He had learnt he was produced in a lab and had understood its meaning. He had starved for three nights in the merciless cold. He had been punched and burnt with cigarettes, and had woken up to a searing pain from being cut for a kidney. But what he felt right now was more painful than the combined agony of those events.

It was a pain felt for someone else, a concept so alien to him that it terrified him.

When he was back to his plank, it was dark outside. The plane was descending. He fastened his seatbelt and dabbed his eyes. The walls and the ceiling of the airplane turned transparent, revealing a canvas of black sky. Below, under the thick layers of smog, VacaRealm magnified. A magical land inside a stained snowglobe.

The holiday capital of Cream emerged like a tangle of garlands made from tiny thousand lights. The amusement parks, theaters, casinos, hotels, and skyscrapers looked like a playground of sparkling concrete.

Aryabh reached Asnofi station, one of the few VacaRealm areas accessible to NonCreamers. It was his first time in the 2nd Stratum. His head spun as he walked past people not so different from his city. Even on the outskirts, the place bustled with movement and luxurious chaos.

He had spent the night in a capsule right outside the airport. He needed time to research on the place he had come for. Upon digging deeper, he had found old maps from the year 2003. That, and the locations and remarks from Lyra's great-grandmother's diary, had helped him figure out a few things. First, a giant portion of VacaRealm was called Paris before the Political Fumigation. Paris was the capital of a country called France. Second, Forêt de Fontainebleau, the place that Lyra wanted to visit, was a small Trunk, or town as it was called in those days, not too far from Paris. Bois le Roi was another neighboring town mentioned in the diary. And lastly, neither of those names were present on the current map. But Aryabh at least knew where he had to look.

On the current map, the area where he believed Forêt de Fontainebleau and its surrounding Trunks should be, was marked by one wide location called VintageRealm.

Aryabh boarded a train that was headed south from one of the thirty-two platforms of Asnofi station. Inside, he scanned his widget at a slot machine to buy food. He clicked on multiple options, including flavors and nutrients. The machine dispensed two thick bars. He shoved one inside his bag and hogged one down.

VacaRealm passed by as the train weaved through pale-colored buildings, old-Earth architecture, and dark tunnels. Aryabh ignored the holograms of the popular celebrities that approached his seat with an invitation to talk about top-ranking products or the Pacamounts.

When he got down at the last stop, he walked to a bus station. Everything he had tracked ended there. From here on, he had to ask people for help.

He despised the idea.

The bus station differed from what he had expected. It was nothing like the stations in Sonmanto. It didn't have interactive maps or Self-Pleasure Booths. Nor was it slathered in slot machines. Instead, it stood in the middle of a secluded area with bare minimum features, and instead of a horde of impatient commuters, less than a dozen people surrounded the station.

Aryabh studied their faces. None seemed inviting. It didn't help that he couldn't pronounce the names of the locations from the old map.

"Fuck it!" he muttered to himself and walked to the first person he found the least annoying. When the woman saw Aryabh approaching, she moved to the other side of the waiting area. "Bastard." Aryabh grumbled.

Twenty minutes later, a bus with a driver came to a halt. Its destination—Baingo. All the passengers walked to its door and stood in a queue. The driver stepped down and loaded their luggage.

Aryabh watched it all, wondering why everything in this Trunk was so ancient.

The driver looked like a person who wouldn't answer a question without asking one, and so Aryabh joined the other passengers and pretended to wait in the queue.

"Hey," Aryabh said to the man in front.

"What?" he yelled.

"Do you know any of these places?"

Aryabh showed the man a list of names on his widget. He was prepared with a response should the man report him for asking about old-Earth places.

"Do I look like a hundred-year-old?"

"Your brain does," whispered Aryabh.

"What did you say?"

"Just talking to myself."

Aryabh slid his hand inside his coat pocket and punched Kenai's tally counter. His friend had asked him to use it every time he was mean to people. He used the counter one more time for calling the woman a bastard even though he thought she had it coming. It was a cathartic release. Aryabh felt as if he had punched someone.

The bus driver walked up to him. "Where to?"

Aryabh shot an arrow in the dark. "Fohret day Fountainblue?"

"What blue?"

"Boys lay Roi?"

"Are you not speaking English?" the driver threatened.

"Hi. Heading to KingsWood." A young boy approached them and gave his bag to the driver.

"Last stop for me," said Aryabh and got inside the bus.

An automated voice announced all the stops. None of the names matched the old-Earth places. However, he was certain that one of them would take him to Forêt de Fontainebleau.

The first stop was a small tourist Head. It looked like a miniature version of VacaRealm. A few people boarded the bus. Among them was an old couple. Aryabh grabbed his backpack and moved to the seat adjacent to them. He leaned towards the old man.

"A question," he said.

"Ask away," the man replied with an enthusiasm that surprised Aryabh. He noticed the man had a slight accent. English wasn't the first language of the people who had lived here ages ago.

"You know of a place called Fohret day Fountainblue or Boys lay Roi?"

Aryabh felt a set of eyes on him. He looked behind their seats and found the young boy from the queue. He was staring at the Advert Screen near the driver's seat with the bluest set of eyes.

"That doesn't ring a bell. Old-Earth Trunks?" asked the man.

"Yes, small Trunks from before the Political Fumigation. Their names are changed now."

Aryabh scanned the bus's camera. It didn't move in his direction. From what he had observed, the surveillance in these areas wasn't as advanced as Sonmanto.

"No, don't know any place like that. Only lived here for forty years. It wasn't much then. Now look at—"

"Yeah, yeah," Aryabh cut the man off and fell back in his seat.

The bus coursed through the Head and entered the Trunks. The scenery outside Aryabh's window transformed. Small-scale stores replaced the mammoth hotels. Compact Trunk-houses lined up against a backdrop of mountains instead of skyscrapers. A parade of beech and chestnut trees appeared in the landscape, their auburn leaves clinging to their dry branches.

Aryabh watched in surprise as he sailed through Tails full of rolling hills, vineyards, green pastures, and fields swaying with wheat, barley, and sugar beets. He had heard of the change in seasons, but Sonmanto barely adhered to the laws of nature. It looked and felt the same year-round except for scorching heat in summer and bone-numbing cold in winter. To him, the view outside the bus was a fictional realm. He wondered why the Pacamounts let these lands be the way they were. Maybe the 2nd Stratum Pacamounts weren't as ambitious as the 1st. Or there might be another agenda—a psychological game plan, maybe.

He imagined Kenai judging him for not enjoying something as simple as this.

When the bus stopped a few stations later, the young boy glanced at Aryabh with slight hesitation and got down.

Before Aryabh could decide if he was in trouble, there was a knock on his window.

"Excuse me." It was the boy. "I can help you," he mouthed and signaled Aryabh to get down from the bus.

After going back and forth on his decision, Aryabh met him.

"I heard you on the bus. Why are you looking for those places?" the boy asked. Aryabh noticed he was dressed as a Header, but his mannerisms screamed Trunk.

"You got me down from the bus to ask that?"

"I am just curious. How do you know those names?"

"Do you know those places?"

"Please answer me first."

"I don't have time for this." Aryabh turned around to get back on the bus.

"Wait!" said the boy. "Yes, I do and I can help. All I need is to know why you are looking for those places." Then he whispered, "For safety reasons."

Aryabh read his face again. He looked not a day older than nineteen. There was a softness in the way he moved and gentleness in his tone, which people his age never do. It made him both trustworthy and suspicious.

"My great-grandmother met her husband there." The words bled out of Aryabh. "She had written about it in her diary. Just wanted to check what all the fuss was about."

"Diary?"

"I don't have it anymore, of course." Aryabh quickly realized he was talking about a contraband, an illegal object that he had smuggled inside a hidden compartment of his backpack. "My father used to talk about it."

"I don't know about Forêt de Fontainebleau, but you mentioned Bois Le Roi." His pronunciation of the places seemed more accurate to Aryabh. "I have heard my grandma talk about a place like that before. This is my home Trunk." He signaled at the station's name on the screen next to them. It read Kings Wood. "I am here on a break. You can come to my house and ask her about the place."

"What's in it for you?" Aryabh asked.

"Just trying to help you. I'll learn something new too." The boy offered his hand. "My name is JB."

"Sagan." Aryabh introduced himself and shook his hand. It baffled him how easily trust formed within him for the boy. "So, what do you do?" he asked, looking at JB's backpack.

"I am a student at Ancome Paca University."

"That's far from here."

"Yes. I live there but visit here often. I like it here."

Aryabh took a few moments to think about it. "Fine. Let's go."

They walked almost half a mile on a narrow road and then

entered a smaller lane.

Aryabh noticed the boy walked just like him, looking at the ground. It gave Aryabh a chance to scan his surroundings.

Trees lined both sides of their road with the sounds of birds, wind, and modest conversational noises dabbling in between. Grocery stores, small bars, restaurants, and cafes in ancient shapes and unique colors stood independently, unlike the boxed stores that shared walls in Sonmanto. Aryabh thought an open space like that would make him more vigilant, but he felt relaxed. The stressing aura that loomed over his city was absent.

JB turned to a dirt path. In the distance, Aryabh saw a golden field. Huge, round bales of hay were piled in its corner next to a dense thicket. He breathed the chilly wind that brought along the forest's mossy scent.

"You might not be used to this," JB said.

Aryabh ignored the remark.

"Do you understand old-Earth languages?" he asked.

"I think we better talk about such topics after we reach home."

Aryabh stepped on a soft muddy land and his vigilance returned. Before he could ask another question, JB asked his. "Where are you from?"

"Ancome."

"You don't look like a 2nd Stratum citizen," the young boy said without looking at him.

"What do I look like?"

"Pure Sonmanto breed," JB answered with a polite smile.

Aryabh didn't display offense and continued thinking of a fallback plan should JB turn out to be trouble.

The next path brought them to a neighborhood. None of the houses looked like the other. They all differed in size, color, design, and personality. Bold colors and intricate designs embellished their doors, while the windows sat like art pieces. Real plants and trees guarded each house, and vibrant flowers adorned their gardens. What shocked Aryabh the most was adults and children sitting idly and playing around the houses, the features on their faces moving more than usual. To him, everything looked ancient and fantastical, as if he had time-traveled to a different era.

"How are people allowed to have houses like these? You don't have to follow the PHS?"

"I don't know how to answer that. For now, let's just say the Pacamounts Housing Standards are different for us. My grandma will explain that much better than I can."

"Fuckin' know-it-all grandmother," Aryabh mumbled under his breath and punched the tally counter inside his pocket.

"We are here."

They stopped at a rustic two-storied stone house. JB opened the gate and entered. Aryabh followed up on a stone path that was paved between patches of lush green lawn. The grass glittered with morning dew. On the right was a peach tree, its leaves crisp from autumn. Underneath it was a quaint picnic table.

Aryabh turned his sight away from the surroundings and looked at the house. It glimmered as the tender morning sunrays flashed on its windows. Smoke puffed out of its tall chimney. Green and maroon vines slithered on its exterior walls and tiny shrubs covered the entrance of the house.

On good days, he had dreamt of a house like this. But instead of this mysterious place, he had pictured it on Zenith.

JB opened a navy blue door with his key. "Have a seat. I'll be back." He dropped his bag on the couch and went inside the house.

Aryabh hung his coat on a funny-looking rack and looked around the living room. It was twice the size of his entire apartment. Potted plants and glass cabinets full of random items crammed the corners of the room. The walls were covered in art, mostly of landscapes. When he touched the frames, he realized the paintings were old and were retouched to look digital.

The spot that allured him the most was a small, dimly lit space underneath a staircase. It pulled him like a secret. When he looked carefully, his eyes widened, despite himself.

There were empty, identical racks which he was certain were bookshelves. Nothing left perfectly lined stains on racks like old, dusty books that have sat on them for too long. He knew that more than anyone.

After inspecting everything, he walked to the couch and took a seat. A stone fireplace faced him; only he didn't know what it was. On its mantle were dozens of digital photo frames. He squinted to identify the faces. One photo was of a pre-teen JB standing alongside an old woman with a burn scar on her face.

Aryabh regained his posture as soon as he heard footsteps.

A plump woman in her late forties entered the room. She wore a cactus-print apron over a long brown dress with her dark hair tied in a tight bun. Her face appeared stern and yet restful. She made signs with her fingers and palms.

"I don't speak sign language," said Aryabh. He doubted the intentions of the woman who was okay with a stranger sitting in her house.

"Maman! Uh, Mom..." JB appeared from behind her and hugged her. "Sagan, my mother, Helene."

Aryabh gave a slight nod.

JB signed to his mother to explain. Not knowing what they were communicating was eating Aryabh alive.

Helene looked at him with a blank face and then smiled. She signed again.

"Mom says, 'nice to meet you'."

"Okay."

The woman scrunched her brows at the response, her stiff posture transforming into a shiver. She folded her arms and looked at the main door. Aryabh had left it open, just in case he had to run. Helene closed the door and picked up a cardigan from a chair. She walked up to her son and pressed the sweater on his chest.

"I am not cold."

She shot daggers at him.

JB shook his head and wore the cardigan.

Aryabh looked away from the mother-son duo and hugged his cold arms. He removed an AwakeTab bottle from his pants pocket. Helene noticed it and asked him to stop. She motioned a food sign and went inside the house.

"Grandma is in the backyard," JB said and sat next to Aryabh. "She'll join us soon."

It was almost eleven in the morning. Aryabh was famished. All he had had was a slot machine bar at Asnofi. He was thinking about eating the remaining bar he had in his bag when Helene brought in a food trolley. JB took the cart from her and placed it in front of the couch. Helene knocked her palm four times and left the room.

Aryabh didn't believe his eyes when he noticed the trolley. It was a smaller, yet more flamboyant exhibit than Caspian's table.

"Here!" JB picked up a mug from the trolley and handed it to Aryabh. "Drink this first. It will warm you up."

Aryabh looked inside the cup. The liquid was barely visible under its steam. He brought the beverage up to his nose and smelled. Nothing familiar.

The lingering doubt wasn't leaving him alone. He was thousands of miles away from his comfort zone, sitting in the 2nd Stratum, in a stranger's house whom he asked about old-Earth places. Should he be eating their food?

"At this point, you have more on us than we have on you," JB said when he read Aryabh's hesitation. "It's just hot chocolate."

Aryabh's lips curled into a slight smile. "So, coffee?" he asked.

"No. The chocolate doesn't have caffeine. You carry enough of it in your pocket."

Aryabh noticed it was the third time that JB had remarked something about him, something he hadn't shared since they met. His wall of vigilance raised higher. "From where do you get so much water?" he asked.

"We..." JB hesitated, "we have our own borewell. It's a method of retrieving water from the earth."

Aryabh made a mental note to research about it later.

He watched as JB blew the fuming steam from his mug and mimicked. The white froth cleared and a dark, velvety brown liquid surfaced. His first sip hit him with a memory of Kenai. He felt a knot in his throat, which he drowned with a few more gulps. The warmth of the beverage relaxed his tensed shoulders.

An object moved inside his cup, a cylindrical bark. He pulled it out. "That's one small straw."

"That's not a straw." JB leaned forward and suppressed a hearty laugh. His shiny, blonde hair cascaded down his head and grazed his temple. "That's a cinnamon stick. It's a spice. Adds flavor."

Aryabh recalled Kenai's ramblings about this spice. He had died longing for its taste, as if the spice were too mighty for his noble heart. With a clenched jaw, he used the bark as a straw. It didn't deserve the glory. It was meant to be used as a trashy tube of plastic.

"That's Sonmanters for you." An old woman strolled into the living room and took a seat on the wooden chair next to the fireplace. "You give them food; they turn it into plastic." She covered her legs with a shawl and grabbed a mug of hot chocolate with her pink hands.

"Grandma," spoke JB.

The old woman frowned at the greeting and faced Aryabh.

"Sagan. Insightful name," she said. "You can call me Maminours." Her voice sounded as if she was talking between rigorous bouts of coughing.

"Grandma!" JB shot a warning look at the woman.

"What's going on?" Aryabh asked, ready to get up from his seat.

"See, he doesn't even know what it means," said the grandmother.

"That implies it's not English! He can—"

"Calm down, mon chou. I've seen the world. I know a vermin when I see one." The old woman tilted her head and eyed Aryabh again. "He is alright. Besides, I don't like how the word 'grandma' sounds on your tongue. I like it when you call me Maminours." A childlike grin spread across her face. "Maminours is a made-up name in French, our native language, that JB started calling me as a child," she explained to Aryabh. "Mamie, means grandma. Nounours means a soft bear. I am JB's grandma soft bear. Maminours." She jiggled her shoulders and gauged Aryabh's reaction.

He didn't flinch.

"See, I told you, he is alright."

JB sat back on the couch, defeated.

Aryabh glanced at the grandmother with a pretense to emptying his mug. She was the oldest person he had ever met. Despite her age, her head was full of hair—gray, short, and immaculate. Her speech was slow, yet confident. Her skin was withered and back bent, and yet a sense of power radiated on her face, a distorted face that was half covered in a pink burn scar. Aryabh felt reluctant to test her.

It took him some time, but he recognized what it was about Maminours that reminded him of Kenai. She too wore eyeglasses. But unlike Kenai's, her glasses stayed put on the bridge of her nose.

"How old are you?" Aryabh asked in a direct tone, his head titled backward. He wanted to set a sense of authority.

"Ah, that's one unique form of greeting, I see." Maminours's rimless oval glasses shone in unison with her teeth. "I turned eighty-three today."

Aryabh veiled his shock. He had read about humans living above seventy a century ago, but had never known about Earthlers this old.

"It's gran... Maminours's birthday today."

"Is facial hair legal here?" Aryabh asked another question.

"Boy, you are a master communicator. Thank you for your wishes." Maminours scratched the wispy white hairs on her chin and pulled its ends to form a neat tiny triangle."

"It's an alien concept to them," said JB. "They don't celebrate birthdays."

Aryabh wanted to point out that he knew well what a birthday was and had celebrated one, but he stayed mum.

"I see. Well, you boys should eat some grub. We'll discuss concepts later." The old woman looked at her grandson. "Mon chou, feed this boy well. He looks deficient." She stood. "I am going for a much-needed afternoon nap. See you in the evening. Dinner is on me." With that, she left through the stairs above the secret bookshelf.

"Every year on her birthday, Maminours makes her special raclette and tarte aux pommes."

JB read Aryabh's face again.

"Uh... a cheese dish and apple pie."

"What? I don't care for that! You brought me here to tell me about those places."

"Only Maminours can tell that, and she won't if you disrupt her naptime. So, for now," JB pulled the trolley towards them, "help yourself. These are fresh fruits from the backyard, cherry tomatoes, raspberries." He popped one in his mouth. "Apples. Here, have these." A basket of fresh pastries rolled towards Aryabh. "Mom baked them. She runs a bakery in the Trunk center. These are croissants and pain au...chocolate bread."

Aryabh stared at the food, a crowd of unrecognizable objects.

'You've never tasted an apple?!' Lyra's voice rung in his head.

He picked up a plump red apple and took a bite. From its shiny exterior, he assumed it would be too hard to chew, but his teeth sunk into its crispness effortlessly. Sweet and tart juices leaked from the corner of his mouth.

Aisle after aisle of Sonmanto's PacaMarkets were filled with desserts, but Aryabh had never needed them for survival. He couldn't even remember the last time he had eaten something sweet.

They ate one item after the other until the trolley was empty. Aryabh rested his back on the couch and closed his eyes. Not even once had he experienced his stomach so delightfully full.

I've always had a transactional relationship with food. I ate it, it helped me survive. There was no love there, because it didn't come easy. Kenai explained the importance of it many times, but food never earned my respect.

But at Maminours's house, when I had my first taste of real food, I felt like a human. It seemed as if I insulted their food by putting it in the same system that was a graveyard of AwakeTabs and slot-machine filth.

Everyone deserves that. Real, clean, healthy food. It's our right.

"You eat this every day?" Aryabh asked.

"No. I mostly survive on what all Headers eat, but I make it a point to eat real food when I am here."

"How do they afford this?"

"Nothing on this trolley was bought. Here, in KingsWood, we, the Trunkers, grow our own crops, fruits, and vegetables, we bake our own bread, and craft our own cheese. What we can't make, we stop using it."

Aryabh snorted.

"What?"

"You folks have a lot of time on your hands," he said, as he tried to dislodge a raspberry seed from his molars.

"Don't say that in front of my grandmother," said JB as he stood. "Rest for a while. We'll talk in the evening." He lent Aryabh a thick blanket and drew curtains on all the windows. The bright room turned dark and cozy. "Take a nap." He build a fire in the fireplace and disappeared to the back of the house with the trolley.

Aryabh had a lot of questions. Most importantly, he wanted to know about the places in Lyra's diary. On a regular day, he would have marched up to the old woman's room and gotten the answers out of her. But he lay on the couch and wrapped himself in the warm blanket.

'You don't have to keep fighting all the time. Sometimes you just quit and take a nap,' He remembered.

With a contented stomach, he watched the dance of flickering fire on the ceiling. Within seconds, sleep enveloped him.

His eyes shot open to a whispering argument at the back of the house. The clock on his lenses told him he had been asleep for almost six hours. He got up in a flash and pushed his ear towards the kitchen. None of the words were recognizable. They were not talking in English! Aryabh also noticed one more voice that sounded like a woman's.

JB's mother didn't speak.

"You can join us, boy," announced Maminours from the back of the house.

How did she know? Aryabh thought as he crossed one room and stepped into the kitchen.

It was almost the same size as Caspian's. Three big refrigerators, a four-burner stove, two ovens, and a two-person dining table lined the room. In the center of the kitchen was a marbled island cluttered with jars of pickles, fruit preserves, and loose teas.

JB was slicing a block of cheese and his grandmother was tossing a salad. The only woman present was Helene. She was untying a bundle of firewood as if she were alone in the room.

"You stopped snoring," Maminours said, "in case you are wondering how I knew."

Aryabh decided he could not be around this woman for long.

"Get ready for dinner," she added. "Fresh air is waiting for us." She carried the salad bowl and left the kitchen through the back door. Helene followed her, lugging a sack full of wood.

"I am okay with eating in stale air," Aryabh said to JB and folded his arms.

"It's nice outside this time of the day. Wear that coat and help me carry this trolley."

Chilly air hit them as they stepped outside. Aryabh noticed that the coldness smelled distinctively different from the winter of Sonmanto. The medley of burning wood, scented flowers, and hot food only made it better.

They walked by a patio covered in creepers. Birdhouses and wind chimes hung from above it. Right outside it was a small patch of ground full of plants. Each had a label poked next to it. Aryabh squinted to read them. Parsley. Tarragon. Chives. Chervil.

"Herbs," helped JB.

Aryabh nodded and glanced at the backyard as they carried the trolley towards it. On one side was a well, behind which stood a grove of trees. Helene had lit a bonfire in the middle, and JB's grandmother was setting a table next to it.

They all took their seats; Aryabh shifted in his. A pleasant smell, however, overshadowed his uneasiness. He looked at the source.

Helene was pouring lustrous red wine into the glasses. It carried notes he couldn't even identify.

Maminours pointed at the items on the table. "Bread, salad, ham, potatoes, cornichons, and cheese. Bon appétit!"

Aryabh helped himself and stared at his crowded plate.

"Let me show you," said Maminours. "This is a baguette." She lifted a long, thin loaf of bread with a toasty crust. "You cut it into whatever size your heart desires." She cut a small chunk, halved it, and placed one piece on a table grill. "Toast it." From a plate full of cheese slices, she picked one and dropped it in a tiny pan. "Let your cheese do its work too." She set the pan under the grill. Its flaming red coil melted the cheese under it and toasted the bread above it.

"Now you take this heartwarming bread." The old woman fetched her piece from the grill. "Layer it with salad, potatoes, and ham, and pour this on top." She grabbed the tiny pan. The cheese in it had melted and turned gooey. "The trick is to pour it in a way that it seals all the contents to the bread like a nice, trusty blanket."

Aryabh replicated the process. When it was ready, he gripped the sandwich and brought it to his mouth. The fat of the melted cheese glistened and its aroma overwhelmed him. He shut his brain and took a bite.

So many textures and flavors! The bread was crisp and the layer of ham moist and chewy. The potatoes and the salad—carrots, corn, peppers, and lettuce—were tender and perfectly seasoned. Then came the gooey, nutty cheese that coated its mouth. At last, he mimicked Maminours and bit into a sour cornichon. He washed it all down with a sip of the robust wine.

Aryabh couldn't tell if the tears in his eyes were because of the scalding cheese or missing his friend. Kenai would have lost it if he were here.

"Where you come from," spoke Maminours, "food is supplied by machines. There is zero human contact. You know why?" She sipped her wine. "Because that was the goal, to distance people from one another, so that they could never unite to fight against them. Food is remarkably intimate. It binds us."

It made Aryabh think of Kenai again.

After a lengthy dinner, they moved their chairs towards the bonfire. Helene sat between her mother and son, still spaced out. Aryabh took a seat next to Maminours and thought about the woman's voice from the argument. JB's mother could definitely talk. Why was she pretending otherwise, then?

There was a weird tension in the air.

A breeze passed through the backyard, playing a melody on the wind chimes. Aryabh moved closer to the fire and toasted his hands.

"Ah," Maminours said as she warmed her hands too. "Like old friends sitting at a table and remembering stories of their childhood." She rubbed the warm hands on her knees. "So, why were you looking for Bois Le Roi?"

Aryabh was glad he didn't have to make the small talk. He

prepared to parrot the same story he had told JB. Lyra's story.

"Not the great-grandparents malarkey," the old woman said. "Give me the real story."

"I don't do malarkey. That's exactly why I'm here."

Maminours folded her hands, the fire glow twirling on the shiny burn scar on the right side of her face.

"Look," Aryabh spoke again. "The faster you help me, the sooner I'll be out of your house."

"Bois-le-Roi was a small town near Paris," Maminours began. "Paris was a part of what people now call VacaRealm." She grunted with displeasure. "Who names a place VacaRealm? Anyway. Fontainebleau was a town next to Bois-le-Roi. It was famous for its art and history."

"What about Fohret day Fountainblue?" Aryabh asked.

"It's not Fohret, it's Forêt." Maminours pronounced it in a manner Aryabh couldn't even imitate. "A thick forest surrounds Fontainebleau. Forêt de Fontainebleau means the forest of Fontainebleau."

Aryabh felt like a fool.

"I will show you the way to it."

"Okay."

Now that he had what he had come for, he could shut up, pass the night, and flee the next morning before anyone was up. "What do you do here?" he asked. "How do you keep a land and house like these?"

"After they took over—"

"The Pacamounts?"

"Yes, Sagan. Them." Maminours said through her denture. "After them, a lot of our people moved to the Heads to make a living. My father was a well-respected man. He convinced a small crowd to stay here. They did, even if it meant being lowly. He believed it was better to eat one piece of bread in the open air than feast on a flamboyant menu in a cage. I agree with my old man. I could never slave for them and be able to enjoy luxury."

Aryabh smirked. "Luxury is the last word I'd use to describe what we have there. *This*," he looked around, "is luxury."

"I know, son. But that term has a different meaning to you and me, and the rest."

Aryabh's heart raced at the sound of 'son'.

"So, where was I?" Maminours took a sip of wine. "Yes. Some people stayed here. The government needed people in Trunks too. A powerful machine runs on well-oiled components. So they allotted managers to Trunks like ours. Cream. My father found out that the Kings Wood's manager ran multiple businesses. So he made a deal with him. The Trunkers would supply him with cheap labor for a few perks. It was a small price to pay for an extra ounce of freedom. Luckily for us, greed is an immortal beast. They always want cheap labor. And, here we are, two generations later."

Maminours pushed a log of wood into the fire and continued, "Our properties are under their name, but we can keep them as we like it. They believe we are too naïve and fragile to cause harm. You come from a Head; you know what they think about Trunkers. Well, we take advantage of this misconception and make the best out of it."

The old woman flashed her wine-stained teeth.

"Are there other Trunks like this?" Aryabh asked.

"A few. Maybe more in the third Stratum."

"How long do you think you can go on living like this? Sooner or later, they are going to come for you."

Maminours smiled and placed her hand on Aryabh's knee. "Son, we always got to have more confidence in us than in them."

The yard went quiet. They all stared at the fire as the wood crackled. Aryabh felt a desperate need to have an empty room and a few hours to process everything he had learnt.

He followed the path of an ember and looked above. Infinite, brightly lit stars packed the dark, moonless sky. His lips parted. Even in his wildest dreams, he could not have imagined a sky so generous. He searched for a particular group of stars.

"Lyra," spoke Maminours.

Aryabh's head cocked in her direction. "What did you say?"

"That's constellation Lyra." The old woman pointed at a cluster of stars. "Its name was derived from Lyre, a harp-like musical instrument from ancient Greece."

Aryabh didn't understand many of those words, but he was relieved. He thought of Lyra and missed talking to her terribly.

"Although," Maminours spoke again, "Keid named her after the constellation, not the instrument."

Without missing a beat, Aryabh's survival instinct kicked in. He glanced at Helene and JB. They were still in their chairs. No weapons. He looked around the garden to spot the exits. Apart from the patio, there was a flimsy wooden door next to the trees. But it looked like it would take him to the neighbor's house. He thought of where his backpack was—on the floor, next to the couch in the living room. How reckless!

He would jump out of the chair, run across the patio to the living room, grab his bag, and escape from the main door.

"You are one of a kind, Aryabh," the old woman addressed him with his real name and flashed a smile again.

Chapter 30

"Don't panic," JB broke his prolonged silence, "if you were in trouble, you would already have been in some."

All his life, Aryabh had set traps for people. It angered him to be on the other side.

"You are impeccably astute, Aryabh," Maminours said. "I admit, you can fool me on a bad day. But, smart girl, Lyra. She knew what to share with you and what not to."

Aryabh's chest tightened. Did Lyra set him up?

"I'll tell one last story," said Maminours. "This one will be quick."

She emptied her glass and rubbed her hands.

"Simon, my grandfather, was friends with Lyra's maternal

great-grandparents. My father maintained that friendship with her grandparents. Lamentably, they moved to the asteroid and their friendship withered. Lyra's foreparents were not from here nor were they related to us, but such were the old times that love and camaraderie turned strangers into a family. When they came to confiscate old-Earth belongings, my grandparents dug a ten feet hole in this very backyard and hid everything they imagined their offspring would appreciate—old pictures, letters, books, paintings, heirlooms. That was how I learned about Lyra's family and saw their pictures. Until his last days, my father regretted not being able to speak with his friends. Earth had barred communication with Zenith at the time. Then, one fine evening, my petit-fils—my grandson JB, came to me with news I could not have imagined in a hundred years," she said, her chin rising higher with each word. "There was a girl on the asteroid. A Zenither called Lyra."

Aryabh wanted to get up and run, but he sat still.

"She was snooping around and leaving messages on various portals of the neighboring VacaRealm Trunks. Sending the same messages and asking questions about our family and Fontainebleau. I knew who she was in a heartbeat. JB didn't like the risk of getting involved, but I wanted to help the little girl. So we contacted her. Told her we knew Simon's family and decided to keep mum about everything else until she was here. She was reluctant in trusting us, but we gave her proofs and told her we would help her here on Earth. JB threw in some buffer words, the usual Pacamounts-worshiping so that our communication didn't stand out."

Aryabh looked at JB, impressed and repulsed.

"Then she told us about an Earthler she had befriended. Aryabh. A kind man from Sonmanto who was helping her with paperwork. I apologize for the brazen prejudice," Maminours leaned towards Aryabh, "but we don't trust Sonmanters here. I conveyed that sentiment to her once and kept our communication to the minimum. We were happy like we had found an old family and all we wanted was for her to get here safely. JB was prepping to receive her at Ancome when we got her message. Her documents had disappeared at the transit station."

Aryabh looked again at the flimsy door by the trees.

"We knew it had Aryabh written all over it. I didn't have the heart to tell her that. Besides, she stopped all communication with us after the incident. Maybe she was heartbroken. But we were furious for her. We tracked your location and followed your every move."

"How?" Aryabh puked the question, his nostrils flaring.

"My petit-fils here is a wizard too, much like yourself. You should have asked him what he did in his free time. He is terrible at lying." Maminours looked at JB with significant pride in her knowing, raven-like, gray eyes. "After Lyra talked about you the first time, we helped her build a locator to track her and make sure she stayed safe once she landed on Earth. When you stole her documents, you stole the locator too. Good thing that you didn't destroy it."

Lyra's diary, Aryabh thought.

"A compass. It was a sticker of a compass. Clever, that girl. She had stuck it on her great-grandmother's diary. We tracked the locator in Sonmanto. It was too risky to come there and confront you. We didn't want to be involved in whatever you were doing, but we kept a constant eye on you."

"Did she know?" Aryabh asked.

"About you stealing? No. She did ask us to track the locator. It was her last message before she stopped replying to us. It was when she had noticed that her diary was missing too. We couldn't tell her the truth. People react impulsively when they are surprised by betrayal. Even smart people. The littlest mistake on her side would have caused a lot of trouble, to us and to her. JB did, however, warn her about you; asked her to at least see the face of the Earthler who was helping her."

Aryabh burned with anger. That was the reason why Lyra had insisted on meeting face to face. She had always doubted him. It was fake—all of it, the conversations, the laughs, and the friendship. He slumped in his chair as a profound sadness overtook his anger.

Maminours turned her chair towards him.

"Boy, we have been tracking you since. Then, lo and behold, you are in VacaRealm! It got me thinking. Why did this fella not dispose of a dangerous contraband? It was only a diary, after all. Why was he headed here? Then it hit me." The old woman leaned back and beamed a kind smile. "Something changed. Didn't it?"

"You stalked me!" Aryabh pushed his chair back and advanced towards Maminours. Helene propped herself between them. With eyes fiercer than the fire, she motioned Aryabh to sit.

"We wouldn't have if you didn't commit the theft," said JB.

Aryabh sat back in his chair. "What do you want?"

"Lyra contacted us yesterday. She apologized for cutting all communication with us. A lot had happened in her life. She is, in fact, giving a big speech right now as we talk!" Maminours shook her head in amazement. "She said she still wants to come here and told us the truth about you. So, we spilled some of our secrets too. We told her about the locator and that you were heading here. It surprised her as well. We discussed your motive, but none of us could come up with one. Except me, of course." The old woman grinned. "I underestimated her, Aryabh. Lyra didn't react impulsively when she found out the truth. She is too insightful and honest with herself to punish you. When we asked her how she wants to deal with you, she said she wants *you* to decide that; to see this side of Earth with an open mind if it helps you in rebuilding your beliefs. Those were her exact words. Can you imagine the emotional strength it takes to give that kind of forgiveness to the person who has destroyed your biggest dream?"

Shock clasped Aryabh. Lyra had forgiven him?

"So to come back to your question," said Maminours, "what do I want? I want you to finish what you came here to do."

"And what's that?"

"Redeem yourself."

The old woman knew his plans, Aryabh thought. "I will once you stop singing sagas," he said.

Maminours cackled. She placed her hand on Aryabh again. "What are you going to do after you are done helping Lyra?"

Aryabh wanted to state it was none of her business. But he said, "I don't know that, yet."

"Well, you did one good thing. You left the Farm."

Aryabh did not even try to get mad. It was the uncertainty about his future that concerned him more. In his vision, the possibility of Zenith glittered enticingly, yet he found himself unable to move towards it.

"You should know one thing, Aryabh. History has proven that authoritarian governments are always temporary. Their system doesn't work in the long run. The Pacamounts, regardless of the rebellion, will perish one day. My guess is sooner than later. Do you know who suffers longer than the generation who has been at war?"

Aryabh shook his head, the smell of the burning wood overwhelming him.

"The generation after that. We leave them poor, hungry, angry, and broken. They survive on the infected aftermath only to create a new generation that wants to go to war again. Cruelty and suffering both have a way of traveling through generations. The anti-Pacas don't see the big picture. Their heart is in the right place, but their hatred and animosity blind them from seeing what needs to be seen at this time."

"And what's that?"

"Children." Maminours pulled her chair closer to Aryabh. "Have you seen the schools and universities lately? They are like their own different Stratums. Why do you think the Pacamounts spend an enormous portion of their budget on education? It's an optimum time in the human lifecycle to inject strong thoughts and beliefs, to create future followers. To these children, they relay their version of history, announce fabricated news, teach destructive science, they...they impart regressive notions, tutor mediocre English, and self-glorify on a daily basis. They distance them from humans and equip them with slogans, flags, bots, and chants. If all they need are compliant adults, why are they wasting important resources on children? The most effective way to create a submissive adult is to raise a brainwashed child. That's why they have PacaChildren."

Maminours paused to refill her glass, took a sip, and spoke again. "Even if we take down the Pacamounts in coming years, what kind of society do you think these kids will create in the future? Everyone is busy axing the branches and tearing down the tree. We need to disrupt the roots. So, even if we fail to dismantle the shark, there will be a generation they would find hard to manipulate. And above all that," Maminours looked at Aryabh and JB with gentle eyes, "children need to be loved, not exploited."

"That's some idealistic BS," argued Aryabh. "A lot of these children grow up in Heads. You have no idea what goes on there."

"Of course, it's not easy. But it's not impossible." Maminours gestured at her grandson. "He was never kept away from the Heads or from accepting what kids of his age were given. We never alienated him from the world. All we did was showed him the path and gave him a choice. I have no doubt that he would impart the same wisdom if or when he has his own children. It's a lengthy and tiring process, but so far, it's the most effective method there is. It's fighting it the right way, not the fast way, even if you don't live to see the victory."

Aryabh didn't speak for a long time. Then asked, "Where does one start?"

"The biggest mistake a lot of anti-Pacas are making is targeting Cream. It's not always the people with money who have the most power. No. It's also the people with influence who make a notable difference, good or bad, for their weapon is people themselves. It's the influential that the Pacamounts used to anchor their government. Through TV, the news, and the Internet, they tunneled their way into the head of every Earthler and spread their propaganda. Think about who and what influences kids. Books, parents, friends, teachers, schools. Write them. Find them. Be them. Try—"

"I am not capable of doing that," said Aryabh.

Maminours leaned back and crossed her legs, gazing at the fire. "Ce que je ferai ici aura au moins le mérite de ne ressembler à personne, parce que ce sera l'impression de ce que j'aurai ressenti, moi tout seul," she said as if she were reciting a poem.

Aryabh listened with an impressed gaze.

"What I do here will be unique because my actions will be based on my own unique feelings and experiences. A prominent French painter said that. You know what is the best thing about humans, Aryabh? We can go to bed being the most arrogant, the most sinister person there is, and can still wake up with the ability to be good and kind. Lyra forgave you because she saw a part of you that you don't see yourself. You are capable of great things, son. Choose your own way. In a world where not speaking English is a death sentence, I resist every day by speaking my native language. I rebel by teaching it to my daughter and she did it by teaching it to her son. Helene here is even stronger than I am. She is not mute."

Helene shot a warning look at her mother.

"She refuses to speak English. She has, ever since she was a child. My daughter was barely thirteen when she made her decision. I was not happy with it, but I gave her the power and freedom to make that decision. We made up an accident and told everyone she lost her voice. She has pretended to be non-verbal ever since." Maminours's proud eyes turned wet, the creases on her throat undulating. "No words can express the pain I've felt watching my child face this world without her voice."

Aryabh looked at Helene. Her stern face perched on her mother's shoulder. Maminours held her hand and kissed her on the head.

"You hate English so much that you chose not to speak your whole life?" Aryabh dared to strike a conversation with Helene. The look on her face made him regret his mocking tone.

"It's not the language that's bad," Maminours answered instead. "It's what it represents—the lack of freedom and choice. Moreover, our language kept us anchored to our convictions. It reminded us who we are every day. Search what keeps you grounded and still gives you the power to fight."

Aryabh rested on his chair and looked above. He felt lost.

"I don't believe any of this makes a difference," he said, as if to argue with himself. "Earth is a ticking time bomb that's running on its last few seconds. It will explode and reset on its own."

"Not everyone has the privilege to have that mindset. Forget about Earth. What do *you* feel?"

"I feel..." Aryabh swallowed a lump in his throat and looked at the ground. Three suffocated words propulsed from his core. "I feel broken." The words reminded him how alone he feels in this world.

"Oh, son." Maminours grabbed his freezing hand and squeezed it between her warm palms.

Aryabh tried to stop his hand from shaking.

"It's okay. You've been through a lot. No one deserves that. It's okay."

He took a shaky breath and fought the urge to sob.

"Your pain is your strength," said the old woman. "Use that."

"Pain is strength?" That pushed the sob away. "Bullshit! Preach that when you've experienced nothing but pain."

"I see why you feel that. But if it wasn't for the strength from your pain, how else would you be here? Think about it."

Aryabh thought about Kenai, as the grief of his death sprung again.

Maminours stroked Aryabh's shoulder and got up. She went into the kitchen and brought everyone a slice of warm apple pie. "Tarte aux pommes, a delightful thing to make."

Aryabh stared at the caramelized apple slices on his plate and asked, "You said you know about Boys...bois le Roi. How do I get there?"

"Mon chéri," Maminours stretched out her hand. "You are sitting in it."

"What?" Aryabh's eyes stood still.

"Yes. Bois-le-Roi means 'woods of the king'. KingsWood." Maminours pulled down her glasses and winked. "Imagine the trouble you'd have saved yourself if you knew French."

Helene burst into a blaring laughter.

"I had a hunch you'd be gone when we woke up," Maminours spoke when she saw Aryabh climbing down the stairs the next morning.

Aryabh had had that hunch too.

"I hope my bed was comfortable," said JB.

"Very."

They ate breakfast as Maminours sent a map to Aryabh's widget. When they were done eating, Aryabh grabbed his back-pack and stepped outside into the golden Trunk morning. Maminours, Helene, and JB followed him to the gate.

"Catch up with you someday," Aryabh told JB.

"I hope so. Keep us updated."

"I will."

They shook hands.

Helene handed Aryabh JB's coat and a small bag. "Un encas pour la route," she said, her voice coarse yet firm.

Aryabh looked at the others.

"Snacks for the road," explained JB. "And your coat won't do where you are going. You'll need this one."

Aryabh removed his coat and put on JB's. After being satisfied with the size and placement of its pockets, he shoved his old coat and the snacks in his backpack.

"Thank you," he said to Helene.

She smiled and bobbed.

"There is another pocket," Maminours pointed at Aryabh's coat sleeves. "It has a letter in it. Read it later."

"Okay."

Aryabh offered his hand to the old woman. Maminours pulled him into a tight hug. She stroked his hair and patted his back. "Stay safe, son."

Even though his eyes stung with hot tears, Aryabh felt as if everything was going to be okay. He found it incredible how a genuine human touch of assurance could flood a sense of security through him.

"Bye," he said, taking a final glimpse of the house, and left.

"Was this wise, Maminours?" JB spoke as soon as Aryabh walked away. "I wasn't even sure if it was the right decision to bring him to our house, and you told him almost everything."

"Don't fret, mon chou," Maminours, almost sang. "He is special. Our world needs him."

"But we didn't have to open our whole house to him or share stories of our ancestors. Or tell him about maman!"

"Some people need a reason or a purpose, some need guidance, and some need materialistic rewards to fight. This boy has a brain many people would kill for but he is also disturbingly stubborn. He," Maminours tugged at her chin hairs and looked at JB, "needed proof. I gave him that. Now he knows that change is possible."

"Penses-tu qu'il rejoindra Jean?" Helene asked her mother.

"Oui," answered Maminours as she gazed at the back of Aryabh's head, which then came to a sudden stop.

Aryabh turned and walked back towards them. They all stood still in their tracks, Helene holding the arms of her mother.

"Why is he coming back?" JB regained his stiff posture.

Aryabh stood facing them and stared for a second. "Forgot something," he said. "How do you say 'fuck you' in French?"

Maminours hung to Helene's arms and roared with laughter.

CHAPTER 31

THE EARTHLER NEWS

November 13, 2125

THE PACAMOUNTS WILL COLONIZE THE MOON!

156 years after the moon landing and 75 years after Zenith's colonization, The Pacamounts are now ready to plant the shark on the moon. In the CEO assembly that was held yesterday, The Pacamounts have decided to use Zenith as...

"When we reached the forest, we found an enchanted kingdom waiting to welcome us," Aryabh read from Lyra's great-grandmother's diary as he stood by the forest of Fontainebleau.

Maminours's map had brought him right up to its entrance. It was exactly how it was mentioned in the diary more than a hundred years ago—a discreet arch of trees on the side of the road. Aryabh jotted the coordinates on his widget and entered the forest.

For hours, he wandered in the thicket, soaking everything—the auburn canopy of pine, beech, and oak trees, the drizzle of their autumn leaves, the vibrant dance of the sunrays on the forest's foggy landscape, the sweet-smelling silence, rocks shaped like random animals, and the crisp chill in the air that felt cozy instead of cruel under JB's coat.

He walked through the orange forest like a shadow, adding the crunch of the leaves to the chittering of birds and the hissing of wind from needles and twigs.

A while later, the main path forked into two smaller roads, just as the diary said. Lyra's great-grandparents had taken the road on the right, and so did Aryabh. The path led him to a cliff.

"Woah!" Air escaped his mouth as he took in the view.

Below him, not too deep, was a wide-open valley, its swaying pastures surrounded by toy-like houses. Aryabh was reflecting on how the view resembled the paintings at Maminours's house when he heard a sound.

He looked to his left. Behind a conglomerate of rocks, he found a babbling stream that merged with a river near the valley.

Aryabh looked behind at the forest and then back at the valley. It was the biggest radius of vacant space he had ever been in. He breathed a lungful of fresh air and climbed on one of the big rocks by the stream. A silly cackle came out of him as he struggled to find a comfortable spot.

Once he was settled, he removed his backpack, and stretched his fingers to touch the glassy stream.

"Fuck!" He retracted. The water was ice-cold. He grinned and submerged his whole hand. Water glided through his fingers. He made a fist and tried to hold the liquid. Then he chuckled again at his foolishness and cupped his hand to drink the water.

> The forest was beautiful. I will never forget the experience. But what finally gave me strength and a sense of power was the stream. It's hard to understand its significance if you have not lived your whole life worrying about every single drop of water that you use. Seeing clearer and cleaner water flow unlimitedly in front of my eyes filled me with hope. I felt the combined energy of a hundred AwakeTabs.

Aryabh took pictures of his surroundings. When a small blue and yellow bird perched by the stream to drink water, he clicked its picture too. Watching the bird relish the beverage made him hungry. He feasted on the bread, cheese, grapes, and a small bottle of juice that Helene had packed for him.

After he was done, he unzipped the edge of his sleeves and pulled out a folded sheet of paper from it. He looked around and unfolded the paper. Maminours had penned a handwritten letter.

Precious Aryabh,

Conviction without purpose is a waste. The reason I brought you to my house was to show you a part of the world that you didn't believe existed, to introduce you to people who still carry conscience in their hearts. Trust me when I say this. There are many places and people like that hidden in the pockets of Earth.

The Pacamounts sat at a table and divided the map of Earth like they were slicing a piece of cake. But they couldn't split connection and camaraderie.

The CEOs are trying hard to hide it but the Pacamounts are losing control over the 3rd Stratum. It is brewing with resistance. I've listed an address below and the way to get there. It's located in Western 3rd Stratum. Before the Political Fumigation, it used to be in a country called India. That's where Lyra's great-grand-mother and ancestors are from. There is a group there that works towards the goal we talked about last night. If you ever feel lost or don't know where to channel your pain, go there. Look for a man called Jean Baptiste. He is JB's father.

Don't worry about Lyra. We will take care of her when she is here.

Aryabh, it is okay to be broken. We are all chipped and cracked in some way. But you are more than those shattered pieces. I believe in you.

Love,
Maminours

Aryabh tucked the letter in his coat pocket and placed his arms and chin over his knees. He reflected on Maminours's words as he caught a whiff of the fire smoke from the previous night still emanating from his skin. Before he gets engaged in forming his next new plan, he had to do something.

Aryabh took a deep breath and turned on his widget to write his own letter.

Dear Lyra,

I am not going to pretend everything is okay. I knew how this was going to end, and so I will save my sorrys for the end. But before I walk away from your life for good, I want you to know a few things, things I never shared, even to myself. Things you need to know before you move to Earth.

I don't even know where to start. Ever since I can remember, I despised my life on this planet. I abhorred humans. Earthlers.

I hated them. Every single face. The mere sight of them nauseated me. I saw faces that were deep-fried in stress and loneliness with no dreams or ambitions of their own. They moved about, wearing ignorance and indifference like a winter coat. I didn't see people walking or driving to their jobs; I saw customized robots trudging to their programmed destinations to fulfill their programmed tasks. I didn't see homes; I saw warehouses that stored these robots when they were not in use. I pictured them returning to their storage rooms and plugging themselves into outlets to recharge for the next day. I saw a man getting on the bus and knew that the only goal of his life was to provide surplus blind loyalty. To exactly what? He wouldn't know.

I saw children who didn't know they were children. They moved and talked like adults, carrying the lack of innocence in their hearts.

From where I saw, it was a big pile of muck and it suffocated me. I knew that one day this planet is going to suffocate too and burst into a hot volcano of wrath and agony.

And I sure as hell didn't want to be here to witness it.

Chapter 32

Zenith

November 13, 2125

"You might as well cook with a blindfold," Sagan told Lyra when she dumped sugar, cardamom, and chopped roasted nuts into the saucepan without measurements. He stood on tiptoe next to her in the kitchen with his hands in his pockets. "Cooking is chemistry. It requires each component in the exact quantity."

"Good that your sister isn't making a living out of it, then." Lyra stirred the mixture of the cooked grated carrots and avoided thinking about the cold response she had gotten after her speech yesterday.

But at least one person was happy with her. Ms Tara had given Lyra her gajar halwa recipe.

"You promised you wouldn't be sarcastic with me," said Sagan.

"Sorry."

"It's okay." Sagan stood on his toes again. "Then how do you determine the exact amount for each ingredient?"

"I just know...like with sugar, I can visualize the crystals spreading across the food particles. I can...imagine its taste on my tongue. It's easy to understand it when you think of cooking as an art and not science. It's like how a painter knows exactly how much yellow the blue will need to achieve the desired green."

"Interesting."

Lyra took some pudding with a spotted spatula. Hot steam wafted from beneath like the aftermath of a space shuttle.

"See...ooh," she waggled the hot halwa she had shoved into her mouth with her tongue, "perfect sugar. Taste it."

"I'll take it like a civilized being." Sagan planted a scoop of the creamy orange pudding on a plate and nibbled at it. "This is the most delightful plate of dessert I have ever had."

"Save some for Sipa."

"I asked him to arrive at four. He said he will be here at three-thirty." Sagan narrowed his brows. "And do we really have to play video games? Can't I just show him my books?"

"You can, but you also have to respect his interests, Sagan."

"Kids." Keid interrupted them.

Lyra and Sagan turned around and found their father standing by the couch in slacks and a Button-down shirt. He was wearing his work shoes, the ones he had not touched in years.

"I was heading out to pay a visit to your mother. Let's go together."

Sagan spoke first. "Would you be willing to also head to the restricted sanctuary section?"

"You got it."

After two decades of Colonization, the Terraformers had accepted that cremating or burying corpses was not practical for their environment. They needed an eco-friendly and yet a respectable method for disposing of the dead.

The scientists ended up innovating the old Promession method. Dead bodies are suspended outside the walls of Zenith. Within hours, the bodies freeze-dry and become brittle. The frozen bodies are then retracted inside the walls and crushed into fine powder. A hundred-pound body would yield only twenty pounds of powder, or as the 1st G called it, 'ice-remains'.

Lyra and Keid sat under a fig tree in an orchard next to the sanctuary forest. It was where the farmers had spread Poona's ice-remains. Her family knew she would not have liked a tree turn into a tombstone and so they had never placed flowers or cards or her paintbrushes underneath the tree.

"Did you know," Keid rubbed his neck and broke the silence, "that it took us only two years to grow this forest, but twenty years to formulate the right soilbed for it?"

"Yeah, I read some of your thesis," said Lyra. "It's impressive."

Keid threw his hand in the air and let out a humorless laugh. "What?"

"That's my biggest problem, Lai. It's hard being an interesting dad to two brainy kids who already know everything. You cannot impress them with your stories."

"It's not like that, Dad." Lyra looked at her father, surprised by his revelation. She wanted to hold him and ask for more stories.

"It is. It's why you never liked my company growing up. Always disinterested in what I had to say." He tried to fake a smile. "You would enter a room and leave immediately if you didn't find your mom around me."

"Dad..." Lyra reached out her hand. "I don't even remember that."

"It wasn't intentional, I know. But that's how you've always felt. You even told me I wasn't clever enough to be your friend. I think you were Sagan's age."

"Whoa. Some brat I was. You still remem..."

"Forget that." Keid waved his hand. "Now, I get that you know everything, but you surely must not have read this. Sometime in the 80s, the botanists discovered that the ice-remains could be turned into powerful fertilizer. So, we started urging people to spread the remains of their loved ones across the forest and our crop fields. But no one would. People wanted their dead family closer. So the remains went into their private gardens or potted plants or sat in their freezer."

"I remember tha—" Lyra stopped midsentence. "Sorry." She flashed her teeth.

"I am not finished." Keid shuffled closer to his daughter and folded his legs under him. He took a bite of one of the fallen figs, Poona's favorite fruit, and passed it to his daughter. Lyra bit into it, and like every time, imagined the wasps that figs usually digest as they ripen. "To change that attitude and spread awareness about how important the remains were for our ecosystem, your mother started a campaign. She created a Remains Right declaration. It was like a permission form signed by people themselves giving away the right to their body after they die. That way their remains would not be handled by their emotional family. I thought it was a bit manipulative."

They both smiled.

"But she said it was needed, that people themselves, and not others, should have the right over what happens with their bodies."

"I agree." Lyra placed the half fig by her father.

"She was the first to sign. Hundreds of people followed suit. It was annoying how easily she could get people to change their minds without coercion." Keid clasped his hands on his lap and looked at them. His eyes brimmed. "I miss her strength so much."

Lyra cleared the lump in her throat. "Me too. She was able to do that because her actions were as powerful as her words. She always led by example. I wish I had that in me."

"You do, Lai. By admitting you have been wrong in front of everyone, you did just that. It was brave, your speech. I saw Poona on TV yesterday. You..." Keid stopped when he found Lyra staring intently at him. "What?"

"You are talking like you used to...like before Mom died."

"I—"

"You didn't even come to support me yesterday. It was

so...hard for me to do that." Lyra wanted to stop, but she noticed that she wasn't shaking. Her words came out calm and honest. "I've always been by myself, failing and hurting." She broke eye contact with her father.

"You are never there."

"Oh, Lai, I know." Keid lowered his eyes. "I realized that when I heard you yesterday. You had all that buried in you for years and I never saw it."

Lyra wiped her cheek. "It's okay. You were also...burying things."

Keid wanted to hug his daughter, but the same awkwardness that his kids had inherited from him stopped him. "There is no excuse for this," he said. "I should have acted like an adult and gotten help. You asked me to. And I know this sudden apology, is not going to solve everything. Things don't work that way. But I got you something." He removed a file from his bag and handed it to Lyra. "I hope it's a good start."

"What is this?"

"Our signatures, including Zaif and Clia's. It means that we support you going to Earth and choose you to be our analyst. I don't want to put you in a dangerous position, and so this is not going to be official or governmental."

Lyra stared at the sign-up sheet filled with hundreds of names and signatures.

"You convinced them?"

"You did, Lai. I only took help of some of your friends and canvassed the signatures. Look here." Keid pointed at the last column. It showed the amount the signees had donated for Lyra's ticket to Earth.

Lyra was speechless. The collective generosity stunned her. More so because it was directed towards her, someone who was never a part of them.

"Dad, this is...I was going to start saving again. I can't take this money. No one owes me anything."

"It's nothing if you think of the individual amount. It seems like a big number because so many people donated. I wish I could give more."

"Thank you!" she crawled to her father and half-hugged him. "But I feel uneasy taking this."

"I knew you would feel that way." Keid stroked his daughter's back. "You have always been very methodical with people. Just like me. You are afraid you can't give more, and so you ask less, take less. Take more, Lai. Then learn to give more. We both need to do that. We can't survive without others. There is nothing wrong in needing someone's help. Isn't that what you have been telling me all this time?"

"I don't have a good track record in obeying my own advice." Lyra grinned.

"Like father, like daughter." Keid picked up the fig from the ground and took a bite. "Now, let's get you packing again."

The words alone were enough to fill Lyra with unbelievable excitement.

"But, Lai, you are doing it differently this time," he said. "No lies, no secrets. You have to tell me everything. What you plan to do once you get there, where you'll live..."

"I didn't tell you something the last time I was leaving." Lyra sat back on the ground and folded her legs under her. "When I was trying to find the places from great-grandma's diary, I came across some people. A guy and his grandmother. They weren't ready to talk much. Maybe they didn't want to get in trouble. But I think their family either knew great-grandma or they know someone who does."

"See, this is why I have stopped you before." Lyra watched her father turn into the man she had known for the past decade. "You trust strangers more than you trust your friends and family. They could be lying, Lai. How can you trust them?"

"Dad, calm down." She stopped herself and policed her words. "You are right. I can't trust strangers, and I won't. I am more cautious than you know." Her tone became calmer. "Trust me. They have sent me enough proof. I wouldn't have talked to them otherwise. I am also verifying one last thing. I'll know soon if they are legit."

Guilt smacked Lyra in the gut. She did want Aryabh to visit this family for his own benefit, but there was a selfish reason too.

When she found out that Aryabh was headed towards them, she saw an opportunity in it, a way to verify the authenticity of the two people she had met on a portal. If there was someone who could scrutinize strangers on her behalf, it was Aryabh. He had cheated and stolen from her, but she knew he would tell her if there was something wrong with them. The fact that she had manipulated both parties, Aryabh and the two people who were probably risking their lives to help her, evoked a familiar troubling feeling. She felt the monster stirring inside her.

"But Lai..."

"I will be okay, dad." She placed her hand on her father's knee. "I promise. I know how incredibly terrifying it must be for you to imagine me living on Earth."

Keid let out a breath and closed his eyes. "Okay. It's good to know that you are aware of that. But hear me. If I die early, it's because of you."

Lyra flashed her teeth. "Come on, I am finally fulfilling your dream," she said.

"What's that?"

"Being a scientist. I am going to do a research on Earth for Zenith."

Her father chuckled. "Well, that is true, and I am proud. But what will you do for a living?"

"I don't know. I do want to travel, learn more about their geography, about old-Earthler ingredients and cuisines. I'll know better once I am there."

"Sounds like a nightmare to me." Keid shook his head. "But I have accepted that we are different and what doesn't work for me might work for you." He squeezed his daughter's hand. "Now let's get your brother before he starts a spider revolution."

Lyra picked up the fig's stem to throw it in the compost pit and got up. She was dusting her pants when her phone vibrated.

It was a lengthy email from Aryabh. She froze.

"Let's go, Lai."

"I haven't seen T. rex in a long time. I'll see you at home?"

"Okay, come soon."

Lyra exited the orchard, crossed the pathway, and entered the bamboo forest. T. rex was inside his hut.

"Hey, dude." She peeped inside and placed wild celery at the gorilla's feet. Then she sat on the ground outside the hut and pressed her knees against her breasts. With a pounding heart, she opened Aryabh's email and then read it for what seemed like eternity.

It wasn't just a letter; it was Aryabh's memoir. The account of his life shook her. She read about Kenai and how he was executed as well as about the Farm and the Pacamounts. The email showed her facets of Earth she could not have imagined. She read why and how Aryabh had targeted her for the badge and how much she meant to him.

T. rex came outside the hut, chewing, and sat behind Lyra. When she didn't notice him, he nudged her. Lyra rested her back on him and read the rest of the email.

> And lastly, thank you! I came here because I wanted answers. For both of us. But instead, I found another dimension. I am sitting in Forêt de Fontainebleau right now. I have found it, the exact place where your great-grandparents had decided to marry. I am attaching a picture and the coordinates of this place. It is just the way you had imagined it and it's still here, waiting for you.
> I have to say, you did well, Ms Lyra. Managed to fool me. Can't say, I am not annoyed at all. But a big fan.
> Kenai died thinking I had left the house to help

you. Maybe that is why I urged myself to do this. I want to rebuild the dream I have destroyed. In a few hours, you will receive a code with which you'll be able to buy yourself a new ticket to Earth. Your bank account will also receive a small amount, a generous tip from an Earthler guest at Faraway Paradise. It should be enough for a few weeks when you get here. Don't think of this as charity. I am only returning the money you lost when I stole your documents.

The day when I discovered your asteroid was both the happiest and saddest day of my life. I was happy there was hope somewhere. A pie in the sky. I was sad that I wasn't a part of it. Zenith kept me alive. I believed I deserved it. But I never asked whether Zenith deserved me. It doesn't. I am not coming to Zenith.

I know that after reading this email, your weird mind will force you to feel guilty. You would start considering your own dream vain after learning the gravity of my situation. Don't. Wanting to escape your prison is not vain. Being able to live a life on your terms is not unimportant. In fact, your dream was better than mine because you wanted to escape your limitations so that you could grow and be better. I was trying to escape from what I had become, without knowing that my toxicity would have followed me to Zenith too.

I don't know what awaits me or where exactly I'll decide to go. At the moment, the most sensible option seems to be the one where I can stop the breeding and raising of more Aryabhs. I have learned that we, the Earthlers, don't need a reset or extinct button. We just need to hit refresh.

I have to get off the grid and take time to find

the things in me that I have lost. I was a frog in a haunted well. I need to walk the Earth and discover its different facets. But know that I will always remember you.

I went from living a lonely, meaningless life to living among people who gave up their voice for their beliefs, who risk their lives to speak their language, who sacrifice their own meal to soothe a sick friend, and who forgive even the worst mistakes easily. All because of you.

Without you, I would still be me.

Stay safe and alert once you are here. It's not going to be easy. You'll be stepping into a world that is entirely different from yours — a ruthless, merciless world that will try to change you at every instance. You will see things that will break and terrify you. You'll be forced to do things that will haunt you every night. Don't let that change you. Stay Lyra.

As for me, I will live my life knowing that on the outskirts of Earth revolves a humble asteroid of my dream. A place filled with hopeful people. In it, lives a person called Lyra, who dared to expect good from Earth. I will live my life trying to make that true.

Thank you for everything. You were a friend I didn't deserve. I am sorry for stealing your documents and the trauma it caused you. I'll miss your company.

Alice, come find your wonderland!

171-2098-1102-8A (Not Aryabh. Story for another life.)

Lyra read the email twice. A wave of nauseating heat orbited her ribs. It was too much information at once. Her mind couldn't grasp it in the manner she wanted.

She looked at the picture of Fontainebleau and gasped. It looked like a surreal painting.

She placed her phone in her lap and looked at the asteroid's roof, her head still leaning on T. rex. There were a million things she wanted to tell and ask Aryabh. She grabbed her phone and hit on 'reply', her legs shaking out of restlessness. What would one say to an email like that? She couldn't frame a single sentence. The thought of Kenai and his execution had frozen her mental faculties.

T. rex sensed her distress. He swayed his body as if to rock Lyra like a baby. It was enough to shake the grief out of her.

Lyra sat until the rooflights dimmed, drowning in and fighting a nebulous mixture of emotions. Then she cried for Aryabh.

CHAPTER 33

Zenith

November 19, 2125

"Did you take enough warm clothes? I read it's going to be winter there soon."

"Yes, Dad. We packed them together."

It astounded Lyra how quickly Mr Zaif was able to arrange for her new Earth visa. She barely had the time to pack and prepare for the journey.

"Just making sure." Keid picked up litter from Lyra's bed. "I've placed the PacaDollars in the side pocket of your bag. Don't forget."

"Thanks, Dad. Oh...I forgot to tell you. I've given away the living-room rug to the recycling center. It was getting old. The floor looks just fine without it."

No more shoving dirt under its corners, Lyra thought.

"Good," said Keid distractedly as he dusted the bedsheet.

Lyra looked at him. His face lacked the light he had possessed when they sat in the orchard. The pain was still as stubborn on it as it was the last time she left.

Keid's grief drifted Lyra's attention to the memory of when she had met Kenai. The thought of his execution barged into her mind again like it had many times since she had read Aryabh's email. And now she was willingly walking into a world that had radiated him to death.

She shook her head and compartmentalized. This was not the time to contemplate.

"Dad, don't forget your promise. Dr Jine, thrice a week."

"I won't."

"Good. Therapy will help you."

"Lai," Keid sat on the bed, "I met the university dean at Sonji's boutique yesterday when I was buying your jacket. He wants me to teach Plant Ecology to the grad students twice a week."

"What?"

"I think I will accept it. Teaching should be good, right?"

Lyra placed her messenger bag aside and sat beside her father. Her fingers flinched from wanting to hold him. "Teaching will be awesome! You should do it."

"Okay, good." Her father stood. "I'll see if Trac can give you a ride. Get ready, now."

He'll be okay, Lyra consoled herself.

"Sai." Keid called out while going down the stairs. "Come, let's eat lunch. Your sister is leaving in two hours."

Sagan sat at his computer, reading an email he had received two days ago for the hundredth time.

Hello Sagan,

We have met before, but for now think of me as your family's well-wisher. I want you to stop your sister from going to Earth. Soon the Pacamounts will be hitting Zenith and occupy it to use it as a base to colonize the moon. I don't know what they are planning to do with Zenithers, but when they come you will need your sister. You have to stop her from getting on that shuttle. My position prevents me from approaching her directly, but she won't leave if it comes from you. You are the only one who can do it. Stop her.

Take care,

The man who taught you to play woodblock at school.

Sagan knew who the email was from—a silver-haired man who had visited their school often. The tall, polished Earthler in a suit who lived at Faraway Paradise. He had asked a lot about Lyra the last time they had met.

"She needs to know," Sagan told his father. They were standing in the living room downstairs.

"No, she doesn't. We have talked about this, Sai. This is her last chance to get away from here."

"But—"

"Why isn't this guy talking to Lyra or me and instead emailing a kid? I don't trust him. Even if he is right, why would you want her to be here?"

"I am not some naïve kid who trusts random people," Sagan retorted without looking at his father and sat on the couch facing the door. "Sister needs to have all the facts before she makes a decision. She would want to know; I am certain about it. That's how she operates."

"If you think it's wise to stop your sister from fulfilling her only desire just so you could keep her here, then...go ahead."

Sagan did not respond and shrunk his small body into the couch cushions.

Keid sat next to him and stroked his head. "I am sorry. I am scared too, Sai. But we will get through this together. We will even talk about this with Ms Clia. But after Lai is gone. Your sister has given up a lot for us. If you show her the email, she will not leave. We need to let her go. I will soon arrange for you to join her, okay?"

"That's not the concern." Sagan got away from his father. "The issue is that we are deciding for her. That's not how our relationship works. Sister and I give each other the liberty and space to make our own decisions. We do not decide for each other."

Keid felt like an outsider in his own family. "I understand that, Sai," he spoke in a soft voice. "But think about this. When you tell her, she will realize that you had the option to let her go but you didn't. How do you think she will feel?"

"She is the brightest person I know. She does not take things personally. You wouldn't know that." Sagan stood from the couch and headed upstairs.

He stopped at Lyra's bedroom door and observed the view. She was sitting amid an ocean of her belongings, mainly her books.

"What are you doing?" asked Sagan.

"Hey, come here." Lyra said without looking at him. "I am compiling a bunch of books for you. I want you to read them. These here are my favorites." She pushed a stack. "I know you will like them too. Don't touch this." She grinned as she hid a pile of disturbing books behind her. "Come here."

Lyra took Sagan to her desk with a childlike gait. She turned on her desktop screen and clicked on a sticky note.

"This is a list of sites for your free time. I started curating them when I bought my ticket. Entomology, chess, music...everything you like. I also found some cool Earthler sites we didn't know before. And I think you should take up technical writing. You are great at stating a straightforward fact. You'll be good at it. It will keep you busy. This is my writing software that you can borrow. Don't read my files. And, Sagan, I know you don't like changes, but I think you should move to my room after I'm gone. It has better lighting."

Sagan stared at Lyra. His sister who barely mumbled words was talking without taking a moment to breathe.

"Or you can..." Lyra noticed his face. For as long as she remembered, she had never seen it contort. "Hey, what's wrong?"

"There is..." Sagan glanced at the books on the floor and her computer. Then he looked at her again. The pure joy that radiated from his sister's well-rested, content face was hard to miss; her voice was rhythmic and her eyes were brighter than ever. She was happy. "Only two hours to go," he said, forcing the usual smugness to his voice, "and you are playing in your clutter? Get ready. Dad is calling you for lunch." He turned around to leave.

"Wait." Lyra held Sagan's wrist and pulled him closer. "Are you okay?"

"I will be. You are leaving and it is evident I am going to miss you. I will miss having the only brain that understands mine. But I am happy for you." Sagan patted his sister's head thrice. "I will see you downstairs."

When Lyra got down, her bags were ready at the door. Keid had written her name and contact details in large fonts on white papers and taped them to the luggage. Sagan had packed her a sandwich wrap for the trip, which was sitting atop one of the bags in a neatly folded paper bag. Beside it was an apple.

They ate lunch telling stories and making promises, as Keid kept his hand on Sagan's knee under the table.

When Trac's loud auto-horn interrupted the silence of their neighborhood, they walked to the door and said their goodbyes.

"Lai, no more old habits." Keid patted Lyra's disarrayed hair and stroked her head. "You have to call regularly and reply to all the messages on time."

"Yes, Dad." She hugged him. "I will visit you soon."

"Arrange something for Sagan too. I want to send him as soon as possible."

"I will." Lyra noticed that her brother's eyes were wet. "Oh." She looked at her father and gave a worried smile. "I don't even remember when I last saw him crying."

Sagan hugged her and patted her head. Lyra hugged him harder.

"Keep your clothes clean," he said in a muffled tone, "and don't trip on your shoelaces. But also don't use the sides of your shoes as compartments to store them."

Lyra laughed. "Okay, Lord Sagacious."

"Take proper care of yourself."

"I will. You take care too." She rubbed his temple and kissed him. "Be nice, okay? And take care of Dad."

Sagan nodded.

Lyra stepped out of the house and looked back. Tears rolled down her cheeks as she saw her brother's sorrowful face.

She walked back and hugged him.

"Lai." Keid held her quivering shoulder. "I will take care of him."

Lyra nodded, her wet face buried in Sagan's neck. Down inside the auto, Trac wiped his own tears.

Sagan kissed Lyra on the head and smiled. "Go rattle the stars, sister."

Outside the spaceport gate, Lyra met a big crowd. Balin, Gryffy, Ms Clia, Rahi, and a few of the Zen Mavericks, including Hawk, were waiting to say their goodbyes.

She got out of the auto and walked towards Gryffy. When Lyra had told her about the changes she had made in the speech and her plans, Gryffy had not been pleased. "I don't get it. But for what it's worth, you finally found your voice," she had concluded.

Lyra indeed had. She had used her voice to raise awareness about the issues at Holding Hands and urged the council to secure more funding for the institute.

"Thank you again for everything," said Lyra.

"Thank *you*, again!" Gryffy shook her. "For the funding. I can't believe you were listening all this time."

"Don't flatter me."

"Sorry. Just kidding. But no, really. It...means a lot that you remembered all my rants. We badly needed that money."

"I know. I should have helped earlier. I was too self-absorbed."

"Shut up." Gryffy hugged her. She gave Lyra an oversized sweatshirt with messages scribbled on it by the entire kitchen staff. "Your parting gift."

To Gryffy's surprise, Lyra removed her sweater and wore the gift.

"You are gonna wear that to the spaceport?"

"To Earth." Lyra pulled the ends of the sweatshirt and grinned a foolish smile.

"You look like a cartoon."

"Thank you!"

Gryffy also handed Lyra Ms Tara's gifts—some written tips on Indian cuisine and a set of handwoven socks, both of different colors.

Ms Clia reminded Lyra about her tasks and Rahi showed her the picture of her baby.

Hawk walked up to her and said, "Bursting out of the hollow balloon at last."

Lyra twisted her lips. "It doesn't seem so hollow anymore. Partly, thanks to you."

"Why?"

"I had always wondered if you felt the same alienation as me, because you never joined michaiyos, or mingled with people..."

"Or fit in."

She let out a silly laugh. "Or fit in. But when *you* did that, I saw myself as the part of the society that you didn't fit in. After all, what's society if it's not the amalgamation of you and me, right? So...in a way, we both are the problem. Maybe all non-fitters are, because they too are someone else's society."

"Interesting. The ability to drop wisdom bombs with casual goodbyes."

"Burdens of a know-it-all bomber."

Hawk guffawed. "I'll think about what you said. While I wait for my eighteenth birthday."

Lyra winked and pointed her finger at him. He pointed back and went back to the crowd.

Balin, who had been standing on her toes for her turn, gave Lyra a box of homemade teas. She held her hands with hope in her eyes. "Lyra, honey. I have to ask you something."

"Sure."

"Did you...really never crush the limes before shifts?"

Gryffy snorted a loud laugh.

"No." Lyra held the worried woman's arms and showed her teeth. "Sorry."

Balin's hands went to her hips. "Oh, boy."

They all laughed and cheered until Trac cursed at everyone and made Lyra sit back in the auto.

CHAPTER 34

PacaSpace Transit Station

November 19, 2125

When Lyra entered the transit Station, the familiar panorama engulfed her—a ginormous, curved metal room packed with opulent shops and Cream tourists. The crowd that had intimidated her the last time, now seemed insignificant and cruel, and the pressure that had overwhelmed her before had vanished.

She collected her luggage from the carousel. When she turned around, she found people staring at her scribbled sweatshirt. Unbothered, she glided through them as a vibrant ink trail on a fresh sheet of paper. With her head held high, she walked straight to Spacebucks, hoping to see Shiaya.

The café, Lyra noticed, had a completely new staff and Shiaya wasn't among them. Disappointed, but relieved, she placed an order for Estlechino and sat at the same table as last time.

Taking sips of the comforting drink, she collected her thoughts. When her head was finally clear, she switched on her new tablet, grabbed her stylus, and wrote an email.

Aryabh (looking forward to the story of your name),

I've been wanting to message you ever since I received your email. I tried many times, but words failed me. Then a lot happened at once and I didn't even realize a week had passed.

I am currently sitting at the same Spacebucks where you changed my life forever. I never thought I would be back here so soon. But here I am. I am coming to Earth, Aryabh. Right now!

Thank you for sending me the money. But it's your life savings. You'll take it back when we meet. I received financial help from people here the same day you emailed me. That's how I bought the ticket.

Before I ask for my own apology, I want you to know that I forgive you. I have been furious, I am not going to lie. There is a part of me who is still sitting in a corner, offended for being cheated that way. But let's ignore her for a while. For now, let me relish the fact that if it hadn't been for your interference, I would have entered the Earth perimeters without ever knowing the importance of Zenith. I would have spent my life without the wisdom I've gained over the last few months. I would have never met you.

Also, thank you very much for finding the forest for me. It means a lot. As for my own dark deeds, I am sorry for the part I played in luring you to their house. I needed assurance and wanted to know if I could trust them. I did want you to step into something different and clear your mind, but you didn't deserve to be used that way.

What I read in your email is still running erratically in my head. I can't even imagine what it can do to someone who has endured it. I am sorry about Kenai. I still can't wrap my mind around it. It makes me wonder if I am in the right state of mind for still wanting to come there.

But I feel different this time. I have learnt that I am more than my dreams or ambitions. I am more than my need to come to Earth. So are you.

Zenither scientists and poets often talk about how small and insignificant we are compared to this gigantic universe. But doesn't an infinite universe also reside in each one of us? There is stardust in every single cell of ours. We carry trillions of those cells and within them lie infinite molecules, atoms, electrons, protons, and neutrons. We carry a whole different universe within us. How are we tiny or insignificant? We are the universe. You and I, both.

I don't know if Zenith deserved you or Earth deserves me. I don't even know if we have the right to make demands about how our worlds should be, for each demand will differ from the next. But we do deserve the quest to figure that out, and then we have to accept the truth even if it detonates us from within.

Aryabh, we were bound by theft, manipulation, and pain. Together, we have to turn this into something better. Even on the nights when I hated you more than anything, your friendship stayed with me; your words had empowered me. Despite these ups and downs and all this lonely wandering, I was pulled into your orbit, just like Zenith got pulled into Earth's. We have a long way to go. No goodbyes yet.

I will contact you as soon as I land on Earth. Attached is my itinerary. After my incubation period at the elevator station, I'll be taking the PacaOcean train to Sonmanto. I will stay there for a day and then fly to Bois-le-Roi. We'll meet there.

I know you feel lost, but please do not make any decisions right now. Stay put. I spoke with Mr Zaif. He has read the letter you sent him pretending to be a Zenither citizen. He is willing to help you. Do not give up yet.

You are an ever-evolving dynamic entity. Don't worry about not having a Constant. There IS no constant, Aryabh. The only constant is change.

I'll see you down the rabbit hole.

Lyra

Once she sent the email, Lyra finished her coffee and pulled her feet to the chair one by one to retie her laces. The immigration counter was open. It was time to board the PacaSpace Elevator.

She grabbed her luggage and walked towards the queue. Standing there at the checkpoint was the same security officer who had escorted her the last time. With a face as frightening as before, he verified the documents of the passengers. "Get moving," he commanded the people in the front.

When it was Lyra's turn, the officer's eyes came in contact with hers, and for a moment she thought he recognized her. "Clear," he returned the documents, "Get moving."

After passing two more security checkpoints, Lyra reached the elevator boarding gate and stood alongside other passengers. As she waited, the reality of what was happening hit her.

She was finally traveling to Earth, the planet of her dreams, the land of her ancestors, and the origin of humanity. Her heart bounced in her chest and her nails prodded her cuticles.

A voice announced the opening of the elevator. Lyra tapped her feet and blew air. The doors slid away revealing a circular room. It was large enough to fit a crowd of fifty people. The seats, however, were only placed at the border of the room, leaving the center vacant for a refreshment hub.

Lyra stepped on the transparent floor of the elevator and looked below. The sight froze her. Protruding beneath her shoes was planet Earth, a giant bright ball in space with sun's light gracefully hugging its atmosphere. A thick, long cord extended from alongside the room to Earth's Atlantic Ocean in the equator. It reminded Lyra of the time when she was studying at the university and wanted to imagine the view from the space elevator. She had stirred methylene blue with activated carbon in a round bottom lab flask and squinted down its long neck to see a ball of teal liquid.

"Move!" an Earthler passenger whined behind her.

Lyra let out the breath she had held and went to her assigned seat. She put on her seatbelt and looked through the floor again. A big patch of the marbled planet stared back at her.

All the things that she had learned about Earth in the past swarmed to her mind's eye—the planet's colossal size and its huge population, its flora and fauna along with its prodigious forests, oceans, and mountains, the water that showers from its sky and the lava that erupts from its core, its extraordinary ecosystem, its art, languages, and sciences, its expansive history and its terrifying wars, the humanities and the atrocities, the life that began on its surface almost four billion years ago and its evolution from single-celled organisms to primates to modern humans who branched into diverse races and then created and flocked towards different tribes, religions, nationalities, and Stratums.

Lyra imagined all of it in the view beneath her feet as she held the arms of her chair to restrain the adrenaline. It was unnerving and inspiring.

"I am finally going," she whispered to herself as if wings had shot out of her spine.

Inside her pocket, her phone vibrated with an email notification-

Failure Delivery Notice. Invalid Email Address

Stay Tuned For Book Two In ASYMPTOTE
UNIVERSE

Meanwhile, I would deeply appreciate a review. **It will help other readers find their way to this book and allow me to continue writing full-time.**

Scan the QR code to leave a review on the website of your choice.

And if you'd like more stories to sit with, I also wrote a short story collection called **<u>Take a Seat at the Cosmic Campfire.</u>** Find it at your favorite online bookstore.

Acknowledgements

First and foremost, I want to thank the amazing Hollis Robbins for penning a thoughtful foreword for this book. She is an essayist, a literature scholar, a poet, the Dean of Humanities at University of Utah, and most importantly, an oracle for speculative and science fiction. Hollis has opened spellbinding dialogs about the elements of these genres and made it possible for sci-fi nerds like me to communicate with the greatest minds in this space including Neal Stephenson and Kim Stanley Robinson.

I owe a heavy gratitude to Dr. Laird Whitehill, a wealth of knowledge and a brilliant astronomer, for not only verifying the science of this book, but also teaching me the power of 'I don't know.' By agreeing to be my eternal scientific adviser, he has pulled me into the same constellation as Carl Sagan for he was Laird's thesis adviser!

I want to thank Anand Gandhi simply for existing. He has inspired a legion of creators, including myself, with his extraordinary mind and the bounteous knowledge it holds. Despite that, he lives as the most humble and intellectually generous person I have ever known. Thank you for trying extremely hard to be a part of this book and giving me the opportunity to write for Memesys.

This book is for my suspiciously caring sisters, Megha and Vaidehi, the Rock and Roll to my silence. To my beautiful Mum, who supported and believed in my dreams and to Papa, for bringing me the world's best olives. For Mitesh, a brother I never had and a cover designer we all need. To Dharati didi who is so intricately crazy that she inspired the character of Gryffy. And to my big, lovable extended family who championed me at every juncture of my life.

For Nidhee who was here and cheered me when the seed of this story was planted, but is not with us anymore. Stay spectacular in whatever form you are.

I owe the progress of this story to Greeshma Giresh, an agent I had but didn't deserve at the time.

A huge thanks to my forever cheerleader, Shehzeen, for reading this big book twice before I had even finished my last draft. She has conducted interventions, bought me Boba tea, told me I will be famous one day, and made me uninstall video games just so I would finish this novel.

Unearthing Idyll wouldn't be what it is without the invested hours of my terrific beta-readers—Bhavesh Patel, Shehzeen Bustamante, Vaidehi Soni, Rinku S. More, Amy Levens, Ris Young, and Adarsh Srivastava. I am similarly grateful to Adarsh Verma, Estelle Gallas, Shaun Mazarell, Simon Bras, and Aaditya Menon for helping me at different stages of the book and getting things correct. For Vedant, the Mythwala, for injecting every second with unbelievable cheer and motivation.

I thank my writing squad, Anna, Yasi, Grace, Cara, and Dianne, with whom I wrote the first draft of this book, discussed plots and characters on train rides, played D&D, did word sprints on countless Discord sessions, and hexed a demonic curse on Justin Bieber for his loud songs at the café where we wrote.

To the Sci-Fi Matters club for giving me a safe space to shamelessly nerd out and keeping the fire alive.

To Sujeet Sharma, an ex-colleague from thirteen years ago who was the first person to tell me I would write a book one day. Sorry for laughing in your face.

To all the losses and calamities that happened during the writing of this novel—the pandemic and lockdowns, the job I lost, the knee I damaged, the depression, and the passing of my remarkable grandmother, Tara baa. Even though they wrecked my heart, they urged me to finish my book in some way or the other.

To that dismal train ride that prompted me to write my first poem on its ticket and triggered this phenomenal journey of words.

To everyone who made it to this page. Thank you for sitting around the figurative campfire and lending an ear to my story.

And lastly, to all the seekers and misfits who are unearthing their own idyll—let's keep building it!